JERSEY SIX

Jewel E. Ann

Copyright © 2019 by Jewel E. Ann
ISBN: 978-1-7337786-2-6
Print Edition

Cover Designer: Jennifer Beach
Cover Model: Javier Ruiz Montoro
Photo: Rafael Catala
Formatting: BB eBooks

Dedication

For Cleida

Playlist

Build Me Up From Bones, Sarah Jarosz
The Blower's Daughter, Damien Rice
My Arms Were Always Around You, Peter Bradley Adams
Wicked Game, James Vincent McMorrow
Awake My Soul, Mumford & Sons
Love is Madness (feat. Halsey), Thirty Seconds to Mars
One Track Mind (feat A$AP Rocky), Thirty Seconds to Mars
Rescue Me, Thirty Seconds to Mars
Dangerous Night, Thirty Seconds to Mars
Someone You Loved, Lewis Capaldi
River Flows In You, Yiruma

CHAPTER ONE

A SIMPLE BEE *sting can set off a chain of reactions to stop a human heart.*

The man glanced at the stormy blue eyes taking pity on him, and he chuckled to ease the worry in the young nurse's mind. "I think I was stung by a bee. Years ago ... maybe as a child." He shrugged, scratching his dirty-blond bedhead while lowering his gaze to his feet, clad in blue canvas sneakers, dangling from the side of the hospital bed. "I remember a sting and burn on my neck. Before I knew it, my whole body started to turn red, and I felt itchy everywhere. Hives appeared out of nowhere. My face began to swell; my throat constricted. I couldn't swallow ... I couldn't breathe."

"You remember that?" Faith asked.

Faith—the perfect name for a nurse.

"Yes. I think. I mean, why would that pop into my head if it didn't happen to me?" The nameless man feathered his fingers over the burns on his hands. After countless surgeries, months of unimaginable pain, and the emotional tragedy of losing his memory, he stood on the precipice of being thrust into an unknown life.

"I'm not an expert on amnesia, but I would imagine

any memory is a good sign. So yeah, that's good." Faith's encouraging smile brought a tiny bit of light to the darkness. For months she had bestowed unconditional kindness on the man covered in scars.

Unrecognizable as a human. At least, that was what he thought.

A monster.

Something a young child could create with crumbly, dry, Play-Doh.

Ugly felt like a compliment. Hideous and unsightly better described his appearance. Thick, raised, and uncomfortably stiff scars covered eighty percent of his body, making him unrecognizable. Erasing fingerprints—dissolving his identity.

"Good, huh?" He wondered if anything in his life would ever be *good* again. "Good that I remember something? Good that I know to watch out for bees? Because let's be honest ... I survived a fire. The doctors said it's a miracle that I'm alive. I've lost my memory. It's unknown if I'll ever get it back. Yet ... my one solid memory is that I nearly died from a single bee sting."

The man chuckled. Glancing up at Faith, he found her wrinkled-nose expression rather cute. "So let's review what we know. I can walk through an inferno, my skin literally melting from my body, but if on the other side there happens to be an angry bee ... I'm a dead man."

"Unless you have an EpiPen, which I highly recommend."

He liked Faith. She had a husband and a two-year-old little girl named Izzy. They just got a dog, a doodle of some sort, and named it Gingie. He liked her all-American story. She was the best part of his day.

"So how's this all going to go down?"

"What do you mean?" Faith cocked her head to the side, exposing two tiny moles on her neck. They were familiar because she comprised a large part of his new memory. The citrus scent of her rich golden hair pulled into a high ponytail, the pink lipstick, and the neon yellow sneakers would forever remain embedded into the working parts of his brain.

"No one has claimed me."

No memory.

No identification.

And sadly, no one seemed to be looking for the name-less man.

"And I don't have anything—money, a social security number, a bed. Just … nothing. How do I pay for the hospital bills? Where do they even send the bills? Where will I sleep tonight?"

Faith rested her hand on his hand. The scars made it difficult to feel certain things, but he felt her warmth, and it felt like everything.

"I'm going to have someone talk to you about all of this. They will help you figure it out. A place to stay. Maybe a payment plan. And the police will continue looking for some leads on your family."

"What if I don't have family? That would explain why no one is looking for me. What if they died in the accident? What if …" He shook his head, pinching his eyes shut. "What if it wasn't an accident? What if I'm some sick serial killer who killed my family, blew up the home, and myself in the process? What if I hobbled incoherently to the hospital? Did they check? Do you think the police checked for arson, murder … something like that?"

Faith squeezed his hand. "You are the sweetest patient I have ever had the pleasure of helping. You never complained, even when I had tears in my eyes watching you endure the hardest parts of the debridement and healing process. Maybe you don't have family looking for you. Maybe they assume you died. It happens. But you are definitely not a serial killer. Besides …"

Removing her hand, she stood straight and shot him a tight-lipped smile. "They said someone literally dropped you off at the entrance to the ER. Right?"

He nodded. "Supposedly. But they didn't take me all the way into the building. Why would they just drop me off? And when the people here looked at the security cameras, all they could get was a make and model of the vehicle. It didn't have license plates. What if I had an accomplice?"

Faith crossed her arms over her scrub-clad chest and lifted a single eyebrow at the man.

He shrugged. "Fine. It's farfetched. I mean … I don't feel like a murderer. That has to mean something, right?"

She giggled a beautiful, life-is-good giggle. "If they arrest you, I'd go with that defense."

He couldn't hide his grin nor could he *fully* grin because his body was nothing more than a heap of stubborn scar tissue and bones.

"You wouldn't believe how many injured people get dropped off at the ER entrance or even the fire station. Gunshot wounds, stabbings, *burn* victims ... we see it all too often, like taking an animal out in the middle of nowhere and just leaving it. A cruel act, but not entirely inhumane. Clearly these 'Good Samaritans' don't want the victim to die, but they also don't want to be questioned for many reasons that might not have anything to do with the victim."

He nodded, eyes squinted.

"I'll be right back. I'm going to see who's available to meet with you to discuss further care, rehabilitation, finances, and so on. Okay?"

The nameless man swallowed hard and nodded slowly.

When Faith disappeared, his hands started to shake, and his pulse took off like it needed to cross a distant finish line. Her words jumbled in his mind, and her smile and that laugh he loved replayed on repeat, but it was no longer cute and endearing. It mocked and berated him. Faith's eyes lost their sparkle, rolling in annoyance that she had to stare at his wretched face all day and pretend that he had a family who would be looking for him. Paranoia attacked him.

Warm.

Sweaty.

Dizzy.

Nauseous.

He needed out of there before anything bad happened. Sliding off the bed onto wobbly legs, he pinched his eyes shut to silence the voices. They were louder than before—screaming at him to get out. His mastery over ignoring them began to slip. They would no longer be silenced.

So he did the only thing he could.

He ran.

Screeching tires, deafening horns, and echoes of profanity poured over the man as he staggered through the busy streets of Newark.

Whispers, cringes, pointed fingers ... they fed the voices, giving them more power than they deserved.

He weaved his way down an alley, the flickering streetlight never fully penetrating the darkness. Stumbling over empty liquor bottles, water-stained crates, and crumpled wrappers and cups, he collapsed onto a pile of leaflets in a corner. When light from a passing car on the street washed over the opposite wall, he caught sight of a tattered blanket.

"Christ ..." He wretched, hugging it to himself to keep warm on the late November night. It reeked of sour vomit.

He surrendered to sleep once the meowing cats, slamming trash lids, and flittering dance of the wind sweeping more trash in his direction silenced the voices.

THE NEXT DAY he discovered people were quite generous to homeless burn victims. An elderly man handed him a full pizza and a twenty-dollar bill. A young girl gifted him a half-full juice box, making her mother quite proud. By the end of the day, the empty half of his pizza box resembled a tip jar, but he didn't have to do anything to earn the money. Looking pitiful proved to be his best talent.

Unfortunately, winter in New Jersey showed no mercy. After a week of living on the streets, he needed something warm. An unlocked car under an overpass worked fairly well, until the owner returned the following morning with a tow truck and chased the homeless man away.

Then, as if there was some higher power who gave a tiny shit about the homeless man, he passed an old building—a familiar building.

Marley's

The angry, fighting voices in his head stopped, and one single voice—a new voice—whispered to him.

"Chris." He exhaled, tears burning his eyes. "My name is Chris. I used to box at this gym. Oh god …" A hard lump formed in his throat. He wasn't lost anymore. And he wasn't a nameless nobody.

CHAPTER TWO

T HE STENCH OF sweat and leather mingled with antiseptic, packing a punch of its own for anyone who walked through the door of Marley's boxing gym. In just over two decades, it went from a popular gym that churned out some well-known professional fighters to a haven for the worst criminals, human monsters, and housing for the occasional homeless person if Marley took pity on them.

However, everything changed for the worse when Marley died.

Laminated member passes evolved into simply showing a concealed weapon to gain entrance. Nobody dared to walk through the door without a loaded gun or one hell of a respectable left hook.

A constant string of profanities danced to the *thud, thud, thud* of gloves beating against bags or fists ripping flesh while lawless sparring stained the rings with shades of red.

"Who's Fuck Face over there?" Judd wiped his bloodied lip while climbing the ropes to find his unsteady legs after the only female member dropped his ass in under thirty seconds.

Jersey Six shrugged, ripping the tape from her hands. "Your gold tooth?" She nodded toward her feet.

Judd glanced behind him at the blood-covered gold crown on the mat. His tongue made a quick inspection, poking through the gaping hole in his already gnarly smile. "Jesus Christ, Jersey. Ya ain't gonna give me a break, huh? Thanks a lot."

"Mouth guard. Dumbass. And stop saying *ain't gon-na*." She kicked the tooth closer to him, knowing he wasn't working with enough brain power to consider the simplest of precautionary measures—not that she could point fingers with her eighth-grade level of education. But she knew mouth guards saved teeth, and "*ain't gonna ain't going to college.*" A Dena Russell quote. Jersey's attention shifted to "Fuck Face" looking around the place like a lost tourist. Jersey had no idea how he managed to get through the door.

Hopping down, she rolled the tension out of her shoulders and headed toward the back room to wash up.

"Excuse me?"

A cringe distorted Jersey's face, making the rest of her body tense in response. No one said *excuse me* at Marley's. He might as well have bent over and asked to have a dick shoved up his ass. "You're clearly lost." She turned. "Can I make a suggestion? If you want to leave with four working limbs and your asshole intact, I suggest you slither back out the front door without attracting any more attention."

"I used to train here."

Jersey's unkempt eyebrows slid up her sweaty forehead while she released her tangled, black hair from its ponytail.

He cleared his throat. "Obviously, no one would still recognize me."

"Obviously." Jersey inspected him. "Fuck Face" wasn't an exaggeration. The guy's face looked like the lone survivor of an atomic explosion. Layers of thick, pearly scar tissue made his blue eyes appear sunken into his skull. It crawled down his face and along his neck like dry, cratered earth. His gray hoodie and matching sweatpants hid most of his body, but the burn-like scars covered his hands as well.

Maybe he had trained there. Members of Marley's wouldn't have the money for a cosmetic surgeon if their bodies were distorted like the one standing before her.

"I need a place to stay." He held out his hand.

Her gaze held his desperation-filled eyes.

After a few seconds, he let his hand drop. "I wouldn't want to shake my hand either." He scratched his dirty-blond head—the one part of his body that looked somewhat normal. She thought he might be in his thirties, maybe forty or so. It was hard to tell with his skin severely scarred.

"I don't shake hands with anyone." Jersey shrugged.

"I need a place to stay."

"You said that. I'm not the owner." She turned.

He grabbed her arm. Jersey didn't think. She just re-acted.

Smack!

"Fuck Face" hit the floor with a *thunk*. A few chuckles

drifted from the distance. There were no heroes at Marley's Gym. No one stopped a fight, saved a life, or blinked at death.

"Chris …" He groaned, planting his hands next to his head, peeling himself from the grimy concrete. Blood oozed from his nose. He wiped it with the hood of his sweatshirt, unsteady on all fours. "My name is Chris." He lumbered to his feet, bringing him nearly a foot taller than Jersey's five-seven stature. "I wasn't trying to frighten you."

She grunted. "Frighten me? You didn't frighten me. You grabbed me."

Chris flinched. It was hard to notice with his distorted face, but she caught the slight reaction.

"Sorry." He pressed the hood of his sweatshirt to his nose again. "I get it. You don't like to be touched. I'm sure you have good reasons. It won't happen again."

Jersey responded with an easy nod as she focused on the blood smeared down his face. "Your blood's in the water. I'd get out of here before the sharks circle."

"It's cold. I need one night."

"It was cold last night." She shrugged. "November in New Jersey."

"Last night I slept in a car."

"Sounds like a solid choice." Low on sympathy and high on the memory of knocking Judd out, she strutted toward the back of the gym.

"The owner of the car kicked me out and called the cops."

"Again," she said on an exasperated sigh, "I don't own

the place."

"The guy in the front office said I could stay one night if you agreed to it."

"No." Jersey's feet screeched to a stop, keeping her back to Chris. As Marley's only son, George took over the gym after his father died.

George didn't box.

George didn't take out the trash or hire anyone else to do it.

George didn't do math.

George had no clue how to run a business.

Marley left his gym to a forty-eight-year-old with some sort of mental disability. Nobody knew what exactly was wrong with George; they just knew he wasn't all there. He mumbled to himself and spent most of the day coloring superheroes in warped, water-damaged children's coloring books with broken crayons piled in a grease-stained, fast-food bag.

"That's bullshit because George doesn't share that many words." She continued into the back room.

"Fair enough. He didn't say that. I asked who was in charge and he nodded toward you. I'm good at reading between the lines." Chris shadowed Jersey like a pesky fly.

"Your lips are still flapping. You're still in the build-ing. I don't think you have any clue how to read between the lines." She peeled off her sports bra.

"Oh jeez …" Chris turned his back to her. "What are you doing?"

"Washing off the blood and sweat. What's wrong? Never seen a naked woman before?" She flipped on the cold water to the rusty sink. All memories of hot water or an actual shower died when she skipped out of the system eight years earlier at fifteen.

"Uh … of course I've seen a naked woman. But anyone could walk back here."

She ignored the pesky fly. After years of living on the streets and doing *anything* for a meal or mismatched gloves and a soiled blanket, she welcomed a five-by-five square of an old boxing ring mat in the back corner of a rundown gym, a shit-smeared toilet, and a dinky sink with partially running water. It was worth the lack of privacy.

Squeezing soap from a bag she stole from the bathroom dispenser at the gas station down the street, Jersey sudsed her body and sponged it off with a well-used rag and frigid water.

By the time she finished and slid on a pair of gray sweatpants and an oversized sweatshirt, Chris faced her with his hands crossed over the front of his pants.

Bed, shower, toilet. Jersey never took for granted the very basic things in life.

"Don't you think you're asking for trouble?" Chris cleared his throat. "This place isn't exactly filled with guys who respect women."

"True." Jersey ran her fingers through her sweaty hair which received weekly washings. "Do you respect women, Chris?"

He adjusted himself, not outwardly proud of his unavoidable reaction to her. "I think so."

She twisted the rag, releasing the excess water. "You

don't sound too confident."

He shrugged. "I was in an accident."

"You don't say."

The scar tissue on Chris's face thwarted his attempt to frown at her reply. "I don't remember anything from the accident. In fact, I didn't remember anything at all until I saw this building. My name is Chris, but I *just* figured that out. I used to box here, and I was good. Marley was like a father to me." He shook his head, closing his eyes. "I don't know. It's coming together, but it's not all there yet."

Snatching a half-eaten banana from the side pocket of her camouflage duffel bag, Jersey plopped down onto the mat—her bed—and crossed her outstretched legs.

"So you grew up around here?"

Chris meandered around the dingy room lined with a few lockers, minus actual locks, a row of three urinals and a toilet, a broken vending machine, and a buzzing fridge filled with water and beer. It smelled like death. "I'm pretty sure. As sure as I can be. I think I grew up in the system," he mumbled.

"Were you homeless before your accident?"

Chris stopped, scratching the back of his head. "I'm not sure. At times, I think I left town for a while. Then I came back after …" He continued to shake his head. "I'm not sure. I think I had enemies. I just …" Chris shook his head, pinching his eyes shut. "It's like my memory has no inception."

"Real enemies?" Jersey paused her chewing. "Not like the obvious one which is life."

He chuckled. "Life, huh? You think life is my ene-my?"

"You said you grew up in the system. You're here, looking for a warm place to sleep, and I saw you practical-ly drooling over this banana when I pulled it out of my bag." She held up the black peel. "And let's not even get into what must have happened to you that left you looking like you do. Clearly ... life hates you." Jersey sucked at subtle. She sucked at a lot of things, like patience, restraint, kind words, and giving a shit.

"And it likes you?"

She shrugged. "I don't think it knows I exist."

After a few silent moments, Chris faced her again, sliding his hands in the front pouch of his hoodie. "Come on. I just bared my soul to you. What's your deal? Why would you say life doesn't know you exist? You have to elaborate."

"You should go. Really."

"Probably. But it's warm in here..." he drew his shoulders inward "...well, warmer. So I'm in no hurry to go back out into the cold. I've met a bad-ass boxing girl with a story that I think parallels mine. And let's be honest ... when I don't disgust you, I intrigue you."

"You annoy me, but I enjoyed hitting you. If you stay here—annoying me more—I might hit you again." Jersey flopped onto her side, closing her eyes. "Go away."

Chris squinted at her bag, inching his way toward it so as to not get his ass kicked again. He bent down, plucking a photo peeking out from the side pocket. "Where did you get this?"

Jersey opened her eyes. On a frown, she snatched the photo from his loose grip. "I'm going to end you, asshole, if you don't get the hell out of here."

"Dena and Charles …"

Pressing a hand to the mat, Jersey slowly sat up, keeping her squinted gaze glued to him, unsure if she heard him correctly.

"They died," he mumbled, pinching the bridge of his nose. "Gah! Stupid voices." The rest of his words tumbled out of his mouth like he couldn't keep up with them. "I lived with them. Charles put me in basketball; that's how I met my best friend. He … his family had so much money, yet he befriended me, bought me shoes, treated me like a real friend. But then …"

"You lived with the Russells?"

Keeping his eyes pinched shut, he nodded. "But they died. He killed them."

"Who killed them?" Jersey bolted up from the mat, fisting her hands as adrenaline made its way through her body, ripping open old wounds, awakening a dormant hunger for revenge.

"My friend." Chris opened his eyes.

CHAPTER THREE

Eight years earlier ...

Two DEAD. FOUR homeless. And a Friday—pizza night.

Jersey endured six nights of stomaching low sodium casseroles and bitter greens with lemon juice and olive oil in exchange for one night of greasy pizza and the health food store's version of carbonated soft drinks.

She never complained. After six failed foster homes in fifteen years, sodium didn't matter. Dena and Charles Russell loved her and the three other foster children in their care. So, why did she focus on pizza while shoving tattered clothes, worn boxing gloves, and two knives into a soiled, camouflage duffel bag? It distracted her from the drift of incessant chatter down the long hallway from the living room.

A hallway lined with photos of foster children, spanning twenty years.

A hallway haunted with the ghosts of Dena and Charles Russell.

And pizza.

Cheese made Jersey gag. She used to scrape the toppings from the crust, pluck off the sausage and mushrooms from its rubbery sheath, arrange them back onto the crust, and sprinkle it with parmesan—because parmesan was salty and didn't make her gag like mozzarella.

"Jersey?"

Hearing the unfamiliar voice calling her name, Jersey closed her eyes, gripping the bag. She no longer needed salt. There was nothing she wouldn't have given up to change the events of that morning. Even pizza.

A heartless, gutless person killed her foster parents along a winding road, a mile from home. Hit-and-run.

With an all too familiar sense of foreboding, she shuffled down the hallway for the last time.

Goodbye gold picture frames.

Goodbye lavender candle scent.

Goodbye vomit green paint.

Farewell creepy buck head above the fireplace.

Coo-coo ...

The old cuckoo clock in the kitchen was the one thing Jersey wouldn't miss. Dena inherited it when her mom died. It didn't distinguish between 2 p.m. and 2 a.m. Dena said it comforted her. Jersey dreamed of it falling off the wall and shattering into unrepairable pieces.

But in that moment, she missed the contented sigh that fell from Dena's chest every time that bird sprang from its perch inside the bottom of the clock. She missed the eye roll of Charles who hated it as much as Jersey did.

The thrumming heartbeat of the Russell home ceased to exist and so did all hopes Jersey had for the future.

"Jersey Six?" A brunette with a high bun, tailored black pants, and a fitted, pink blouse studied the contents of an open manila folder. She nibbled on her clear-glossed lower lip.

Several other strange adults, along with two police officers, clogged the pocket-sized living room as the three other foster children scuffled down the hallway, carrying belongings that could fit into a single bag: gently worn clothes, a doll or superhero figurine, a Dena Russell original hand-tied fleece blanket, and a toothbrush.

For the first time in many years, Jersey wanted to cry. She'd resided with the Russells for six months. The best six months of her miserable life.

"You." The brunette snapped her blue manicured fingers at Jersey. "Roll call. I'm really sorry for your loss, but I'm a bit crunched for time. Are you Jersey Six?"

She nodded once, curling her straggly, coal hair behind her ear on one side, lifting her sable-eyed gaze to make eye contact with the social worker.

The sky spit a few raindrops into the late September air. Jersey diverted her attention to the front window—a clean window.

Dusted blinds.

Vacuumed beige carpet.

Shiny, faux-tile linoleum.

Not only had it taken fifteen years to land in a home where love was not laced with hard slaps and inappropriate touches, it took fifteen years to experience cleanliness, smoke-free air, and doors with locks meant to keep bad people out—not innocent children locked inside.

Mason, Sophie, and Wyatt followed another social worker to the door, shooting doe-eyed glances and trembling lower lips over their shoulders at Jersey.

Three, four, and seven.

They couldn't comprehend reality, so they looked to Jersey for some sort of explanation or reassurance.

"Be brave and run fast."

That's the advice she followed years earlier after an older girl they called G used a baseball bat to crush the skull of the fifty-year-old man who liked to do sick things to young girls. Jersey ran, just like the girl told her to do, and she didn't stop until a police officer snagged her by the waist in a park nearly two miles from the scene of the homicide.

CPS quickly placed Jersey in a new home with a new, demented fuck of a man and his wife who liked to screw the window washer.

Jersey knew Mason, Sophie, and Wyatt were destined to follow in her footsteps because, just like her, they had at least one living parent who was not willing to get their shit together but also not willing to completely surrender their parental rights.

As their social worker opened the door, Mason ran to Jersey, clinging to her leg. He pulled her pants down several inches because Jersey liked baggy jeans that hid her willowy body. She rested one hand on Mason's head as her other hand tugged up the waist of her jeans. He cried but said nothing. Mason didn't speak. Ever.

Not for one second did she think about lying to him, telling him everything would be okay. It wouldn't be okay because Dena and Charles were dead.

Mason wailed when they tore him away from her and hauled him out to the dirty, white SUV.

"Let's go, Jersey." The roll-calling brunette jerked her head toward the door.

"Amy, search Jersey's bag." A partially bald police officer didn't even look up from his flip phone as he barked his request. Jersey recognized him. He'd questioned her about different *incidents* on more than one occasion.

"Her bag?" Naïve and obviously-new-to-the-job Amy questioned.

Without hesitation, Jersey dropped her bag. *Thud!* The unexpected eviction left no time to make alternative arrangements for the contents in her bag.

Amy eyed her for a few seconds before squatting down and unzipping the bag. "Drugs? What exactly am I looking for?" Inexperienced Amy stabbed her hand into the contents of the bag before Jersey could warn her. "Ouch!" She seethed, jerking her hand from the bag.

Lips twisted, nose wrinkled, Jersey's gaze followed the blood oozing down Amy's hand, right onto the clean, beige carpet.

"Knives, Amy." Jersey laced her fingers behind her back. "Officer Dickhead wanted you to inspect my bag for knives. But his lack of respect for you—probably because you're a woman—prevented him from suggesting you use caution."

One of the knives was sheathed. Amy managed to find the one that was not. And a third knife Jersey carried on her. Officer Dickhead retrieved a towel from the kitchen and wrapped Amy's hand while scowling at Jersey. "Johnson will take you to get this stitched up. I'll deal with Jersey."

"How did you know she'd have knives?" Amy hugged her wrapped hand to her chest.

"Less than a year ago, Jersey gutted a man from groin to throat when he tried to take photos of her naked in the shower."

Amy gasped, meeting Jersey's gaze.

On a heavy sigh, Jersey rolled her eyes. "Gutted is not the correct word. It implies I removed his organs. Slashed, sliced, cut, maybe even lanced … but definitely not gutted. That's gross." Jersey had a limited vocabulary, except when it came to knives. She knew everything a knife could do.

Amy cringed as every ounce of sympathy drained from her rigid body. It didn't faze Jersey. She doubted Amy's genuine sympathy anyway. It was a job. Jersey was Amy's job—and not her only one that day.

That was fine. The fifteen-year-old didn't want sympathy; she just wanted Amy to get that hand stitched up before she dripped any more blood onto Dena's clean, beige carpet.

The officer dumped out the rest of the bag's contents, using more caution to retrieve the knives. "I'm not going to lie … the asshole deserved it. But, we still can't let little Jersey take the law into her own hands whenever she sees fit."

Little Jersey mumbled a "fuck you very much" as she hiked up her oversized jeans before bending down to stuff everything back into her bag. The asshole did deserve it. Jersey wasn't his first victim, but she was his last one. She never feared going to jail for murder—it would have been a welcomed opportunity at that point—but they didn't charge her with a crime. Instead, she won the lottery ... They placed her with the Russells.

Officer Dickhead waited for everyone else to leave the house before turning toward Jersey. "No one wants a fifteen-year-old delinquent."

Her hard gaze remained affixed to him. He wasn't sharing any new information.

"Jersey Six ..." He shook his head, scratching his scruffy chin before running his hand over his dark, buzzed halo of hair. "Did anyone ever tell you why that's your name?"

She narrowed her eyes, clenching her jaw.

"You weren't swaddled in a number six jersey. It's not the day of the month. Or any other rumor you've probably heard. You were dropped off at the door to the fire station, a New *Jersey* fire station, on Christmas. And you were the sixth abandoned baby that month. A foot of umbilical cord was still attached to you, pointing to a trail of bloody tracks that ended at a bus stop."

Dipping her head, Jersey took slow steps toward the officer.

"No."

She halted, glancing up.

"It ends here. If you can slaughter a grown man, you don't need anyone to take care of you."

Slaughter. Not a terrible description. Jersey thought it

was better than gutted.

"I know you don't want to see what's behind the next door. The system is flawed. Most homes are good. Most foster parents are loving. How you've managed to find the rare exceptions …" He shook his head. "Well, it's beyond me."

Searching for the true meaning behind his words, Jersey canted her head. Was he going to draw his weapon and put her out of her misery? Kill her with her own knife? So many questions kept her from speaking or moving another inch.

"What did you say to those other kids before they left?" His expression mirrored hers as he cocked his head to the side. "Be brave and run fast?"

Jersey nibbled the inside of her cheek, wondering where he was going with his questions.

"No one will miss you. Run, Jersey. Don't stop. Keep your head down. Stay out of trouble. And maybe you'll live. Maybe you'll find some way to turn this shit life of yours around."

Her eyes flitted between him and the door. He stepped to the side and opened it for her.

Fifteen. A police officer encouraging a *fifteen-year-old* girl to run, nowhere in particular, had to be wrong on too many levels to count. But that's exactly what he did.

That girl took cautious steps, waiting for the trap to snap on her. There had to be a catch.

"You could freeze to death in one night or be raped and left for dead in a week. Tell me you understand."

Jersey's steps faltered at the threshold. "I understand."

Her voice was soft but sure.

"And we never had this conversation. If you're not clear on that, then you can choose to get in my car, and we'll find you a home."

She nodded, putting one foot in front of the other until she stopped at the squad car. Maybe the next home would be like the Russells'—the good kind of love. That possibility gave her a moment's pause. It was the other kind of love that kept her feet moving down the driveway.

Him. Before she cut him open with her knife. Him. With his creepy, old man funk. The putrid smell of his breath, something in between garlic and cigarettes mixed with a bit of booze.

Was that good?

The way she was made to sit next to him, at the table, on the couch, or in the car. Close enough for him to touch her with his rough, filthy hands and move her closer to him so she could touch him for his pleasure. The smell of him was always so overwhelmingly enhanced by the terrified moments of wondering how far it would go this time.

Was that good?

Love didn't exist.

As the memories of that kind of *love* crawled up her throat from her churning stomach, she picked up speed until her legs took her far away from an awful past.

CHAPTER FOUR

Present

"THE RUSSELLS WERE good people." Chris hugged his knees to his chest, sitting next to Jersey on her mat. "I … I still can't remember much, but I remember that. I remember they were good. I feel like I have more feelings than actual memories."

Everyone else was gone, and it was a little after midnight. A single light in the corner by the sink flickered a few times, casting shadows on Chris's swollen face.

Jersey crossed her outstretched legs, sliding her hands between them to keep warm. The heat in the building barely kept things from freezing, always dropping a good twenty degrees after the sweaty bodies exited at the end of the day.

Chris continued, "Fifteen. You must have felt so lost."

She nodded. "Your friend …" Jersey brushed off his comment because lost wasn't even close to how she felt. Eight years later, she still couldn't find the right words. Of course she felt lost, but it was more. Lost felt like her normal. "How do you know it was your friend who killed them? Is he in prison? Please tell me he's in prison."

"He told me he did something—a mistake, an accident. He begged me for help." Chris grimaced. "I ... I told him he needed to go to the police. If..." his voice shook "...if it was an accident, then there wasn't anything to fear. Right?"

Chris met Jersey's gaze with pleading eyes as though he needed her to agree.

"No." She shook her head with sharp jerks. "Running over innocent people and then just ... taking off is *not* okay. What if they weren't dead? What if he could have called for help and saved them? But he didn't!" Jersey's heart hammered with anger. "He left them to die. *That* he did on purpose. *That* wasn't an accident."

Resting his elbows on his bent knees, Chris dropped his head into his hands. "He didn't go to the police. He must have told his parents. And I know they helped him. His *wealthy* ... influential parents. Then he just disappeared. We were supposed to be friends, but he just left."

"Left?" Jersey whispered. "You didn't turn him in? You didn't go to the police?"

"No ... no ... I just ..."

"You just what?" She shoved him.

He fell to the side, pressing his hand to the icy floor to keep from losing the rest of his balance.

Jersey shoved him again. "What is wrong with you? He ran over Dena and Charles. You knew, but you didn't do one fucking thing?"

"Stop!" He held up his arm to protect his face. "I don't ... I don't remember. Just stop! I-I just remembered my own name today! My name. Do you get that? Do

27

have any idea what it's like to really have nothing?"

He wiped his nose with the back of his hand, eyes red with emotion. "I wasn't just homeless. I was nameless. Unrecognizable, even to myself, in every way possible. Look at me!" He pointed to his face. "I …" his voice lost all fight, falling to a whisper "…I'm tired. And I hurt all over. I'm physically lost and emotionally hollow. So can you give me one night? And maybe when I'm not so cold, exhausted, and hungry … maybe I'll remember more."

Jersey had a mat. A roof. An occasional meal. And boxing … She had an outlet to fight her past, a method to defend her future—no matter how insignificant it seemed to most people. And even if her name was nothing more than a sad statistic, it was hers.

"One night?" she whispered, studying the vacant eyes of the lost soul in a battered body.

"One night."

ONE NIGHT TURNED into one week. One week bled into the next month. She couldn't kick him out over the holidays. Even Jersey wasn't that awful. And he managed to scrounge a cake for Christmas, which was also her birthday. Her first cake since Dena and Charles died.

"Firefighter, huh?" Judd stared at Chris sitting in the office with George. Neither one talked to the other, but they shared a mutual fondness for coloring—two fucked-up adults armed with a shit-ton of issues and a broken palate of crayons to bring superheroes to life.

"Yup." Jersey sprinted through a hundred sit-ups as Judd held her feet.

To keep Chris from getting killed for being at Marley's without the willingness to step in the ring, Jersey told everyone that he used to box—truth—but he had to quit after he was badly burned in a fire. The PTSD ruined his marriage, and he ended up losing his job too. Truth? No one knew, not even Chris and Jersey. But it seemed like a solid story.

Chris possessed a patchy memory at best, a crazy man's chattering about voices, and a Jekyll and Hyde personality. But Jersey let him stay because they shared a bond. That, and Chris agreed to do the shit work like cleaning and keeping an eye on George so Jersey could spend more time in the ring training for fights she'd never see, goals she'd never reach, and a future that most likely included jail time.

Everyone who hung out at Marley's ended up doing time, and most were repeat offenders. Crime sort of rubbed off in that place.

"Ya fucking him?" Judd smirked. "He sleeps with ya, yeah? Does his wiener look like the rest of him?"

"I'm not going to say. If you want to know about his wiener, you'll have to ask him out like a real gentleman. You'll have to buy him dinner and give him some sort of intelligent conversation. Chris is smart."

"Smart? Like he don't says ain't?" Judd coughed a laugh.

When she reached her hundredth sit-up, Jersey collapsed, resting her arm across her sweaty forehead. "Yeah.

Smarter than all of us put together. When he's not bat-shit crazy, he's smart. Uses big words. I think he might even use them correctly." Dena drilled Jersey on proper grammar. Six months wasn't long enough to amass a large vocabulary, but it was long enough to get rid of *ain't* and *gonna*.

"*Ain't gonna ain't going to college.*"

Judd laughed, standing and offering his hand to Jersey.

She took it, letting him pull her up.

"So if ya *ain't* letting him get you off, then why ya letting him hang out here?"

"He does the shit work. And he's helping me with something." She started to wrap her hands, ready to kick Judd's ass in the ring.

"Helping ya what? You two gonna make weird porn videos in the back room?"

Jersey let Chris stay for several reasons, but revenge sat at the top of that list. Eventually, he'd remember more details about his friend. They would find him. And they would kill him.

An eye for an eye.

"Might be the only way to keep the gym open." She winked.

Judd frowned as Derek, one of the older guys, tied his gloves for him. "Ya heard?"

She nodded. "Marley's is closing. Developers want to make this part of town safer, which means we're getting kicked out. Yeah, I heard." Jersey slid between the ropes and tapped her gloves together twice. "Ding. Ding." She smiled with her black mouth guard puffing out her lips.

Judd threw the first punch. Predictable.

Jersey bobbed to the right and returned with a quick one-two combination, knocking Judd off balance. Before he could recover, she pummeled him until he landed face down on the mat.

Ten seconds lapsed.

Jersey kicked his foot. "Dead?"

Judd grumbled.

Nope. Alive.

She sighed. "Chris is going to find me a worthy opponent. Your size just makes you slow. It means when you fall, it takes longer for you to get up. And I don't want to kill you, so it's not as much fun."

Judd lifted his bloodied face, stretching the cords of muscle in his thick neck. "Ya wanna kill someone?"

Jersey turned her back to him, tugging off her gloves. "I want revenge."

CHAPTER FIVE

"WHERE ARE YOU going?" Chris looked up from his book.

Jersey had to give him credit. He read absolutely anything he could get his hands on. "Self-help book?" She squinted at the title, not able to see it very well.

Chris flopped back on the mat, using Jersey's blanket—their blanket—as a pillow. "Yeah. It's missing the first few chapters." He tilted it to show her the mangled book. "But they put all the valuable stuff at the end anyway. Figured since we're going to be on the street soon, we might as well figure out something now."

"We?" Jersey released her hair from its ponytail. "Does this mean you're looking to help me?"

He shrugged, keeping his gaze on the book, hiding most of his face. "Maybe. Or at least I'll let you borrow the book when I'm done."

"I hate reading." She scraped a handful of change from the bottom of her bag and shoved it into the front pouch of her hoodie.

"Aw, that just means you haven't found the right book."

"No." She sauntered away from him. "Just means I

hate reading."

"You didn't say where you're going!" Chris called.

"Out." Jersey pushed open the front door, squinting against the midday sun but welcoming the hum of cars and buses instead of the bitching. Ever since George posted the closing announcement for the gym, whining, bitching, and idle threats filled the stagnant gym atmosphere as if it was her fault wealthy developers decided to invade their part of town.

With nowhere to go and no means to get there even if she did, Jersey made her usual stroll around the block to clear her head and absorb some sun, even if it was freezing outside. The coins in her pocket meant she'd get a meal that day. The Underdog hot dog stand managed to stay open year-round, a fixture in that part of Newark for over a decade. While the demolition in Jersey's neighborhood brought a boost in business with hungry construction workers, she wondered if the rundown food truck would last once the *trash* got taken out.

Pulling her hood up, she hugged her body and shivered as winter showed its potential, biting her exposed skin and rattling her bones as she waited in line.

"Just one," she mumbled while digging the change out of her pocket.

"Drink?" The new guy manning the stand asked as he fished out a hot dog from the warmer and plopped it into the white bun.

She shook her head.

"Chips?"

She continued to shake her head.

The guy beside Jersey rammed into her as he jumped back to avoid the ill-aimed spray of mustard from the pump.

"Shit!" Jersey's change took flight, some of it landing on the counter, but most of it bouncing off the front of the truck and ricocheting in all directions.

"Two dollars," the new guy manning the stand said as he fixed the mustard pump while the grumbling patron who bumped into Jersey wiped the splatter from his shirt, giving zero shits that he made Jersey lose her change.

She crawled around on the filthy ground, collecting as much of the money as she could find.

"Hurry up! I have a line."

She missed Tye, the owner of the stand. He would have taken pity on her—even if she didn't want it—and handed her the hot dog with a kind smile and a "don't worry about it this time."

"I've got it."

Jersey ignored the deep, unfamiliar voice above her as she reached for the nickel a foot under the food truck.

"Make it two." Three more words fell upon her from that voice.

She glanced up from her hands and knees, giving up on the five cents. A tall man in distressed blue jeans and untied gray boots smiled at the grouchy hot dog stand guy. His white teeth complemented his scruffy jaw. His sunglasses hid his eyes beneath a gray beanie matting dark bangs to his forehead. He slipped several napkins into the pocket of his puffy, space-blue jacket before cradling two hot dogs in one hand while offering his other hand to help Jersey up from the ground.

She could do one-arm pushups. There was no need to play damsel in distress, so she stood, brushing her hands on her sweatshirt while squinting up at him. He owned a crooked and undecipherable smile. After sharing it with her, as if his smile alone was some sort of gift, he proceeded to deposit a squiggly line of ketchup on each hot dog before handing one to Jersey.

"Thank … you …" She accepted the hot dog without taking her eyes off his smirking face. "What if I don't like ketchup?"

He eyed the scar on her right cheek for a few seconds, his grin faltering for a breath, as if it somehow distracted him.

"I said, what if I don't like ketchup?"

He tore his gaze away from her scar, meeting her eyes and blinking at her for another few really uncomfortable seconds before taking a bite of his hot dog while moving a few steps away from the food truck. "Then lick it off and forget about it."

Jersey laughed. "If I didn't like ketchup, then why would I lick it off?"

His long legs took tiny steps, as if walking and eating a hot dog could end in disaster. "You said *if* and *didn't,* not *since* and *don't,* which means you like ketchup, but you're just trying to bust my generous balls by throwing out some hypothetical situation."

Taking a massive bite of the hot dog, Jersey followed a few steps behind him. She liked ketchup on her hot dog. Only ketchup.

"Are you stalking me?" His strides lengthened toward the stoplight.

Jersey took another bite. One more bite and it would be gone. She chewed slowly, the only option with a third of a hot dog and bun shoved into her mouth. "Well..." she mumbled, swallowing twice to get the partially chewed food into her stomach "...I need to know about your generous balls. They wouldn't happen to have some spare change, would they?"

Hard work, a paycheck, job promotions ... and a million other things imparted a sense of pride to the average person. People who lived on the street could be proud and starve to death, or they could swallow their muted pride along with a hot dog and possibly some spare change for their next meal.

"You live around here?" The man wadded up his napkin, proving to be a faster eater than Jersey.

"Yes. You?"

He turned, sliding his sunglasses down to the tip of his nose and sizing her up with his dark eyes. "I used to."

Jersey finished her hot dog and wiped her mouth with the sleeve of her sweatshirt. That seemed to elicit that undecipherable grin again. Men like him didn't grin at women like Jersey, especially after being solicited for money. But after a few more odd moments of just staring at her, his grin faltered.

"Do you have a job?"

"Why are you looking at me like that?" Her eyes narrowed into slits.

He pushed his sunglasses back up his nose. "Like

what?"

"Like I confuse you?"

On a shrug, he shook his head. "You don't confuse me. You didn't answer my question. Do you have a job?"

Her lips twisted. "Sort of."

"But it doesn't pay well?"

"Doesn't pay at all. I work for benefits."

"Benefits, huh?" He glanced around the neighborhood before returning his attention to Jersey. "Well, sounds like good old bartering."

"What do you mean?" Her gaze sank to her feet.

"What do I mean by bartering?"

"Yes … no …" She pinched the bridge of her nose and shook her head. "Never mind. I was just looking for spare change. Thanks for the hot dog." Hugging her arms to her chest while denying him one last glance, Jersey fled in the opposite direction.

"I have change."

Her steps faltered. The hot dog satisfied her hunger. She could figure out the next meal later, but she thought of Chris and wondered if he needed something to eat.

She turned.

He held out a twenty-dollar bill. "What are your benefits? What do you do in exchange for them?"

The girl who took off her clothes and gave away the last piece of her pride for a sack of groceries, a blanket, and a gently used pair of shoes had no good reason to withhold simple information with twenty dollars at stake. "A gym membership and a bed." Her chin lifted, heavy with her life's reality. "I clean a few things and help out where I'm needed."

He slipped the twenty dollars into the pocket of her hoodie. Jersey stiffened, holding her breath. Lifting his hands up slowly, palms toward her, he offered her a soft smile.

Jersey asked for spare change. He gave her more than a buck or two. She felt foolish for her reaction.

"I'm Ian."

"I'm not going to buy drugs with this, if that's what you're thinking."

His head inched side to side. "I wasn't."

Lunch. Twenty dollars. A real smile. No judgment.

There had to be a catch.

"Well … again … thank you." Her gaze bounced around to avoid looking at him and the way he studied her like Chris studied the pages of his books.

"You're welcome. My name is Ian."

She nodded, watching the cars just over his shoulder. "You said that."

"I know. I'm just wondering how many times I have to say it before you tell me your name."

Her lips betrayed her, letting the cute stranger pull a smile from her. "Jersey."

"Jersey … good name."

"No." She chuckled, relinquishing eye contact to go with the smile. "It's not. It's a lazy name. It's the name they give an abandoned baby from *New Jersey*."

"Could have been Mississippi. You know, that poor kid who never gets to see their name in alphabet magnets on the fridge because some dimwit gave them a name with four S's and only two S's come in a bucket of those rainbow-colored magnets."

People like him didn't have conversations with her. For a long moment, she inspected him—his dark eyes, his gleaming smile, his relaxed posture.

"Are you a reporter?" she asked.

"What?"

"Are you doing a story on Newark's homeless population? Are you wondering what's going to happen to me when Marley's shuts down and I have no place to go? Is that what you need? My story?"

"No. I—"

"An undercover cop? Are you going to offer me money for sex to see if I take it?"

Ian flinched, rubbing his neck while shaking his head. "No to all of the above. Uh … Marley's? That's the gym?"

Jersey kept her invisible shield held high. "Yes. You heard of it?"

"That's…" Ian pointed in the direction of the gym "…where I'm headed."

She squinted. "Why?"

On a soft laugh, he shrugged. "I'm not sure. To say goodbye to memories, I suppose." His head circled slowly. "I just wanted one last look at everything before it undergoes this *image rehabilitation*. That's what they're calling it, correct?"

Jersey lifted her shoulders to her ears. She had no clue what politically correct term they used to justify running businesses into the ground and displacing poor people. "Maybe just walk by Marley's. If I were you, I wouldn't go in there."

"No?" Ian's head tilted to the side.

"Everyone's in a shitty mood because of the closing. Not that the people there are ever particularly welcoming, but today they'd have no tolerance for someone like you popping your pretty head into the gym for *one last look*."

Ian shared his easy grin. "You think I have a pretty head?"

"I think your hat looks warm."

"I see … so popping my warm hat into Marley's isn't a good idea?"

"Not if you want to leave with your hat." Jersey gave him a sly grin before pivoting and strutting back toward the gym. The wind blew her hood off her head. She tugged it back up, but it blew right off again.

"So you're just going to eat half of my lunch from my favorite hot dog stand, pocket my twenty dollars, and leave me feeling vulnerable on the streets with my warm hat and pretty head?"

"Yes," she hollered on a very uncharacteristic giggle. "Even if you have good taste in hot dogs." Jersey tossed a flirty smile over her shoulder. At least it felt like that. She had no experience with actual flirting.

As she attempted to wipe the grin from her face, the scuffing of shoes behind her grew closer.

"Under Dog is still the best. All these years later … it's perfection."

"Ian, are you stalking me?"

"Yes." He picked up his pace, sidling next to her. "I'm going to Marley's."

With a quick sideways glance, she grunted. "You're stupider than you look."

"Ya think?" Ian cupped his hands at his mouth and blew into them. "I haven't been here in years. Yesterday, someone saw me wearing an old shirt that said Marley's on it. They told me that it's shutting down. I have part of the day off, sort of … so I felt compelled to come say a silent goodbye to some of my past."

"Marley is dead."

"I know. I heard that." Ian stopped twenty feet from the door to the rundown gym.

Jersey halted several feet farther and turned around.

Slowly, almost reverently, Ian removed his sunglasses, focusing on the faded, burnt orange sign missing the M and L.

"You coming inside?"

Ian's head inched side to side. "No. Some people would be a little pissed off at me if I risked my pretty head."

"I'll protect you."

His right brow inched up his forehead as his focus shifted to meet her gaze.

"Twenty bucks will buy you ten minutes to look around. I can keep you unscathed for that long."

"What are you? Five-six?"

"Five-seven." She pushed her shoulders back, struggling to show him her true strength. Yeah, five feet seven inches of bones wrapped in hard-earned muscles—but where muscles didn't hide bones, those bones protruded. Bony hips. Knees and elbows. Her cheekbones protruded.

Lack of regular meals made it impossible to hide her angular face, gaunt and emaciated.

"You couldn't keep ahold of two dollars in change for your lunch, yet I'm supposed to trust you with my pretty head?"

Jersey crossed her arms over her chest and flipped out her hip.

Ian smirked. "It's fine." His gaze made a slow sweep along the length of the building. "This is good. This is enough."

Good.

Enough.

Nothing kept her there, yet she didn't walk away. In many ways, life ended at fifteen for the girl who couldn't turn around and walk away. In the span of thirty minutes, Ian gave her a glimpse of something. What? She didn't know.

"You really sleep here?"

Jersey's gaze lifted from the ground, her concentration trying to define the unfamiliar feeling in her gut. "Yes."

"Where will you go when it permanently closes?"

"I don't know."

He studied her more, pressing his lips together, slipping his hands into his front pockets. "What if I offered you a job? Would you be interested?"

"Um … you're offering me a job?"

His eyebrows squeezed together. After a few seconds, he returned an uneasy nod.

"We just met … on the street."

He continued with his slow nod. "I realize this."

"Something legal?"

Ian grinned. "Yes."

Jersey waited for him to say more, change his mind, withdraw his knee-jerk offer. "I'd take it ..." her lips twisted to the side "...well ..."

"Well what?"

"I have a friend. We kinda agreed to look out for each other. So it would have to be something close by."

Ian released a slow breath as he hooked his sunglasses onto the top of his jacket. "What if ..." he narrowed his eyes, pausing again like something in his head was at war "...I can get jobs for both of you?"

"Are you serious?" Her head jutted outward.

He glanced around uneasily. "Serious."

"Sold."

He widened his eyes, lips parted. "O ... kay then. I'll have a car pick you and your friend up..." he cocked his arm out in front of his face, glancing at his watch "...around three. Have your stuff packed."

"Stuff packed? What do you mean? Where are we going?"

"It's a traveling gig."

"Traveling?" Jersey's nose scrunched.

"Yes. You'll stay in a bus or at hotels."

"I can't afford—"

"You won't have to pay for them, and food will be provided."

"Traveling around New Jersey?"

Ian bobbed his head side to side. "Think bigger."

"I can't think bigger. I've never left New Jersey."

"Ever?"

She shook her head.

Ian pulled his charcoal gray beanie from his head, leaving a messy case of hat head. He took five long strides and slid the beanie onto Jersey's head.

"Why?" she whispered.

"You said it yourself; it's a warm hat."

"No. Why are you offering a complete stranger a job?"

His gaze swept along her face and up to the hat on her head of long, dark hair. It rested there for a few silent seconds. "Just a feeling."

No person had ever made her feel more vulnerable than Ian did in that moment. After years of having nothing, the homelessness became its own comfort. She accepted her life's circumstances.

Nothing felt like something.

Lost became its own home.

Dreams died.

"Three o'clock. Out front. Okay?"

Jersey returned a single, wide-eyed nod.

Ian smiled. "Do you have a last name?"

"Six."

That made his smile swell another inch up his pleasant face, letting his teeth shine. "Jersey Six…" he reached up and gave the hat a gentle tug "…I'm going to show you the world."

"What does that mean?"

He let go, taking a step back while maintaining his confident grin. "It means I'm going to show you the world." Ian took two more steps backward. "The world, Jersey."

CHAPTER SIX

"PACK YOUR SHIT." Jersey grabbed the soap by the sink, a spare roll of toilet paper, and several waters from the fridge.

Chris peeked at her from behind his book as she shoved everything into her bag.

"What did you do? Are we on the run? Did you kill someone? Steal something?"

She paused, huffing out a quick breath. "Jobs. I got us jobs."

"I see. You're going to have to elaborate. And nice hat."

Forgetting that she had Ian's hat, she pulled it off her head, bringing it to her nose for a few seconds. It smelled good—clean-guy, expensive good.

"Did you seriously just sniff that?" Chris laughed, closing his book and sitting up.

In their month together, Jersey stopped seeing Chris's scars. All she could see was her new friend. And earlier that day, she felt like Ian saw *her*—not a homeless woman in need of twenty bucks and a meal. That meant something because she had no idea what he saw since her own reflection looked so foreign to herself. Then again …

there wasn't a mirror in the joint, so Jersey rarely witnessed her own reflection.

Her eyes narrowed. "Someone gave me the hat. I was just making sure it didn't smell funky."

"Jers, this place is the epitome of funky smelling. Unless someone pissed on that hat today, it can't smell worse than the air we breathe daily."

"Epitome?"

"A perfect example." Chris never made fun of Jersey's limited education and vocabulary. Not once. That was why she made them a package deal with Ian.

"The guy who gave me this hat offered to give us both jobs. And we're being picked up at three."

"Why are you packing?"

"It's a traveling job."

"What's the job?"

She rolled her eyes and shrugged. "I don't know. But it involves a place to sleep and food. And it's legal."

"Doesn't feel right. A stranger offering you a job on a whim is a little worrisome. And offering *me* a job having never met me—seen me." Chris shook his head. "It's not right. It has to be some kinky shit."

"I told you it's legal." She zipped the bag, and it crept back open because the zipper was broken.

"There's a lot of kinky shit that's legal."

"Chris …" Jersey frowned. "We share a mat and what amounts to one and a half blankets. We take food and money from strangers, dumpsters, and places that are just too embarrassing to admit. At this point, I'd exchange a little kinky shit for an actual bed and regular, hot meals."

He sighed and resumed his reading. Jersey ignored the occasional scowls he tossed her way while giving her the silent treatment.

"I'm going to tell George goodbye. Just George. I don't trust anyone else around here to not screw up this chance for us."

Another silent scowl.

Jersey smirked.

At three o'clock, Jersey *and* Chris snuck out of Marley's, unnoticed. A tall, broad man sporting buzzed, reddish-blond hair held open a door to a black sedan that looked too nice to be in Marley's neighborhood. For three full seconds, Jersey contemplated the sanity of getting into the car. Ian hadn't given her the kinky vibe, but Jersey wasn't an expert on more than boxing and knives.

"Jersey?" the tall man asked.

She nodded, taking the final steps across the littered concrete to the cracked sidewalk curb.

"I'm Shane." He smiled, even at Chris, without a lingering gaze or second look at her disfigured sidekick.

"This is my friend, Chris." Jersey hugged her bag to her chest.

"I can put your bag in the trunk."

"I've got it." What little she had to piece together and call her life or belongings wasn't going in the trunk. If kinky shit went down, she wanted her bag and the spare knife in it. Chris didn't have a bag. He had the ripe, soiled clothes on his back and a few toiletries in the pocket of his hoodie.

"Suit yourself." Shane shrugged.

They slid into the backseat of the car. Another smiling face greeted them from the front passenger seat. Her blinding-white teeth seemed a bit too big for her mouth—in Jersey's opinion—but her beaming dark eyes, penciled eyebrows, and perfectly glossed lips made the whole poster smile work. She could have been in a commercial for toothpaste or maybe some sort of allergy medication ad.

"Hi! I'm Max. Ian's assistant. I'll need you both to fill out these forms. When one of you is done, click *next* and it will bring up a new form." She tucked her stick straight, chin-length black and gray hair behind her diamond-studded pierced ear and handed Jersey an electronic tablet.

Jersey stared at Max's perfect Asian skin and dainty hands. She didn't look like a Max. The car pulled away from the curb as she set her bag between herself and Chris and glanced at the tablet. It had been eight years since she'd held a fancy electronic device. Dena used to let Jersey use her phone to play games if Jersey finished her chores on time.

First name.

Last name.

Date of Birth.

That's all she could fill out. No address, phone number, emergency contact, previous employment, list of references … nothing else.

Occasionally, Max glanced back, shooting them more toothpaste-commercial smiles. Jersey returned a tight grin, feigning confidence in her ability to fill out the employee information form.

"Here." Chris grabbed the tablet from Jersey and filled in all the empty blanks with unfamiliar numbers, street names, reference names like Billy Bob and Heidi Ho. He typed in his name as her emergency contact, pausing at the last name spot.

Chris didn't have a last name. His memories of some things were colorful and sharp, but simple details like his last name stayed hidden in the unreachable parts of his memory. Maybe they were gone forever.

He glanced at her, and a tiny, tight grin pulled at his lips as his eyes filled with wickedness.

Ten, he typed in the last name box.

Her narrow-eyed glare bounced between his eyes and the tablet.

"Ten?" she whispered.

He shrugged. "You're a six, so I'm going to be a ten."

She fisted her hand, leaving it in her lap, with her middle finger stretched long for him to see.

He chuckled, leaning closer so only she could hear him. "It's perfect. Chris Ten … get it? Christian?"

Shane and Max cracked their windows an inch. Jersey waited for them to light up, but they didn't. Shane glanced back at Jersey in the rearview mirror, answering her questioning expression with a slight smile and wrinkled nose.

"We stink," she said under her breath to Chris.

"Of course we do." He continued to fill out several other pages of her employee information, including a digital signature. Then he moved on to the next form for himself—Chris Ten.

She couldn't remember the last time she'd been in a car, but she definitely remembered the last time she'd crossed over into New York—never. Her mind raced with all the ways she could get back to Newark if Ian's job offer didn't work out. After all, she had the twenty dollars from him and maybe another five dollars' worth of change in her bag.

"What did he say?" Chris muttered, staring out his own window after finishing the forms and returning the tablet to Max.

"Who?" Jersey shifted her attention to him.

"George. When you said we were leaving, I didn't say goodbye. My money is on us being right back in that dump before the end of tomorrow."

Max glanced over her shoulder again, and Jersey eyed her with caution until she turned back around.

"He didn't say anything, of course, but he tried to hand me fifty dollars. I couldn't take it. I really don't know what's going to happen to him after the gym closes. Somehow I doubt the guys will financially look after him the way they managed to pool their money together to keep Marley's open."

Chris hummed in agreement.

"And where did you get money to bet on how soon we'd return?"

He shook his head on a soft chuckle and returned his attention to the window and the skyscrapers welcoming them to Manhattan. "Oh, Jersey … I love you."

She scowled at the back of his head, irritated at herself

for letting him worm his way into her barely existent world—and even more irritated at herself for liking his place in it. Jersey loved how he'd read her books at night, even if she pretended to plug her ears, telling him to shut up. Sometimes he'd have a bad dream, nightmares about his disoriented past, and she'd comfort him. That made her feel needed.

Feeling needed meant more to her than she ever imagined it could. Maybe the only purpose to life was having a purpose.

"We're going to stop for some essentials. You good with that?" Max asked.

Jersey and Chris stared at each other.

"Essentials?" Jersey repeated.

"Ian thought you might need some clothes and other *everyday* things. His treat."

"He's going to dress you up as his whore, Jers," Chris whispered in her ear.

"For both of us?" Jersey asked.

Max nodded.

"Okay."

Max faced forward again.

Jersey stuck her tongue out at Chris. "Looks like you'll be his whore too," she whispered back to him.

CHAPTER SEVEN

C HRIS IGNORED THE second looks and not-so-subtle glances as they trekked through the posh hotel lobby carrying several bags of clothing and other essentials.

"Chris, we'll find room for you on one of the buses over the next few days. Might have to do some shuffling. For now you'll stay with us." Max stepped into the elevator, chin tipped toward her phone as Jersey and Chris followed her.

"Buses? I'm getting shipped back already?"

Leaning against the back wall of the elevator, Max glanced up, penciled brows drawn tightly. "No. The tour buses. Can you lift heavy objects?"

He peered at Jersey's clueless expression, and he answered Max, "Depends on how heavy. I have some physical limitations."

Max nodded, chewing on her bottom lip. "Listen, people are going to be … *people*. Human. They're going to be curious about what happened to you. I'd like to put all the whispers to rest as soon as possible so everyone can just focus on their jobs. What can I tell them?"

"I was badly burned," Chris replied, sounding more condescending than he meant to sound.

The elevator dinged and the doors opened. He and Jersey stepped off the elevator as Max returned a frown.

"Clearly. But can I ask *how* you were badly burned?" She took the lead, and they followed her around a sharp right corner and down a long hallway.

"You can, but if you want an honest answer, then you're going to be sorely disappointed because I don't know how it happened."

Tapping the room key card to the sensor, Max pushed open the hotel room door, stepped inside, and held it open for Jersey and Chris. Jersey hugged her duffel bag and shopping bags, making a wide-eyed inspection of the room while Chris plopped his shopping bags onto the first of the two queen beds.

"So…" Max threw open the curtains, exposing a stunning view of Manhattan "…it's safe to say you have some memory loss of the trauma?"

Some memory loss.

Chris inwardly grinned. "That's a very safe answer."

"And your family doesn't know?"

Hugging her bag, Jersey remained planted to her spot three feet inside the door. Chris tore her bags from her grasp, one at a time. She stiffened, hands balled into fists.

"You just purchased us new clothes." He managed to tug Jersey's shopping bags from her, but he didn't fight her for the duffel bag. Instead, he rolled his eyes at her and returned his attention to Max. "And I assume you'd like us to take a shower to wash the filth and stink from our bodies. Surely in the back of your pretty mind you have to think we don't have family … a home … or any other belongings to our names. Right?"

Max glanced at her watch and clasped her hands behind her back. "Listen, Ian disappeared for several hours today, and he came back with instructions to pick you two up and get you set up with jobs. He requested I not ask any questions that don't need to be asked. So I'm navigating this carefully. But honestly, I have a million questions screaming in my head. All I'm asking is for you to help me help you."

Chris didn't question her sincerity because her defeated posture and the surrender in her voice left little room for doubt.

"Tell people whatever you think they want to hear."

Chris and Max turned toward Jersey's voice. She loosened her grip on her duffel bag and took cautious steps toward the window, not making eye contact as she squeezed by them. Jersey's body jerked with an audible gasp at the sight before her.

"If you need anything, here's my number." Max set her business card on the desk, next to the hotel phone. "Otherwise, I'll be back in an hour to get you. I'll have some food sent up right away. Is there anything else you need?"

Jersey remained statuesque at the window as Chris inspected Max's business card. It was all black with just a phone number, not even her name.

"We're good. Thank you. Um …" He held up the business card. "You don't strike me as a Max. Is that your real name?"

She smiled, a soft one that held some sadness. "My

father is from Japan. My mother is American. She had a sister who died at a young age. I was named after her, Maxann."

"Sorry." Chris let his gaze fall to the black card.

"Me too."

When the door clicked behind Max, Chris stood next to Jersey at the window. "Well ... at least your new friend, Ian, set us up with a sweet view, new clothes, and clean sheets. I'm just worried he's trying to get us to lower our guards before the kinky shit begins."

Jersey's jaw clenched, but it couldn't hold back her grin.

"Bus ... did you hear her say I might stay on a bus? We're joining the circus, Jers. You get that, right? In another few hours, you'll be decorated in sequins, traipsing around on a giant elephant while I'm three steps behind with a bucket, scooping its shit."

She giggled. Chris liked her giggle. He'd seen her knock out men twice her size, leaving them bloodied and gasping in the middle of the boxing ring. He knew what it felt like to be on the receiving end of her fury, so sharing space with her during a rare moment of giggling made him feel normal, even special, and anything but lost in the world. When he wasn't experiencing nightmares, voices in his head, cold sweats, and heart palpitations, he imagined what his life was like before the accident. A woman, maybe a family, a job he loved ... could it have been possible?

TWO SHOWERS AND two chicken sandwiches later, Jersey and Chris sat on their respective beds watching television, dressed in new jeans, white T-shirts, hole-less socks, and well-fitted sneakers. It had been eight years since her hair experienced shampoo and conditioner and a hairdryer that didn't also double as a hand dryer in a public restroom.

"It was disgusting." Jersey kept her gaze on the television, some action movie.

"What was?"

"The water in the bottom of the shower. The last time I took a shower, the water wasn't black."

"Well, that's what happens when you're forced to live in a shithole and bathe out of a sink."

She nodded. "I shaved. Kept clogging the razor. The guys used to stare at my hairy legs and armpits. They didn't dare say a word, but I knew they were staring."

Chris shrugged. "I didn't mind. The hairy version of you helped keep me warm at night."

She flipped him the bird, and he chuckled. Jersey shot him a nervous smile as three knocks hit the door.

"Let the circus begin." Chris shut off the T.V. as Jersey opened the door.

Max's eyes widened. "Night and day difference." She smiled. "Let's go."

Jersey grabbed her duffel bag.

"Oh …" Max shook her head. "You'll be back later. You can leave your bag here. Just bring your purse if you want it."

"I don't have a purse. I have a bag. And I'm not leaving it behind."

Max cringed when Jersey lifted the bag onto her shoulder, smudging black marks onto her new white tee. "Alrighty then. I'm out of shits to give today. Let's go." Max pivoted, striding down the hall in her black skinny jeans, ankle boots, and white wool coat tied in front. "Maybe we can find you a new bag."

Jersey didn't want a new bag, but she kept that to herself.

Fifteen minutes later, the vehicle stopped at the back entrance to a huge building. Security dotted the area. The driver opened Max's door and then Jersey's door.

When they climbed out, Max slipped lanyards around their necks. "Keep these on at all times. Follow me." She wormed them through people scurrying in all directions, all wearing the same type of lanyards around their necks.

"What the hell, Jers …" Chris nudged Jersey as they raced to keep up with Max's long strides. "We're at a concert." He held up the badge around his neck.

Jersey hadn't stopped to read hers. She had too much to worry about with people bumping into her. The urge to push back gnawed at her, but the concert news explained the music vibrating around them in the cold, hollowed hallways.

"Dalton!" Max whistled and held up her hand.

A dark bearded man with tattooed arms turned around from several yards in front of them. Max sped forward with Jersey and Chris in tow.

"Dalton, this is Chris. Use him where you need him. Message me if there are any issues."

The guy looked like a monster with graffiti and a beard as he held out his hand to Chris, not seemingly bothered by Chris's appearance. Jersey wondered if Max spent her hour away from them forewarning everyone.

"Welcome."

Chris shook his hand, giving Jersey a look she hadn't seen except when he woke from his night terrors. She shot him a reassuring smile. They were showered, clothed, and fed. And apparently at a concert venue.

Jersey shrugged. "It's not a circus."

Dalton's and Max's lips turned up in amusement at Jersey's comment.

"Follow me." Dalton continued several steps forward and opened a door to his left.

Chris shot Jersey one last nervous glance before following Dalton.

"This way." Max lead Jersey in the opposite direction. "First concert?" she called over her shoulder.

Jersey gripped her bag tighter, dodging glances from a few people who passed them. "Yeah."

"Have you been a big fan of Ian's for a while?"

"Um … I'd say just since he bought me lunch and offered me a job."

Max stopped without warning, sending Jersey into her back.

"Sorry." Jersey stepped back, and Max turned.

"Name one Ian Cooper song."

Jersey curled her lips between her teeth.

Max coughed on her reply. "You ... you've never listened to his music?"

Jersey shook her head. Maybe she had heard his music. The guys at the gym played a lot of music, but she didn't know artists, pop culture, current events, or anything that didn't involve boxing or the means to get a meal.

"Have you even heard of him before today?"

Another headshake.

Max curled her black and gray hair behind her ear. "Ian ... Ian ... Ian ..." She shook her head a half dozen times before turning toward a door. Next to the door was a white sheet of paper with *Ian Cooper* printed on it.

"How old are you?" Jersey asked.

Max glanced back over her shoulder. "Why?"

Jersey shrugged. "Just curious. Your skin looks young, but your hair looks old."

On a chuckle, Max's penciled eyebrows slid up her forehead. "Old hair, huh? Well, thanks for the skin compliment. I'm fifty-one. But I don't feel a day over thirty." She winked just before knocking twice and opening the door. "Heads up, gentlemen."

The doorway opened to a spacious room, double the size of the hotel room, which wasn't tiny in Jersey's eyes. It was filled with sofas, chairs, lit vanities, a television, several tables covered with food and beverages, and three men all close to Ian's age—maybe late twenties/early thirties.

Two men sat on a sofa, playing video games. They gave Jersey and Max a quick "hey" without actually tearing their attention from the battle playing out on the T.V. screen. A blond guy with wavy shoulder-length hair glanced up from the edge of his chair where he sat strumming a few chords on a guitar.

"Thanks, Max."

Jersey's attention shifted to Ian's voice from the opposite side of the room where his long jeans and T-shirt-clad body engulfed a sofa as he slid off a pair of neon blue, wireless headphones. When Jersey turned back toward Max, the door was already shut with no Max in sight. The blond guy playing guitar gave Jersey a smile and polite nod as she tightened her hold on the bag and inched her way to Ian's side of the room.

Ian sat up, stretching his arms above his head on a big yawn. Jersey remembered a guy who came into Marley's Gym several years earlier: Racer. Ian's body resembled his—tall, lean, and intricately cut to perfection. Racer treated his body like a million-dollar performance machine. And he was the first person to knock Jersey out in less than two minutes. He made her stronger, made her work harder and fight smarter. Then someone took him out with a single gunshot to the head on his way out of the gym on a Friday night.

Jersey remembered it was a Friday because Dena and Charles died on a Friday.

"Jersey." Ian smiled at her like he did earlier that day. Not a you-look-better smile like the one Max gave her at the hotel, just a nice-to-see-you-again smile as if he wasn't seeing her in a different light. No night and day.

She smiled back at him, not because she wanted to,

just because she couldn't help herself.

The grin on his face doubled. "Would you like something to eat or drink?" He nodded toward the tables of food and beverages behind her.

"We ate at the hotel." Her lips twisted to the side. "Mind if I stick some stuff in my bag for later?"

A tiny wrinkle formed between Ian's eyes, just below the long sweep of his black bangs. "There will be lots of food available later too. But..." he shrugged, leaning forward and resting his elbows on his knees "...take whatever you want."

Jersey glanced over her shoulder at the food and the three other men in the room. She decided to wait a little while before shoving as much as possible into her bag like a free-for-all. "Thanks." Jersey returned her attention to Ian. "So ... you're a singer. Like ... are you a big deal?"

Every word she spoke seemed to feed his level of happiness. "Well ..." He rubbed his chin, twisting his lips. "We play music. People like to listen to our music. But no ... it's not a big deal. We're not saving lives or anything like that."

She eyed him with suspicion for a few seconds. That smile of his didn't feel worthy of complete trust. "Um ... what exactly do you need me to do? What's my job? They already took Chris. Will that big, bearded guy come for me too?" Jersey couldn't remember his name.

"No." Ian stood, pushing his elbows out from his shoulders, twisting side to side. "Tonight you are just going to watch the concert from backstage. Tomorrow night you'll sell merchandise."

"Drugs. You mean drugs, don't you?"

Ian paused his stretching, letting his arms fall limp to his sides. "Merchandise—T-shirts, posters, keychains, phone cases, hats, guitar pics …"

"To who?"

"Fans." Ian grinned. "Okay. I might have understated all of this to you … can you name a famous singer? Old or new. Doesn't matter. Just a famous singer."

"I had a foster parent who used to listen to Josh Groban." Jersey gnashed her teeth, still feeling so much anger. Dena wasn't just a foster parent; she was Jersey's friend.

"Okay. Well, Josh has sold millions of records, and he's a huge star in his genre of music. Thousands of people pack venues all over the world to see him sing live in concert. And they sell merchandise of his at those concerts."

Jersey gazed unblinkingly at Ian as he scratched his jaw.

"Well, I sing a different genre of music, but I, too, travel the world, singing to sold-out concert venues, *and* I have people who sell my merchandise at these concerts."

Jersey dropped her bag to her feet and planted her fists on her hips. "Listen, Coop. Stop talking down to me. I'm not an idiot. I know what a concert is. But earlier today you didn't say what you did or what the job was you were offering. You bought a homeless person a hot dog and offered her a job. Of course, I'm going to think something sketchy might be involved."

Tipping her chin up, she held her breath to puff out her chest, pretending the recent revelation of Ian Cooper being a famous singer didn't faze her one bit. Inside, Jersey's heart hammered into her ribcage, and her mind reeled trying to figure out the day's events.

"Coop?" His lips twitched into a tiny grin.

"It's short for Cooper."

"Clearly." Ian chuckled. "But my name is Ian. Everyone calls me Ian."

"I busted the nose and jaw of a kid named Ian. He tried to stick his cock in my ass. I'll call you Tom, Dick, or Harry, but I'm not calling you Ian because that makes me want to physically harm you."

Ian's eyebrows shot up his forehead as his head whipped back a few inches. "Coop it is."

A knock at the door sent the other guys in the room into a frenzy, jumping to their feet.

"Let's do this!" The messy redhead yelled as he tossed his game controller onto the sofa and chugged down the rest of his beer.

The three men filed out the door without looking in Ian's direction.

"Band members?"

Ian nodded, grabbing a clear glass bottle with a blue lid. He screwed off the top and took down the whole thing.

"They left without you."

He sighed, wiping the corners of his mouth with his hand. Jersey could hear a surge of cheers and rhythmic clapping thundering through the venue.

"I'll catch up. I'm the last one to go on stage. Walk with me."

She lifted her bag onto her shoulder.

"You can leave your bag."

"Nope." She shot him a challenging look.

"My bad. You should definitely bring it. That was my second suggestion. Do I have anything in my teeth?" He bared his teeth and pink gums.

The room was lined with vanities, mirrors, and lights. Jersey blinked in disbelief for several seconds.

"No? Good. Let's go." He winked and strutted to the door.

Jersey hiked her bag up higher and followed him. Two guys waited outside his door. She recognized Shane. He led the way, and the other guy lagged behind Ian, speaking into his wrist. The intensity of noise grew deafening as they wound their way through a maze of halls and doors to a set of stairs caged in by black scaffolding.

Ian turned around at the bottom of the stairs. "Wish me luck, Jersey."

She shook her head, cupping her ear.

He leaned in so close his lips brushed her ear, and his warm breath burned her skin. "Wish me luck." Ian pulled away just enough to see her face.

He was close. Too close. Jersey didn't let men get that close to her without asking to get knocked on their ass or stabbed in the gut.

Except Chris. She let Chris lie close to her, sometimes even touch her in an innocent way. But Ian wasn't Chris, and surrounded by bodyguards, he was off limits for hitting or stabbing. So she matched his smile, not knowing what to do with the foreign flutter of something in her stomach.

"Luck, Coop."

He reined in his smile, wetting his lips just inches from her face as he gave her one more slow wink before ascending the stairs. Max waited for him at the top, handing him another glass bottle with a blue lid. He drank it down, gave a few people high fives, and disappeared from Jersey's sight.

Max waved Jersey up the stairs just as the lights dimmed. The roar of the crowd demanding their rock star escalated to a level beyond pandemonium. The stairs vibrated beneath her feet, and she clutched the railing with one hand and her bag with the other hand. At the top, Max handed her earplugs and led her off to the side where they had a perfect view as a Technicolor of lights lit up the stage and the band started to play.

Ian strummed an electric guitar, watching his hand slide along the neck, pressing and picking the strings as the crowd surged forward out of control. Security held the women off as they cried.

Actually cried.

Jersey narrowed her eyes in complete disbelief.

When Ian started to sing, that was when it all clicked—the song, the voice. She'd heard it a million times playing over the speakers at Marley's.

"Oh my god …" she whispered to herself.

Jersey spent two and a half hours with her jaw hanging open. It felt like a dream, only she knew it wasn't because she didn't dream about rock stars. After every few songs, he'd jog off the stage and hydrate, not making eye contact with anyone or anything except the glass bottle of water in his sweaty hand.

Ian owned the stage, his guitar, and the crowd. Everyone wanted to see him, have a chance to touch his hand, look into his eyes. All Jersey wanted was to know why he bought a homeless woman lunch and offered her a job.

After an encore performance, the band exited the stage. Jersey stayed close to Max. "Where's Chris?" she yelled over the noise.

Everyone seemed pretty jacked up after the concert.

"He's going to help tear down and load up the buses. We'll make sure he gets back to the hotel. Wait here." Max turned and pointed at the floor like an owner telling their dog to heel.

Jersey obeyed out of a lack of other options. She had nowhere to go and no clue what was going to happen next. She hated feeling so out of her element and out of control.

Two guys walked toward her, laughing it up. "Dude, did you see Deadpool drop that fucking case?"

The other guy cringed. "I can't even look at him."

Six *thunks* followed:

One—Jersey's bag hitting the floor.

Two through five—a quick upper cut and jab to the first guy, quickly followed by the same to the second guy.

The final *thunk* was her body hitting the ground as security closed in around her.

"Stop!" Max yelled, shoving her way into the crowd

gathered around Jersey's reprimanded body on the cold concrete. "Oh my god … get her off the ground. What the hell happened?" Max's frantic voice matched the rapid ping-pong of her gaze going from Jersey to the security guards to the two victims.

"She assaulted them." One of the security guards nodded to the two men.

Max's head jerked back. "Excuse me?"

Jersey held a stiff poker face as they helped her upright. It wasn't her first time in handcuffs or her first time being accused of assaulting someone. She could have hit them harder. No one seemed to notice that the damage was minimal—no blood and nothing broken but two male egos.

"*She* hit *you*?" Max questioned the two men leaning against the opposite wall, rubbing their minor wounds. "What did you do?"

"Nothing. That's just it!" The stumpy guy wearing a baseball cap on backward shot Jersey a scowl.

"You were picking on my friend! Assholes."

"Chris?" Max questioned the two men.

They didn't reply, but their set jaws and firm glares answered her question.

"Are you pressing charges?" a security guard asked.

"Yes…" Max folded her arms over her chest "…*are* you pressing charges? Do you want everyone else to know that you got your asses handed to you by *her*?"

Jersey took offense to Max's implication regarding her gender, but she managed to bite back her defense since she liked Max.

Both men dropped their gazes to the ground while mumbling, "No."

The guards removed her handcuffs. Jersey grabbed her bag and followed Max without being asked to do so. She knew the next step involved getting fired. Chris was right. They'd be back at Marley's in less than twenty-four hours.

"Where's Chris?"

"I told you, he's still tearing down." Max worked her long, angry strides toward the exit.

"I'm not going back to Newark without him."

Max ignored her.

"Did you hear me?" Jersey's voice carried an edge to it.

Max stopped at the doors and whipped around. "Listen up, Jersey. Ian Cooper is not impulsive. He's meticulous with his music, his business, and his personal life. But today he took off without telling me a thing. Then he hires two strangers off the street. You're here because I trust his judgment. You're here for a reason, even if he's not ready to tell me what exactly that is … but nonetheless, I'm trusting him. That means it's my job to protect you and Chris, but you have to help me out a bit. Okay?"

Jersey stared at Max for a few seconds, jaw set.

"I'll take that as a silent yes." Max pushed open the exit doors, tying the belt to her white coat as she strutted to a black SUV. Shane opened the back door. From the far side of the backseat, Ian glanced up from his phone and smiled at Jersey.

"Your special request for the day tried to beat up two members of your crew. I'm not saying they didn't deserve it, but you know we can't let that happen again."

Ian's smile faded. Jersey climbed into the backseat, holding his eye contact the whole time. She felt no regret for her actions.

"Goodnight." Max shut the door.

The SUV took off as Jersey hugged her bag, eyes squinted a bit daring him to say something. Ian's gaze moved along her face and the rest of her body. As much as she didn't want a lecture or to get fired, his silence felt like a greater punishment than any words. After he seemed satisfied with his silent assessment of her, he leaned his head back and closed his eyes.

THEY STOPPED AT a back entrance to the hotel. Ian slipped on a black beanie, like the gray one he gave Jersey, and hopped out of the SUV as Shane opened Jersey's door, giving her a wry grin.

"Are you laughing at me?" She slid out and tried to get up in his face, which only amounted to her face meeting him mid-chest.

"Admiring your feistiness." His smirk grew into something that she wanted to punch, but Ian cleared his throat behind her.

Jersey turned toward Ian, and they had another little stare off that Ian broke when Shane opened the back door to the hotel.

"Get your ass in the hotel, Jersey." Ian grinned.

Jersey hated that grin—him dismissing her anger. She also loved it. And she hated herself for loving it, wanting it, feeling it on a visceral level.

Shane took them up the elevator and escorted them to a room at the end of a hall. Jersey inspected the doors. She didn't remember her room number, and she didn't have a key to it anyway.

"Inside, Jersey," Ian called from the room where Shane held open the door.

"I think that's my room." Jersey pointed to the door to her right.

"You're on a different floor." Shane gave her a tight-lipped smile.

"But this looks like the hallway we went down earlier.

"It's a hotel. All the hallways are identical."

She frowned, feeling stupid but daring him to mock her for her lack of hotel experience—after all, it was her first time in a hotel. By the time she swallowed her pride and scuffed her feet into the room, relenting to Ian's request and Shane's shocking revelation, Ian was already in the bathroom with the door shut and the shower running.

"Night, Jersey." The door slammed shut behind Shane.

CHAPTER EIGHT

I AN WASHED OFF the day, giving thanks for his life—
every dream that came to fruition, every fan, every
single breath.

Pay it forward.

He toweled off, dressed in a T-shirt and jogging
pants, and ruffled his messy hair, making a mental note to
get a slight trim before the next concert.

"What can I get you?"

Jersey jumped, tearing her gaze away from the window and the lights of Manhattan. "Get me?"

Ian twisted off the cap to a bottle of water. "Food?
Drink?"

She nudged her chin toward his hand. "What is that?
I notice it's the only thing you drink. Clear bottle. Blue
lid. Is it vodka?"

"Spring water." He took a few gulps.

"You don't drink?"

He shrugged, twisting the lid back on the bottle and
folding his tired body onto the sectional, stretching out
his long legs on the coffee table. "Occasionally."

"Sooo ..." Jersey set her bag on the floor and perused
the room. "You're a star. A really big deal. Incredibly

popular. Rich, I'd imagine." Her nose wrinkled as her gaze landed on him.

He laced his hands behind his head.

"Yet, you picked me up off the street and offered me a job, but I didn't actually work tonight like Chris did. And now I'm in your hotel room … alone with you." She balled her hands, cracking her knuckles.

"I sense a burning question coming."

"Am I here for sex?"

Ian willed his face to remain stoic, but he inwardly cringed. "No." He narrowed his eyes a fraction. "Would you have agreed to the job had that been what I was asking?" The possibility that her answer could be *yes* made him nauseous.

Jersey held eye contact for several unblinking seconds before averting her gaze to the floor. "I don't know." Her shoulders lifted into a slight shrug.

"I'm sorry. I should have been more clear. Instead, you've been thinking I befriended you to sell drugs and have sex." He tried to chuckle, but it came out as a disgusted grunt. How many people had asked her to sell drugs or her body?

"Befriended?" She squinted at him. "We're friends? Why? Why me? The sex actually makes sense; the friendship does not. And really, for someone with as much money in the bank as you probably have, I'm not sure the sex really makes sense. Who drives to Newark to pick up a homeless person for sex?" A ball of nerves, she paced the room, hugging her arms to her body, fingers digging into her skin.

He watched her, the moment blindingly surreal. A tiny body with a big punch. A young woman sculpted from bones, skin, and a few defined muscles. Every edge rough. A hundred years of wear on a twenty-something body. Tiny scars scattered along her skin, ghosts of the past.

Jersey had a story to tell, a story Ian needed to learn to silence the voice in his head.

He sighed. "*Why me* is my favorite question in the world, but only when asked after something good happens. You know … there's the glass-half-empty people who always ask *why me* whenever something goes wrong, like they are more deserving of a flawless life than some other person. But when someone asks why me because something good has happened to them, it just makes the answer that much sweeter."

Jersey stopped pacing. "What's the answer?"

Ian smiled. "Why not you? That's the answer. Today I stumbled across a young woman in need of lunch, some money, a place to live, a job … a chance. So I offered what I had to offer. So why *me*? Why would I do that?" He shrugged. "Well, why not me? I have the means."

She eased onto the opposite end of the U-shaped sectional, sitting on her hands, shoulders next to her ears. "You do this a lot?"

"Help people?"

"Hire homeless people."

"I do have a few people working for me that were jobless before I hired them, but I don't think anyone before you and your friend was homeless."

"So let's go back … why am I here? In your hotel room? Don't you have parties? Don't you hang out with your band members?"

"Sometimes I go to parties. Sometimes I hang out with my bandmates. But I've been doing this for over ten years now. My buddies in the band have wives and kids that sometimes travel with them. The party scene takes a toll on you after a while. And it's late, as you can see, but the adrenaline won't let me sleep, so adding any sort of stimulation isn't a good idea. Also, I like my privacy. When I'm on tour, there's always someone demanding my time, talking at me, touching me, dragging me where I need to be. So I take my alone time when I can get it."

"Why me?"

He knew what she meant with the repeated why me. But he couldn't share the answer. Not yet.

"Why do some people run into burning buildings to save complete strangers? It's just an instinct—an impulse."

"I'm an impulse?"

He laughed, rubbing his face and his tired eyes. "Ask Max. She'll confirm you were definitely an impulse."

"Last time …" She sighed with a little more aggravation. "Why am I here *in your hotel room*? Are you fucked up? I've met a lot of fucked-up people. You said no to sex, but there's a lot of weird shit you might have in your head that's not exactly sex. Your wealth and status don't fool me. Mental illness doesn't give a shit about social status."

"Jersey—"

"And just so you know, I was kind to those two assholes tonight. I could break you. And after I'm done breaking you, I will literally carve your fucking heart out of your chest with my knife."

Ian waited until the muscles in Jersey's fists and jaw relaxed. Then he nodded several times. "You remind me of someone I used to know. Not in a messed-up way. Not in a sexual way. Not in a way that will require you to break me or literally cut my heart out of my chest." He rested a flat hand over said chest. "In a good way."

She deflated a fraction. His confession softened her face.

"I enjoyed lunch with you. I know it was a short amount of time, but it awakened this feeling of familiarity. You triggered something, and I liked how that something made me feel—at lunch and again before the concert. So…" he rubbed his lips together and shrugged "…I brought you here because there's an odd comfort I get when we're together."

"What's odd about it?"

Ian let his thoughts play in his head, deciding what to say that would protect his vulnerability as well as hers. "The obvious. We met at a hot dog stand twelve hours ago." His eyebrows knitted together. "That, and it's a little odd that you so quickly threatened to cut out my heart. That's at least third or fourth date material."

"So this is a date? I think dating my boss is a bad idea. And I've never dated anyone, so you're going to be really disappointed."

"I was using it as a figure of speech."

"Food," an unfamiliar voice called, following several

hard knocks at the door.

Ian opened the door. "I'm starving."

"Sorry. There was a delay in a few of the things I requested." An average-height man with light brown hair and bags in his hands brushed past Ian. "Oh, hello. I'm Nick." He smiled at Jersey while depositing the bags onto the coffee table.

"Jersey," she replied with a cautious voice, eyes flitting between the bags and the two men.

Nick proceeded to pull containers of food out of the bags as Ian returned to his spot on the sectional.

"Help yourself." Ian shot Jersey a small grin and an easy nod toward the food.

"How are you feeling?" Nick turned down the bed and set out alcohol, swabs, and needles.

Ian bobbed his head side to side while plunging a plastic fork into a black plastic container of pasta. "Not too bad. My right shoulder is tight."

Nick poured some of Ian's bottled water into a glass and added several drops of herbs before handing it to him.

Ian set his bowl of pasta to the side and chugged down the bitter water. "Still tastes like shit." He scrunched his face.

Nick met Jersey's wide eyes. "Herbs to help him sleep."

"Best pasta in New York. Try some." Ian scooted another black container to the opposite side of the coffee table.

Jersey eyed it and then him for a few seconds. When

she reached for the container, Ian grinned around his plastic fork. She knelt on the floor and opened it, using her fingers to scoop up the long strings of spaghetti, sucking it into her mouth.

"There are more forks in the sack."

She paused, glancing up at Ian while slurping the last inch of spaghetti into her mouth. Her cheeks turned red. He didn't mean to embarrass her. Without giving it a second thought, Ian kneeled on the floor at the opposite side of the coffee table, pitched the fork over his shoulder, and dug his fingers into the pasta, bringing it to his mouth and slurping it up.

A tiny laugh slipped out of Jersey when sauce splattered onto his face and into his right eye.

"Clearly I'm out of practice." He grinned, wiping his eye. "What else do we have?" Ian pulled out another container. "Yes! My favorite." He opened the container of olives and popped one into his mouth, moving it side to side while chewing it before spitting out the pit into the empty bag. "The salt ..." He licked his lips. "I crave the salt after sweating so much."

Jersey eyed him with curiosity as she slurped more spaghetti. He liked her even more in that moment. She wasn't just a reminder of his past. Jersey brought back memories of so many of Ian's firsts—the curiosity, excitement, and thrilling fear of the unknown.

Her gaze dropped to the bowl of olives, and the gleam of curiosity died as a frown stole her smile.

"Have some."

She shook her head.

"You don't like olives? I didn't like them until my agent and a producer took me to a vineyard in Italy. We had pasta, bruschetta, and olives ... lots of olives. They went on and on about the olives, telling me to try them. I hated them, but I wanted to impress them." Ian shrugged. "I don't know if it was all the wine, or just forcing myself to eat dozens of those damn olives, but weeks later, I found myself craving olives. Isn't that crazy?"

Jersey's focus remained on the olives as she nodded slowly. "I like them. I just don't eat them." When her dark brown eyes met his, it sent cold chills cracking along his spine. She had more than one look that did that to him. Maybe he couldn't see the pain in her vacant eyes, but he could feel it.

"We're flying to Charlottesville in the morning. Is there something specific you'd like for breakfast?"

She shook her head, retaining that vacant look in her eyes like it had settled in for the night and there was nothing Ian could say or do to change it—except give her time.

"Do you drink coffee?"

A single nod.

"Cream? Sugar? Black?"

She shrugged.

"Eat. We'll figure it out tomorrow. There's always tomorrow."

Her lips parted.

"What?" Ian slipped another olive past his lips.

Jersey shook her head. "There's not *always* a tomorrow."

Ian took the olive seed from his mouth and tossed it into the bag. "You're right."

"I should see if Chris is back." She licked her fingers and wiped them on her jeans.

He studied her for a few minutes, the drift of her gaze to the floor then over his shoulder to Nick sitting on the edge of the bed, reading a book. "Nick, I'm walking Jersey to her room. Then you can stick me with needles."

Jersey jumped to her feet and grabbed her bag.

"Can I carry your bag for you?" Ian opened the door.

She shook her head, stepping out into the hallway.

"Want me to sharpen your knife?" He walked beside her.

Jersey shot him a quick sideways glance. He kept his eyes on the length of the hall in front of them, biting his lips to keep from grinning. Ian pushed the button to the elevator. A few seconds later, the doors opened, and Jersey stepped into it.

"How about a song? I can sing you a song."

Hugging her bag, she kept her gaze downcast as he followed her into the elevator and pushed the button to her floor.

Ian hummed.

Jersey twisted her lips to the side, tipping her chin farther down.

"I met a girl…" he sang.

"In the heart of Newark—"

"Stop!" Jersey snorted a laugh. "No. Just … no."

"Come on. It's a good start."

"It's not." She giggled.

Ian liked that giggle so much it constricted his chest. Once again, she reminded him of someone from his past—a bittersweet, breathtakingly beautiful flash of a yesterday long ago that ended tragically.

She stepped off the elevator before the doors completely opened, leaving him to catch up with her.

"You know, most women would feel honored to have me write a song about them."

"Then you should write them a song." Jersey looked left and right. "God! Why are all the doors the same?"

Ian grinned. "What's your room number?"

"I don't know."

"You didn't pay attention to your room number."

"No!" She whipped around, stepping into his space, neck strained upward. "I didn't look at the room number. I don't stay at hotels and eat fancy food. I don't jump around on a stage and write silly songs."

Ian's jaw unhinged, and he jabbed a fist into his chest, making a stabbing motion while falling back into the wall. "Silly songs ... Jersey, I didn't think you were serious about cutting out my heart. But that was brutal."

Jersey tried her best; he could see her giving it her all to hold firm to her scowl, tiny lines wrinkling the corners of her eyes, but she lost the fight. "Jerk." She shoved him.

He stumbled again, holding his belly while chuckling.

"You are mental. I can't believe people pay to watch you." She shoved him again, dropping her bag and strutting toward him as he moved away from her.

"Whoa ..." He brought his fists up, mirroring her. "Really, we're going to duke it out here in the hallway?"

"Maybe." She smirked. "Ever been beat up by a girl, Coop? Or do you always have bodyguards protecting your delicate little ass?" She shadowboxed him, only gently striking him in the gut and arms as he kept his fists by his face and twisted his torso side to side, laughing more with each retreating step.

"Should I feel violated that you've been paying so much attention to my ass to know that it's delicate?"

She added a little more power to her punches until his back hit a wall again. He bobbed his head to the side, peeking at her from behind his arms and clenched fists. Blowing out a slow breath, she relaxed her right fist, the one shoved into his gut, and kept her hand pressed flat to his abdomen. "Why didn't you fire me, Coop? Send me back to Newark after I assaulted those workers of yours?"

"Because they probably deserved it," he murmured, afraid to move with her hand pressed to him. He didn't want to scare her away. Ian wanted her trust, even though he had no idea what he would do with it.

"Thank you." Jersey worked her gaze up his body.

"For?"

"I'm going to sleep in a real bed tonight. I took a shower today, not a birdbath. Two meals … I had two meals today."

Ian couldn't hold back the twitch of pain pulling at his brow. Bed, shower, food … so basic.

"Jers?"

They turned toward the deep voice and the scarred face peeking out of the doorway to a room close to where Jersey left her bag.

Her hand dropped from Ian's abdomen. "Chris." She smiled, a genuine, happy to see him smile.

Ian followed her as she retreated to grab her bag. He caught a better look at her scarred friend who eyed him without blinking. They said nothing. Ian didn't know what to say. All he could do was stare and wait. Wait for her *friend* to speak, to see if his words matched the hard look in his eyes, wary and conflicted.

"Chris?" Jersey cleared her throat and nudged his shoe with hers. "This is Ian Cooper, our boss." She wedged herself between Ian and Chris's body halfway out the door. She snapped her fingers in front of his face. "Hello? Can you speak? Maybe a 'thanks for hiring us' or something besides your cow-eyed stare? Are you drunk?"

Chris shook his head a slow inch at a time, not moving his focus from Ian. "Generous of you to give us jobs," he mumbled.

Ian could barely hear him.

"He doesn't like it when people stare at him. And he lost most of his memory in an accident, so he's very distrusting." Jersey lifted her eyebrows, giving Ian a tight-lipped smile.

Drawing in a slow breath, Ian held out his hand to Chris.

Chris ignored it, unblinking as his lips parted a bit. Ian pulled back his hand and slid it into his pocket.

"I see you survived your uh … first night." Ian scratched his jaw. "If you're new to this, it's probably a little overwhelming. Just let Max know if you have any issues."

Jersey cocked her head to the side, peering up at Chris. Without giving her a single glance, he grabbed her arm, pulled her inside the hotel room, and slammed the door shut.

CHAPTER NINE

JERSEY LEANED AGAINST the inside of the door as Chris rested both hands just above her head, breaths quickening like impending heart failure, or an asthma issue, or maybe even a panic attack. "I'm going to knock you on your ass if you don't back off. And if you're dying, nod or give me some sort of signal so I can call for help. Otherwise, you'd better tell me what the hell is going on with you."

"It's ... him," he whispered like someone had their hand around his throat.

"Ian Cooper. Rock star. Rich dude ... yeah, yeah, so what? I didn't take you for the type to be starstruck and acting all breathless over someone famous. And he probably shouldn't have stared so long at you, but it's hard at first to pretend like you haven't experienced some serious physical trauma."

Chris shook his head. His Adam's apple bobbed with a hard swallow. "It's *him*. The one who killed Dena and Charles."

Jersey's nose scrunched as she jerked her head back until it bumped the door. "What? No. You're losing your shit, Chris. I'm patient with you when you have your nightmares or something simple sets you off and you start rambling about the voices in your head. I let your craziness slide, and I even defended you to the guys at Marley's. But *this* I'm calling bullshit on. There's no way Ian was your friend. No way he killed Dena and Charles." Jersey shoved his chest to get around him.

She sighed, a longing smile stealing her lips at the sight of the bed. A bed …

Grabbing her toothbrush, she squeezed past Chris to get to the bathroom, ignoring his shocked face. After brushing her teeth and peeing, Jersey again passed Chris, who seemed to be frozen in place. She slipped off her shoes and jeans to slide under the sheets.

"Oh … my … god. I'm never leaving this bed." A contented sigh escaped Jersey's nose as she tucked the sheets under her chin and closed her eyes.

"Jersey …" Chris's strained voice held so much pain.

She opened one eye. "Don't do this. I've had the best day. I'm in New York with a full belly and a *real* bed. Don't ruin this tonight. We'll talk in the morning and sort through what you think you know about him. Maybe after you sleep on it, things will be a little more clear for you. Okay? Can we just go to sleep?"

Chris pressed the heels of his hands to his temples and squeezed his eyes shut, releasing an indecipherable grumble. Then he flipped off the lights and crawled into the other bed. After a few minutes, Jersey realized how much she'd grown used to a warm body beside her.

"What are you doing?" Chris asked.

Jersey climbed in bed next to him. He rolled toward

her. She didn't say anything. She didn't have to answer him. He pulled her back flush to his chest and rested his chin on top of her head. Always being defensive, alert, and guarded took its toll on her. Jersey never realized, until she met Chris, just how badly she needed to rest from her own demons and surrender to a safe haven.

THE FOLLOWING MORNING, just after five a.m., Jersey slipped out of bed and went for a jog, making a mental note of the room number. A cold blast of frigid air stifled her lungs as she emerged from the revolving door onto the sidewalk. She imagined Manhattan being busier, but then again, it was quite early.

"Good morning." A uniformed man smiled at Jersey.

"Where's the nearest park?" she asked.

He chuckled, pointing to his right. "First time here?"

She nodded.

"Well, there's a great park straight that way. Central Park. You can't miss it."

"Thanks." Jersey jogged in the direction of Central Park. The sidewalks weren't bustling yet, but she wasn't the only fitness buff fighting the onset of winter in the park. She sprinted, skipped with high knees, boxed the air, breezed through fifty pushups with her feet elevated on a park bench, and found the Holy Grail of her workout—pull-up bars.

Blowing on her hands and rubbing them together a few times, she jumped up and muscled a quick thirty pull-ups.

"Damn … and I mean d-a-mn!"

Jersey released to the ground, shaking out her hands before blowing warm air on them again while glancing at the broad-chested man with dark skin, black running pants, and a white hoodie.

"I never seen that kind of shit before from someone so small." He hopped up, clenching the bar next to Jersey. "Now just move along before you make me look bad."

"If you can't keep up with me…" she jumped back up and gripped the bar with her hands in the opposite direction to reach a different group of muscles "…then maybe you should move along before I make you look bad. Which … I will." Jersey shot him a sideways smirk.

After she kicked his ass, showing off on the bar long after the dead weight of his body *thunked* to the ground, Jersey let go.

The stranger shook his head and grinned, massaging his forearms and hands. "I'm not worthy." He held out his hand and she shook it. "Enjoy your day, young lady." The stranger walked off, picking up his pace to a jog.

Behind her, a slow clap sounded like the rhythmic slaps of a horse's shoes against the pavement. Jersey turned.

Ian.

"Impressive." He continued a slow clap.

Weird, fluttery things happened in Jersey's belly when Ian grinned. "I impressed one person. You sent thousands of women into a frenzy by just stepping into the spotlight." The wind gusted, attacking Jersey's face. She winced.

But his face … it was chiseled to perfection, shadowed with a light outgrowth of stubble, slightly softening each sharp angle. Ian wore a kind smile with a hint of mischief like he kept the best secret ever. Jersey couldn't believe that secret involved killing two innocent people.

"What's it like to have that effect on people?"

He shrugged, tugging his blue beanie down over his ears. "I don't care about their reaction. I'm just so fucking happy that they show up. It's that simple for me. I want to sing—to one person or twenty thousand people. It never stops blowing my mind that they just … show up."

"That's it, Coop?" She erased the space between them with several calculated strides. "Just showing up does it for you?"

He curled his lower lip into his mouth, scraping his top teeth over it. "I think I could listen to you say my name like that all day."

"Yeah? Well, *Coop*, I slept like the dead last night in that bed you paid for, so I'll chirp on repeat whatever you want if it leads to a warm bed and a hot meal."

Ian gave her a full grin that reached his eyes. "That's it, Jersey? A warm bed and a hot meal does it for you?" He rocked back and forth on his heels, shoving his hands into the pockets of his jogging pants, shoulders lifted toward his ears.

In that moment, he didn't look like a rock star. Ian Cooper resembled a young man Jersey met on the streets. He left an abusive situation—a boy too young, like Jersey, to be on his own. But unlike Jersey, he didn't have what it took to survive in a world where right and wrong didn't exist. He chose right over necessary. And Jersey mourned over his dead, badly beaten body behind a dumpster before anyone found him.

So many people had come and gone from Jersey's twenty-four-year-old life.

That boy flirted with her, curling his bottom lip between his teeth like Ian. Grinning to his eyes like Ian.

No. The man before her didn't kill anyone. Killers didn't find joy in the simplicity of someone showing up. Jersey knew this … she was a killer, and she didn't know joy. She knew how to breathe in and breathe out and live life looking over her shoulder, one hand curled into a fist, the other clenching a knife.

"So … your friend. How long have you known him?"

She shrugged. "Not quite two months. Why?"

"Just curious. He seemed angry with me last night and protective of you."

"Yeah, well you wouldn't stop staring at him."

"Sorry." Ian frowned. "It … *he* was just unexpected."

"Like a rock star in a rundown Newark neighborhood?"

He smirked. "Fair point." Pulling his left hand out from his pocket, he looked at his watch. "We have an hour before Max drags us to the car by our ears so we're not late for our flight."

Jersey glanced around, making a complete circle in place.

"You're lost." He chuckled.

She chewed the inside of her cheek, trying to gain her

bearings. "I'm *so* lost."

"This way." He nodded to her left. "Are you a runner, or were you just here putting on a pull-up clinic?"

Her eyes narrowed.

"It's a compliment. It means you're better than everyone at something. You were schooling that guy." Ian took off jogging, and Jersey caught up. "Shredding his ego, slowly ripping apart his manhood." He grinned.

She glanced over at him for a few seconds before returning her attention to the paved path before them. A grin crawled up her face. Jersey liked his compliment—very much.

"Have you always been a runner?" he asked as they approached the crosswalk at the end of the park entrance.

"Yes." She slowed to a stop as they waited for the light to change. "When I was much younger, I lived in a foster home, and the husband wasn't very nice. He liked knocking his wife around as well as me and the three other foster kids that lived there at the time. The oldest girl tried to watch out for us, took the brunt of the abuse."

The walk light illuminated and they took off jogging again.

"I was the youngest, and I hadn't been there as long as everyone else. So when Mr. Fisher decided to do … um … really bad things to me, G beat him over the head with a baseball bat. Then she told me to be brave and run fast." Jersey grunted a painful laugh. "So, yeah … I'm a runner. I've been running ever since that day."

Ian remained quiet for several blocks. Jersey thought

maybe she shared too much. Stories of sexual abuse to children weren't the best conversation starters.

"G?" He tossed her a quick glance as they slowed to a walk a few yards from the entrance to the hotel.

"Yes." She shrugged. "I never knew her name. Everyone called her G. And she didn't ask us to call her anything different than that because she didn't really talk much, but neither did I." Her brows drew inward. "I don't know what happened to G. Mr. Fisher ended up in the hospital, and I heard rumors that he died. So maybe G ended up in juvie or prison if she was tried as an adult."

Ian's concentrated expression mirrored Jersey's when she glanced up at him as they stopped just inside of the hotel lobby. Whispers and giggles surrounded them as a few women abandoned their rolling suitcases on their way out of the hotel to stop and take photos of Ian—not so discreetly trying to capture a distant selfie with him.

Jersey let their shameless photo op pull her attention away from Ian and away from her ugly past.

"Can I get a picture?" A teenaged girl sidled up to Ian as her parents gave him an apologetic smile.

Ian rested his arm on the girl's shoulder and posed without hesitation. She was one of them … one of the people who would show up so he could sing, and he clearly felt grateful for her.

After several pictures, he rested his hand on Jersey's back and guided her to the elevators. Her spine stiffened, unsure what to do with him touching her. The girl with a past of sexual abuse didn't like people touching her, except Chris. She came to find comfort in his touch, maybe because it wasn't sexual. But what made her most uncomfortable about Ian's hand on her back was how it made her feel those flutters in her stomach again.

"Oh …" Her lips formed an O as he used his room key card to access her floor.

He lifted a single brow, smirking at her as the elevator doors closed. "You still don't have a key card, do you?"

Jersey's head inched side to side.

"Did you tell Chris where you were going?"

She continued to shake her head, gazing straight at the mirrored elevator doors and the reflection of the tall and distractingly sexy man beside her.

"Max?"

"Nope." She pursed her lips to hide her grin.

"So you wanted to be homeless in New York instead of New Jersey. I see … because the plane was and is leaving with or without you in less than an hour."

"Lesson learned," she mumbled, sporting a tight grin and wide eyes.

The doors opened to her floor.

"Do I need to help you find your room?"

"Six-one-nine." She stepped off the elevator with her chin held high again as if remembering three digits made up for her other missteps that almost lead to abandonment.

Ian followed her, grabbing her hand as she took a left instead of a right.

Her hand. Not her arm—like the gentle nudge with his hand on her back in the lobby. Ian Cooper took Jersey's hand and her breath in one quick move.

It was warm against her cold. She couldn't find a full inhale of oxygen as he pulled her down the hallway. "We're on the ninth floor, Ferdinand. So your room number has to start with a nine. So maybe 916? Or 961?"

Nope. He didn't kill the Russells. Murderers had cold hands. Jersey knew this because she had cold hands, except when she was boxing.

At room 916, Ian released her hand like it was no big deal. But it was a big deal—a big, warm, tummy-doing-weird-things kind of deal. He knocked twice on the door.

"For the love of god, where have you been?" Chris leaned against the door to keep it open while pressing his palms to his temples, his signature reaction to too much stress.

The butterflies in Jersey's tummy died. She worried Chris. Had she just told him, the unnecessary worry could have been prevented. "I'm sorry." She eased her hands around his wrists, gently pulling his hands away from his head, waiting for him to look at her and see the sincerity in her eyes, the true apology on her face.

"Why were you with him?"

Glancing over at Ian, she attempted to brush off Chris's harsh question with a nervous smile. "I wasn't. We just ran into each other while jogging. I didn't have a key to get up the elevator."

Chris clenched his jaw, refusing to look at Ian.

Jersey pressed her hand to Chris's chest. "Get dressed or grab another shower. Yes, a shower. Go take a shower to relax your mind. I'm fine. We're leaving in less than an hour."

Chris's nostrils flared as he blew out a long breath. "M-maybe." He nodded.

"Go." Jersey pushed him toward the bathroom. After Chris slid the door shut, she wrinkled her nose and faced Ian. "He has some PTSD."

Ian lifted his chin as his brows slid up his forehead. "I … see," he replied with apprehension to his voice. "What happened to him?"

"We don't know. He has no memory of anything. No family … nothing."

"I'm sorry."

She returned a half smile.

"I need to go shower. I'll meet you guys out front in…" he glanced at his watch again "…thirty-five minutes. But I'm guessing Max will be knocking on your door in less than fifteen."

"Okay."

"Okay." He shared his mischievous grin one last time before heading back down the hallway.

"Coop?"

He turned.

"Who's Ferdinand?"

Ian chuckled. "Ferdinand Magellan. First explorer to circumnavigate the globe."

"Were you making fun of me? Because I seemed lost?"

"Seemed?" He laughed again while continuing to the elevator. "Thirty-five minutes."

CHAPTER TEN

"I NEED YOU to believe me." Chris sat at the end of the bed in the hotel room after giving Jersey the silent treatment. They hustled to get ready while Max tapped her foot outside of room 916.

Jersey spit out the toothpaste and shoved the rest of her stuff into her bag. "About what?" She sighed.

"It's him." He rubbed circles on his forehead, eyes closed. "I know you think I'm crazy, and maybe some days I don't think clearly; some nights, things from my past haunt me in my dreams. But I knew it when I saw him and heard his voice last night. I didn't get to see him up close at the concert, and his singing voice is different—deeper, grittier. But I knew it last night, and I still know it today. One hundred percent. It's him. I need you to believe me."

Jersey closed her eyes with her back to Chris. She didn't want to believe him. Nothing about his claim made any sense.

"He came from a wealthy family. How do you think he got where he is today? I know he's this big rock star, and you, like every other girl out there, can't keep from getting ensnared in his charm and his appearance."

"I'm not ensnared, whatever the hell that means. Don't ever accuse me of being like the women fainting at his feet or freaking out because he steps onto a stage holding a guitar. That's not me, and you damn well know it."

"I see you look at him."

"You don't see shit." She lifted her bag onto her shoulder, bearing its heavier weight after overstuffing it with her new clothes and shoes.

"Then why won't you believe me? He killed them. His family helped cover it up. Sent him off ... and I never knew where he went, but I do now. They changed his name and his image and gave him a new life. Money did that. Money buys freedom from accountability. Money buys fame. Money erases guilt ... if he ever even felt any guilt."

"No ..." Jersey shook her head and turned toward him. "Eight years ago, almost nine. That's when they were killed. Ian said he's been performing for over ten years. What you're saying doesn't add up. I'm not calling you a liar. I'm just saying you're not remembering correctly. You're piecing things together the wrong way."

"You're taking his side. Wow ... you've known him for all of twenty-four hours and you're—"

"His side?" She gasped before laughing. "There are no sides. There can't be sides until you can prove your point."

"You said it yourself." Chris jumped to his feet and paced the room. He paced more than tigers at the zoo. "You said you wanted to destroy ... to *kill* the person who did that to Dena and Charles. Well, fate just dealt you the winning ticket, Jers. He's so fucking untouchable to the rest of the world—bodyguards, security, a village of people keeping constant tabs on him. But by some miracle … *fucking fate,* Jersey … you're in his life. A homeless girl from Newark has access to one of the world's biggest rock stars. And not just access, you have his attention. You've been alone with him on more than one occasion in less than twenty-four. Fucking. Hours!"

"Chris …" She felt bad for him. The PTSD. The nightmares. The paranoia. The assholes who had made fun of him the night before. Jersey was homeless and had been homeless for over eight years, but she knew how she got there. She knew every hideous detail of her past. And her past most likely involved bigger monsters than Chris had ever encountered.

However, she couldn't imagine losing her memory, no matter how awful some of her memories were. And for that reason, she refused to give up on Chris.

Max knocked on the door. Chris picked up his department store bags, a disappointed frown pinned to his face. *She* had disappointed him. Jersey didn't feel bad about much. Years of abuse followed by years of surviving on her own left her emotionally crippled and calloused, but Chris affected her. She felt something real with him. They shared a vulnerability as much as they shared a survival instinct.

"I'll see what I can get."

Chris paused before opening the door. "Get?"

"Out of Ian. I'll fish for something that tells me

you're right about him. And I'm sorry I can't blindly trust you on this. It's not you personally. It's your memory I don't know if I can totally trust. I just can't target a man—*this man*—risking so much without being absolutely sure."

After a few seconds of studying her, maybe gauging her honesty, he nodded.

"And he didn't seem to recognize you at all. That doesn't feel right."

Chris's face collapsed into a sullen expression.

Jersey shook her head. "You know what I mean. Your eyes, your voice … something about you has to be the same. Right?"

He continued to frown. Of course, he didn't know.

"Ready?" Max greeted them with all smiles when Chris opened the door. She tapped her watch. "Let's get out of here."

They followed Max to the elevators.

"There's room for you on one of the buses, after the concert tonight. Are you good with that or are you two …" Max's gaze bounced between Jersey and Chris as the elevator descended to the lobby.

Chris ignored Jersey when she turned to him for an answer.

"No. I'm not fucking Jersey. Look at me for Christ's sake. Only a blind woman would have sex with me, and even then … only if I paid her. The bus is fine."

Jersey drew her head back and winced as his words pulled a bitter smile from her. Her gaze dropped to her feet until they reached the lobby. She liked Chris, finding comfort in his friendship. Not caring about his skin. She didn't think of him like anything more than a brother. And she wanted to believe it wasn't based on his injuries. Just like she wanted to believe the flutter in her tummy around Ian wasn't because he looked like a god.

Was she that superficial?

She pushed that thought away. No … she wasn't that person. Jersey knew what it felt like to be judged based on looks or life's circumstances. Chris brought his own brand of crazy into her life. *That* was the unattractive part, not his skin.

And Ian … well, he looked at her like he understood her, even though there was no way he had an inkling what her life was really like. He felt like the day to her night and a promise on the distant horizon. The last time she felt so alive and filled with hope was during her six months with the Russells.

"The bus it is." Max tucked her chin, focusing on her phone—or maybe hiding behind her long bangs.

Chris gave everyone the silent treatment on the way to the airport. He boarded the private jet without one look back at Jersey. Was he angry about Ian? Angry about riding the bus, or not having sex with Jersey? She didn't know.

"Coming?" Max peered over her shoulder, paused halfway up the stairs of the jet.

Jersey stood idle at the bottom of the stairs, cracking her knuckles while swallowing hard. Then she chewed the inside of her cheek.

"First time flying?"

A nod.

"It's fun. Safer than driving. And this is a short flight down to Charlottesville. A blink."

Another nod, but no other movement on Jersey's part.

Shane appeared at the top of the stairs. "I can carry her."

Max held up her hand and gave him a subtle head-shake before retreating back down the stairs. "You roughed up two guys twice your size last night. Get on the plane while you're still my idol."

Jersey rolled her shoulders, stilling her darting gaze on Max's face and the mildly arrogant smirk tugging at her lips.

One step.

Two steps.

She swallowed her fear. It wasn't the plane crashing. Jersey feared letting go of control, the familiar, a short train ride from the only place she'd ever known. After a brief stare off with the cheery blonde just inside the door to the plane, Jersey relinquished her heavy bag and followed Max around the corner.

Ian sat to the left, chin tipped to his phone with an empty leather seat facing him. Max took the seat on the right, facing Shane. Behind Shane there was a sofa and two more seats facing each other on one side, a grumpy Chris taking up one of them. Jersey ignored everyone else as she made her way to the seat by Chris. He lifted his feet, claiming the empty seat—giving her the proverbial middle finger without looking up from the magazine in his hands.

Jersey scowled. "You're being a dick," she mumbled while turning around. Instead of sitting on the couch so he'd be forced to look at her, she retreated to the nicer people on the plane. She couldn't wait for him to go on the bus later that night. They needed a break from each other.

Ian glanced up at her when she plopped down into the seat facing him. His brow wrinkled, and he glanced over his shoulder at Chris, who ignored everyone and everything but the demons polluting his mind and the gossip magazine in his hands.

"Everything okay?" Ian asked, returning his attention to Jersey.

"Yup." She stared out the window.

"Please fasten your seat belt, miss." The blonde in black pants and a white blouse smiled.

Jersey fumbled for the two pieces to her seat belt. The metal clicked and scraped together, and her shaky hands made repeated failed attempts at fastening it. Her stomach churned and chest tingled as her breaths accelerated. Then she froze, ceasing to breathe as Ian unbuckled and kneeled in front of her, resting his hands on her armrests without physically touching any part of her body.

He leaned in so his face hovered a few inches from her face. Ian smelled fresh. It was the most accurate description she could find to describe him. That fresh smell probably had some fancy soap or cologne name and scent to go with it. But to the girl who recently took her first real shower in years, the only word that came to mind was fresh. Intoxicatingly fresh—and minty. Ian had minty breath, not the dragon breath Chris had when he exhaled in her face every morning in the musty, damp corner of Marley's back room.

What a difference twenty-four hours made in Jersey's life.

"Hi." Ian smiled.

Jersey stared at his mouth. Did her breath smell like his? Did Max buy her the same potent mint toothpaste that Ian used? She hoped so.

"You're in my space," she whispered in an unfamiliar, breathy voice.

"You're in my plane. We need to take off. I'm going to fasten your seat belt for you. You're going to let me without feeling the need to do any sort of physical harm to me. Okay?" Ian's gaze dropped to Jersey's mouth.

She closed her lips, biting them together for a tight seal in case her toothpaste wasn't the same as his. The fact that she cared set off a multitude of foreign emotions. The butterflies returned. The nerves and anxiety remained, but they shifted their focus to the specimen before her instead of the dread of leaving the ground.

"Breathe, Jersey," he whispered.

She jumped, gripping the armrests when his hands grazed her jean-clad legs to fasten her seat belt. They weren't baggy, three-sizes-too-big jeans. Max insisted on fitted jeans that felt like a thin second skin. She called them sexy. Jersey didn't feel sexy, but she also didn't feel like she had much of a say in the matter because she wasn't the one paying for the jeans.

Her cheeks burned as she relinquished a false smile that hid her trembling lips. She averted her gaze to the window when Ian tightened the seat belt. And she held her breath until he returned to his seat.

Closing her eyes, she imagined a fight—the adrenaline before the first punch and the way her body thrived on fear, gobbling it up, transforming it into strength, and conquering its fucking ass.

Once they were wheels up, two women appeared from an area at the back of the plane with two carts. One stopped bedside Chris and the other stopped next to Jersey.

"Manis-pedis." Max smiled.

"What?" Jersey eyed the friendly redhead who placed a tray in front of Jersey and covered it with a warm towel.

"Manicure and pedicure. They're going to get your hands and feet looking and feeling fabulous."

Jersey cringed at Max. "How embarrassing."

Max chuckled, glancing up from her phone. "Relaxing. Pampering. Amazing. Those are better descriptions."

Ian's eyes were closed, headphones covering his ears.

"Chris isn't going to want his nails painted. Or probably anyone touching him."

Wrong … Jersey craned her neck to see Chris. The cute, short-haired blonde already had Chris's hands and feet soaking in something, and he was all smiles about it.

Much like the first shower, but thankfully not *as* much, Jersey watched the water in the basins darken as her hands and feet were submerged. The young redhead perched on a small, three-legged stool went to work on

Jersey. She asked about several sores on Jersey's feet and offered some type of herbal salve. Jersey had no idea what she meant by salve, but she couldn't say no to something the woman promised would be soothing and healing.

"What color would you like?" She showed Jersey a rainbow of nail polish bottles. Jersey let Dena paint her fingernails and toenails once—light pink. She rolled her eyes at Dena, not wanting to admit that deep down she liked it because, despite the abuse, the murder, and the awful hand of cards, Jersey went through much of her life wanting to fit in. Normal felt like an unreachable dream, but nonetheless, still a dream.

What would Ian say? Or what if they ended up back at Marley's and Jersey had pink polish on her nails?

"No polish."

"You sure? What about clear?" The redhead seemed really enthused about putting polish on Jersey's nails.

She wasn't sure why. Jersey felt nauseated by the disgusting amount of dry skin the woman filed off her feet. Jersey prayed Ian would stay asleep and not see that.

"Or … black." Shooting Jersey a wicked grin, nail lady held up a bottle of black nail polish.

Jersey's lips twisted. "Whatever." On a huff, she turned her attention to the window, giving Ian a quick glance first to make sure he wasn't consciously witnessing the polish conversation.

As promised, they were back on the ground in no time. Two vehicles waited just beyond the plane. Without saying a word, Ian hopped into the back of the first SUV as Shane held open his door.

"This way." Max ushered Chris and Jersey to the second vehicle. "Rex will get you both where you need to be. Jersey, Dani will show you the ropes for merch. I'll see you later."

"Where are you going?" Jersey stared at the SUV with Ian in the back of it.

"Ian has a jam-packed day of interviews and appearances. We'll see you at the venue later."

Before Jersey could respond, express any apprehension, or wrap her head around the whirlwind of events, Max slid in the backseat of the SUV, next to Ian, and the vehicle sped off into the distance.

Rex, the short, dark-haired man with a stalky build and an indifferent smile, held open the car door for Jersey. She hugged her bag and slid in next to Chris. He stared at her, which felt like progress—except his hard expression held more contempt than any sort of surrender.

"Don't give me that look," she said as Rex shut her door. "You're being an asshole. I said I'd ask him questions, but I'm not going to do it on a plane with his assistant and bodyguard just feet away. And in case you haven't noticed, he's a busy guy. Not to mention the surprise washing of our hands and feet they sprung on us. I bet Max knew I wouldn't go for that shit unless she pinned me in a corner on a plane a gazillion miles off the ground." Jersey silenced her tongue when Rex opened the driver's door.

Chris rolled his eyes. "I liked being pampered. And if you didn't, then something is seriously wrong with you.

And … you like him." He lowered his voice to a whisper. "You like the fucking rock star who murdered the Russells."

Jersey returned a dismissive headshake while focusing on the back of Rex's head instead of the agitated man next to her. "I don't like *anyone*, but definitely not you at the moment." She stared at her black fingernails. They weren't entirely awful.

CHAPTER ELEVEN

P INK-AND-GRAY HAIRED DANI opened Jersey's door and slipped the pass around her neck. Jersey wondered why anyone would intentionally go gray in their twenties, but Dani's half long and half buzzed hairdo somehow made it work and even fit her bubbly personality. "Leave your bag. They'll put it on the bus."

"She's not going on the bus," Rex corrected Dani with more information than Jersey had been given. "If you don't need anything from inside it, then leave it in the car."

Jersey hugged her bag tighter.

Before they could usher Chris off in the other direction, he stepped in front of Jersey, lowering his face to her eye level and his voice just above a whisper. "If I'm being an asshole, then you're being a paranoid bitch. Leave the stupid bag behind."

She narrowed her eyes, teeth clenched. After a brief and silent stare off, Chris turned and strutted away.

Jersey huffed out a quick breath. "Give me a few seconds." She slipped into the backseat again and closed the door, grateful for the darkened windows. After sliding her favorite, sheathed knife into her sock and tugging her too-tight jeans back down her leg, she zipped the bag and climbed out.

"We good?" Bubbly Dani asked.

Jersey nodded, feeling naked without her bag, vulnerable hundreds of miles from Newark.

"You ever used a credit card machine?" Dani power walked into the building.

"No." Jersey clenched her hands several times, contracting the muscles in her arms to draw her shoulders inward as they slid past workers hauling equipment.

"I can show you. Or you can be in charge of the cash. Max suggested it. However, if things don't balance at the end of the night, it's on you. Or if someone steals it while you're running it between stands and backstage … it's on you."

"No one will steal anything from me." Jersey murmured, trying to focus on Dani's questions, but the chaos split her attention.

"You sure about that?" She shot Jersey a wry grin.

"Positive."

Dani chuckled. "Let me guess … you take Krav Maga or some type of fitness class that's given you an overinflated sense of confidence and security."

"No …" Jersey had no idea what she meant by Krav Maga. "I know how to cut off the hand of anyone who tries to take something from me … or I can simply break their nose, shatter an eye socket, or bust ribs. I'll decide which fits best if the situation comes up."

Dani choked on a small laugh, eyeing Jersey for some sort of cue that she might be kidding, but Jersey's divided attention made her threats sound calm and calculated, like muttering a list of five things she needed at the grocery store.

"O … kay then. You'll run the money."

After grabbing coffee and bagels behind the stage being constructed by a massive crew, Dani showed Jersey the locations of the merchandise stands, the order in which she should make her rounds, and where to take the money. Then they set up the stands, taking several more coffee breaks, and a quick lunch of sub sandwiches that arrived around twelve thirty.

"This is my favorite part."

Jersey jumped as Dani whispered in her ear. She didn't hear her sneak up behind her as Jersey watched the band trickle onto the stage, sipping drinks and laughing as they messed around.

Dani continued, "Sound checks and a final run through. They try to reconstruct the stage and everything the same way for each concert. But venue sizes vary, so sometimes they have to make minor adjustments. Ian is a perfectionist. I love watching him."

Jersey liked watching him too.

"Dani? We're missing hats. Where are they?" One of the other crew members poked his head into the stage floor doorway at the far end of the stage where Jersey stood, entranced by everything.

"Ugh … I'll be back."

Jersey nodded slowly, not caring if or when Dani returned.

Could a man who murdered two innocent people

stand on a stage, wear a carefree, crooked smile, laugh at jokes, and mess with the strings to his guitar? Jersey couldn't imagine. She killed a man who was not innocent—a horrible man—but his death plagued her every day. It robbed her of her own innocence. With each smile that tried to form on her lips, the memory of him gurgling his blood, choking on his last breath, haunted her.

"Ask him about his childhood."

Again, a voice startled her. Jersey turned. "Where are you supposed to be?" She narrowed her eyes at Chris.

"Where are *you* supposed to be?" He slid his hands into the pockets of his jeans, scowling at Jersey's black, Ian Cooper Crew tee that Dani told her to wear. "It's like you've forgotten." Chris tore his gaze away from her shirt and made eye contact with her.

"I haven't forgotten anything."

"Killers … they come in many different forms. It's not just poor people who take lives. Rich people do it too … only they are more likely to get away with it. Nobody wanted to believe the handsome Ted Bundy could be a serial killer … but he was."

"Who's Ted Bundy?"

Chris grumbled, shaking his head.

"Did you just call me stupid?" Jersey puffed out her chest and made a fist with her right hand while stepping closer to him.

His face twisted as he sighed, rubbing his temples. "Fifteen. You were fifteen when you ran away. Weren't you in school before that? Didn't you learn how to read? You seem to enjoy it when I read to you. Well, it wouldn't kill you to pick up a book, a magazine, a newspaper … really anything to sound a little smarter."

"Fuck you!" She shoved him and he stumbled back a few steps as she charged him, cocking her arm back with a rock-hard fist ready to reacquaint itself with his face.

"Jersey!" Max rushed between them, holding up her hands to stop Jersey while turning her head to the side like her face was the new target.

"So fucking gullible …" Chris shook his head and disappeared around the corner.

Jersey relaxed her grip, letting her arm fall to her side.

"I'm confused." Max let out a nervous laugh. "He's not your boyfriend or your husband … at least I'm assuming since his last name is Ten and yours is Six." She raised a knowing eyebrow that Jersey ignored. "But Ian made it clear that the two of you are a package deal. Yet … you don't seem to like each other. I can't have you throwing punches every day. This crew is a family. Disputes are settled quickly and quietly. Understood?"

As the band started to play part of a song, Jersey turned back toward the stage. "What do you know about Ian's past?"

"Just what he tells everyone else."

"And what's that?" Jersey asked, raising her voice so Max could hear her over the music.

"It's none of our business."

Jersey's head whipped toward Max. "You know nothing about his past?" Reality hit hard. For the first time, she opened the door to her mind, letting in the tiny possibility that there could be truth to Chris's claims.

"He's private and protective of his family ... or his past. I'm not sure which one. But I get it. I'm not exactly an open book either. Inevitably, one day someone will be successful at digging up something from his past and smearing it all over the tabloids. For as long as I've known him, Ian Cooper has been nothing more than a rock star in the moment, like he appeared out of nowhere and just landed on the stage, holding a guitar. And I've been with him longer than anyone except his manager who saw him perform at a bar in New York and picked him up—no questions asked."

Jersey swallowed hard. Just the possibility made it difficult to breathe as a prickle of rage stirred to life, stomping all the stupid butterflies in her stomach.

"How did you get hired?"

Max curled her hair behind her ear, a nervous, somewhat sad smile finding its way to her lips. "I was a nanny for Ames's kids. Ames is his manager. The kids got shipped off to boarding school. Ames signed Mr. Control Freak Cooper and decided the person best suited to keep a neurotic rock star in line was the same person who basically raised his three little hellions. And most of the time, I'm certain I do the bulk of Ames's job."

Max sighed. "Neurotic was the term Ames used. Ian's not really neurotic. He's disciplined. There's a huge difference between the two. I've known him for years. I love him to death. No one works harder than Ian. No one has a bigger heart."

"No wife? No kids?"

"No—" She held up her hand and dug her phone out

of her pocket with her other hand, bringing it to her ear. "I'm coming ... I'm coming ..." Without another word, Max scurried off toward the side of the stage as the band stopped playing.

"Jersey Six."

Her heart skipped the next five beats as her name echoed over the speakers, sending an instant rush of red-hot embarrassment crawling up her neck.

Ian extended his arm, maybe crooking a finger or giving her the middle finger. She couldn't see that well.

"Jersey Six, champion of the pull-up bar, please come to center stage."

Most of the people around him kept working, but a few lifted their gazes to the embarrassed young woman dragging her feet toward the stage. Again, she found herself stereotyping a murderer. Was Chris right? Did killers come in all shapes and sizes, from all walks of life? Did she live with occasional regret for killing a sexual predator, while Ian Cooper mowed down two innocent people on a road without a single ounce of regret or accountability?

Step, step, step ... she dragged herself to the stage as all kinds of scenarios played in her mind. No one knew anything about his past, not even those closest to him. How was that possible? Did he never go home for the holidays? Never see his family? Or did they help him get away with murder, creating a new life for him, knowing he would never be able to go back. Like someone in witness protection?

There was only one way to know for sure ... she had

to get close to him—closer than anyone else. Closer than Max. Closer than Ames. She needed to draw him in like she did her opponents, giving him a false sense of strength and trust.

When she was sixteen, Jersey had sex in a red sports car for a bag of groceries, a blanket, and a pair of shoes. Another time, she exchanged a blowjob for a tube of antibiotic ointment for a festering wound on her heel. Jersey and desperation had an intimate relationship.

For revenge … she would do *anything*.

"What's up, Coop?" She climbed the stairs, imagining the stage was her ring, and she always owned the ring.

"Coop?" The other guy holding a guitar winked at Ian.

Ian wore his signature lopsided grin.

"Make it quick. I'm supposed to be working. And my boss can be a real dick. If he sees me slacking, we're all in trouble."

Jab, jab, jab …

No man liked to go down without a good fight. If he killed her people, Ian Cooper would go down hard, and he wouldn't get back up.

When the naïve little girl inside of her liked him, Ian owned the stage, orchestrating the dance of butterflies, making her knees feel like jelly. With the new revelation, the gut-wrenching possibility that he got away with murder, Jersey owned him, his fucking stage, his words, his songs, his reputation, and everything that made him want to take his next breath—even if he didn't know it yet.

White teeth peeked out from his lips as she obliterated his personal space by stopping when the toes of her white sneakers tapped the toes of his unlaced, neon blue tennis shoes. She tipped her chin up and grinned—a sweet and very poisonous smile.

"I'm a dick?"

She shrugged. "I imagine you have one."

His grin doubled in size. "I have; therefore, I am?"

She had to think of Dena and Charles, and she had to imagine Ian killing them, anything less made her vulnerable to him. Every single thing about *him* had the power to destroy her if she didn't destroy him first.

"Guys," Ian took a step back, reclaiming his space. "This is Jersey Six. Jersey, this is Alex." He nodded toward the ponytailed blond holding a guitar. "That's Jordan on the drums."

Skinny, bald Jordan nodded and smiled, twirling a drumstick between his fingers.

"Bryson on the keyboards."

"Hi, Jersey." He winked at her. Bryson and his wavy, dark hair—slightly longer than Ian's hair—rivaled the rock star who stood center stage. Jersey made a note to never hit Bryson's beautiful face, even if Ian had to die.

Jersey Six.

He introduced her by name, with no reference to their relationship, and nobody seemed to care. Was that because Ian demanded privacy in all aspects of his personal life, like any good killer would do? Or was she the flavor of the month in their minds?

"Did you get lunch?"

She nodded.

"Great. Let's go grab some water." He turned and exited the stage at the back.

Jersey paused for a few seconds before jogging after him. "You drink a lot of water."

"I sweat a lot. Don't you … when you're in the ring?"

The ring. She already missed hitting a bag or an opponent—without getting in trouble. "I sweat when I'm training, but in the ring, I just get the job done. It rarely requires breaking a sweat."

Ian stopped at the door to the green room and turned toward her. "Is that so?" His eyes made a slow inspection of her. She couldn't tell if they admired her or doubted her. The former made her job easier; the latter made it more fun. She liked people who sat back and smirked, never seeing it coming—seeing *her* coming.

"Coop, if you keep questioning my ability to put people in their place, I'm going to be forced to knock you on your ass, and I know Max will not be happy with me. But both of you will have no one to blame but *you*."

Ian grinned, again brushing her threats off like playful banter. He opened the door to the room, a tinier room than the previous night but still well-stocked with places to sit, mirrors, a T.V., and tables of food, beer, and clear glass, blue-lidded bottles of spring water.

"Is that what you're wearing tonight?"

"No." He unscrewed a bottle of water.

Jersey grabbed a handful of chips and walked around the room as Ian stood in the middle of it, watching her.

"How old are you, Coop?"

"Thirty-one."

"You married?"

"No."

"Girlfriend?"

"Sometimes." He eyed her while finishing the bottle of water.

"Sometimes you have a girlfriend, or you have a sometimes girlfriend. Like she's at home or in some fancy place you bought her, thinking she's dating a famous singer, but when you're traveling and women give you their panties, it's a time you choose to be girlfriend-less because it eases your conscience?"

"Are you stereotyping me, Jersey?"

She stopped in front of him and frowned, eyes narrowed.

He tossed his empty bottle into a bin. An inch shorter and it would have landed on the floor, shattering everywhere. "Are you building me up in your mind to be what you think famous people are like?"

She wasn't. Famous singers didn't pick up homeless people off the street and reword things to make them easier to understand without ever making the homeless and undereducated young woman feel stupid.

When her resolve started to crack, she retreated several steps and plucked a carrot stick from a vegetable tray. "Are your parents musical too?"

"Musical?" He grinned and shrugged. "I don't know."

"What does that mean? That you really don't know or that it's none of my business?"

"Maybe."

"Maybe's not an answer. I told you about G. I shared something personal with you. Don't you feel like you should share something personal with me?"

"I think I should get changed before Max brings back fans with backstage passes for photos. And unless you're wanting to watch me change my clothes, you should go sell some tee shirts and shit like that."

On a slow exhale, she turned and shuffled to the door, but instead of opening it, she pivoted back around and leaned against it.

Ian pulled a shirt from its hanger on a rolling clothes rack and stilled, glancing over at Jersey.

She tucked her thumbs into the tight, front pockets of her jeans.

"What?" He cocked his head to the side, eyes narrowed into slits.

"I want to watch."

He studied her in silence, unmoving from his spot twenty feet away from the door.

"At Marley's … I slept in the back room on this old mat. A room much smaller than this one, much dirtier and smellier. There was a toilet that everyone used, but I'm pretty sure I'm the only one who flushed it. A rusted sink with only cold water. Even the water had this odor to it, but after a while, I got used to the smell. Chris noticed it when he arrived and started staying with me."

Jersey's gaze slid to the floor between them. "I dressed in that room, stripped down and washed my naked body with the cold, smelly water and really potent hand soap that left bad rashes on my skin if I didn't get it washed off good." She lowered her voice and slowed her words. "Men would come and go from the back room. Sometimes they just needed to take a piss, but sometimes, they stood there and watched me. I let them because they let me stay there, even after Marley died. And some of them brought me food and stole things for me … things I needed to survive. So … I let them watch. If they didn't try to touch me … I let them watch."

A deafening silence shrouded the room, leaving the meaning of her words suspended in the stagnant air—whatever the meaning was supposed to be. Even Jersey felt conflicted over her intentions when she volunteered such a personal part of her life. She waited for Ian to say something, but he didn't speak or even move one tiny inch. He just stood there with a blank expression holding his face hostage.

"I want to know what they felt. Did it bring them joy to watch me? Did they feel guilty? Did they forget me in the next blink, or did the image of me run through their minds when I wasn't taking off my clothes? I don't know why men in my life have needed this … but I want to understand it."

More silence.

Ian glanced away, staring at the shirt in his hand, eyebrows drawn tightly. He draped the clean shirt over the back of the tall chair by the vanity mirror before removing his worn shirt.

He didn't look at her.

After toeing off his shoes and socks, he unbuttoned his jeans and pushed them down his long legs, stepping out of them and folding them before setting them on a black bag.

He didn't look at her.

Just as slowly, he slid down his black boxer briefs.

Jersey swallowed hard and held her breath as emotion grated her conscience.

He didn't look at her.

Ian stood tall, turning toward the mirror as he closed his eyes, holding completely still.

Naked.

It wasn't seconds … it was minutes later that he opened his eyes and dressed for the show.

Clothes.

Hair.

Deodorant.

Teeth.

Ian primped for his performance—never looking at Jersey.

When she realized there was no sense to be made, no non-perverted reason to watch what she had witnessed— what so many men had witnessed with her—Jersey left the room.

As she turned the corner at the end of the hallway, looking for Dani, Max almost ran into her.

"Oh! There you are. Dani is looking for you. Have you seen Ian?"

"Yeah. I've seen him." And right then, another question got its answer. The image? It stuck. She would always remember what Ian looked like naked, just like so many men walked around with clear memories of Jersey naked and vulnerable.

Max chuckled. "Okay ... where? Is he in the green room? I hope he's getting dressed."

"He is." Jersey nodded slowly, chewing the inside of her cheek as what just happened started to fully come to life in the part of her brain that wasn't fucked up from an unspeakable past.

Ian did that for her. No questions asked. Why? Why did he do that?

CHAPTER TWELVE

C HARLESTON.
Atlanta.
Nashville.
Birmingham.
Indianapolis.
Detroit.

The following weeks flew by. Ian Cooper put on unforgettable concerts. Jersey didn't see much of them, but she heard them—or more accurately, she heard thousands of screaming fans. After they ended, she wasn't beckoned to the green room or an SUV behind the building. She helped tear down the pop-up merchandise stands, gorged on food catered to the crew, and looked for Chris. But she rarely found him in the mix of local crew and Ian's traveling crew bustling to get everything taken down, packed up, and on the road.

Chris traveled by bus. She traveled by plane. Ian treated her well, like a friend. So did Max, Shane, Rex, and Ian's bandmates. Since the stripping incident, Ian kept a safe distance from Jersey or at least made sure they were rarely alone together.

Max did nice things for Jersey, but she had no idea if

they were Max's ideas or Ian's generosity—like the trip to the hair salon before the last concert. Jersey acted like she didn't care if she got a haircut, but there were no words to describe the feeling of someone washing her hair, cutting it measured and carefully, instead of the way Jersey had occasionally butchered her own hair over the years with dull scissors.

"Ready?"

Jersey turned toward Max just as Dani finished telling a story about her drunkenness from the previous night. Just because Ian wasn't a partier didn't mean his crew ran a sober ship after hours.

"Yeah." Jersey followed Max toward the exit.

"Yo, Jersey?" Dani called. "I heard a rumor that you've been flying with Ian all this time, and that's why we never see you on the buses. That's fucking crazy, right? I mean … are you holding out on your girl?"

She wasn't sure when Dani became her girl, but Jersey agreed with her about the first part. "Yeah," she nodded and kept walking, "it's fucking crazy alright."

Shane drove them to the airport. They weren't staying the night in Detroit. They were heading straight to Chicago.

"I'm so damn tired." Max climbed the stairs to the plane with Jersey right behind her and Shane bringing up the rear.

Jersey stopped just inside the jet. Shane stored her bag in the bin above her head to the right and folded his large body into the seat on the opposite side of the aisle as Max. A closed curtain divided their seats from the other two seats and the sofa in the back of the plane. She had never seen the curtain closed.

"Go on back," Max muttered on a big yawn as she stretched her legs out on the seat in front of her. "If he didn't want you back there, you'd be on a bus right now."

Was that true? Did Ian really want her there? He had a weird way of showing it.

Weeks of traveling with the star, but why? Naked Ian consumed her thoughts. Every perfectly defined inch of his body. Yet, he treated her like a friend, a sister. Not like the woman who asked him to strip for her. It was like it never happened.

"We're taking off. What's it going to be?" Shane nodded to the seat facing him.

Jersey collapsed into that seat and fastened her seat belt, gripping the armrests as they took off. Shane closed his eyes like the force of the plane didn't affect him, and it probably didn't. He'd done it hundreds of times.

Once the plane leveled out, and Jersey felt convinced that Shane and Max were asleep, she unbuckled and peeked through the closed curtain. Ian's reclined body engulfed the sofa to her left, so she eased into one of the leather seats on her right.

When she looked at Ian again, two dark, wide eyes stared back at her. The way they burned her skin didn't change her intentions. If he was a killer, she would end his life. But in that moment, she didn't *know* anything. Weeks of digging and subtle questions left her with no more information about Ian and his past than she knew after their first time sharing spaghetti in New York.

And she'd been dodging the one thing she knew might get her somewhere—offering him something new. Something he couldn't refuse. The only way to uncover the truth was to get as close to it as possible.

When he didn't blink or say a single word, Jersey stood, nervously stroking her ponytail a few times, still in awe of how soft her hair felt since the haircut. Ian had no idea how much all the little things he did for her added up to something too big to describe.

Slipping off her jacket, she let it drop to the floor. Ian eased himself to sitting in the middle of the sofa with his broad shoulders squared to Jersey.

How close?

Ian helped himself to every inch of her without moving anything but his eyes.

How close could she get?

Jersey kicked off her shoes and locked gazes with him as she unbuttoned her jeans.

How close could she get to the truth?

Ian's hands rested on his legs, and his gaze moved only with Jersey's eyes as she lowered her body to peel the jeans off her legs, leaving them to rest by her jacket, along with the knife she had planted in the sock of her right leg. Not even a discarded knife made Ian as much as flinch.

The slick material of her new panties still felt foreign to her after years of wearing worn, ripped, and stained cotton. Wearing only the black satin panties and her black, fitted Ian Cooper Crew shirt, she straddled his lap. Ian eased his hands to the side, resting them on the sofa as she lowered to his lap, balancing herself by holding the back of the sofa. With a stone face and even breath, Ian lifted his hand so very slowly, reaching for the back of her head.

Jersey's lips parted and her jaw lowered an inch as he tugged her ponytail. It radiated heavily in her breasts and between her legs. The feeling intensified when she thought of him naked.

He pinched the rubber band and eased it from her hair, allowing the long strands to fall around her shoulders and face.

She let a man fuck her with the handle of a hairbrush while he videotaped her. After six days locked in a room with a gallon of water and no food, she realized her body was nothing more than a tool. Weak and emotionally dead, she stopped fighting him. For a ham sandwich, she let him do it to her—the brush in one hand, the video camera in his other hand. Pride had no place in her life.

Survival.

Basic human needs.

Revenge.

They fed the person she had become.

Ian let his gaze drift to Jersey's mouth. He would kiss her. She would let him.

But he didn't move his mouth. He moved his hands.

She gasped, her whole body recoiling without actually pulling away from him as his hands palmed her ass, his fingers curling into her muscled flesh and satin panties. Her hands tightened on the back of the sofa as he lifted her, pulling her closer, and guiding her over him.

The part of him she saw in the dressing room, the

part of him that showed no pleasure in her seeing him naked weeks earlier, vanished. Dragging in a ragged breath, feeling intoxicated, willingly drugged by the way he looked at her in silence, she slowly blinked.

Slowly, like the way he rubbed her against him.

Slowly, like the hypnotic dance of a serpent.

Slowly, like unearthing the truth.

Time paused as it always did when Jersey let herself fall and surrender to achieve something greater than a moment. A small trade in a much bigger game. A single line of a long story.

Again, he rocked her pelvis against his erection.

Again, the denim teased the satin.

Again, she blinked heavily.

Her tangled thoughts fought to break free, to comprehend the stolen moment.

Control slipped. She needed to take it back, but she couldn't because the lie felt too good. It poisoned her mind and manipulated her body.

Before long, that body took over. Jersey didn't need him to guide her. She did it all on her own. Her eyes glossed over as her jaw dropped another inch. And with a final jerk of her pelvis, she stilled, pressing hard against him. Wave after wave of pleasure surged through her. Jersey's strong hands dug at the leather, and her head dropped to Ian's neck. She moaned, biting and sucking his skin to keep from waking Max and Shane. It felt so intense, bordering on pain.

Jersey liked pain.

When her breath evened out and her hands unclenched from the back of the sofa, Jersey lifted her head, hair matted to her face. Ian's hands slid from her backside, resting again on the sofa.

No words.

No emotion on his face.

Nothing.

The truth she sought remained buried in the man—a stone-cold crypt with no entrance. She would have to break in, chip away at it until it cracked, until *he* cracked.

Easing off him one leg at a time, Jersey pulled on her jeans, socks, and shoes. While sliding the knife back into her sock, she stared at the wet spot she left on his jeans. He stared at her.

Jersey dropped into the chair. Then Ian folded his hands on his lap, tipped his head back, and closed his eyes. It felt like mere minutes before they landed. By the time she managed to peel open her eyes, the only other person left on the plane was Max with her arms crossed over her chest and a scowl pinned to her face.

"What time is it?" Jersey mumbled, pulling her tired ass out of the leather seat. The only light she could see out the window was from a vehicle parked near the plane. "What?" She rubbed her eyes when Max refused to move out of her way.

"In five hours, Ian has a live televised interview with a morning show."

Jersey squinted against the overhead, fully illuminated lights. "Okay. Whatever."

"He's not a turtleneck guy, and I've never seen him wear a scarf. It's not his look. If we try to change his look too much, it will distract from the promotion of the album and tour."

"Jesus …" Jersey sighed. "Can we just find a place to crash for a few hours? I don't give a shit what you decide to do with Ian's look. Why are we having this conversation?"

"Because he has a massive hickey with bite marks on his neck that wasn't there when he boarded the plane. I went to sleep, and as far as my husband has shared with me, I don't unknowingly suck and bite people's skin at night. Shane just got married to a woman, so I didn't even question him about it. The pilot stayed glued to his seat, and Eve, the attendant, didn't fly with us tonight. See where I'm going with this?"

Another sigh escaped Jersey's hickey-giving mouth. "It won't happen again."

Max shook her head, lips pulled into a firm line. "I can't ask him this, but I'm sure as hell going to ask you … did you two use a condom? It's usually something I provide while picking up miscellaneous things for him, but he didn't make a request, which makes me think this wasn't planned. And there are *a lot* of unplanned people walking this earth."

"We didn't have sex."

Max narrowed her eyes, disbelief radiating from her entire body.

"We didn't." Jersey forced herself to look Max in the eye, in spite of the lights burning a layer of her corneas.

When Max seemed satisfied, albeit still pissed off, she pivoted and exited the plane. Shane waited by the vehicle with the back door and the front passenger door open. Max hopped into the front, and Jersey climbed into the backseat.

Ian eyed her briefly, again with no expression or hint of emotion. Then he leaned his head against his window and closed his eyes. They parked at a side entrance to the hotel and shuffled through the door and down the hallway in a single file line, with Max leading the way, followed by Jersey, Ian, and Shane.

When the elevator doors opened, Jersey stepped inside and turned toward Ian and Shane as they followed her. Her gaze homed in on the huge mark on Ian's neck. She cringed. He turned around, standing beside her. Again … no reaction. Not his signature smirk or even a fleeting moment of anger that matched Max's irritation regarding the interview in less than five hours.

Five hours.

Jersey knew a lot about bruises. That mark on his neck would look much worse in five hours.

To Jersey's surprise, they all exited the elevator on the same floor, which meant their rooms were closer together. Max flashed the face of her phone over the sensor to a room and opened the door. Ian slid past her, with a simple "goodnight" mumbled.

"Goodnight," Max replied.

Shane used his phone to open the door to another room.

"You're with me since he didn't invite you to stay with him." Max smiled at Jersey as she shut the door to Ian's room.

Jersey ignored the smug expression on Max's face. Lack of sleep robbed her last fuck to give that night ... or morning. It was morning, just early, before-Jersey's-jog early. Max opened the door to their room, and Jersey tossed her bag on the ground at the end of the bed near the window.

"It's not you." Max pulled off her white coat and draped it over the back of the desk chair.

Jersey removed the knife from her sock and set it on the nightstand. Max had a much more visible reaction than Ian did.

"If someone breaks into the room ... I've got it handled." Jersey smirked while slipping off her shoes and jeans and crawling into bed.

Max cleared her throat, peeling her gaze away from the knife and lifting her jaw off the floor. "As I was saying, it's not you. What we discussed on the plane? I don't want you to take it personally." She unzipped her suitcase, grabbed a smaller bag and a nightshirt, and disappeared around the corner into the bathroom. As she droned on about Ian and what's best for him, his life choices, his future, and his reputation, Jersey fell asleep.

"WHAT ARE YOU doing?" Max mumbled from her bed.

"Pushups. Sorry. I didn't mean to wake you." Jersey finished her last ten and jumped to her feet. "I wanted to go for a run, but I don't have a room key, and I assumed you'd get all pissy if I stole your phone. What I *really* want is to beat on a bag for a while. Are there any places around here I could find one?"

Max retrieved her plugged-in phone from the nightstand and squinted at the screen.

"It's ten to five. Are you kidding me? I deserve another hour of sleep."

"A punching bag, Max. I'm starting to have withdrawals. If you don't figure out something soon, I'll be forced to find a live one amongst your crew."

Max buried her head underneath her pillow. "Go tell Shane to find you a punching bag. I'm sure he's awake and already caffeinated."

Slam!

The door shut behind Jersey as she crossed the hall and knocked on Shane's door at least a dozen times. Just the promise of getting to hit a bag made adrenaline burn through her veins, building so much anticipation, making her jittery like an addict in need of a hit.

"Shane!"

Bang! Bang! Bang!

The click of a door opening to her right stopped her fists from pounding on Shane's door.

"What the hell, Jersey?" A groggy, messy-haired Ian peeked out from his hotel room.

Shirtless. He had a perfect smattering of hair on his chest.

Shorts. They rode low on his hips, displaying a lot of a happy trail.

Two days' worth of stubble darkened his face.

But … the hickey. It stood out like a new, ugly tattoo

on his neck.

"Jersey!" The irritation in his voice cut through the air.

Her gaze snapped up to meet his. "Max said Shane would take me somewhere to box. I need to hit something ... really, really badly. If I don't hit a bag soon, I'm going to hit actual people. No one wants me hitting people. Do you, Coop? Do you want me to use an actual person for a punching bag?"

Chain-smokers and heroin addicts had more control than Jersey did at that moment.

"Well, clearly Shane's not in his room. So you don't need to wake the whole goddamn hotel. Just a minute ..." Ian started to close his door then pulled it back open. "Wait in here while I get dressed."

Jersey pumped her hands, working the adrenaline as she stepped into his dark hotel room. From the light of the bathroom, she could see the room was much smaller than some of his previous rooms, but still twice the size of Max's room. Hers didn't have a sitting area or a kitchenette.

Ian closed the bathroom door, leaving Jersey in complete darkness. She dropped down and pushed through fifty more pushups, side planks, mountain climbers, and finished with jump squats just as Ian emerged from the bathroom, wearing loose-fitting jeans and a long-sleeved, fitted, white tee.

Breathlessly, she eyed his messy, damp hair ... and the hickey.

"Why are you doing that in the dark?" he mumbled

with a groggy, morning voice.

Jersey flipped the light switch by the door. Ian tucked his wallet into his front pocket, his phone in his back pocket, and grabbed two bottles of his special water from the kitchenette's counter.

For a few moments, Jersey forgot what they were going to do. Ian moved toward her, looming over her as her back melted against the door.

"How tall are you?" she whispered, straining her neck to look up at him.

"Six-five." He shoved one of the bottled waters into her chest.

Jersey dropped her chin to stare at it for a second before taking it from him.

Ian had large hands that fit perfectly with his tall frame. Chris said they played basketball together. She could imagine Ian palming a basketball with those large hands—the same ones that easily palmed her ass on the plane.

She swallowed hard from the memory of it.

Ian's nose wrinkled. "Why do you keep wearing the same clothes you wore when I met you?"

Jersey shrugged. "Because I'm not wearing tight jeans to work out."

"Why didn't you get new workout clothes when Max took you shopping?" Ian sounded exasperated, like everything about Jersey irritated him.

Another shrug. "Because I didn't see any at the store, and she said we needed things for me to wear while working."

He frowned. Jersey's body stiffened when his hand brushed her side, reaching for the doorknob. She squatted down to grab her bag.

"Let's go."

IN THE TAXI on the way to the gym, Ian texted Max to let her know their whereabouts and instruct her to go buy new workout clothes for Jersey ASAP.

She wasn't the only one in need of a bag to hit that morning. A crowd of men and women filled the space. Ian purchased a day pass for Jersey, drawing more attention to himself than he wanted that morning. He wasn't ready for autographs and selfies, but without a hat and sunglasses, it was unavoidable.

After the last picture, he found a dark corner to hide in that still gave him a good view of Jersey. In her baggy sweats and a soiled, white-ish tank top, she beat the hell out of a large punching bag before moving on to a speed bag.

Ian narrowed his eyes as another boxer, a woman a little older and a lot bigger than Jersey, approached her. She wore a cocky grin, pointing to the empty ring in the middle of the room. Jersey twisted her lips and shrugged, following the woman to the ring.

A guy who worked at the gym stepped into the ring as well, chatting with Jersey and the other woman as they stood huddled together. Both women nodded and tapped gloves. The guy stepped back against the ropes and hit a bell.

The larger, taller woman slipped in a mouth guard. Jersey didn't have one in her mouth. Ian eased out of the shadows, feeling a twinge of concern for Jersey's teeth. Her opponent had to be at least twice Jersey's size. His new employee carried nothing but hard muscles on her bones. Jersey wasn't soft and curvy, but rather five feet, seven inches of sharp bones and steely muscles with a thick, dark mane.

Jersey reminded Ian of a racing horse, a filly less likely to win but filled with as much determination as the favored colts.

Her confident challenger threw the first punch. Jersey bobbed to easily avoid the hit. Her opponent had fast feet and good form. Jersey stood idle like a bright red target, her hands limp at her sides instead of up by her face—protecting her teeth!

Ian's phone vibrated. "Yeah?"

"We're out front. You're going to be late if you don't hurry up." Max's scolding tone nipped at his ear.

"Okay." Ian ended the call and weaved his way toward the ring, planting himself in Jersey's line of sight.

She dodged another attempt by her opponent and glanced at Ian. He held up his wrist and tapped the face to his watch. Jersey nodded several times and dropped the larger woman with one hard, fast hit. The employee rushed to the woman's aid, waving another employee over to the unconscious woman.

Ian cringed.

Jersey? She ducked between the ropes like nothing

happened and tugged the ties to her gloves with her teeth, trapping one glove under her arm to pull it off and then the other.

"You knocked her out." Ian watched in concern as they tended to the woman. By the time Jersey stuffed her gloves into her bag and pulled on her hoodie, they had the woman on her feet, pressing a towel to her bloodied nose.

"Coop, it's boxing. What the fuck did you think I was going to do to her? Braid her hair?" Jersey made her way to the exit.

Ian shook his head, still in shock, and followed her out of the building to the SUV waiting for them.

"Morning. Did you get your shit worked out?" Max twisted her body to scowl at Jersey. With a quick sniff, her scowl deepened.

"It was okay." Jersey drank from the bottle of water that Ian gave her.

He eyed her, waiting for her to share the story of how she knocked that woman out, but it didn't seem to faze Jersey one bit.

"We have an hour and a half. We'll go back to the hotel so you two can get showered ... separately," Max murmured.

Jersey turned her head toward Ian, studying the hickey on his neck before meeting his gaze. A smile played along her lips. That ... *that* was what made her smile? Ian couldn't believe the fight did nothing, but a hickey made her happy.

His dick stirred in his pants. After Jersey's striptease

on the plane, he needed something. A quick lay. A hand job. A blowjob … or just an extra five minutes in the shower. The woman possessed something he didn't anticipate—a look. Jersey had a subtle beauty, one you might miss if you didn't look closely. Over the previous weeks, her body had gained a few soft curves, her face began to fill out, taking the edge off, no longer gauntly. But it was her eyes, it had always been her eyes, that told her story, shared every emotion. Earthy browns, rich like shades of clay, deep, and full of wonder and desire, heartbreak and determination. She could ball her hands and clench her teeth, but her eyes never lied.

Shane pulled up next to the side door, and Max handed Jersey a room key card. "You two have forty-five minutes. We'll grab food and…" Max rubbed her nose "…new workout attire."

Jersey rubbed her nose too, but only using her middle finger. Ian bit his lips together and opened the door before he landed on Max's shit list for laughing at Jersey's not-so-gracious response.

"Yes, boss." Ian winked at Max while shutting the door.

"I stink." Jersey dropped her head as Ian held open the side door to the hotel.

"You do." He smirked, but she didn't glance up at him to see it. "I stink too when I exercise. Max will get you some new workout stuff so you only have to wear around one day's worth of stink." He pushed the button to the elevator.

"Fuck you," she whispered.

The doors opened and they stepped into the empty elevator. Ian grunted a laugh, resting his hands on his hips and tipping his chin down on a slight headshake. "You're trying, Jersey ... you're definitely trying to fuck me."

She was a million things he could never really explain—least of all his motive for the previous weeks.

A feeling.

An impulse.

An underlying need.

So he kept it to himself, in spite of the looks from Max and Shane. The curiosity of his bandmates. Even the rational part of his own brain questioned his rationale.

Why he felt drawn to her that day in Newark. Why he offered her a job. Why he stripped for her. Why he helped her get off on him on the plane.

Ian ran away from his past. Killed it. Burned it. Scattered the ashes in the middle of the ocean. Then ... one day, someone on his crew *had* to mention Marley's, and Ian *had* to drive to Newark.

Newark. Dead is just dead; it's not really gone.

Forever doesn't exist. It's just what people tell themselves to make the now a little more bearable.

Jersey charged off the elevator the moment the doors opened. Ian gave her space, staying several steps behind her. She tapped the key card on the sensor. It didn't open. She waved it quickly in front of it. It didn't open.

Then she punched the door and jerked her hand back against her chest, cradling it. Ian rested his hands on the door above her head, caging her with his body, his chest to her back.

Jersey leaned forward and rested her head on the door. "Why did you do it?" Defeat weighted her words. "Why did you take off your clothes?"

"Why did you take off yours?" he whispered back to her.

She didn't take all of her clothes off, but she would have … that much Ian knew.

Jersey rolled her head side to side, eyes closed. "On the plane … you … you didn't say one word. Why? Why didn't you say anything?"

"Jersey …" he sighed. "I'm just trying to give you what you need."

Her head stilled. "W-what?" Jersey pushed away from the door, forcing Ian to take a step backward. She turned to face him. "What I need?" she sneered, pinning him with cold eyes and widening her stance.

"Forget it. Go shower." Ian refocused on the schedule he needed to keep. Sliding his phone out of his pocket, he used his digital key to open the door to his room.

"Don't just blow me off," she spewed through gritted teeth.

"Not blowing you off. Just staying on schedule." He slipped into his room and shrugged off his shirt to get into the shower. While tossing it on the bed, he paused. The door didn't click behind him. He sighed. "Fuck, Jersey, just …" He turned.

The door clicked behind her as she stalked toward him, hands fisted. "You should have left me on the street."

He shifted right to avoid her fist, but she landed a

hard hook to his ribs instead, followed by another, and another …

"Back the fuck off!" He guarded his face and twisted his body, stumbling a few steps. When the back of his legs hit the bed, he blocked her jab and shoved her with enough force to knock her on her ass.

"There are no shiny rewards for adopting the homeless, you rich, fucked-up asshole!" She scrambled to her feet. Blood oozed from the cut by her eye where she hit her head on the leg of the barstool.

Ian cringed, finding it hard to defend himself without hurting her.

Jab. Cross. Hook. Uppercut.

Jersey exploded onto him like a tornado touching down in a crowded town. He fell back onto the bed. She straddled him, using every inch of him as a punching bag.

He hid his face behind his arms, wincing at the stabbing pain in his ribs from her relentless jabs. Ian rolled to the side and shoved her from the bed.

She came at him again.

Again, he shoved her away. When she stumbled to the floor, he grabbed her arm and twisted it behind her back, forcing her onto her stomach. Then he lay on her. Just … restrained her with his sheer size and bodyweight, needing a few moments of reprieve to assess the damage.

He underestimated her mental stability, her self-control. That was on him. But he couldn't let her do that anymore. Licking the blood from his lip, he blinked both eyes. The left one throbbed, along with his jaw and bruised ribs.

"I'm not yours to fix." She grunted, trying without success to free herself from the weight of his body.

Ian rested his cheek on the backside of her shoulder. "I never said you were broken."

She wasn't broken, just really damaged.

"Here's how this will go … I'm going to let you out from under me. You're going to walk out that door, shower, and wait for me in the hallway—on time. And we're not going to speak of this again. And it's *not* going to ever happen again. Understood?"

Jersey moved her head into a tiny nod. Ian released her arm and eased off her one inch at a time, readying himself for her to lose it again. He lumbered to standing, and so did she. They faced each other, both bloodied and bruised.

"When's the last time you spoke to your family?" Her question gave him whiplash.

"When's the last time you spoke to yours?"

Jersey's mouth turned downward. "What makes you think I have a family?"

"What makes you think I have one?"

"You're an asshole." She pivoted and retreated to the door.

"Yeah, well, so are you." He didn't wait for her to respond, leave his room, or figure out how to open her hotel room door with the key card. Ian closed and locked the bathroom door, removed the rest of his clothes, and stepped into the hot shower.

CHAPTER THIRTEEN

J UST AS JERSEY unplugged the hair dryer, Max opened the door to the hotel room. She paused, blinking several times at Jersey's reflection in the mirror—the unmistakable cut by her eye and red bruise along her jaw.

"Ian's going to fire me." Max stepped the rest of the way inside of the room, and the door shut behind her. "He's going to fire me and keep you. Which is insane!" Max tossed her purse onto the desk. "Because I do everything for him so he can focus on the one thing he loves most in life. I am the keeper of schedules, the fixer of catastrophes, the right brand of crackers, the two-dozen room-temperature, glass bottles of spring water neatly lined up and ready to go before he even realizes he's thirsty."

She tore open the blinds to the room and sighed while staring out the window. "And I do it because I love my job. I do it because he loves his job. I do it because I respect him. I genuinely respect him and how he chooses to run his business. I respect the way he treats his employees, his fans, and other musicians."

Jersey shut off the bathroom light and slid around the corner, unable to make eye contact with Max.

"But here's the issue ... I don't know why a man worth millions of dollars picked up a stranger off the street, clothed her, fed her, employed her, did whatever it was he did to or *with* her in a private jet last night, then allowed her to assault him, and still ... refuses to let her go or explain to anyone around him his reasoning for keeping her. I ... I ... I just can't wrap my head around this.

"But he just kicked me out of his hotel room for *caring about him*. Have you seen him? Have you taken a good look at him? The hickey is the least offensive thing he has going for him at the moment. I just stood in the hallway canceling his appearances for today. The silver lining is he doesn't have to perform for two more days, and hopefully makeup will do the trick by then—*unless* you decide to take out your anger on him again!"

Jersey rubbed her bruised knuckles. *If* Ian killed Dena and Charles, she knew death would never be enough. People like Max held him too high on an unreachable pedestal. One blow, one cut ... it would never be enough. Jersey would bring down his whole world, killing him slowly, so slowly he wouldn't even realize the end was near.

But ... if he didn't kill them, then the man down the hallway genuinely cared for her and her *needs*. Either way, she had to dig deeper and find that truth.

"I'm sorry." Jersey turned and opened the door.

"For what?" Max asked on a chuckle.

"I'm not sure yet." Jersey let the door close behind her and took the ten steps to Ian's door, slapping it several times to save her knuckles from more misery.

When he didn't answer, she slapped it several more times. He opened the door, holding a glass tumbler in his hand and a vacant look in his eyes—the good one and the slightly swollen eye.

No shirt.

No shoes.

Dark jeans.

Wet hair.

"Nice hickey."

Ian stared at her, maybe trying to lift his eyebrow in disbelief, but the swelling prevented his attempt. He turned, letting the door begin to close.

Jersey shoved her foot into the space before it clicked and followed him inside the room. The knocked over barstools and displaced coffee table were back in their spots. Ian collapsed onto his bed, leaning against the turquoise padded headboard, gaze locked to the basketball game on the television.

Basketball … clearly, he liked it. Did that mean he played it? Did he play it with Chris?

Ian sipped his drink while expertly ignoring Jersey.

What would he say if she just asked him?

Did you accidentally run over two people eight years ago and let your rich family keep you out of prison? Did you take away my entire future? The only people I've ever loved and who ever loved me?

Would his reaction give her the truth? Or would it land her on the street again, with no answers, no job, and no way to get back to Newark?

Jersey slipped off her shoes and crawled up the bed, in uncharted territory, with her thoughts warring between revenge and redemption—a second chance at a life lost eight years earlier.

Was Ian the Devil or her savior?

He leaned a few inches to the side to see the screen past her. She straddled his legs, this time wearing jeans and a gray, fitted tee, more clothes than Ian wore.

Jersey took his glass from his hand, bringing it to her lips. It burned her mouth as she swallowed it. "Not water," she mumbled, setting the glass on the nightstand.

Ian's gaze followed the glass, lingering there even when Jersey released it.

She ghosted her thumb over the red haloed bruise around his eye. "I'm nothing…" she whispered "…insignificant … forgettable … no one would miss me if I died. No one would look for me if I were lost. No human has ever cried for me."

With her index finger, she used a feather's touch to trace the cut on his lip. "I am unloved." Her words snagged in her throat. They hurt a lot less when they were just thoughts. "I am unlovable."

His inward gaze focused on her as if her words woke something up inside of him. She gave him her truth. Maybe he would give her his truth. A risk she had to take, knowing she might fall for a lie.

Was Ian a lie?

"So why …" She brushed his cheek with her nose, closing her eyes. "Why do I feel like you're making up for something? Why do I feel like you didn't simply meet me by chance? Why does it feel like you *found* me?" Her lips touched his mouth.

"Jersey …"

Her hands pressed to his cheeks as she kissed him.

Softly.

Slowly.

A shy kiss.

An inexperienced kiss.

A simple touch that made her tremble.

Pulling back an inch, their gazes locked. "Tell me to go, Coop."

His eyes flitted along her face. "I can't."

"Then ask me to stay."

Ian's brows turned down. "I can't."

Revenge held its own intimacy. Jersey felt it when she killed the man who sexually abused her and took photos of her. Before he completely bled out, she kissed his cheek and thanked him for making her a little bit stronger. For a single blink—a second, a flash—she felt the intimacy between them. He came into her life. He took something that wasn't his to take. And she returned the favor. They both learned from each other, a messed-up symbiotic relationship that ended when she no longer had anything to take from him.

Jersey slid her fingers into Ian's hair. "Then give me what I need." There was only one way to find out how much she needed to take from Ian Cooper.

"What do you need?" He brushed his nose along her cheek the way she did to him.

The truth. She needed the truth. But something told

her he wouldn't hand it to her. She would have to take it from him, one piece at a time.

Jersey pulled back just enough to see his eyes. "I need you to know I'm not sorry."

"For what?" A slight crease formed along the bridge of his nose.

Her gaze swept along his face and neck, taking in all the marks she left on him. "For anything."

Ian nodded in tiny increments for several seconds before pressing the pad of his thumb to the cut by her eye. "Neither am I." He pressed it with enough pressure to make her flinch, as if he meant to draw pain from her.

The tremble. The weak moment of insecurity that she surrendered to his touch minutes earlier vanished. Jersey grabbed his wrist and jerked his hand away, narrowing her eyes.

Ian smirked.

"You're going to lose your hand, Coop."

He expressed everything through a look, a code waiting to be cracked, a challenge waiting to be accepted.

The truth.

Just get the truth.

Jersey leaned in to kiss him again. Ian pulled away, leaving her hanging and slightly off balance in her mind. She clenched her teeth, her gaze hard and fixed to his. He taunted her again with his silence and indecipherable expression.

Swallowing her saliva instead of spewing it in his face, she climbed off his lap, shoved her feet into her shoes, and made slow steps to the door, pumping her fists and fighting the urge—the need—to control him. Ian Cooper liked control. He liked the game. Little did he know he would never win.

"Oh!" Max jumped back with her fist ready to knock on Ian's door as Jersey opened it. "I wondered where you went." She craned her neck to see past Jersey to Ian.

Jersey returned a tight-lipped smile. "Might want to get me a pregnancy test and some condoms and an STD test for your rock star."

Max's jaw fell open as her eyes bulged from her head. Bumping Max's shoulder, Jersey returned to their hotel room.

IAN TURNED UP the volume to the basketball game as Max let the heavy door slam shut behind her.

"I was coming over here to apologize for crossing some invisible line with you earlier, but if I need to get that girl a pregnancy test, then you need to get your shit together and tell me what's going on with you."

"She's not pregnant." Ian kept his attention on the game.

"Did you use a condom?"

"None of your business, Max." He shot her a quick glance.

She curled her hair behind her right ear and planted herself at the end of his bed, blocking his view of the television. "Did you cancel your appearances for today?"

When he didn't answer her, she crossed her arms over

her chest and twisted her lips for a few seconds. "Hmm ... oh, that's right. I did that. I do everything but wipe your ass, but you knocking up a homeless girl who works for you ... that's none of my business? Really? That's how you want to play this?"

Pinching the bridge of his nose, he shook his head. "We didn't have sex."

"Then why would she say that to me?"

"I don't know."

Max coughed a laugh. "You don't know? So there's a zero percent chance that she's pregnant with your baby? A zero percent chance that you've contracted an STD from her?"

"Correct."

"Then fire her, Ian. Fire her before she walks out of this hotel to a crowd of paparazzi and tells them she's pregnant with your baby. This isn't you. If it's sex, Ian, we'll find someone to meet your needs without the—"

"Jesus, Max ..." He shook his head, eyes squinted. "No. I don't need you to hire someone to have sex with me. But thanks for the vote of confidence."

"Ian ..." Max exhaled, releasing her posture into a slump of defeat. "Why this girl? Don't get me wrong, I like her. She's a hard worker. She's feisty. Refreshingly uncensored at times. And I catch glimpses of her looking at you like your hand personally hung the moon in her favorite bedtime story. But I don't see the appeal from your lenses. Out of millions of women ... why her?"

The answer should have been simple, and when he saw Jersey at the hot dog stand in Newark, it felt simple.

Fated.

A chance to right wrongs.

As the weeks passed by, the answers became more complicated. Motives blurred. Reality twisted and tangled good intentions into a mess.

A dangerous mess.

"I know what I'm doing."

"You do?" Max's head canted to the side.

Ian nodded.

He had no idea what he was doing. But he felt no need to burden Max with that truth. She was right.

"Do I need to talk to her?"

Ian shook his head.

"Do I need to get her pregnancy tests? Condoms and a STD test for you?"

Another headshake.

"Did you donate a kidney to this girl?"

Ian tilted his head, refocusing on the television as a tiny grin stole his lips. Max grumbled and pivoted on an eye roll before leaving his hotel room.

CHAPTER FOURTEEN

J ERSEY SAT IN on a few meals with Ian, Max, and Shane while Ian healed from their little dispute. Other than the occasional prolonged, expressionless glance, Ian never spoke to her. Max kept the conversation focused on business.

After the Chicago concert, Chris found Jersey and tugged the back of her shirt. She whipped around, not fond of anyone touching her. He gave her a sad smile. She mirrored his sadness, and after a minute or so, she stepped into his embrace.

If revenge could be intimate, then separation felt torturous.

"Cash. I got paid in cash because I don't have a real identity," he mumbled, resting his cheek on her head.

Jersey nodded. She, too, received an envelope of cash earlier that day after Max confirmed that Jersey didn't know her social security number or have a bank account.

"What are we doing?" Chris pulled back and met her eyes.

She knew what he meant. Were they just working because that was the only job they had, or was there a purpose to the coincidence—to Chris's claims about Ian?

"It might have been him." Jersey frowned. "He's too …" She shook her head. "I don't know. It's hard to explain, but he's hiding something from me. I can feel it. I can see it in his eyes. It's guilt and something else I can't quite figure out. Anger? Resentment? I don't know. But I'm afraid to mention Dena's and Charles's names, and—" She watched some of the crew squeeze past them.

Chris nodded toward the other hallway. She followed him into the dimly lit area.

"People don't like to keep this shit to themselves." Chris leaned close to her so no one could hear him. "The guilt. It's too much. He's dying to tell someone. He has to be. All these years of keeping it to himself, there's no way it's not taking its toll. You … he'll tell you. But he has to trust you more than anyone else. You have to gain his trust, Jers."

She shook her head. "I don't know how to do that. I've tried to get close to him. He pushes me away."

"He's a guy. Crawl into his bed. Suck his dick."

Jersey scowled.

Chris held up his hands. "I'm not pimping you out to a murderer. I'm giving you a chance for revenge. Don't look at me like I've offended you, like you're too goody-goody for the job. I've seen where you live, how you bathe, the dumpsters where you find food … it's called survival, and you damn well know it."

Chewing on the inside of her cheek, she averted her gaze. "For your information, I've tried to crawl into his bed. He dismissed me."

"Because you didn't suck his dick."

"Not my thing."

Chris grinned. "It's not any woman's thing. It's not supposed to be. It's a guy's thing."

"Then *you* suck his dick."

Chris shrugged. "Statistically, he's most likely going to want you to do it, but if you try and he stays limp in your mouth, let me know. I'll see what I can do."

"You're disgusting." Her nose wrinkled.

"Every guy is disgusting. Even the ones who have a wife and two bratty little kids sitting next to them at church every Sunday morning. If you think for one second that they're focused on salvation instead of their secretary blowing them in their office the next morning, then you're just too damn naïve."

Jersey blinked several times. "Do you think of me blowing you?"

"I jerk off to the image of it at least twice a day."

Her eyes narrowed into menacing little slits as she balled her fists.

"No." Chris laughed. "You don't get to be pissed off about that. If anything, I should get points for honesty. But if it makes you feel better, I've imagined Max doing it to me wearing nothing but her fancy white wool coat, and definitely your buddy Dani because she has her tongue pierced and that's gotta feel like fucking nirvana."

"I thought you were different than all the perverted thugs at Marley's." Jersey stepped away from him, walking backward down the hallway.

"Different? No. More self-controlled? Yes."

Jersey stopped, tugging on her ponytail to tighten it.

"Am I good?"

Chris lifted his chin, squinting his eyes.

"In your fantasies … am I good?" She smirked.

Even with the dim lighting, she could see his cheeks turn red. "Yeah, Jers … you're my favorite fantasy."

As she turned the corner to find Max, Jersey saw the band members exiting the building at the far end of the hallway. Everyone except Ian.

"Max!" Jersey jogged toward the door to the green room just as Max grabbed the handle. "Is he in there?"

"Yes."

"I need to see him."

"No." Max winked at Jersey. A stupid wink like they were playing a game or telling jokes.

No game.

No jokes.

"Why are you telling me no? And what's up with the winking? You suck at it in a really creepy way like your fake lashes are tickling your eyeball."

Max returned a twisted grin. "Funny. And I'm telling you no because he's having a muscle spasm in his back, and Nick is working on him, trying to get him comfortable enough to get to the hotel."

"Oh, well I just need a few minutes with him."

"Nope. Sorry Jersey, maybe later."

"Can you at least give him a note for me?"

"Text him."

Jersey scowled at Max.

Max rolled her eyes and dug through her handbag for a receipt and a pen. "You should use some of that newly earned cash of yours to buy a phone."

"I don't have anyone to call."

"Ian … apparently you could call him, so I don't have to pass notes during study hall for you."

Jersey returned a sour face as Max handed her the receipt and pen. Deep down, she liked Max. Hell, she wanted to be Max. What a life to have?

Hi Coop. I was thinking of sucking your dick. Have a few minutes to spare?

Jersey folded the receipt and handed it with the pen back to Max. "I'll wait outside for his response." She shot Max a toothy grin.

"Don't hold your breath. I think he's in too much pain to be your pen pal tonight." Max slipped inside of the green room and shut the door.

Jersey leaned against the opposite wall with her hands in her pockets and one ankle crossed over the other ankle. Less than a minute later, the door opened. Max exited followed by Nick.

Max glared at Jersey and her victorious smile. "What did your note say, Jersey?"

She shrugged. "What did Ian say?"

"He told us to send you in and give him ten minutes."

Chris was right. The perverted bastard was right.

Jersey winked at Max, making it look awkward and exaggerated like Max's crazy wink earlier.

"Make it quick. We need to get him back to the hotel," Max grumbled.

"As quick as I can." Jersey made an invisible cross over her chest with her finger before going into the green room and shutting the door.

"Lock it." Ian's deep, slightly strained voice startled her from her cloud of gloating.

Jersey locked the door.

"Do you have any idea how many 'I want to suck your dick' notes I get after my concerts?"

Jersey prowled toward him, feigning more confidence than she actually felt in her gut. "Three? Four?"

Ian cringed, rolling from his side to his back on the sofa. "Times a hundred."

"So … lucky me …" She eased his legs apart and kneeled on the couch between them. If she had to infiltrate a man's life to the point of doing absolutely *anything* to gain his trust, there were far worse choices than Ian Cooper. He personified sexy in a way Jersey had never experienced in her secluded life on the streets of Newark.

Ian swallowed hard, staring at her with a dark look in his eyes. "I'm not letting you suck my dick."

She kissed his abs along his shirtless torso to the top of his happy trail. He tasted like salt. He probably needed a shower, but Jersey wasn't an expert on smells either. Maybe if Ian had gone months without showering, she might have detected something unpleasant about him.

"Yet … you told me to lock the door." Jersey dipped her tongue into his belly button as she unfastened his jeans.

"Jersey …" Ian protested in a pathetically weak voice.

"Coop …" She pulled him free from his boxer briefs.

Ian was fully aroused for someone claiming he wasn't going to let her do that to him.

"Just shut up." Her tongue teased him. "And close your eyes. I can't do this with you looking at me."

He seethed, maybe from the feel of her warm mouth on him, maybe from actual back pain. She didn't care. Pain wasn't worth an apology.

Ian closed his eyes and caressed her hair as she did her best to do something she detested beyond words. It wasn't the dick that made her want to vomit, it was his gentle touch, the way he petted her like a good animal.

"That's it, Jersey. You're such a sweet girl to make me feel good. I'm going to make you feel good too." Her past could never be silenced.

Without stopping her motions, she grabbed his wrists and pinned them to his chest, gripping them tightly so he kept them out of her hair. She wasn't a pet. She didn't need stroking and praise.

"Jersey …" Ian's voice cracked like it pained him, but as his pelvis made tiny thrusts toward her, she knew he was just a guy sitting by his family in church thinking about the secretary blowing him in his office the next day.

She hated that Chris was right.

Ian Cooper was just a guy. And his weakness would become her greatest strength. A few minutes later, his abs constricted. He moaned as he tried to sit up, as he tried to pull away from her. Jersey pushed him back and took everything he gave her.

Keeping his eyes closed, lips parted, hands relaxed on

his chest, Ian whispered, "Why?"

Jersey grabbed the half-empty bottle of water on the floor and poured the rest down her throat before climbing off the sofa. "Now we're even." She exited the room before he opened his eyes.

Jersey shouldered her way past Nick and Max without making eye contact.

"Jers?" Chris passed her, wearing a concerned expression while trying to grab her arm to stop her. She jerked away and stumbled into the single-stalled ladies' room, falling to her knees and vomiting in the toilet. When men raped women by thrusting their dicks into women's mouths and spewing their disgusting bodily fluids down their victim's throats, vomiting was the only way to numb the pain, silence the guilt, and regain some sense of control.

Ian didn't rape Jersey, but he didn't stop her either. She needed to remember that beneath that appealing exterior and seductive voice lived a man.

A simple, predictable, self-serving, dick of a man.

"Jers …" Chris's voice sounded behind her.

"Get out!" She wiped her mouth.

CHAPTER FIFTEEN

"WILL YOU CONSENT to STD testing?" Max casually asked while looking over the breakfast menu in their shared Madison, Wisconsin hotel room two days later.

Jersey hadn't seen Ian since their encounter in Chicago. Nick kept him behind for extra acupuncture treatments and physical therapy while Max drove Jersey to Madison.

"It was a blowjob. What could I have possibly given him?"

Max's cow eyes peeked over the menu at Jersey. "Too much information. And that's not why I'm asking you."

"Shit." Jersey sighed, flipping through a Madison travel guide. "It's him. You're worried that he gave me something, and you don't want it in the media."

"Listen …" Max laid the menu on her lap and wrinkled her nose. "I don't need the details of your relationship with Ian, however crazy it might be. He asked me to get you tested. Also, we need to find your social security number and birth certificate to get you a passport. Same with Chris *Ten*." She rolled her eyes.

"Well, good luck with all of that." Jersey tossed the

travel guide onto the desk and swiveled side to side in the chair. "I ran away at fifteen. I have no idea where my social security card and birth certificate might be. And just a heads-up … if you happen to scrounge mine, which might not be impossible since I know my legal name, birthdate, and place of birth, the chances of you finding Chris's are probably less than zero. I mean … if you did, you'd be solving a huge mystery about his past that's stumped detectives for months."

"What if you both stay here while Ian finishes his tour? Then we don't have to figure out the passport issue. I'm sure Ian will find something to keep you both busy and employed."

Jersey didn't have much to offer. How could she argue with Max when she and Chris were completely reliant on Ian and his willingness to employ them? "How long will he be gone?"

"Three months. Twenty shows from Portugal to Belgium."

"Three months?" Jersey cringed.

"Yes. Can you two lovebirds stay apart that long?"

"Lovebirds? I hardly think dry humping on the plane and a quick blowjob in Chicago makes us lovebirds."

Max ran her hands through her hair, tugging on it while pinching her eyes shut. "I don't need that kind of detailed information, Jersey."

"I'm just saying … don't label us like that. But to answer your question, no … I don't want to stay here, even if Chris stays here. Ian promised to show me the world."

And I can't inflict revenge upon him if we're in different countries.

Max frowned, lifting the menu to hide her face again. "I'll see if I can get you a passport." She lowered the menu again and grabbed her vibrating phone. "Hi. Yeah, suite 2533. You have two radio interviews, a podcast, and a photoshoot. How are you feeling?" She nodded several times. "Good. You have an hour. Are you hungry? Are you sure? Okay."

"He's here?"

Max bit her lips together and eyed Jersey for a few minutes. "Mmhm."

"Great. Room 2533?"

"No. Don't you dare! He has a full day of—"

Jersey let the door slam behind her. Perfect timing. Shane and Ian rounded the corner.

"You good?" Shane asked, eyeing Jersey for a second before returning his attention to Ian.

Ian nodded, letting his gaze linger on Jersey as Shane opened the door to a different room. "You're all kinds of trouble." He held up his phone screen to the sensor on room 2533 and opened the door.

"Missed you too, Coop." She followed him into the sprawling corner suite.

He lifted his suitcase onto the luggage holder and opened it.

"How's your back? Sounds like such an old-man issue." Jersey walked around the room, grabbing a granola bar from the basket of food on the counter by the coffee maker.

"The injury is old. Me? Not so much. But thanks for

your take on the matter."

She took a bite of the bar and nodded, sliding open the tall, gray and royal blue curtains. "Your room always has the best view."

Ian hummed like it was no big deal. Every new view was a big deal to the girl who had seen very few views in her lifetime.

She took in the moment—the view, the fancy hotel room, the opportunities at her disposal thanks to Ian Cooper. Then she imagined it all vanishing for murdering him.

Prison.

Maybe the death penalty.

Did she care?

The greatest opportunity in her life was a chance at revenge. Not college. Not love. Not success. Vengeance for the Russells.

Revenge.

If Dena and Charles knew, would they understand? Would they be proud of her?

"Coop, can you even remember a time in your life that something took your breath away? I bet not. People who have always had everything can't possibly imagine what it's like to have nothing." She stiffened, feeling him at her back, hovering over her, trying to taunt her with his size and authority, high on the false sense of power that she gave him.

"You think you know me, Jersey?" he whispered in her ear.

She sucked in a sharp breath as his hand pressed to

her hip, sliding around to her stomach. Swallowing hard, Jersey nodded once.

"I don't think you do."

Jersey pressed her left hand to the window as her drumming heart made it hard to breathe. Ian's other hand slid around her waist too.

"How much, Jersey?" His breath singed her skin, frying her nerves and making her dizzy. "How much did you miss me?" Ian slowly unfastened her jeans.

Her poorly concealed knife, shoved into the back of her jeans, fell to the floor. Ian paused, and Jersey glanced back at him. They grinned at each other.

Jersey's lips parted, one breath chasing the next as his right hand slid down the front of her panties. She dropped the granola bar and pressed her other hand flat to the window. Could she let him do that to her and still keep her mind focused on the end game? She needed him close, needed him to want her with him, by his side, in his bed, wrapped around his life so she could find his truth and close the noose.

"Jesus …" Her forehead *thunked* against the window, eyelids heavy, conscience cringing with guilt. Was it okay for her to enjoy it? Was it okay for a killer's hand to give her that kind of pleasure? She fought it, his touch, the building need in her body, the teetering edge of control. But he wouldn't stop, so Jersey let him poison her with pleasure.

For several minutes the hum of the heater and their dueling shallow breaths filled the room. If he said something to her, asked her how she liked it, if she wanted him to stop, anything that felt nauseatingly familiar from her past, she would have pulled away.

But he didn't.

When it was over, she kept her hands and forehead on the window, shoulders slumped. Ian slid his hand out of her panties and refastened her jeans. When he stepped back, she turned. His tongue grazed along his lower lip before he rubbed them together as if he needed to restrain his next words. And he did.

Jersey bent down and retrieved the knife and the granola bar. Picking off a few pieces of lint first, she took another bite, chewing with her mouth shut while shoving the sheathed knife back into her jeans and wearing a challenging expression on her unavoidably flushed face.

Ian rubbed a hand over his mouth several times, studying Jersey. "I'm going to take a shower and get dressed. I have a busy day."

Jersey shrugged, glancing down at her granola bar before taking another bite. Was he waiting for permission? A thank you?

"So..." he scraped his teeth along his bottom lip "...Jersey two, Ian one."

She choked for a second, covering her mouth with her hand, eyes wide. They were keeping score?

Ian waited.

Jersey didn't blink.

He waited some more, suppressing his smirk.

She slowly started chewing again and returned a single nod. When Ian seemed satisfied with her level of discomfort, he sauntered off to the bathroom.

"DO YOU HAVE siblings?" Jersey shot Ian a question the second he emerged from the bathroom, hair wet, ripped jeans, black tee. Perched on his bed, she finished the second bag of chips from his basket of food and crumpled up the foil wrapper.

"You're getting crumbs in my bed."

"Brothers? Sisters? Childhood pets?"

"Thanks for asking if you could eat the chips." He set his neatly folded dirty clothes on the right side of his suitcase.

"Did your mom bake cookies? I had a foster mom who baked cookies, but they were a sugar-free kind ... well, sweetened with dates and bananas. I didn't complain because it was food. Ya know?" She didn't say Dena's name, but she wanted to say it, see how he might react.

Ian stood at the end of the bed with his arms folded over his chest. Jersey tried to ignore her attraction to him. It had no place in her plan.

"Yeah. I know." He pulled his phone from his pocket.

"No." She grunted a laugh, tearing open a box of fancy chocolates. "You don't know."

Ian gave her the hairy eyeball for a few seconds before returning his attention to his phone. "Let's go."

"Can I go with you today?"

Ask you a million more questions that you refuse to answer?

"You have a job to do and so do I." He headed to the door.

Jersey hopped off the bed and chased after him. "Co-op, if I don't go with you, how will I even the score?"

Ian stopped with his hand on the doorknob, his back to Jersey. He glanced at her over his shoulder. "You have chocolate on your face."

She wiped both sides of her face with the back of her hand.

He turned around and shook his head. "It's still there."

A frown pulled at her lips as she scrubbed both cheeks with the palms of her hands.

Ian chuckled. "Why would it be on your cheeks? Did you roll in my chocolate?"

Jersey started to narrow her eyes, ready to punch his pretty little face.

"Stop giving me that scowl." He grabbed her face and leaned down, stopping a breath away from her mouth.

She grabbed his wrists without pulling him away as she held her breath. He licked the corner of her mouth like an overly friendly dog.

Jersey's nose wrinkled. "Yuck!" She tried to shove him, but he tightened his grip on her face and kissed her, fusing his mouth to hers like they were stuck together. Tasting the inside of her mouth like his tongue was on a treasure hunt.

"Time to go!" Max called, knocking three times on the door.

Again, Jersey tried to push him away with her hands even though her mouth fully participated in the kiss.

"I don't like this silence!" She pounded on the door

again. "Is Jersey in there with you? Please … pretty, pretty please don't let her mark you today. You have a photoshoot." Max's voice simmered into a painful plea.

Ian released Jersey's mouth, rubbing his lips together and wiping the corners of his mouth with the back of his hand like Jersey had done.

She lifted her shirt and wiped her entire face as if she *had* actually been attacked by a slobbery pet.

Ian rolled his eyes. "You liked it."

She swallowed the lie because she *did* like it. "You're taking me with you." She squared her shoulders and tipped her chin up.

He opened the door. Max deflated with relief.

"Jersey's hanging with us today." Ian strutted down the hallway toward Shane.

"Oh good. I like it when you're thoroughly distracted," Max mumbled to Ian while pointing two fingers at her own eyes, and then pointing them at Jersey.

Jersey whipped her head around to glance behind one shoulder then the other before gesturing to herself while mouthing, "Who? Me?"

"I'll give you fifty bucks if you're good today," Max murmured, giving her attention to her phone as they followed Ian and Shane.

"Define good." Jersey adjusted the knife shoved into the back of her jeans.

"Do I really have to?"

"If Ian is in a good mood, does that mean I'm being good?"

"No. If he's sexually frustrated and not bruised or

bleeding, then I know you're being good."

The doors to the elevator opened, and the two men stepped into it followed by Jersey and Max. Everyone faced the doors except Jersey. She faced Ian, hands in her pockets, glancing up at him with all kinds of mischief—hidden revenge—in her eyes. Chin tipped down, Ian kept his gaze on her, eyes slightly narrowed and his lips in a firm line. Distrust bled through his expression. Jersey liked that about him even if it made her job a little more challenging.

"Max offered me fifty bucks to be good today."

Ian's brows inched up his forehead. "Is that so?"

Max didn't budge, not a single flinch as Jersey called her out on her bribe. "Yup. Fifty bucks for you too, Ian, if you behave today." She swiped along her phone screen like bribing people to be well-behaved was part of her everyday duties.

"And what did you say?" He cocked his head to the side, a playful glint in his eyes.

The elevator doors opened.

"Game faces, kids. A mob of paparazzi awaits." Max and Shane stepped off the elevator.

"Why didn't we go out a side door?" Jersey asked Max.

"They're at all the entrances. Word got out where we're staying." Max looped her arm with Jersey's arm and dragged her toward the entrance, distancing them from Ian and Shane.

A few people snapped photos of Jersey as Max stuffed her into the back of the SUV, but most of the attention went to Ian. He stopped for a few autographs and smiled for the cameras before Shane opened the back door, and Ian hopped in next to Jersey. Even after the door closed, the camera flashes continued.

As Shane shoved the vehicle into drive, Ian glanced over at Jersey and rested his hand on her leg. "You okay?"

She stared at his hand. Jersey liked the feel of Ian touching her, but she hated the memories of being touched—a polarity of emotions that warred inside of her. "Of course. I used to deal with that popularity crap at Marley's. I couldn't leave the building without someone snapping my picture or asking for my autograph. I was kind of a big deal around there. You know … my undefeated title and all that."

Ian squeezed her leg. "I can see that about you."

Jersey hugged her arms to her chest, unsure what to do with them while he continued to use her leg as a rest for his hand. After several stiff minutes, he retracted his hand and fetched his phone from his pocket. She relaxed her arms a tiny centimeter at a time to conceal her relief.

"I don't know, Ian. Last year's cover is going to be hard to beat." Max held up a magazine with Ian on the cover—naked except for a guitar covering his man parts.

He chuckled. "Squint all you want, Jersey. You're not going to see past the guitar."

She leaned closer, continuing to squint. "Shut it, Coop. I'm just trying to see the title of the magazine."

"Coop?" Max twisted her lips to hide her amusement.

Ian grabbed the magazine from Max and held it up— as far away from Jersey as possible. "Can you read the title?"

Jersey shook her head and squinted.

He moved it a bit closer. "Now?"

"No." She leaned closer and took it from him, bringing it less than two feet from her face. "Now I can."

"Jesus, Jersey ... you need glasses." Ian shook his head.

She knew that. Dena took her to the eye doctor. They got her a prescription and picked out a sleek pair of frames for her new glasses. The day Dena died was the day she was supposed to take Jersey to pick up her glasses.

Twenty-twenty vision and pizza on the same day. A day that should have been one of the best days of Jersey's life turned into the worst day of her life.

Worse than the day she took a man's life.

Worse than every day she was abused physically and sexually.

Worse than any day she exchanged her body for something like food or antibiotic ointment.

Jersey nodded, handing the magazine back to Ian. "This one time, Marley let me look through his thick glasses. It was like a whole new world to me. He said they probably weren't the right strength for my eyes, and that I shouldn't look through them that long ... like they could have messed with my sight or something, but I didn't care. So sometimes when he'd doze off in his chair, I'd ease his glasses from his face and wear them outside just to see all the shit that I'd been missing."

Ian frowned and so did Max as they stared back at Jersey.

"We're going to get you glasses," Max said without even looking at Ian.

Jersey's gaze shifted to him. Ian nodded several times. His expression held an uneasy sadness.

"It's fine. I just got paid. I can probably afford a pair of glasses if I don't buy a phone like Max suggested. I can just send you messages on receipts. Right, Coop?"

"Pfft …" Max faced forward again.

A smile cracked Ian's frown as the car stopped at an old warehouse. They spent two hours at a photoshoot, grabbed coffees on the way to a radio interview, more coffee and a clothing change before a television appearance, and finally a thirty-minute podcast with a young woman who was some sort of social media influencer.

"Where to now?" Jersey asked as they piled in the SUV after taping the podcast.

"The venue for the sound check. And then you'll clock in and explain to Dani where you've been all day. And your coworkers will hate you. So there's that fun." Max glanced back at Jersey as Shane gunned it out of the parking lot.

With a solid fifty-fifty chance of killing everyone's favorite rock star, Jersey wasn't concerned about winning any popularity contest. When they got to the venue, Jersey started to walk in the direction of the long line of tour buses, but Ian grabbed her hand and pulled her in the opposite direction.

"I have to work."

"You will. In a bit." He pulled her into the building as Shane led the way and Max followed behind them.

Their locked hands drew a few lingering glances from some of the crew as they made their way to the lower level and the green room. "Hey." Ian greeted his bandmates, who were in their usual spots, playing video games.

They returned their half-interested greetings, not giving Jersey more than a quick glance and polite nod as Ian pulled her to a sofa back in the corner of the room. Ian shut off the lamp next to it, giving the corner a feeling of privacy compared to the rest of the room.

He opened a bottle of water and drank half of it. Then he handed it to Jersey. She stared at it for a few seconds before taking it from him and drinking the rest.

"You didn't even the score today. I'm a little disappointed." He plopped on the sofa and leaned back, propping his feet up on the opposite end.

Jersey returned a nervous laugh, setting the bottle on the small table next to the sofa. "Well, we were never alone."

"That's my life." He held out his hand.

After a few seconds of hesitation, she rested her hand in his. He pulled on her until she stumbled into the sofa, landing on top of him.

"You have to get creative," he whispered as her face hovered over his face, the ends of her ponytail brushing his cheek.

She swallowed the rush of anxiety that came with her body pressed to his. "You have sound check."

"In forty-five minutes." His gaze swept along her face.

"I have to help set up the merchandise stands."

"Someone else can do it."

"I could get fired."

Ian grinned. "Then your boss is a dick."

Jersey didn't want to smile, because no matter how much she tried to convince herself to treat Ian like an opponent, like the enemy, she couldn't stop herself from liking the way he looked at her or the way she craved his next move—his next touch.

Not giving a second thought to the onlookers, she brushed her lips over his mouth, baiting him while slowly torturing herself. He took the bait, lifting his head up just enough to capture her lips.

He kissed her with a patience she didn't expect. That was *his* strength, giving her a hook when she expected a jab. Throwing her off balance. Making her question her true intentions. Jumbling thoughts. Casting doubt.

"Coop," she whispered between kisses, "I like kissing you."

He grinned against her lips. "Say that again." Ian teased her bottom lip with his tongue.

She flicked her tongue out to meet his. "I like kissing you, Coop."

Ian rolled them onto their sides, pinning her back to the sofa as he kissed her harder but still slowly. He bent his top leg, wedging it between her legs as his hand slid down her hip, guiding her top leg over him until they were scissored, a tangled mess of limbs.

His hand drifted from her hip to her face where his thumb brushed her cheek before he stroked her hair.

Jersey pulled back, a little out of breath. "Don't do that."

"Do what?" His brow wrinkled.

"Stroke my hair."

"You're stroking *my hair*."

And she was. The slightly curled fingers of her left hand combed through his dark hair in slow strokes, even as he brought it to her attention.

"Don't stroke my hair," she repeated on a soft whisper as her gaze focused on her hand moving on its own accord through his hair.

Ian closed his eyes, stilling both of his hands. His lips parted and he sighed softly as she continued to do the exact thing to him that she forbid him to do to her. After studying every curve of his face, including the exact spot high on his cheeks where his long eyelashes rested, she let her eyes close and her fingers slow to idle in his hair.

Jersey dreamed of the handful of moments in her life when she felt so safe, normal, content: when G let her sleep next to her, when Dena and Charles welcomed her with love into their home, when Chris kept her warm and read her soothing passages from his books.

"Jersey?" A while later, Max's voice brought her out of her dreams.

Jersey's eyes fluttered open.

"You have to work, and Ian has sound check. Have him out that door in five minutes." Max smiled before pivoting and exiting the room.

No lecture.

No frowning.

She could have woken him herself and kicked Jersey out, but she didn't. As Jersey moved her leg to untangle them, Ian shifted, opening his eyes and making another quarter turn with their bodies, pinning her beneath him, wedging his pelvis between her legs.

"Are you trying to escape?" He nipped at her lower lip.

She rolled her eyes, trying to contain her own amusement. "Coop, if that was my goal, I'd already be gone. You have less than five minutes to get to sound check, and I have to go sell your stupid shit to gullible people who think you're something special."

He grinned, pushing himself off the sofa. "Get out of here." Ian grabbed a new bottle of water, twisted off the cap, and brought it to his mouth with his grin still in place.

Jersey peeled herself from the sofa, straightening her shirt and adjusting her knife as she eyed him through a contrast of emotions. Why did everything good in her life have to morph into something bad. Chris labeled her chance meeting with Ian as simply fate. Jersey considered it plain fucking cruel.

"Jersey?"

"Yeah?" She stilled at the door.

"Wish me luck."

With her back to him, she let a grin slide all the way up her face. "Luck, Coop." She eased open the door. "And Coop?"

"Hmm?"

"Do you like to play basketball?"

"Yeah. Why?"

The fire burned hotter as she edged her way toward

the truth. "No reason." The door clicked behind her.

Jersey soared through the night, transformed by his touch, haunted by his truth. The slow drip of revelations gathered in the pit of her stomach, nauseating her conscience, drowning her ability to pretend he didn't kill the Russells.

"Hey," Chris whispered at Jersey's back.

The smile fell from her face as she snapped the lid onto the last plastic container of hats. The lingering fans trickled out of the venue as security made its final sweep through the venue at the end of the concert.

"Hey." She drew in a slow breath and faced him.

"I heard some guys talking tonight about the first cars they owned when they were teenagers."

Jersey stacked the containers onto the cart. "Sorry, I can't help you. I've never owned a car. Never had a driver's license."

Chris peered at her with a blank expression. He failed to appreciate her need to make assumptions and end the conversation before granting him the opportunity to make his full case.

"Fine." She huffed a full night's worth of exasperation as she crossed her arms at her chest. "Tell me about the cars."

He shook his head. "Just one car. Of all the makes and models of cars being tossed around in the conversation, the one that stuck—the one that triggered a memory—was a black Dodge Charger. Ian drove a black Dodge Charger. I bet it was the car that killed the Russells."

Like her friend, the ultimate bearer of bad news, his revelation hovered over her, dismal and brooding. "Okay." She shifted her gaze to the lingering crew drifting past them in random directions.

"Okay—"

"I'll handle it," she bit out the words and immediately cringed.

"He's no fairy tale. You know that, right?"

Jersey nodded.

"I bet he's never killed anyone beyond them. I bet he funnels money into some heartbreakingly worthy causes. Clearly, he plucks homeless people off the street and gives them jobs. It wouldn't surprise me to find out he visits young cancer patients or grants end-of-life wishes to them. I don't think he was born a murderer. But you can't undo certain wrongs, and this is one that will never be undone. You *have* to remember that. You have to remember that when he's nice to you. When he touches you. When he makes you feel special. When he gives you pleasure."

She swallowed hard, clenching her jaw and balling her hands.

"Jersey …"

Her head jerked when his finger lifted her chin, forcing her to meet his gaze.

"He might even fall for you, promise you the world."

"I'm going to show you the world, Jersey."

"But he destroyed your world. He killed it. He can't undo death. He can't make something from nothing. He left you with nothing. And you can't let him try to fill that void with *things*. Ian has all the *things*. And they're bright and shiny, soft and comfy, physically rewarding like soft beds, warm meals, and intimacy."

"I know what I'm doing."

Chris studied her. "Do you?"

Jersey's eyes narrowed into slits.

"Have you let him inside of you? Did you let yourself enjoy it?"

She held his gaze, letting it slide over her like a stone honing a blade. "I fear you mistake my lack of education for weakness—gullibility. If he killed them, it wasn't intentional. He's not a killer, and neither are you. I think you might take a bullet for me, but I don't think you'd actually take a life for me."

"I've got this." Dani strode up next to Jersey and started pushing the cart of containers. "Max said to meet her at the back entrance." Her words evaporated in the distance.

Jersey nodded once, keeping her attention on Chris as her hardened expression softened into her greatest asset— control. "You see … I've taken a life. Courageously. Brutally. With a steady hand and a numb conscience. And I was only fourteen. I don't fear death *or* value life anymore. Not my own. Not Ian's. And not yours. So when you and your ex-BFF use me as a tool to make sense of your own miserable lives, just remember … I lost my soul before I ever knew I had one. And that makes me everyone's worst fucking nightmare."

Before Chris could respond or even blink, she brushed past him and out the back entrance to Max in the front seat of the SUV and Shane holding open the back door.

"Nice of you to finally join us," Max mumbled on a yawn.

The familiar clean-guy fragrance filled the vehicle, and Ian's mop of dark hair looked damp, shower-damp, not sticky with sweat.

"Bryson's family home isn't too far from here. We're going there to hang out for a bit."

"A party?" Jersey questioned with a dull edge of irritation.

Ian's lips twisted as he studied her or maybe her response. "An intimate gathering. Food. Drinks. Conversation." He grinned. "You can skip the conversation. We'll just keep you fed and hydrated."

"Asshole."

Shane chuckled from the driver's seat.

"You're an asshole too." Her middle finger shot up so Shane could see it in his mirror.

"I want to go back to the hotel. If you refrain from calling me an asshole too, I'll let you come with me," Max offered.

"You're my favorite person at the moment, Max."

"We're *all* going to Bryson's for a little bit." Ian shook his head while turning his attention to his window and the fading lights of Madison as they wormed their way out of the city.

"I DON'T LIKE this." Max shot Ian a nervous scowl as he opened her door.

Jersey glanced up at Shane. He didn't look overly enthused either.

"We stay an hour." Ian shut her door and followed Shane's lead through the smattering of people smoking various things and cluttering the front yard of the sprawling single-level home seemingly in the middle of nowhere.

Several high or intoxicated women stopped Ian along the way to snap a quick photo while Max grumbled a few *just greats.*

"What's the deal?" Jersey asked, leaning close to Max as they followed Shane and Ian.

"The deal is Bryson has a history of small gatherings turning into disasters. Fires. Drugs. Prostitutes. Arrests … you name it."

"Then why are we here?"

Max sighed. "He cleaned up his act several years ago. Took months off to go through rehab and then reconciled with his wife. Ian trusts him now."

"But you don't?" They squeezed through the congestion at the front door, shouldering past a thick group of mostly women.

"Look around, Jersey. Of course I don't."

The crowd engulfed Ian as Max pulled Jersey toward the food. "Rock stars and skinny bitches … they only drink and snort shit. So no one hangs out around the food until the potheads smoke their last joint and gnaw their way to the bottom of the chip bowl."

Max was right. The table of snacks appeared untouched.

"You realize you're quite skinny yourself." Jersey eyed Max as they loaded their plates with food.

"It's genetic. I don't drink or do drugs and I love food. If I weren't genetically thin, I'd be morbidly obese."

Jersey lifted onto her tippy toes to find Ian in the crowd that was far from an intimate gathering. She spotted him with a beer clutched in one hand and his other arm draped over the shoulders of a busty brunette.

Sitting next to his wife and children at church, thinking about how his secretary would blow him on Monday morning.

"Ian ever mention what car he drove as a teenager?"

Max laughed, covering her full mouth. "I told you … no one knows anything about his life before stardom."

Jersey shoved handfuls of chips into her mouth as Ian threw his head back in laughter and his blowjob secretary gazed at him with her intentions clear in her doe eyes and teeth planted into her bottom lip.

"Ian slid his hand down the front of my pants this morning."

Max choked on her sushi roll.

Jersey nodded toward Ian and his secretary. "Think he's going to put his hand down her pants before we leave?"

Max coughed a few more times. "You *know* I don't want to hear about this, talk about it, or envision it in any way, right?"

With a shrug like her emotions were dead, and maybe they were, Jersey tore her gaze away from Ian and focused on Max. "Do you realize we would rule the whole damn world if we had big cock swords carving the way for us? Fearlessly and unapologetically impaling anything that got in our way."

"And by *we* you mean women in general, not actually *you* and *me,* correct?"

Jersey licked the salt from her fingers, letting her curiosity return to Ian.

Max moved closer to Jersey. "The girl … Grace … she's Bryson's sister. I don't know what her relationship is with Ian. But if you're concerned about what could happen, then go tell him how you feel—but don't actually do physical harm to him."

Jersey sighed. "Another example why men still out rule us … they don't let petty things like feelings get in their way."

"Where are you going?" Max called as Jersey weaved her way through the crowd to the coveted rock star at the epicenter of the gathering.

Shane frowned, more like a subtle cringe, when he caught sight of her as he stood guard behind Ian and Grace.

"You don't own him," Shane warned, keeping his voice just low enough so Ian couldn't hear him.

Jersey lurched forward as if someone shoved her into Shane. He grabbed her shoulders, keeping her upright. She lifted her gaze, flashing him a toothy grin. "I own all of you; you just don't fucking know it yet." With her right hand she slipped out her knife, squaring her shoulders to Shane while gripping it firmly at her side.

Shane focused on the knife while slowly reaching inside his unzipped, black leather coat. Their little standoff continued, unnoticed by Ian thanks to the shoulder-to-shoulder crowd and the incessant white noise of chatter making it difficult to hear well.

He did a good job playing it cool, but Jersey knew Shane's heart raced with panic behind his broad chest as his hand came up empty. Lifting her left hand, she dangled his gun from her index finger. Jersey wasn't a fan of guns, but Judd trained her well on disarming the enemy.

Shane wasn't the enemy. He was just the enemy's bodyguard.

"Oh my god!" Grace yelped, glancing over Ian's arm still resting across her shoulders.

Ian turned. His gaze ping-ponged between the dangling gun, Jersey, and a wide-eyed Shane.

"Dropped your gun, big guy." Jersey shot Shane a lethal smile as she extended her hand toward his face.

He glared at her for a few seconds before shooting his attention to her other hand, but she had already returned the knife to its concealed spot. Shane grabbed the gun and shoved it back into its holster.

"Jer-sey …" Ian said her name in two slow syllables.

"Dude …" Some drunk guy cackled. "How the fuck did you drop your gun?"

"Dropped your wallet too." Jersey fished Shane's wallet from her front pocket and tossed it into his chest.

Shane's anger simmered into something else? Hurt? Was he hurt that she'd embarrassed him? Did she go too far? Jersey wasn't sure. But his *you don't own him* comment felt like the manly cock jab—the age-old attempt at putting a woman in her spot.

"Let's go." Ian grabbed her arm.

She fought back the urge to jerk away from him and land her fist into his pretty little face. She submitted to his need to steer her through the crowd, down a long hallway, and into a dark bedroom.

Ian released her with a firm shove and shut the door behind them. The second it clicked, a knife landed with a thud into the solid wood mere inches from grazing Ian's ear. He froze with his back to her.

"To be clear, Coop, you manhandle me like that again, shoving me into a dark room, and the tip of that knife will be lodged into your heart."

Ian slowly turned toward her. "You touch Shane again … his wallet, his gun, or one fucking hair on his head, and your ass will be planted in the back of a squad car."

"He's a joke. Nice guy sometimes, but I sure wouldn't trust him with my life. The only person around you who is truly capable of protecting you is the homeless girl you pay to sell T-shirts for you. That's pathetic, Coop, and you know it."

"Is this about Grace?" He tilted his head to the side.

"Grace? Really, Coop? I can't read the letters on your shirt from here, which should make you wonder how I managed to not make you bleed with that knife. I disarmed your bodyguard in less than five seconds. My life is filled with nothingness. Nothing to lose because I literally have *nothing*. Your pretty little head can't even imagine the crimes that have been committed against my body. So do you *really* think I give a shit about some woman at a party?"

Ian swallowed hard, lines digging into his forehead.

"I wanted to ask you what kind of car you drove in your early twenties."

"What?" His head jerked backward.

"Do you have a driver's license?"

He nodded slowly, confusion cemented into his face.

"Then tell me what cars you've owned in your life, specifically in your early twenties." Jersey clasped her hands behind her and rocked back and forth on her heels.

Ian shook his head, gnashing his jaw. Jersey didn't let his aggravation deter her.

"Cars? That's what started this tonight?"

"Yes. I was making my way through the crowd to discuss this with you, and Shane flapped his jaw about some *you don't own him* bullshit. Naturally, it pissed me off that he had to be such an asshole about something as innocent as me approaching you about your car history. Someone bumped into me, sending me into Shane's chest." Jersey shrugged. "And my instincts just took over."

"Your instincts?"

She nodded.

"If you bump into someone, you instinctually disarm them and lift their wallet?"

"Yes, you spoiled dumb-fuck. Some of us have to live on sharp instinct and developed survival skills."

Ian reached across his body and removed the knife

from the door without taking his eyes off Jersey. "Cars …
I've owned three. A red Mustang. A black Escalade. And a
midnight blue Jaguar." His long legs swallowed the space
between them with three slow strides. He reached behind
her.

Jersey grabbed his hand. Ian gave her a firm headshake. She eased her grip from his wrist, letting him
retrieve the sheath from the back of her jeans. He slid the
knife into it and tossed it on the floor.

Her gaze followed it, narrowing her eyes for a few
seconds. "The black car was an Escalade?"

"Yes."

Her lips twisted to the side. "You're sure?"

"Yes. Why?"

"You'll find out," she whispered, not knowing what
to do with that information. Not knowing who to trust.

"When?"

She let her gaze make its way back to his face. "When
I'm ready."

"Ian?" A woman's voice called from the other side of
the door along with quick knocks.

Before he could answer, Grace opened the door, poking her head inside and flipping on the light. "Hey, I
wondered where you went in such a rush. Is everything
okay?" She stepped her large-chested body into the room,
sizing up Jersey for a quick second before wrinkling her
nose at Ian. "There's chatter going on out there that
you're having issues with your new merch girl. Do you
want me to get security?"

Jersey snatched her knife off the floor, pulled it out,

blew on it, and placed it back in her jeans. Grace's eyes and nose flared as her lips formed a nervous O.

"I think you need to find someplace else to be right now." Jersey stepped toward her.

"Jers—"

"Shut up, Coop." She moved closer to Grace.

"But …" Grace's voice quivered. "This is my room."

Jersey's eyebrows shot up her forehead. "Is that so?" She took another step toward Grace, forcing her to retreat a step, then another, until her body crossed the doorway's threshold. "Gracie … go tell the curious people out there that the *new merch girl* is fucking Ian Cooper in your bed." Jersey slammed the door in Grace's face and locked it.

"Grace is Bryson's sister."

Jersey turned. "I know."

Ian slipped his hands into his back pockets; it pulled his jeans down just enough to expose the black band of his boxer briefs. "Thought you said it wasn't about Grace."

"It wasn't." She discarded her knife, shrugged off her shirt, and unbuttoned her jeans while toeing off her sneakers.

Ian's eyes surrendered, trailing down her body as his lips parted. Jersey unhooked her black bra, letting it fall to the floor in the foot of space between her and Ian.

She lifted her gaze to meet his. "But it is now."

"You're not a nice person."

His words sent a thrilling jolt through her veins and etched a tiny smile on her face. "You have no idea …"

Ian peeled off his shirt, and Jersey inched her jeans and panties down her legs. He fished a condom out of his pocket. Complements of Max? Probably. He palmed the back of her head and smashed his mouth to hers. She clawed at his chest, pulling feral groans from deep in his throat.

It wasn't love.

It wasn't payback.

It wasn't a promise.

When they landed on the bed, Ian pinned Jersey's hands above her head and wedged his narrow hips between her thighs, sliding into her in one sharp thrust.

"Coop ..." Her breath caught as she arched her back off the bed.

Her fingers dug into his knuckles.

Her eyes closed.

"We're terrible people," he whispered over her lips before kissing her, moving hard and fast into her, making Grace's bed creak and tap the wall.

Jersey opened her eyes and smiled against his mouth pressed to hers.

A liar.

A thief.

A lover.

Jersey wrapped her legs around Ian's waist, and she let herself pretend for a breath in time that they were beginning. But she knew—no matter what car he drove eight years earlier—they were approaching the end.

"IF I DIDN'T know better…" Jersey glanced up at Ian as she fastened her jeans "…I'd say you like watching me put on my clothes more than you like watching me take them off."

One side of his mouth pulled up into a partial smile as he sat on the end of Grace's bed, tugging his shirt on.

"You're giving me the silent treatment." She shoved her bare feet into her white sneakers. "Coop, if you're trying to find a way to tell me I'm fired, just say it."

He made a weak attempt at a full smile as he leaned forward and grabbed Jersey's hand, pulling her closer until she stood between his spread legs.

She rested her palms against his cheeks, making him look up at her. "You have something to tell me," Jersey whispered. "I can tell. It's the fake smile. I've seen it many times. It always comes right before bad news."

He nodded, covering one of her hands with his hand before turning his head so his mouth pressed against her palm.

"Tell me."

His head inched side to side as he closed his eyes and kissed her hand. "Not yet."

"When?"

Ian opened his eyes. "When I'm ready."

Nerves coiled in her stomach. Nothing could be worse than him confessing to running over Dena and Charles. A confession could cripple her intentions, steal her vengeance. Could she kill him if he told her the truth without knowing how attached she was to the real-life consequences of their death? If he dropped to his knees and begged for forgiveness, would it matter?

Jersey kissed him because she needed to get closer to him. She needed more than a promise for another day.

Jersey kissed him because they were a game and he was her pawn.

Jersey kissed him because she liked kissing Ian Cooper.

And she kissed him because no one told Jersey Six what she could or couldn't do.

He bit her lower lip, trapping it between his teeth. She tried to grin.

"I like…" he released her lip "…kissing you."

She nodded, rubbing her lips together to savor his taste and to keep from grinning too big.

"I'm not ready to do the walk of shame."

"The walk of shame?"

Ian nodded. "Bryson isn't just my bandmate, he's my friend … he's family. So that makes Grace like family too."

"She likes you, in case you're too blind to see how she looks all weird-eyed at you."

He chuckled. "Weird-eyed?"

"You know what I mean."

"Maybe." He leaned forward, resting his forehead against her chest.

Her fingers threaded through his hair.

"I'm certain everyone heard us," he murmured.

"We're terrible people." Her grin matched his. "The

guy she likes just fucked another girl in her bed. What kind of monster are you, Coop?"

"You're such a bitch …" he mumbled just before biting her nipple through her shirt.

Jersey seethed, and if it hadn't felt so good, she would have planted her knee into his ribcage. But it did … It felt good.

"I've been told I don't play well with others."

"Ya think?" Ian lifted his head and grinned.

He felt familiar, like the culmination of the few good dreams she'd experienced between the living nightmare of her life. Why did everything good have to turn into something bad?

"Let's run away."

"Run away?" She stepped back when he stood.

Ian zipped and buttoned his jeans. "Just for another hour or so."

"I'm listening …" Jersey's lips twisted to the side.

He snagged two blankets off the velvet bench along the wall adjacent to the bed and slid open the window. "Side of the house, no one's out here. We slip out and make a run for it."

Before her brain had a chance to play the WWKD (What Would a Killer Do) game, Jersey followed Ian out the window. He closed it, grabbed her hand, and they took off running.

The cold air nipped at her face and made her teeth ache, but she didn't stop grinning and running, and she never let go of his hand. The cracking branches and crunchy, cold earth beneath their pounding feet replaced the music and hum of the party as the lights from the house vanished the farther they ventured into the woods.

"Why are we running?" Jersey laughed.

Ian slowed his pace, and they stopped next to a large fallen tree amongst dead brush. "I suggested we run away. Had we walked, it would have been considered walking away." He dropped one blanket onto the ground, plopped down onto it with his back against the fallen tree trunk, and pulled her onto his lap, facing him with her knees straddling his legs.

She giggled when he completely covered them with the other blanket like a fort. Ian rubbed her arms, building friction to warm them up. Then he kissed her because they weren't done with that—it felt impossible to get their fill of each other. The sex was good, but the kissing blew her mind. Sexual predators were visual; they liked to watch, stalk, touch, record, and masturbate. Sometimes, they liked to force their dicks down young girls' throats.

But kissing … Jersey could count on one hand the number of times she'd been kissed on the mouth, and it was never inappropriate. The sick, awful, morally deranged monsters who abused her never even tried to kiss her on the lips.

"G used to build forts. She was really good at it," Jersey whispered as Ian kissed her neck.

"Oh yeah?" he murmured over her collarbone. Ian's right hand slid up her shirt, tugging up her bra to release her breasts. The pad of his thumb teased her nipple.

"Yeah …" she replied through a gasp. Her hips

rocked against him, her contribution to the warming friction. Denim on denim was a long shot at best, but she couldn't stop trying to find that pleasure again. "In the basement, she'd build elaborate forts over old boxes and storage containers ... sort of a maze. And when he came for us ..."

Ian stilled at her words. "Jersey ..." he whispered like it pained him to imagine what came next.

Jersey stilled her body as well, except her hands—they stroked his hair. "G let him take her first. We'd wait our turn in the dark. It felt like hours sometimes, but I know it was minutes ... maybe ten ... maybe twenty. The stairs would creak beneath his weight. G never cried in front of us. Never said more than a few words. Hazel, she was three years older than me, and always went second. Looking back, I think G and Hazel thought Fisher went easier on me because he exhausted himself with them."

"Jersey ..." Ian's voice cracked.

She wondered if Ian held unshed emotion in his eyes on the other side of the darkness between them. Maybe that's why G built the forts in the windowless basement ... so no one would see her cry.

Truth didn't live in the light; it hid in the dark, dancing with demons, afraid to be set free, afraid to be seen by judgmental eyes.

Maybe someday Ian would find his own safety in the darkness and tell Jersey everything.

Maybe he wouldn't.

She didn't share that moment with him to get anything in return ... and *that* scared her more than a million

Mr. Fishers because it meant she trusted Ian Cooper with a part of her that used to house her soul.

Jersey blindly searched for his mouth, kissing his eyebrow, his cheek, bumping his nose, and finally finding those lips. "Wouldn't it be amazing if we could scrounge enough spare change to get a hotel room? Ya got anything in your guitar case, Coop?"

Ian chuckled, his breath a mix of beer and mint. "I might be able to swing something." He started to lift her from his lap.

"Wait," she whispered, letting her fingertips slide from his head to his face, tracing every angle. "Just … can we wait for a few more minutes? Because …" She closed her eyes.

"Because?" he whispered back against the brush of her fingers over his lips.

"Because I feel safe."

"You are safe."

She wasn't, but for a few minutes, Jersey laid down her weapons in the dark, surrendered her defenses, and allowed herself to be a twenty-four-year-old woman completely enamored with a rock star, under a blanket in the early morning hours.

They wrapped the blankets around themselves and walked back to the house.

"We're not going inside." Ian slid his phone out of his pocket and messaged Max and Shane to meet them at the car. And because Ian wasn't a truly evil person like Jersey, he returned the blankets to Grace's room via the window, unlocked her bedroom door, and snuck back out the window.

"How did you get out here?" Max asked as they piled into the SUV.

"Magic." He winked at Max, but her scowl didn't seem receptive to his charm.

"Want to know the crazy rumor that was floating around the party as to your whereabouts … pissing off your *friend* Bryson?"

"We heard the rumor too." Ian grinned at Jersey. "I think you know us better than that."

"No." Max's phone lit up as she checked the time—3:30 a.m. "I know you both just well enough to believe it was unlikely just a rumor. But thanks for dragging Shane and me to a stupid party, just to embarrass him and crush Grace's heart."

"I'll make it right before we fly out," Ian promised.

Max leaned her head back and closed her eyes. "You'd better."

CHAPTER SIXTEEN

I AN EXTENDED A long apology to Grace, along with a huge bouquet of flowers and a new bed and bedding. Bryson didn't seem quite as satisfied with the gesture, but since the band was a week away from leaving for the international leg of their tour, they made rocky amends.

"This might be a bad idea. We should have gone back to Newark," Jersey murmured to Chris as Shane drove them to Ian's house in Los Angeles.

Ian glanced back at Jersey, sliding his sunglasses down his nose. "Did you say something?"

"Just wondering if you should have taken us back to Newark."

Ian's brows squished together. "Marley's is closed."

She shrugged. "Newark's still home."

"Where would you go?"

Another shrug.

"I'm not returning you to the street." Ian faced forward again.

Chris shot her a tight-lipped smile.

When they pulled into the circle drive of the impressive, two-story home, Jersey's jaw plummeted to her lap.

Chris's elbow jabbed her in the arm. "You can be impressed by him," he whispered when Ian and Shane climbed out of the vehicle, "or you can kill him. But you can't do both, Jers."

Ian opened her door and held out his hand. Her right eyebrow lifted a fraction as she declined his help, which brought a grin to his face when she hopped out, spine straight, chin lifted.

"Just trying to be a gentleman." He shut her door as Shane unloaded everyone's bags.

"Just trying to *not* be a helpless female." She scuffed her sneakers along the driveway behind him, taking her bag from Shane and avoiding Chris's scrutinizing gaze.

She came from nothing. Of course the house impressed her, but that didn't mean the owner had anything to do with it.

"Hey, little bitches!" Ian greeted two dogs—little, half naked, ratty looking dogs. "Was Bria good to you?" He picked up both dogs. "Was she?"

Jersey and Chris shared a look, an indescribable look because there really was no explanation or proper reaction to what played out before them.

Rock star, Ian Cooper, an idol to so many women in so many ways, the voice with so much grit and haunting emotion, had two little dogs.

"Four bedrooms, four bathrooms. The one with clothes in the closet is mine, the other three are available." Ian set the dogs down, and they skittered off into another room.

Shane carried Ian's bags up the stairs, and Chris followed him with his new suitcase. Jersey still had her old bag with the broken zipper.

Ian watched Chris with a scowl. Ian always regarded Chris with a scowl and a general distrust vibe. "You can stay in my room, if you want to." Amusement teased Ian's face once Chris disappeared from sight.

"I don't." Jersey showed no amusement.

"Suit yourself." He sauntered to the kitchen.

She dropped her bag at the bottom of the staircase and followed Ian. "Interesting choice of dogs." Jersey glanced around his open kitchen, meticulously cleaned and decorated in all white with a wall of windows overlooking a pool.

"I lost a bet. Two actually. The first one got me the dogs; the second allowed Jordan to name them. I have a love-hate relationship with my bandmates. They like bets. Me? Not so much." He opened the glass door to the refrigerator.

"What are their names?"

"Lola and Foxy, but I usually just call them my bitches."

Jersey laughed. This wasn't a side to Ian she could have ever imagined. "Were you raised with a strange bottled water obsession? Or did you get the runs from tap water at some point? Happened to me at Marley's. When I first started staying there, I drank the orange-tinted water and nearly crapped out my intestines for a week." Jersey wedged her body between Ian and the open door to his huge refrigerator with rows of perfectly lined glass bottles of water. No food … just water.

He grabbed a bottle in one hand and her ponytail in

his other hand, yanking her back so he could shut the fridge door. She batted him away, and he chuckled.

"I just prefer it." He unscrewed the cap, leaned back against the island and drank the whole bottle as Jersey studied him.

"Anything else?" Shane poked his head into the kitchen.

"No. Thanks, buddy. Go enjoy your family for a few days. We'll be wheels up again before you know it."

"Where's Chris?" Jersey asked.

"Tossed his bag on the floor upstairs and collapsed onto the bed. Said he needed a nap." Shane shrugged. "Later."

Jersey's gaze slid up to Ian's face. He gave her the look he usually wore just before kissing her. That look made her heart race and her skin burn. She hated ... truly hated that any man had that effect on her.

A look.

His spiced wood, mildly scented cologne.

Minty breath.

Hands that played a guitar and her body like they were made to do those exact jobs.

"Tomorrow Max is taking you to a couple of appointments." He turned, ripping away that I'm-going-to-kiss-you look while making his way to the windows overlooking a swimming pool.

Ridiculous. The look she hated was gone, yet it angered her that he let it die as just a look. No kiss. She really needed to stop liking his mouth on hers so much.

"Appointments?"

"A physical and the eye doctor."

"You want to know that I don't have STDs, and you want to know that I can see your dick from across the room. Correct?"

"*You* should want to know that you don't have STDs, and we already know you can see my dick from across the room."

"You're right. As I stand here in this very spot, I can definitely see a dick across the room."

Ian turned, slipping his fingers into the front pockets of his jeans. "You seem a little more … edgy, aggravated … confrontational than most days. Have I done something to upset you?"

Her focus shifted over his shoulder to the pool, and she shook her head. "I … I don't know yet."

"You don't know yet if I've done something to upset you?"

She shrugged.

"When will you know?"

"When I do." Her gaze returned to him.

"And you'll tell me?"

"Oh …" She blew a quick breath out of her nose. "When I know, you'll definitely know."

"Can't wait."

Biting her lips between her teeth, she lifted her eyebrows and nodded several times.

"Hungry?"

Jersey grinned, jabbing her thumb behind her. "I just saw your fridge, Coop. I'm pretty sure I'm only allowed to be thirsty at your house."

"There are nonperishable items in the pantry." He pointed to a large cabinet door and opened it. A light automatically came on in the room lined with shelves of food, wine behind glass cabinets, a second sink, and a counter with a toaster and a coffee pot. "Chips? Nuts? Crackers?"

Her wide eyes surveyed the hidden room. "Where are the non … whatever things?"

Ian chuckled. "Nonperishable items?"

Jersey nodded.

"That's what most of this is considered—nonperishable. Things that won't spoil quickly."

"Then why not just say that? Why try to make me feel stupid?"

Ian shook his head, forehead slightly wrinkled. "That's not what I was doing."

"Never mind. I'm not hungry." She turned, marching out of the pantry. Snatching her bag, she stomped up the stairs.

"Jersey!"

She ignored Ian closing in on her. At the top of the stairs, Jersey spotted Chris sleeping on a bed in the room to her right. Before Ian reached the top step, Jersey slipped into the bedroom, closed the door, and locked it.

Swallowing back a jagged lump of emotion, she slid down the door, hugged her knees, and wiped one single tear.

One. She told herself that was all she got. One weak moment. One tear that no one else saw.

Did slaying monsters make her one too? Could monsters have the heart of a child? Were they born of this earth or born from circumstance? Did monsters forgive? Were they worthy of forgiveness?

The worst thing in Jersey's life didn't happen to her. It happened to two other people. It wasn't a touch. It was two words.

They're dead.

It didn't leave a mark. It left a void.

"Come here."

Jersey lifted her head. Chris hadn't moved, but it was his voice. She climbed to her feet and slipped off her shoes. He opened his eyes and his arms. She settled onto the bed next to him, her back to his chest. Closing her eyes, she let time pause while he enveloped her in the arms she trusted to comfort her unspoken fears.

"Want to talk about it?"

Several hours later, Jersey woke to Chris's voice in her ear. She pushed herself to sitting, letting her legs dangle from the bed for a few moments. "No," she whispered, sliding to her feet.

Leaving Chris behind, she tiptoed down the stairs, drifting toward the rattle of paper and cabinet doors tapping in the kitchen. As she leaned her shoulder against the threshold, Ian glanced up from the grocery bags cluttering the island.

"Hey."

"Hey." She offered a flicker of a smile, hoping he saw

her regret in it.

Ian continued to unload and put away the groceries as Lola and Foxy scarfed down their food next to the patio doors.

"You went shopping?"

He shook his head, dumping apples into a basket next to the fridge. "I had them delivered."

"Why? You can't shop without your fans following you?"

"Something like that."

She waited for him to look her way again, but he didn't. So Jersey opened the backdoor and stepped into the late afternoon sunshine by the pool. The blue water invited her to sit on the edge. She rolled up her jeans and dipped her legs into the cool water.

Leaning back on her hands, she closed her eyes, relishing the warmth, the light, the soft breeze on her face.

"Tell me more about Chris?"

Jersey peeked open one eye as Ian sat next to her, plopping his legs into the pool without rolling up his jeans. She laughed.

He smiled, leaning back on his hands too, his arm lightly brushing hers.

"There's not much to tell. He came into Marley's looking for a warm place to stay for the night. I busted his nose. He got up and kept nipping at my ankles like one of your little dogs." She released a slow breath as they stared at their bare feet stroking the water. "I had nothing … he had less. And we lived happily ever after."

"He's your friend?"

She nodded.

"Is he more than your friend?"

Jersey shot him a sideways glance, squinting against the sun. "Jealous, Coop?"

He twisted his lips, keeping his gaze on the pool, stealing a few seconds of silence before answering. "Nope. Just curious. When I use the wrong word and you stomp off to the bedroom with him and stay there for three hours … it just makes me wonder what you're doing in there with him."

"Well, I'm not being made fun of for my lack of intelligence."

"Jesus! I wasn't making fun of you."

"Chill out, Coop."

"Oh, I'm chill, Jersey. You're the one who needs to chill the fuck out." He shoved her into the pool.

The average person in her situation might have felt pissed off, planning their revenge as they swam to the surface. Jersey found the surface, but only briefly because she couldn't swim.

Her throat burned as her heart raced, limbs flailing. Seconds—that felt like minutes—later, an arm hooked around her body, just under her arms. Ian pulled her to the surface. Jersey tried to take a breath, but it caught, and she coughed. That caught too, making it painful, almost impossible to breathe in or breathe out. He propped her on the top step in the shallow end of the pool.

"Lean forward. Cough it out." He pushed her hair away from her face and gently rubbed her back as she coughed, spitting up some water. When she could breathe without coughing, he framed her face and brought her head up to look at him. "I'm so ... fucking sorry." He kissed her forehead, wiped the tears from her face and the spit from her chin. "Jersey ..." He hugged her.

She rested her cheek on his shoulder, draping her limp arms around his neck. "I—" Again, she coughed. "I can't swim."

Ian pressed a hand to the back of her head and kissed her cheek over and over. "That quickly occurred to me ... after the fact. God ... please, forgive me. I'm such an asshole. I'm so, so sorry." He continued to kiss her face, everywhere except her mouth.

"I'm cold."

"Okay. Let's get you into some dry clothes." He started to pick her up.

"I can walk." She pushed him away.

He ran a frustrated hand through his hair and nodded, settling for resting it on her lower back. "Let's take our clothes off here." He grabbed the hem of her shirt.

Again, she batted his hand away, scowling up at him. She peeled off her own clothes and made eye contact again.

Ian rubbed his lips together and nodded several times, standing in front of her wearing just his boxer briefs. "You could have left on your underwear, but this works too."

Her eyes narrowed. "You could have not shoved me into the pool so I wouldn't be standing here *naked* and freezing."

"I'm sorry." He opened the door. "How many sorrys

will be enough?"

"Sometimes sorry *isn't* enough." She stood at the bottom of the stairs, teeth chattering, and pointed to the upstairs. "You're not walking behind me up these stairs."

He didn't give her any resistance, which was the reason she didn't give in to her impulse to knock his teeth out. That ... and he looked disturbingly good in nothing but wet, blue underwear.

"Where's your bag?" Ian turned at the top of the stairs, his gaze slipping for a second to her naked body before returning to her face.

She nodded to Chris's room and started to grab the doorknob.

"No." Ian grabbed her wrist. "The room at the end of the hallway. Wait there. I'll get your bag."

"Don't make me cut your hand off, Coop."

"With what? You have a knife shoved up your ass?"

"He's seen me naked."

Ian's jaw clenched, but at the same time something vulnerable flashed in his eyes—a pleading of some sort.

"He's seen me naked ..." Jersey repeated in a softer tone.

Keeping his hand on her wrist, he slowly leaned down. "Can he not..." Ian whispered over her lips "...see you *now?* Can you be for my eyes only?"

Jersey blinked several times, feeling tension in her jaw too. But as he eased his grip on her wrist, she released the doorknob.

"Thank you," he breathed into her mouth a second before kissing her.

She kissed him back, wrapping her arms around his neck, letting him slide his arms around her naked body, letting him lift her up, guiding her legs around his waist. Ian kissed her all the way to the bedroom at the end of the hallway. He closed the door behind them. And he kissed her more, taking slow steps toward the king-sized bed next to the glass doors to a private balcony.

"You made fun …" she fought for a full breath as he took it away with his lips beneath her ear "…of me in the pantry."

His mouth paused for a moment and turned up into a smile. "I didn't." He lowered her to the bed and kissed his way down her throat as she arched into him.

"You tried to drown me." She fisted the sheets beneath her and let her heavy eyelids close.

Again, he paused at the swell of her breasts, grinning again. "I didn't." Making his way back to her lips, he rested his forearms beside her head. "Jersey?"

She blinked her eyes open.

"When I realized you couldn't swim … your heart didn't stop beating." He closed his eyes and released a slow breath through his nose. "But mine did."

"Coop …"

"I'm a terrible person."

"You are." She grinned, and it brought a little light to him as well. "But so am I. So let's do what terrible people do."

Ian's gaze swept along her face. Then he smiled and stretched his arm to the bedside table, pulling out a strip of condoms and tossing them on the bed before losing his underwear and taking. All. The. Kisses.

"IT'S NOT TERRIBLE." Jersey smiled as she and Ian rested on their sides facing each other—naked, sleepy, and satisfied. "I mean, we're terrible, but *it's* not terrible."

"What is *it*?" A contented smile played along his lips as he reached over and cupped her cheek, ghosting the pad of his thumb across her lower lip.

No one had ever touched her the way he did. So gently, like his hand was made to rest against her cheek. She liked pretending that. And she liked pretending he didn't kill the Russells. Everything with Ian felt like pretend.

Fairy tales.

Unicorns.

Pixie dust.

And rock stars who fell for homeless girls.

"It," she whispered, kissing his thumb, "is me being for your eyes only."

Those dark eyes shifted to look at her—all of her. "I'm going to miss you. Waiting for you to get your passport and join me again … it's going to be terrible." He smirked. "Not as terrible as us. But terrible."

She pulled away from his hand and sat up with her back to him.

"What's wrong?" He propped himself up with one arm.

Jersey inhaled a shaky breath.

One tear. She already gave her one tear away. No

more were allowed.

Her eyes disagreed, so she hurried to the bathroom and shut and locked the door. Why was she so damn emotional?

"Jersey?" Ian knocked on the door. "What's wrong? What did I say?"

"Nothing," she managed to squeak out while fighting back the demanding emotions. Why? Why did they need to be felt? Life was easier when emotions belonged to other people. Not Jersey. "Everything," she whispered to herself, leaning her head against the door as more tears broke free. Ian brought more tears out of her in one day than everyone else combined over the previous eight years.

She heard a tiny *thunk* against the door, his head pressing to the other side.

"Say it. You don't have to say it to my face. And we won't talk about it again after you open the door, but just … say it," he pleaded with her.

More tears. She let them fall freely. "You're going to miss me?"

"Yes," he said, sounding so close.

"No one has ever missed me before."

"Jersey …"

She felt so stupid, so young, and so weak. Raw— Jersey had never let herself feel so *raw* and exposed.

"Let me in."

"No."

"Shut off the lights and let me in. Please."

After staring at the switch for a few moments, she

flipped it off and unlocked the door, keeping her back to it. Ian slowly opened the door and shut it behind him, leaving them in the dark.

"I'm sorry if you're not strong enough to be missed by me. But imagine being in my shoes. I'm going to leave in a week. I have a full-time job to do, but I'm going to suck at it. It's the only thing I've been good at—and I'm going to suck at it. Because missing you will be my full-time job. And it doesn't matter if anyone has ever missed you before, because I will miss you enough to last a lifetime."

Sometimes … sometimes when you close your eyes, when darkness comforts you, the truth doesn't matter because no one can see it.

Jersey turned, and before she could say anything to the dark silhouette before her, he had his hand against her cheek, his thumb erasing the tears, his lips pressed gently to her lips.

She hugged his naked body to hers and whispered in his ear. "I'm going to miss you too. But don't tell anyone."

CHAPTER SEVENTEEN

"**O**H MY GOD!" Jersey's eyes looked like saucers as she surveyed her surroundings, wearing her new black-framed glasses.

Ian paid to have a rush put on them because he wanted to see Jersey's reaction before he left for Lisbon, Portugal in three days. He also paid a hefty sum to get things rolling on her birth certificate and social security card so she could get a passport.

"So *this* is what you meant when you said you'd show me the world."

It wasn't, but he felt certain nothing would compare to that moment. Chris sat in the corner of the waiting room, refusing to look at Jersey. Ian wasn't entirely sure what to think of their relationship. He just knew that he hated it beyond words. The bane of his existence. But she wanted Chris to stay with her at Ian's place in Los Angeles, so Ian put him to work doing some grounds-keeping around the house. However, Jersey insisted he come with them to pick up her glasses.

"Um … sure. I totally meant *see* in the most literal sense." He winked at Jersey as the technician handed them a bag with the glasses case, some cleaner, and a pair of prescription sunglasses too.

"Coop." She cringed, pressing her hands to his whiskery face. "You are so much uglier than I thought. This is just…" she covered her mouth "…so awkward."

The technician giggled as Ian's eyes narrowed at Jersey. She gave his left cheek a gentle pat before sauntering toward Chris.

"I *see* you, Mr. Ten." She pinched the corner of her glasses and wiggled them on her nose.

"Well…" he stood, hiking up his jeans "…if he's suddenly ugly, I must be flawless through those glasses."

She snaked her arm around him and looked up at him with adoration. It wasn't Chris's scars that disgusted Ian, it was the way he seemed pissed off at Jersey all the time, yet she brushed off his attitude as a bad day. He didn't trust him … for so many reasons.

Four days in L.A.

Four consecutive bad days for Chris.

Ian didn't share Jersey's disappointment over not being able to get Chris a passport. He wanted her to himself, even if it was selfish. And Ian hated that she was staying in his house with her needy male friend while Ian had to leave for the tour.

He hated that Chris had seen her naked.

He hated her blind trust in a stranger off the street.

"Meet you in the car, Coop." Jersey glanced over her shoulder and winked at Ian.

CHRIS TOOK THE dogs for a walk as soon as they re-turned. Ian thought it was a fitting job for him since he found any excuse to nap or take a walk when Ian wanted to spend time with Jersey.

"Want to see something?" Ian smiled at Jersey's reflec-tion in the bathroom mirror as she admired her new glasses.

"I see everything now." She turned leaning against the counter, arms crossed over her chest. "But what did you have in mind?"

"Follow me." His grin swelled while his dark eyes held something playful and mischievous. As they headed down the stairs, he shrugged off his T-shirt, wearing only black jogging shorts and tennis shoes.

Jersey wasn't too keen on the idea of swimming, but if he was stripping for sex, she wasn't in the mood to argue.

Past his workout room, he opened a door around the corner she didn't realize was there. He flipped on the lights to a gym with tall ceilings and a full basketball court. Jersey fought to balance her surprise. He liked basketball, just like Chris said. Every day she waited for Ian to prove Chris wrong. What was next? A black Charger in a hidden garage?

"Wow! Chris would love this. He played basketball in high school."

"Yeah?" Ian mumbled, grabbing a basketball from a rolling cart filled with balls. "Interesting." He dribbled it and shot from the three-point line, nothing but net.

"Why is that interesting?" Jersey grabbed a ball and

shot it from the corner, nothing but net.

Ian's lips parted for a few seconds before they pulled into a tentative smile. "You've played before."

She shrugged. "Just enough to win a few bets, pay for a few meals. Before Marley let me train at the gym, I used several of the parks to exercise. Met some guys who liked to play. They taught me a few things."

Ian made a few more long shots before palming a ball and dunking it.

Jersey froze, unable to blink or speak.

Ian grinned like he knew he was something pretty fucking special. And what could she say? Yeah, he could sing and play the guitar, write lyrics, kiss—man could he kiss—and he could dunk a basketball. Could they fit all of that onto a headstone? Jersey thought they could use small letters and both sides to accommodate his many talents.

"I'm thinking one-on-one or horse. What's your game?"

"Horse, but no dunking."

Ian nodded, passing her the ball.

"Are we wagering something?" she asked.

"What did you have in mind?"

"If I win, you tell me something about your past that you've never told anyone."

Ian's lips twisted to the side. A few seconds later, he nodded. "And if I win?"

She dribbled the ball between her legs several times. That made him smile even bigger. "What do you want, Coop?"

"You relinquish that thing you call a bag and let me get you a new one."

"Wow ... that's a little harsh but whatever." She tossed the ball up in the air, making the first basket.

After some impressive shots, evil banter, and a few stolen kisses, they were tied at HORS, Ian's shot.

"Can't wait to buy you a bubblegum pink travel bag, maybe something with rhinestones on it." He winked, making a three-point shot ... with one hand.

Jersey scowled at him, setting up for her shot. She put a perfect arc on it, landing it in the hoop, but it made a half spin, flying back out.

"Yes!" Ian threw up his hands and jumped up and down before hugging Jersey's waist and lifting her up like they were on the same winning team.

When he finally set her down, she couldn't look him in the eye.

"Oh come on, you can't be that attached to that bag."

She shook her head slowly.

"My past ... you wanted me to tell you something about my past that I haven't told anyone."

Jersey glanced up at him. He had no way of knowing how tortured she felt, how incredibly torn up she was inside from the painful conflict of needing to hate him but wanting something else.

What if Chris wouldn't have shown up at Marley's? She still would have met Ian, taken the job, traveled the world, and spent her nights watching a rock star and her early morning hours kissing said rock star.

Why? Why? Why? Why was everything good in her

life destined to go bad?

She slid her glasses up her nose after Ian's celebration vibrated them out of place. "Congratulations. I can't wait to see my new bag." Jersey turned, taking confident strides to the door in spite of her disappointment.

"My parents died when I was seven."

Jersey stopped, taking in a small, quick breath as something unfamiliar tingled in her chest.

Was it a lie? Ian told stories for a living. He wrote songs, like fictional stories, and sold them to fans with his voice. They were emotional and real … they were relatable. Maybe even believable.

He knew Jersey grew up without a family. Was he just trying to be relatable?

"My father was an only child, and his parents were dead. My mother had two siblings, and her father was still alive, but she was estranged from her family. When they contacted her surviving relatives, no one wanted to take me in and raise me."

Jersey listened, without turning toward him. His story was sad, but not yet tragic. Not by her definition of tragic.

"Nobody else knows this?" she asked.

"No."

Nobody could corroborate his story. Convenient.

"Were your parents wealthy?"

"That's two things. I already shared one, and you didn't even earn it."

Jersey nodded, keeping him at her back. "True. Are you sure you never owned another vehicle like … a black Charger?"

"Who wants to know?"

That made Jersey turn around. "Does it matter?"

Ian returned a blank expression. After a few seconds, he shrugged. "I suppose not, since the answer is the same either way. No ... I've never owned a black Charger. Hope that helps you sleep tonight."

Was she imagining him talking in his own riddles, saying very little but meaning something worth so much more?

"Yeah. When I dream of that black Charger, I won't put you in the driver's seat."

CHAPTER EIGHTEEN

"H E HATES ME." Chris smirked, tipping back a beer as he and Jersey got a little tipsy on Ian's sprawling deck overlooking the heart of Los Angeles. "Is it wrong for that to please me?"

"You never speak to him, which comes across like you're some ungrateful asshole." Jersey slipped on her new sunglasses as the sun sank lower into the western sky.

Ian had dinner plans with his manager, Ames.

"I'm paranoid that if I talk too much something about my voice might become recognizable to him and blow our whole plan."

"At this point, I'd welcome something recognizable about this whole messed up situation. The black Charger is bullshit—"

"It's not bullshit!" Chris heaved his empty bottle into the pool.

"He didn't even flinch when I asked him about his cars. I asked him again earlier … in his gym."

Chris slid down his sunglasses, peering at Jersey. "His what?"

"Gym. He has a full basketball court just beyond the workout room. He can dunk." She shook her head, finding it impossible to not grin. "Fucking rock star who can dunk a basketball and hit three pointers like he's been doing it since he came out of the womb. Which …" She frowned. "He told me something about his past. Something personal that makes no sense."

"Which is?"

Jersey leaned her head back and sighed, closing her eyes. "I feel like it's a secret I'm not supposed to share."

"You're not serious."

Her nose wrinkled. "Fine. He said his parents died when he was seven."

"No." Chris shook his head. "That's not true. He would have told me. There's no way he befriended me and kept that a secret from me out of all people. Those weren't his adopted parents. No way. He's playing you. One orphan to another. And I'm not wrong about the car."

"Well, either you're not remembering the car correctly or he knows … he knows I lived with the Russells. He knows he's responsible for what happened to me after they died. And sometimes…" she stood, adjusting the ties to her pink bikini and fishing the empty beer bottle out of the pool with the long-poled skimmer "…I think that's it. I think he knows everything. He knows we know. He's testing me or you. Maybe both of us. What's he thinking? If he knows you, why not say something?"

"What the fuck is all over your legs?" Chris nodded toward Jersey's crotch.

She smoothed her fingers over the red bumps near the apex of her legs. "Max sent me to get waxed yesterday.

Apparently, this can happen after the first time. They should disappear in the next few days."

"Waxed, huh? So all of your pubes have been ripped out?"

Jersey frowned, nodding while plopping back down onto the lounge chair.

"Ouch." He shared a sympathetic seething noise.

"I've experienced worse things. And I felt agreeable and quite happy after the STD tests all came back negative."

"True." Chris opened his book. "That's good news."

"I can see the title." Jersey grinned, nodding to his book while adjusting her glasses.

Chris's attempted smile failed, so he held out his hand. Jersey took it, letting him pull her over to lie with him. She nestled her body on its side between his legs, resting her cheek on his chest covered in a long-sleeved swimming shirt that protected his damaged skin.

"It's not enough … the glasses. I'm happy for you that you can see things now, but it's not enough to make up for what he did."

Jersey sighed, closing her eyes behind the glasses. "I know."

After a few silent minutes, Chris started reading to Jersey. He read the murder mystery to her for over an hour. Then he made dinner for her in Ian's fancy kitchen.

"I'm going to bed." He kissed the top of her head as she sipped the rest of her wine, slightly past the tipsy point.

"Thanks for dinner."

"Anytime."

"Chris?" she murmured. "Are you … lonely?"

He stopped just before turning the corner by the stairs. "Lonely?"

"For a woman. Pleasure. The fantasies you said you have."

"Yeah, Jers … I'm lonely. I'd give my right testicle for a trip to a strip club or a computer with access to a good porn site."

"Coop has a computer."

"Sure, Jers … I'll try to remember to ask him for the password tomorrow since we're such close buds."

"Chris—"

"Night, Jers."

A few minutes later, Ian came in the back door as Jersey emptied the last few drops of her wine down her throat.

"Drinking alone?" He lifted a sexy eyebrow.

"Mmhm." She licked the residual wine from her lips while letting her intoxicated gaze slide along the length of Ian's body—dark jeans, a white button-down, and a sharp blue blazer the color of his car. She liked looking at him. That emotion felt new and a little odd. Very little in her life had involved enjoyment and pleasure, so admiring a man who freely returned the sentiment felt like an out of body experience. A dream.

"Chris go to bed?" Ian shrugged off his blazer.

Jersey nodded, propping her bare legs and feet up on the kitchen table next to the empty wine bottle and glass. Her white, sheer swimsuit cover-up slid open.

Ian unbuttoned his shirt with his gaze affixed to her legs. "Nice bikini." He unbuttoned his cuffs and removed his shirt, letting it fall to the floor by her chair.

"It's impractical. All the stupid ties." Jersey's words slurred a bit.

Her foot jerked when he ran his finger along the instep. "I disagree."

Jersey's heart pumped harder, the echoing pulse whooshing in her ears as she felt it surging blood to all the places Ian's gaze touched her body as he stripped her with a single look.

Kneeling on the floor, he moved her feet from the table to the edge of her chair, her knees spread wide to accommodate him. Leaning forward, he hovered a breath away from her lips. "You're so fucking beautiful. Every soft curve, every hard muscle, every tiny scar. And those glasses …" He brushed his lips over hers several times before flicking his tongue out, beckoning her to open up for him.

She did, her tongue meeting his in the middle as he deepened the kiss. Deft fingers worked the lower tie to her top, loosening it enough to pull it up, exposing her breasts. Her heavy eyelids fought the gravity of his touch as he dragged his eager lips and warm tongue down her neck to her breasts, eliciting a drunken moan from Jersey as her fingers dug into the sides of the cream upholstered chair.

"This…" Ian kissed lower, his tongue dipping into her navel "…is what makes this the best bikini design ever." At the same time, he untied the sides of her bottoms, peeling the front away from her body with his teeth and a wicked grin.

She wrinkled her nose, erasing the smile from his face.

"If you don't want me to do this …"

She shook her head, swallowing a ridiculous amount of pooling saliva. "It just looks bad because of the red bumps."

His gaze homed in on her bared, slightly bumpy flesh. After a slow and silent inspection, he turned his head and kissed the inside of her thigh, just above her knee. His gaze locked with hers again. "Tell me it's okay." He kissed higher.

It was easy to despise and even kill a man who sexually abused young girls. It was much harder to think about taking the life of a man who cared about a woman's emotional scars, who asked permission to kiss her in places she might not want to be kissed.

But Jersey did want Ian to kiss her there. It scared her just how much she wanted Ian to kiss her everywhere, touch her deeper than she'd ever wanted any man to touch her. "Yes …" She inched her legs open a little more and closed her eyes as he kissed her intimately. The warmth of his tongue brought her eyes back open, needing to watch him. A shadow, ten or so feet behind Ian, caught her attention.

Chris.

He stood statuesque at the bottom of the stairs.

Even with her new glasses, it was too dark to see his eyes. What were his eyes doing? Why was he standing there watching them?

Then it hit her—water. Chris always needed one last drink of water before bed. But he didn't move toward the sink or the refrigerator. He just stood stone still.

He watched the enemy spread Jersey's legs, his mouth pressed to her most intimate parts, humming his pleasure.

He watched Jersey's mouth fall open while her right hand clenched Ian's hair, encouraging him.

It was a game.

Chris told her to play it … he told her *how* to play it.

He couldn't be mad that she played it so well.

And she couldn't call a timeout just because Chris felt thirsty again.

Ian would be livid with Chris for watching them. He'd be pissed off at Jersey for letting it go on so long … so she said nothing. She let her lonely friend watch them.

Jersey used her other hand to slide her top completely off her head, giving Chris a better view of her.

She arched her back and moaned when Ian made her orgasm.

Her gaze flitted for a brief second to Chris when Ian stood on his knees, digging a condom out of his pocket.

Jersey returned her attention to Ian as he shoved his jeans and briefs down just enough to release his erection and roll on the condom.

She kissed him passionately as he pulled her naked body closer to his.

She bit the tight muscle along his shoulder as he guided her legs around his waist and drove into her.

Her fingers dug into his back while leaving her gaze on Chris's idle body the entire time. Maybe for that one night … she wasn't only for Ian's eyes.

A game … just a game.

A game she enjoyed too much.

A game with a lonely, sexually deprived spectator.

Ian stilled on his final thrust, and Jersey closed her eyes for a few seconds. When she opened them, Chris was gone.

CHAPTER NINETEEN

J ERSEY PUNCHED, KICKED, jabbed, and grunted at the hundred-pound punching bag hanging in Ian's workout room. The wine wore off by eleven. Ian joined her in the shower around midnight. She peeled his limbs from her naked body around two. Stared at the ceiling until three. Slipped on a sports bra, shorts, and her boxing gloves ten minutes later.

"Can't sleep either?"

She turned toward Chris's voice. He stood in the doorway, wearing sweats and holding a glass of water.

"I see you're finally quenching your thirst." She rammed her fist into the bag again.

"Are we really going to talk about that?" He moseyed around the room, inspecting the expensive exercise equipment.

"No. We're not." Jersey grunted with another jab.

"Listen …" He sat in the seat of the rowing machine, with no intention of rowing. "I get that you don't want to kill an innocent man—which he's not. But you're not doing *anything* except letting him crawl between your legs. The plan was to destroy his reputation, turn the world against him, make him *want* to die."

She ignored him, throwing another punch.

Chris shrugged. "I'll play devil's advocate for a minute and pretend that he's not the person who killed them. But he's still not your happily-ever-after. He will despise you on a visceral level for planning his death. He'll know that all of this was an act because you can't honestly fall in love with the man you're planning to kill. He's too smart to be that gullible. So … any way you look at it, this story doesn't end with you both alive and together."

She bent over, resting her gloves on her knees while catching her breath. Chris was right. One hundred percent.

"Tell me what to do." Jersey's sweat-stained face glanced up at him.

A tiny smile curled his lips. "Put yourself on the radar. He's working his ass off to do it anyway by getting you a passport to join him abroad, but being the flavor of the month is not a huge deal. I'm sure he's had girlfriends. However, we don't want his adoring fans to be jealous of you. We want them to hate you because you're bad for their rock star."

"Bad how?"

"Unpolished. Impulsive. Unpredictable. And you have a real doozy of a past. You've been arrested. You've been in juvie. You've *killed* a man. That's not exactly girlfriend material for the world's favorite singer."

"Petty theft. Assault charges. I spent a week in juvie. One lousy week. Less than three days in jail before being sentenced to community service. And the man I killed was a sexual predator. It was self-defense. I didn't spend one night in jail. There wasn't even a trial."

Chris chuckled. "Yes, Jers, compared to the population of Marley's, you are nothing but a white dove with a tiny smudge of dirt on your wing. But to adoring, young fans who might not even have a parking ticket on their record, you are a hideous criminal, a worthless piece of shit from Newark who doesn't deserve their Ian. And that's exactly how we want it."

"So he'll let me go. Game over. Then what?"

"Let you go? No. They'll come after you, and he'll risk *everything* to protect you. Were you not in the kitchen last night?"

She stood, stretching her shoulders while turning her back to him. "Fuck you," she mumbled.

"No. But if you *did* fuck me the way you fucked Ian last night ... I sure as hell would risk my whole world to keep you."

"*But* ... what if he knows? What if he's keeping me close to him so I *don't* kill him?"

"That makes no sense." Chris stood, finishing his glass of water.

"It does. He has a secret too. I see the agony on his face when I share pieces of my past. I ..." She shook her head, closing her eyes. "I need to see him crack, just a little. I'm going to tell him about the Russells. And he won't have to say a word. I'll see the truth on his face. I need that ... I need the truth."

"Fine, Jers." Chris stopped in front of her, using his height and a challenging smirk to try to intimidate her. "You do your thing, and I'll do mine. Let's see who's better at avenging death."

"GOOD MORNING." MAX smiled as Jersey rounded the corner to the kitchen.

"Hey. Where's Coop? I got up really early to exercise. But by the time I went upstairs to shower, he was up and gone. No note or anything."

"He probably couldn't find a receipt and pen." Max shot her a toothy grin. "There." She nodded to a bag on the island. "There's a new phone for you in that bag. Welcome to the world of technology, where humans communicate through texting and emojis. And where handwritten notes on the back of receipts are the equivalent of carving stick people on cave walls."

Jersey poured herself a cup of coffee from the pantry. "Well, Coop got one hell of a blowjob thanks to ancient ways of communication."

"La la la la la ..." Max covered her ears. "Will you ever *stop* oversharing?"

She emerged from the secret room. "If you're bothered by our sex acts, then pick a different chair to sit in because the one you're sitting in is the one I sat in last night when he buried his head between my legs before—"

"Jersey!" Max sprang out of the chair, doing a weird dance like something crawled up her pant leg. "No! Why do you hate me? I'm old enough to be your mother!" She shimmied a bit more before pointing to another chair.

Jersey nodded.

"So where's Chris?" Max wasted no time changing the subject.

"I don't know. Probably taking a walk. He likes to walk. I think that's when memories come back to him. And he needs a phone too so I can communicate with him when I'm gone. Oh … and access to the internet would be great for him as well."

Max nodded. "That can be arranged. Ian's with Nick doing therapy this morning. He should be back soon so I can go over his schedule with him. How are you liking L.A.?"

Jersey sat across from Max, blowing the steam from her coffee. "I don't know. I guess it's all relative. I'm staying in a fancy house. Eating three meals a day. Showering. So in that way, L.A. is amazing. And maybe if I were on the streets, it still might feel like an improvement just because it doesn't get as cold here."

"Well, if your birth certificate shows up, we'll get things going on your passport."

"We'll? Aren't you leaving too, in three days?"

"Yes. Jeanine, my assistant, will take care of whatever you need."

Jersey coughed, setting her coffee on the table. "You're Coop's assistant, but you have your own assistant?"

Max pulled Jersey's phone out of the bag and turned it on. "Yes, but she's part-time. I use her to help me when I can't be in two places at once, like when they're touring. Like when Ian's personal life becomes his priority, but he still has to do his job."

"You think I'm his personal life?"

Max nodded on a chuckle. "If you saw the messages he's sent me since the day he met you, I think it's safe to say he's made you his whole life." She shrugged. "And I don't know why. And that's nothing against you. I genuinely like you. It was just an odd meet cute."

"Meet cute?"

"A meet cute is a first encounter that leads to a romantic relationship."

"Whoa … we don't have a romantic relationship. It's sex."

Max curled her hair behind her ear and reached across the table, resting her hand on Jersey's hand. The smile Max shared, a mix of amusement and sympathy, made Jersey nervous. "Have you ever been in love?"

Jersey shook her head.

"Have you ever thought about a man in a nonsexual way, for no particular reason other than you just liked how it made you feel to think about him?"

She shrugged. "I don't know." Her gaze averted to the windows. "Maybe. But that doesn't mean anything."

Releasing her hand, Max sat back and grinned. "No? Well … maybe not. But when you overshare with me about the sex, you do it in a very matter-of-fact way. In those moments, I might believe it's just sex. However, when I mention Ian, when I watch you watching him on stage, or when you ask where he's at, your cheeks turn pink, you wet your lips, and you can't even look me in the eye. That's romance. And you don't have to admit it, but I know from experience it's an incredible feeling."

It wasn't an incredible feeling, not for Jersey. Had someone told her that the Russells were going to die and there was nothing she could do to stop it … *that's* what it felt like to think about Ian.

"Here." She slid the phone to Jersey. "Enter a six-digit code and remember it."

Jersey stared at the screen a few seconds then tapped it six times.

"You just typed 666666, didn't you?"

She nodded.

Max rolled her eyes. "Okay. Whatever. We'll just make sure you don't keep the launch codes on your phone."

"What launch codes?"

"Nothing."

"No." Jersey tipped her chin up. "Not nothing. I'm sick of everyone around here making fun of me."

"What's going on?"

They turned toward Ian's voice. He dropped his wallet and key fob on the counter, giving them a narrow-eyed inspection.

"Just a misunderstanding." Max smiled.

Jersey grabbed her phone and marched out of the kitchen.

"Jersey …" Ian tried to grab her arm, but she jerked it away and ran up the stairs, slamming the door to Ian's bedroom, tossing the phone onto the floor and pounding the door with her fists like a hammer.

"Ahhhh!!!!" She released her frustrations. When she gave up the door fight, it opened slowly, forcing her to take a step back.

Ian peeked around the corner.

"Get out of here, Coop," she warned, out of breath, and feeling out of control on the inside in a way she hadn't felt in a long time.

"Talk to me." He ignored her request and stepped into the room, closing the door behind him.

She turned her back to him and pulled at her hair much like Chris did when things in life got too overwhelming. "I don't want to talk. I won't have big enough words to say because I'm so fucking stupid. I just want to go back to Newark. I don't care if Marley's is gone. I just ..." She closed her eyes and let the rest of her words burn out on the inside because she didn't really know what she wanted.

Not totally true. She wanted the impossible—the Russells still alive, a bigger vocabulary, a college degree, a normal life, relatives, maybe a boxing title, and girly nail polish. Instead ... she was well on her way to killing a man who made her cheeks turn pink, going to prison, and dying from lethal injection.

"How many broken noses, busted teeth, and cracked ribs have resulted from you feeling like someone's crossed a line and made fun of you?" Ian sat on the bed, so she had to look at him. He rested his elbows on his knees and folded his hands.

Jersey kept her focus on the thick white carpet between them. "Too many to count," she mumbled.

"First: Max wasn't making fun of you. She wouldn't do that. I wouldn't do that. You're safe with us. You don't have to walk around with your fists up and a knife in the back of your pants.

"Second: It's not your fault that you don't always follow what someone is trying to say or what a word means. You weren't given the same chance at an education that so many other people get."

Jersey glanced up at him. "I was. I was in school until I ran away. I didn't have to run away, but I did. That was my choice. Maybe if I would have let them find a new home for me, I could have stayed in school."

"So why did you run?"

She moved to the glass door by the balcony that overlooked the pool. "Because I was done. Done taking my chances on … people. The system. All of it. I was done with the abuse. Done being touched. Done with group homes. After G killed Mr. Fisher, she told me to be brave and run fast." She shrugged. "Since that day, it's just been what I've done. I do it better than anyone."

"Are you tired? Tired of running. Tired of being brave all the time?"

Yes.

"No. It's who I am. It's how I stay alive. It's how I *know* that I'm alive." She looked down toward her crotch and frowned. Without glancing in Ian's direction, she made a straight line to the bathroom.

"Jersey—"

"I need to … go … use … um, the bathroom." She locked the door, shoved down her pants, and sat on the toilet. "Really?" she whispered to herself, scowling at the blood on her underwear. After a quick wipe, she waddled around the bathroom with her pants at her knees, looking in the cabinets for something.

"I hear doors opening and closing. Can I help you find something?"

She closed her eyes and sighed, plopping back down onto the toilet seat. With no other option, she wadded up a bunch of toilet paper for a makeshift sanitary napkin.

Ian took a quick step backward when she opened the door. "Hey …" His eyebrows lifted with an unspoken demand for an explanation.

"Can you just do me a favor?" Frustration bled through her words in spite of her effort to be nice.

"Sure. What do you need?" Ian smiled, seemingly pleased at the prospect of helping her.

"I need you to stay in this room while I talk to Max privately."

His eyebrows squished together as his tongue poked into his cheek. Jersey prepared herself for the resistance and onslaught of questions.

"Okay." Ian's face relaxed.

"Okay?"

He nodded. "Yep. Go talk to Max. I'll stay here."

She pulled her glasses down her nose and peered at him over the frames. "I'm watching you."

"Good." He grinned. "I like it when you watch me."

Jersey backed away slowly, pivoted, and sped down the hall and stairs to the kitchen. "I have a problem."

Max looked up from her phone. "I know you do. That's why I'm not holding your outburst against you."

"What?" Jersey's nose wrinkled. "That's … no." She

shook her head a half dozen times. "I don't even know what you mean by that—and don't try to explain it. I don't give a shit. My problem is I started my period. I haven't had one in years. That doctor you took me to said it's probably because of my over-exercising and lack of food. She said if I started eating regularly and don't overdo it with exercising, I'd hopefully get my period again in the next six to twelve months. *NOT* in a matter of days."

"Okay. I'm following the order of events, but not the actual problem. However, it explains your moodiness."

"I don't have tampons or pads! I'm just bleeding with a wad of toilet paper between my legs."

Max's lips formed an O. "You should have led with that." She dug through her handbag and pulled out two tampons. "I'll get you more after I go over the schedule with Ian."

Jersey grabbed them from Max's hand and headed back toward the stairs, stopping just outside of the kitchen. "Thank you," she said without looking at Max.

"You're welcome, Jersey."

Slipping into the first bathroom, she swapped the toilet paper wad for the tampon before returning to Ian's room.

"I'm done."

Ian glanced up from the bed, reclined back, holding Jersey's phone. "Come here."

She sat on the edge of the bed. He patted his hand on the mattress right next to him. Jersey sighed and crawled over next to him, leaning closer to see the phone screen—

a selfie of him with a cocky grin.

"I'm going to show you how to use this phone so you can reach me or Max if you need anything."

Jersey nodded, giving him a quick glance. His gaze dropped to her mouth for a few seconds.

"Don't look at me that way, Coop. I'm not in the mood."

He coughed on a chuckle. "Look at you in what way? And what aren't you in the mood for?"

"Don't look at me like you plan on kissing me."

"You're not in the mood to kiss me?"

"No." She nodded toward the phone. "Get to the point. Max is waiting for you downstairs to go over your schedule or something like that."

"Since when did you start caring about Max's time?"

"Since she's going to buy me a box of tampons as soon as she's done going over your schedule."

His eyebrows shot up as his gaze snapped back to the phone. "Okay then, let's get through this quickly."

Jersey crossed her arms over her chest and twisted her lips to hide her grin. She *was* moody and irrationally sensitive. But if she were honest, she wasn't really *not* in the mood to kiss Ian. A selfish, indulgent physical act sounded really good.

"This button gets you to your contacts. Max and I are your only contacts at the moment. You can message, call, or—"

"I lied." She snatched the phone and tossed it on the floor. "I'm in the mood to be kissed."

Be kissed. Commit emotional suicide. Blur the lines

with blood and lust. If crazy period hormones were real, Jersey had them in full force—an insect ready to mate and then kill its prey.

"I bought you that phone, and you keep throwing it around."

"Really, Coop? Do I have to ask you twice to kiss me?" She angled her body toward him.

He laughed. "You didn't ask me once."

"Do I really *have* to ask?" She shifted to her hands and knees, bringing her face close to his.

"Yes. Just ask me. Ask me to get you tampons. Ask me to take you boxing. Ask me what something means. Ask me for the world. Or just ask me for a kiss."

"Kiss me, Coop." She grinned, a breath away from his lips.

"*Ask* me," he whispered.

His stubbornness infuriated her, but for whatever reason, she liked his style of foreplay.

"Coop, will you—"

"Yes." He slid his hand behind her head and kissed her.

CHAPTER TWENTY

THINGS STARTED TO unravel the day of Ian's departure for Portugal.

"Good news." Max sat in the oversized chair in the corner of Ian's bedroom as he finished packing.

They had the house to themselves since Jersey went on a walk with Chris.

"I like good news." Ian set a pile of jeans on his bed next to his suitcase, everything freshly laundered by his service.

"Well, enjoy the three seconds it lasts."

"Three seconds?" He squinted.

"Yep. Here we go. Start counting. Jersey's birth certificate and social security card arrived. Three, two, one … and she has a record."

Ian paused for a few seconds before shrugging. "Anything that might prevent her from getting a passport?"

"I doubt it. But it won't take much for the press to find out."

"Your point?"

"She killed a man."

Ian stilled his hands, staring at the bottom of the suitcase for a few moments.

"That's not on her record. I just decided to look up what I could on her once I discovered she had a record."

"And?" Ian replied without any emotion.

"Theft and assault charges. She hasn't done hard time, but she's a repeat offender. And I know you're going to blow this off and say so what. And given her history of living on the street, I tend to agree. So what? She had to survive, right?"

He nodded slowly.

"But she killed a man. Yes, come to find out he was a pretty sick man doing unthinkable things to young children. She wasn't charged or convicted of any crime. But ... she killed him, Ian. At age fourteen, she killed him. Not like shoving him into oncoming traffic or a subway train. Not poison. Not with a gun she found in the house. She cut him open from throat to groin like a butcher. That's not normal. And she always has a knife on her. Hello? This is crazy!"

Ian closed his eyes, replaying the words, letting the images come to life. The girl who just wanted to be kissed ... she brutally killed a man.

"Thank you. Have Jeanine help her get the paperwork submitted to expedite her passport."

"Ian, you can't seriously—"

"That is all."

"Ian—"

"You're dismissed!" He kept his gaze on the bed, jaw clenched.

"As you wish," she replied with poison in her words. "Shane will pick you up in two hours."

"Thank you," he whispered with a tiny sigh of regret.

Twenty minutes later, as he zipped his suitcase, Jersey slipped into the bedroom and wrapped her arms around him, resting her cheek on his back.

He stiffened beneath her touch. "How was your walk?"

"Slow. Chris likes to smell the roses, only not really. He thinks he's deadly allergic to bee stings. The only time he picks up the pace is when he sees a bee."

"Bees, huh? Well, isn't that interesting. And simple," Ian mumbled.

"What's wrong?" She ducked around, wedging herself between Ian and the bed, craning her neck to look up at him.

He chewed on the inside of his cheek, brows drawn together. "Are you running?"

"Running?"

"Running from your past?"

She blinked several times. "I grew up in the system— tossed out of homes, abused, lost—who wouldn't run from that?"

"Max looked into your past. I didn't ask her to do it. She's just looking out for me."

A few more blinks. "Okay." She held his gaze without a blip of reaction.

"You have a record."

She returned a tight-lipped smile. "Yes, Coop, I have

a record. You're not sharing anything new with me."

Ian took a few moments to do his own blinking, studying her for some sign of nerves or regret.

Nothing.

"You killed a man who did something very bad to you."

Not. One. Tiny. Blink.

"I did. G killed Fisher when I was seven. Seven, Co-op. I knew at that age that if I was ever put in the same position, I would kill too. That's been my fucking life."

Ian drew in a slow breath. "Do you regret it?"

"No."

"Were you scared?"

"No."

"No?" He tipped his head to the side. "You were fourteen. You cut open a man from throat to groin and you weren't scared? You weren't scared of the consequences?"

"For the first time in fourteen years, I stood up for myself. I wasn't scared; I was strong. How the hell I ended up with another foster parent as bad as Fisher ... well, beats the hell out of me. But I did. After years of abuse, missing G, feeling alone, being the oldest in the house ... I just snapped.

"I said no. He didn't listen. I warned him. I said I'd cut him open and watch him bleed out. He laughed. So when his wife left town to visit her parents, I snuck into his room while he was sleeping. I restrained his hands with jump ropes, anchoring them to the posts. Then I jabbed the tip of my knife into his throat. His eyes flew open. His hands jerked against the restraints. I carved a straight line and watched him bleed out as blood gurgled at his throat."

Ian swallowed hard. "Then what did you do?"

Jersey shrugged. "I went to sleep. Slept through the night, like a baby, probably for the first time in fourteen years."

"I'm sorry …" he whispered.

"I'm not. Thirty-two. That's the number of girls he sexually assaulted. Photos of thirty-two naked girls on his computer. Thirty-two girls he videotaped taking showers while he jerked off."

"Jersey …" He ached to touch her, but the timing felt off.

"I'm not broken, Coop. But you're right. I'm running. Only you don't see the real picture. I'm not running away. I'm running toward something. I'm chasing something. I am the predator. The captor. Not the prey. *Never* again will I be the prey."

He returned a sluggish nod, mentally chewing on her words, trying to connect the underlying meaning. "Who are you chasing?"

"Not who. What. I'm chasing the truth."

"The truth about what?"

Jersey's gaze slipped for a few seconds. Her intent expression pointed at his chest before glancing back up at him. "My life. Why it's taken the turns it has. And who's to blame."

"You're twenty-four."

"Yeah, so?"

"Okay. You're a twenty-four-year-old with a rocky

past, but you're on the verge of traveling the world with a moderately famous person. And said moderately famous person likes you ... quite a lot actually. So why chase demons?"

Jersey frowned, a silent punch to Ian's gut, leaving him feeling like a failure. What did he miss? Why was his question not well-received?

"I didn't dream of traveling the world with some guy. And no matter how much of the world you show me, it won't erase my past. It won't give me what I've lost. It won't be an education, a useful skill, a sense of independence, a feeling of normal ... ness, a family."

Family. That he understood.

"Are you chasing *me*?" Ian cupped the side of her face.

She closed her eyes, leaning into his touch. "I'm chasing the truth."

He brought his other hand to her face too. Then he leaned down, whispering over her lips, "Am I your truth?"

Jersey's eyes popped open wide, blinking several times. "Yes."

He kissed the girl who liked to be kissed. She slid her hands up his shirt, curling her fingers into his muscles. It felt like a silent claim. Ian ran from clingy women, dodged anything too personal, skirted the issue of love, his past, and his fears. Until ... Jersey.

Her hands descended to the button of his jeans, giving it a hard tug until it popped open.

"Jersey ..." he mumbled into their kiss.

She pulled down his zipper.

A groan rumbled his chest as he tried to step back.

"What are you doing to me?"

Stepping toward him, hooking the waistband of his briefs with her finger, she grinned. "I'm kissing you, Coop."

He took a mental picture of that smile, tucking it into a special place in his memory. For a flash of a moment, she wasn't the abused, defensive, homeless woman he found weeks earlier. In that moment, she was a woman wanting a man, not a fan seducing a rock star. A woman—*the* woman—wanting him. And he wanted her too.

"You're teasing me with something I can't have." He rested his forehead on hers, covering her curious hand with his to stop her from going any further.

"My female issue is done, Coop."

"That was quick."

She chuckled, lifting onto her toes and biting his lower lip as her hand broke free from his grasp and pushed down the front of his briefs. "Do we really need to talk about it?"

His abs tightened as he sucked in a quick breath when she grabbed him with her warm hand. He claimed her mouth, kissing her hard, but afraid to move an inch, not wanting to lose her touch. His tongue slid across hers, deliberate yet patient like her hand moved along him.

When the tension built to the brink of losing his sanity, they pushed away from each other, breathless and desperate. Quick hands tore off clothes. Ian shoved the suitcase onto the floor. Before Jersey could get her pants completely off, Ian grabbed her face and kissed her again.

She stumbled backward, her feet tangled in her pants.

Clinging to each other, they fell to the bed. His hand slid between her legs, and she kicked her leggings the rest of the way off.

"I might die waiting for you to meet me on the other side of the world." He kissed her neck.

She lifted her pelvis off the bed, chasing his touch. It gave him an indescribable high to know that he could strip her down to a simple woman wanting a man.

A beautiful woman with thick, dark hair that she never curled.

A shy smile.

A face with no makeup.

A body riddled with tiny scars.

But she never said no to a mani-pedi with Max. Jersey's raw beauty drew him in, and her teasing splashes of femininity softened her jagged edges. But those eyes … they never lied. They had seen too much to ever be anything but dark.

He watched a killer unravel beneath him with his mouth on her breast and his hand between her legs. An unforgettable sight.

"Jesus … Coop …" Her jaw relaxed, eyelids heavy as she jerked against his hand.

Watching her orgasm was more addictive than a stadium filled with screaming fans. He shifted to the side, retrieving a condom from the drawer and rolling it on. Jersey's sated body came to life again when he settled between her legs and pushed inside of her.

"I don't want you in his bed when I'm gone."

She grabbed his ass, digging her fingers into his muscled flesh to bring him back into her every time he pulled away. "I don't let him do this to me."

Ian slammed into her, his tense face hovering over hers as he moved inside of her. "I don't give a fuck. I don't want his hands on you." He kissed her.

Jersey kissed him back. It was rough and demanding, like her hands on his ass. He tried to make his point, tried to make his mark. But no matter how hard he drove into her, desperate to make his point, it didn't matter. When he finished and she dug her teeth into his flesh, probably leaving another mark while his body went rigid with waves of pleasure, he still didn't have her promise.

Jersey relaxed beneath him, and he rolled onto his back. She jackknifed to sitting, swinging her legs over the side of the bed, barely taking a breath before slipping into her clothes in record time with her back to him. "I don't belong to you, Coop."

He sat up, standing behind her with his chest to her back. Grabbing her face, he turned her head just enough to kiss her, tasting every inch of her mouth once more before pulling back a fraction of an inch to meet her eyes—her hard gaze.

"No. You don't. But you belong *with* me." He released her jaw and sauntered into the bathroom.

IAN TOOK A quick shower. Returning to an empty bedroom, he grabbed his suitcase and carried it toward the stairs just as Chris stepped out of the guest bedroom.

They sized up each other before Ian cleared his throat.

"If you have any questions about your job, have Jersey contact me. If you want to go back to Newark when she joins me abroad, Max will arrange your transportation."

Chris returned an easy nod, and his lips curled into a tiny smirk. "I think I'll wait here for Jersey. She might need me. Besides, we don't know if her passport will get approved. It might just be the two of us here for a while."

Ian narrowed his eyes, tipping his chin up a fraction to look down at Chris. "She sleeps in my room. You stay in yours. You keep your hands to yourself. Understood?"

Chris shrugged, sliding his hands into the pockets of his sweatpants. "She crawls into my bed because she likes my body next to hers and the comfort of my arms. I'm here to give her *whatever* she needs, including a tissue to wipe her watery eyes and drips of vomit from her chin after she lets you fuck her mouth like all the pricks before you."

Ian saw red, so much red. His hands clenched into tight fists. Taking a step forward, he forced Chris into the wall, his right hand taking a firm hold on Chris's neck. "Touch her. I kill you. It's that simple."

Chris took a hard swallow, his cocky grin quivered for a second before he took a full breath. "I'll keep that in mind, rock star."

Ian's eye twitched. It took superhuman power not to crush his airway and wait for him to turn blue or drop him on his ass and kick it to the curb. Ian released Chris, leaving him gasping and rubbing his neck. Then he grabbed his suitcase and descended the stairs.

"Hey." Shane smiled, waiting by the front door. It faded when he saw Ian's murderous expression. "What's up, buddy?"

Ian set his suitcase on the ground by Shane. "I'll be out in a few minutes. There's something I need to do first."

"Sure you don't need me to stay?"

Ian didn't answer as he took long strides to the kitchen. Jersey tore her attention away from surveying the contents of the fridge to give him the once-over with a cautious expression.

"Pantry. Now." He pointed toward the tall cabinet doors.

She paused for a moment as if to let him know she would do her thing on her own time.

"*Now,* Jersey. Don't fuck with me. I need to leave."

She followed him, crossing her arms over her chest as Ian turned toward her in the corner of the pantry, and the door eased shut behind her.

"You're not a whore." His jaw muscles pulsed. "You're not a victim anymore. You're not even homeless, or starving, or at anyone's mercy. So why the fuck did you suck my dick, *vomit*, and tell your friend about it? I didn't ask you to do it. If it's some trigger for you, then why? Why would you do that?" A stomach-turning mix of anger and pain gripped him, torturing him with regret.

Jersey clenched her jaw as well, controlling her response with a few seconds of silence as he scowled, demanding an answer.

Ian waited.

No response.

She stared at his chest.

He wanted to shake the truth from her, but that would make him a hypocrite. So … he gave her time. But when she didn't move or speak, time ran out.

On a painful sigh, he brushed past her, grabbed a bottle of water, and headed toward the front door.

"Coop?"

He stopped with his hand on the doorknob, his back to her voice. Her feet padded toward him, and she wedged herself between him and the door, sliding her hands around his neck. When she tugged on him, he leaned down, resting his forehead on hers and closing his eyes.

"I … I wanted to do that. And I wanted to like it. I didn't want it to be a trigger. I didn't want anyone to see me running to the bathroom to vomit."

"Jersey …" he whispered, lazily rolling his forehead against hers. "Don't let him touch you."

Her head moved into a barely detectable nod, but he felt it, and it felt like hope. She pecked at his lips, but he didn't want to give in so easily. A stubborn part of him wanted to stay pissed off at her. But he couldn't put half a world between them without making things right. So he kissed her until the only thing holding her upright was his arms around her body.

She rubbed her lips together, letting a small grin slip. He smiled, feeling it in his veins like the ultimate high.

"Wish me luck, Jersey." He cradled the back of her head and kissed the top of it.

She rested a flat hand on his chest over his heart. "Luck, Coop."

CHAPTER TWENTY-ONE

JERSEY GAVE CHRIS the silent treatment for the next twenty-four hours. As they ate dinner, she set down her fork and asked the question that gnawed at her.

"Why?"

"Oh. Are we speaking again?" He glanced up from his plate.

"If you want me to get close to him, why say something to piss him off?"

"Him? Are you sure I didn't piss you off as well?"

"Yes. You pissed me off too. You're trying to derail everything I've done."

He coughed, bringing his napkin to his mouth. "Sorry. I'm a little lost. Aside from screwing him, what exactly have you done?"

"Trust, asshole. I'm gaining his trust. If he trusts me, then he tells me everything."

"Fine, buttercup. But while you're fucking the trust out of him, I'm doing the real work. I'm the reason Max looked into your past. I'm the one who put that bug in her ear, innocently expressing my concerns over your past and how it might affect our favorite rock star. I'm the one who sucker punched him with the truth about the post-concert blowjob. And you know…" he leaned back in his chair, pushing his plate away from the edge of the table "…I think good cop/bad cop is the way to go. I plant seeds of doubt in his mind; you swoop in to ride his dick and reassure him that all is well. That way, he'll never see it coming."

"See what coming?" Jersey stared out the window at the pool.

"The end."

She shook her head. "I don't know. I just … I'm not sure we have the right person."

"Oh, Jers …" He chuckled some more. "Let's go into a dark room. Let me bury my face between your legs for ten minutes, and I bet you'll forget what I look like, who I am, and that I was threatened with death if I touched you."

"You're an asshole." She controlled the urge to crawl across the table and bludgeon him with her fists—because a small part of him was right. Ian manipulated her with words, a look, a touch. Only, he wasn't knowingly manipulating her. "Wait … what do you mean threatened you with death if you touch me?"

"He's a little possessive of you, Jers. If you weren't going to kill him, I'd warn you to watch yourself. Guys like him are bad news."

"He said if you touched me, he'd kill you?"

Chris scratched the back of his neck and nodded. "I get it. I want to rip out his vocal cords every time he touches you." He gazed out the window.

Jersey opened her mouth to speak. Then clamped it

shut. Most of the time, Chris did a good job of hiding his insecurities, but in that moment, everything from his broken tone to his inability to look her in the eye reeked of insecurity. Ripping out someone's vocal cords felt possessive too.

Did sleeping next to him cross a line in his mind? Did he misinterpret their friendship?

"Well, if anyone kills you, it will be me. I won't let Ian do it."

He shot her a quick glance, and she returned a toothy grin.

"And you'll make ripping out his vocal cords part of his slow death, right?" Chris looked to her for reassurance.

Jersey chewed on the inside of her cheek for a few seconds before giving him a slow nod. An odd chime sounded from the other side of the kitchen. She glanced over her shoulder.

"Your phone, Jersey. It's ringing."

She looked for her phone, finding it under a kitchen towel. "Hello?"

It continued to ring.

"Swipe right, Jers."

She held it out and swiped right, bringing it back to her ear. "Hello?"

Ian chuckled; it was louder than she expected. "Hold it away from your face. It's a video chat."

Jersey looked at the screen and saw Ian's sexy smile and messy hair. He sipped a cup of coffee. Her grin took over her face. When she caught Chris's frown out of the corner of her eye, she took her tiny live version of Ian up the stairs to his bedroom.

"Coffee for dinner, Coop?" She shut the bedroom door and plopped down on his bed, resting her head on the padded headboard.

"Breakfast. It's early morning here."

"And where are you again?" She turned her head to the side and released her hair from its ponytail.

"Lisbon, Portugal."

"Where is—" She bit her lips together for a moment. "Uh … so when's your next concert?"

Ian set his coffee down and combed his fingers through his messy hair. Long bangs swept low onto his forehead. "Portugal is a southern European country next to Spain." He smiled—a sweet, nonjudgmental smile. "In case you were wondering. I'm terrible at geography. Thank god for the internet and instant maps."

"It's weird that you're that far away and I can see you like you're right here with me."

"Mmm … yes. But if I were in the same room, you'd feel me. In that way, video is incredibly inadequate."

Jersey wet her lips, unsure how to respond. She just liked seeing him on her screen.

"And the concert is tonight. I have a full day of press, so I wanted to seize my chance to chat with you before you went to bed. What did you do today?"

"Worked out—"

"Wait." He took another sip of coffee. "Start from the beginning."

"That is the beginning."

"No. You skipped the part about waking up."

"Um … okay. I woke up. Worked out—"

"Woke up in my bed?"

Jersey cocked a single brow. "I'm not your girlfriend or even your sometimes girlfriend. So if you think—"

"Why not?" He removed the lid from his coffee and blew on the steam. "If I don't have anyone in my bed and you don't have anyone in … well, my other bed with you, then you could be. Right? You could be my girlfriend. My sometimes, anytime, or all-the-time girlfriend. Right?"

"No." She laughed.

"Have you ever had a boyfriend?"

"No."

"I could be your first. You could do worse."

"Which means I could also do better."

"True." He inhaled and let it out slowly as his lips turned downward.

"Coop, you're supposed to say I can't do better than you."

"Well …" He lifted a single shoulder while glancing away like Chris did when he made his awkward confession in the kitchen. "That would be a lie, wouldn't it?"

Jersey didn't respond because she didn't know what to say. So she propped the phone up against the adjacent pillow and rolled to her side, resting her cheek on her folded hands. "What would you do if you weren't in a band?"

"Curl up next to you in that bed."

A shy smile overtook her lips. "That's not a profession."

"I don't know." He sipped more coffee, glancing at

his watch. "I never formulated a plan B. I knew it would hold me back, a safety net. Like the ladder to the high diving board. If you climbed to the top and someone took the ladder away, you'd have to jump. I didn't want a ladder, a safety net, or a plan B. I wanted to play my music. So if I weren't in a band, I'd be somewhere begging for stage time, sending tracks to record labels and producers, playing my music for absolutely anyone who would listen to it."

He glanced at his watch again.

"You have to go?"

He nodded. "I do. Are you going to bed?"

"No." She yawned.

"You sure about that?"

"I'm going to take a shower. Then have popcorn with Chris while he reads to me, if he hasn't given up on me and gone to bed already."

"He reads to you?"

"Yup."

"Why?"

"Because he likes to read, and I don't. But after he forced me into listening to him when we were at Marley's, I started to like the stories."

"Then why don't you read to yourself?"

Jersey picked at a piece of dry skin on her lip and shrugged. "I just don't. I'm not into blowjobs and reading. You have a problem with that?"

"Jersey…" Ian rubbed his forehead as someone knocked on his door. "I have to go."

"Okay." She pressed the red button that said "End."

A few seconds later a message popped up on her screen from Ian.

> **You have terrible video-chatting manners. It's like a phone conversation. We end with a goodbye. So ... goodbye. Goodnight. I miss you already.**

She grinned.

> **Goodbye Coop**

Jersey typed **I miss you too**, but then she deleted it. No need to miss him while he's alive.

SEVERAL DAYS LATER, Ian messaged Jersey, instead of doing a video chat. He strained his vocal cords and wasn't supposed to speak between concerts if at all possible. A week later, the problem continued, but they hadn't had to cancel any concerts yet.

Jersey emerged from the workout room, covered in sweat. Chris glanced up from the kitchen table and the laptop in front of him. He wrinkled his nose.

"What are you doing with Ian's computer?" She fetched a bottled water from the fridge.

"*Things.* I was able to login as a guest user."

"What sort of things?"

"Well, I thought of a way to make our rock star buddy feel a little pain in his life."

Jersey set the bottle on the counter and crossed her arms over her chest, attempting to look curious instead of defensive. Ian wasn't hers to defend. He was the target. "How?"

"You said he had some issues with his throat or vocal cords that were affecting his voice."

"So?"

"Well, I thought it might be fun to start a few rumors."

"About?"

"Lip-syncing."

"Lip-syncing?"

"Yes." Chris took a bite of his toast. "People don't like to pay a premium for concert tickets only to have the artist stand on stage and lip-sync to something prerecorded."

"He's not really singing on stage?"

"No, Jers, he is. But starting a rumor that he's not, coupled with the fact that he *is* having some voice issues, will cause him some grief. Anger some fans. Stir up shit in the media. It won't burn him to the ground, but he'll feel the heat."

The previous night she video-chatted with Ian because she wanted to see him. He did a lot of nodding, smiling, and soft talking because he was supposed to rest his voice. He drank some sort of throat tea and sucked on lozenges. Jersey found the subdued, almost shy version of Ian quite cute.

Cute. Yeah, she found him cute like a young girl crushing on a guy. She spent her young girl years trying to avoid being sexually abused followed by years on the street, so she missed those swooning years.

"What's wrong?" Chris asked.

She shrugged. "Nothing."

"*Nothing* is what you're saying, but I get this vibe that you're thinking *something*. Please tell me you're not feeling sorry for him. We don't have the luxury of sympathy when it comes to a rich guy who got away with murder."

"I know."

"Do you? Because when I told you I knew who killed the Russells, you were ready to tear his balls off. No name. No description. All that mattered to you were the facts. He killed them. He got away with it. Then the good Lord hands him to you on a silver platter—utensils, a cloth napkin, and a bottle of wine. Now, instead of tearing his balls off, you just want to roll them around in your hands and lick them. What has happened to you?"

Jersey tried to clench her hands, readying herself for a fight. But she couldn't hold a fist or her laughter. She rested her elbows on the counter and covered her face with her hands, laughing to the point of tears. "You are so messed up." Her body shook. "Who says that shit? Roll them around in my hands and lick them?"

"Thanks for taking this seriously." His focus returned to the computer. "Don't worry. I'll keep this plan moving forward while you scribble his name in your notebook and twirl your hair around your finger while talking to him late at night. 'You hang up,'" he said in a mocking, female voice, "'No, you hang up first. I love you. No. I love you more. Te he he.' Kill me now, Jers. Just kill me now."

"I've never said any of that. And I don't love him." She regained her composure as his incessant mocking diffused any residual spark of humor.

"Good to know." His fingers moved across the keyboard. "I'd imagine it's pretty hard to kill someone you love. But … if he loves you, then it's just that much sweeter. So really, if you're willing to suck his cock to play the revenge game, sleep in his bed, laugh at his jokes, then don't stop there. Go all the way. Tell him you love him. Don't stop short of an Oscar-winning performance."

"I'm not telling him that."

"No. Don't throw that shit out there unprovoked. Wait until he says it. Men need constant ego stroking. It's true. If he gets the nerve to say the words to you and you don't return the sentiment, his balls—that you enjoy licking and fondling—will most likely shrivel up, like overcooked marshmallows, and fall right off his body."

"No." She headed toward the stairs. "I'm not telling him that."

The legs of the chair screeched across the floor as Chris stood to follow her. "Why? If it's not real, if it's all an act, then you should be able to say absolutely anything. But if you actually think you could love him back, then I can see why you don't want to say it until you're ready. But if that's the case, Jers, then you need to tell me because that's one big fucking problem."

"I don't love him now, and I won't love him ever."

"I don't believe you."

She whipped around just outside of the entrance to the bedroom. "Then you're an idiot."

"Me?" Chris chuckled. "Bullshit. You're in over your head. I can see it in your eyes." He rested his hand on the newel post, sporting a smirk.

"Then you're blind. You can't see shit in my eyes."

"Then tell him. If he declares his love to you, tell him you love him too. Poison him with your words then slay him with your hands."

"Fine." She clenched her jaw.

"Fine?"

Jersey returned a sharp nod.

"You're in?"

Another nod.

"Say it, Jers. I need to hear you say it. *You* need to hear it come out of your mouth."

"I'm in."

"If he killed them, he dies."

Another nod.

"No. Say it!"

Jersey swallowed and narrowed her eyes. "If he killed them … he dies."

"Attagirl."

CHAPTER TWENTY-TWO

"Hi." Jersey tripped over her attempted enthusiasm when Ian called her after nearly two weeks of nothing but short texts. "No video chat today?"

"No. I've only got a few minutes. I have you on speaker while I get dressed. Max and Ames should be here soon to discuss damage control."

"Damage control for what?" She paced the bedroom.

"The stupid lip-syncing claims. I told you this."

"Oh, I didn't realize it was a big deal."

"My reputation—my career—spiraling down the toilet? Nope, no big deal."

"But if it's not true, then I don't see why you're concerned."

Ian sighed. "If your name gets dragged through the mud, even if the claims turn out to be false, it still leaves a mark. And it's the worst timing because I've had issues with my voice. So while the claims are not true, they are believable. It's like claiming you're not having an affair then pulling a woman's panties out of your pocket because you picked up the wrong jacket from the coat check. The fucking stress is killing me."

"Well, don't let the stress kill you."

That's my job.

She pulled her lower lip. "Your voice must be better."

"Yes, but it hasn't stopped the rumors. Any news on your passport?"

"Nope."

"How's Chris?" Ian said his name like he had a piece of sour candy lodged in his throat.

"You know … I've been meaning to ask you about your conversation with him before you left. Did you really say you'd kill him if he touched me?"

"Yes."

Jersey paused her pacing to let her jaw hang in the wind. She didn't really question if he said it. Chris had no reason to lie to her. She just didn't expect Ian to own it without a bit of hesitation, with such matter-of-fact confidence.

"You sound pretty tough for a guy whose most dangerous weapon is a microphone."

"Would you like me to underestimate you the way you underestimate me?" he asked.

"Oh, Coop … I think you do that anyway. But I'm curious. Are we talking poisoning him or something better fitted for a rich person?"

"Like hiring a hitman?" Genuine curiosity carried his words through the phone.

Jersey bit her thumbnail for a few seconds before making her move. "No. I think rich people just run other people over with their cars."

Silence.

More silence.

Her chest tightened, restricting a little more oxygen with each passing second. Why didn't he respond? Joke about the absurdity. Return a cynical laugh. Something!

"I have to go."

"What?" she managed to whisper the word, in spite of the nauseating knot in her stomach.

"Um …" He sounded distracted. "I have to go. I'll uh … call you later. Bye."

Jersey didn't get a goodbye out before he ended the call. She barely got a breath out. The phone dropped from her hand, and she squatted to pick it up, but she couldn't stand. The room began to spin. She covered her eyes. "Coop …"

Did the real bed, daily meals, clean clothes, and actual shampoo make her weak? Chris was right. She'd been given exactly what she wanted—the prime chance at revenge—but she lost her focus.

Ian killed Dena and Charles. He had to die. Jersey couldn't have a sexy rock star boyfriend *and* revenge. She had to make a choice.

THE FOLLOWING WEEK Jersey's passport arrived. "I got it." She held it up for Chris to see.

He set his book down on the sofa next to him and steepled his fingers at his mouth. "We move into the next phase."

Jersey inspected it, flipping through the pages. "Yeah."

"Don't sound so excited."

She grabbed her phone and texted Max.

Got my passport

"Excited … I'm not comfortable with that word. And maybe my limited vocabulary prevents me from finding the right word to express how I feel, but it's not excited."

Max replied.

I'll book you a flight for tomorrow

Jersey continued, "I don't think the executioners in prisons get excited. Well, maybe a few fucked-up ones do, but I think for most of them it's a job. They are doing their part to serve justice in the world.

"When I kill Ian, it won't excite me. It will simply be an end—justice for Dena and Charles. I won't feel any pride. I won't celebrate. After all, I'm most likely going to end up lying on a cold table with a needle in my arm and poison dripping into my veins."

Her eyes glassed over as she sighed. "It's probably how my life is meant to go. But I hope you can walk away and find something that makes you happy. Maybe you'll come into some money and you can pay for the surgeries you said would make your face look a little more …" Jersey's nose wrinkled.

"Human?"

She nodded. "Maybe you'll remember your past. What if you have a family and they just think you're dead? I mean … you could be a dad, Chris. I know I have nothing, but you could have everything waiting for you if your memory comes back. So …" Jersey gave him a resolute nod. "Yeah, let's go with that."

"If I have a wife, she's probably screwing my brother or boss by now."

Jersey smirked. "Probably." She shrugged. "Maybe they'd feel sorry for you and let you watch."

Chris bobbed his head from side to side. "Well, I do like to watch."

Giving him an eye roll, she shoved her phone into the pocket of her jeans. "Max is getting me a flight out tomorrow. I need to pack. Come read to me. I'm going to miss your sexy voice."

"You think my voice is sexy?" He followed her up the stairs.

"Oh yes. After you finish reading to me, I usually find a spot to touch myself."

"I officially hate you."

"You don't." She giggled. "You love me. And … I love you."

"You do?"

She shot him a tight-lipped grin over her shoulder. "Hmm … we'll never know. But the fact that you sound so damn happy at the possibility of it, gives a boost to my confidence. I'm certain I will be able to sell it to our rock star."

"You're one sick chick," he mumbled.

CHAPTER TWENTY-THREE

Basel, Switzerland

S HANE ACCOMPANIED A driver to pick Jersey up from the airport. He held up a sign with just the number six. She laughed, scolding herself for feeling something resembling a sense of belonging. Killers didn't belong.

"Mr. Popular couldn't break away to come get me himself?"

Shane glanced back from the passenger's seat, sunglasses low on his nose. "Not without Max killing him. He had an interview, a chance to slowly redeem his tarnished reputation."

Jersey frowned. Chris did a fantastic job of screwing with Ian's life. Why didn't Jersey share his enthusiasm?

"But he wanted to come. After a ten-minute argument between the two of them, I slipped out or else no one would have been on time to get you."

"That's fine. I'm just here for the free stay and food."

A hearty chuckle escaped him. Evidently, she wasn't that convincing.

They arrived at the hotel ahead of Ian and Max. Shane let her into the large suite. She recognized Ian's suitcase.

"I don't have my own room?" She lifted her brows.

"Not to my knowledge. I just do what I'm told. You'll have to take that up with Max and your boy."

"He's not my boy."

"Sure." Shane winked just before shutting the door behind him.

Jersey ignored the view, the spacious suite, and the chance to rifle through Ian's things in favor of crashing on the king-sized bed. She woke sometime later to the click of the door.

Blinking the sleep out of her eyes, she lifted onto her elbows. "Hey," she murmured in a sleepy voice, admiring the tall, sexy man prowling toward the bed. He shrugged off his shirt and toed off his shoes.

Jersey wet her lips out of instinct, angry at herself two seconds later for showing such obvious signs of need. The only thing she *needed* was to stay strong. There was one job to do, and it didn't involve ogling Ian and his body.

"Where have—" she started.

He held his index finger to his lips just before crawling toward her on the bed.

She fought the onslaught of emotions, especially the fluttery ones, the tingling ones, the ones that made her want to lick his chest and maybe … just maybe his balls too.

Biting back her grin, she let him peel the sheets from her body, exposing her bare legs, fitted white tee, and white panties. Ian grinned, not a cocky rock star grin, a genuine happy to see every inch of her grin.

Jersey reminded herself that he was a job, a mark, and they were a game that he would lose. Ian slid off her panties, reminding her that no game, no job, really nothing at all would ever be more pleasurable.

The first sound he made wasn't a greeting or an explanation of where he'd been. It was a low hum from his chest when his mouth settled between her spread legs.

She kept her upper body lifted onto her elbows, chin tipped toward her chest as he kissed her, keeping his gaze locked to hers until she felt the first wave of pleasure hit, making her feel instantly dizzy and drunk. Her head fell backward, mouth open, eyes closed.

"Coop … oh Jesus … Coop …" She gripped the sheets.

He kissed his way up her body, taking her tee with him, pulling it over her head, leaving her completely naked. "Miss me, baby?" he whispered in her ear before sitting back and pulling off his jeans.

She swallowed over and over again, eyeing his erection, his tight abs—sinewy arms taut, eyes dark.

Jersey let her gaze slide up to meet his, giving him a tiny grin before returning her attention to his lower body settling between her legs.

Baby. She wasn't anyone's baby. No orphan was. But Ian made her feel something no one else ever did, and for that, he could call her anything he wanted.

He kissed her like the final song of a concert. Giving her everything, making a lasting impression. At the same time, he thrust into her, slowly building the tension between them. His hands ghosted along her body, as if she were breakable. Then they framed her face, as if she were a priceless work of art.

That was it. Ian Cooper made her feel wanted.

Honestly.

Deeply.

Undeniably … wanted.

The seemingly endless kiss lasted until they were nothing more than two desperate, naked bodies racing to the end, out of breath, in need of that final moment when everything just erupted with waves of something too powerful to put into words.

She had no idea what time it was when he pulled her to him on their sides, chest to chest, legs scissored, her face buried in the crook of his neck, his hands idle in her hair. G used to hold her until she went to sleep. And sometimes if Fisher only took G to do his sick shit, Jersey would lie behind G in her bed and stroke G's hair, hoping it would comfort her.

Fisher's hands in Jersey's hair made her skin crawl, but a weird part of her needed to do it to G. As if balancing the bad with the good.

The only difference … Jersey cried, not only for herself, but for G too. G never cried. She was silent, strong, and always there for Jersey. She wondered if Ian would be there for her like that. And if he were, would it be out of caring for Jersey or would it be out of pity?

"WHAT TIME IS it?" Jersey mumbled hours later, not having moved from her spot nestled into Ian's body.

He kissed the top of her head. "Dinnertime."

She imagined that moment being one she'd remember for the rest of her short life.

His body dwarfed hers like a protective shield.

The possessiveness—the false security—of his hands, one in her hair, the other low on her back.

The warmth. She'd remember the warmth of his body long after his heart stopped pumping blood.

But more than anything, she'd remember how the same person who took away her future, also filled a physical need and an emotional dream, if only for a moment in time.

In some ways … everything about him felt familiar, like she'd experienced something with him in another life.

A blink.

A whisper.

A flash.

It haunted her in ways she couldn't explain.

"Coop?" Her lips pressed to his neck, lingering there until his pulse kissed her back.

"Hmm?" His large hand drifted just below her butt, pulling her an inch closer to him.

"Are you afraid of dying?"

"No," he murmured, ghosting his lips along the top of her head before kissing it.

"Why not?"

"Because I've always thought living in fear has to be worse than death. We stop living when we let in that fear."

Her head inched side to side.

"No?" He pulled back until he could see her face. "You disagree?"

"I think we only have fear when we have something in life that means enough to us that we can't imagine losing it. That fear is how we know we're alive. It makes us fight to stay alive." Her eyes narrowed as her gaze shifted to the side. "I don't think it has to be a person. Maybe it's a purpose or a chance at something."

Ian scraped his teeth along his lower lip, returning a sluggish nod, contemplating her words as they settled between them.

"Are you afraid of dying?"

"Yeah," she whispered. "I think that fear is the only reason I'm still alive."

"What do you fear?"

Her heart crashed against her ribcage, over and over. Did he feel it? Her fear came like a storm, desperate and destructive. "I fear dying without making things right in the world—in my world."

Ian rolled over, settling his body between her legs, forearms next to her head. "My world has been shit lately, until I saw you in this bed a few hours ago." He brushed his nose along her cheek. "Now everything feels right in *my* world."

Several knocks pounded at the door. He grabbed her leg, hiking it up so he could push into her.

Jersey's breath hitched as the ache of wanting him but needing to kill him feuded in the tiny space that housed the remnants of her conscience. "Th-the door …" She bit her lip and blinked heavily.

"Fuck off!" He yelled over his shoulder while gripping her leg tighter, sinking deeper into her.

The knocking stopped.

Everything about him haunted her. Jersey wondered how much of herself she would have to surrender to make her world right. So she let her conscience work that out while she kissed him.

The kiss. It always felt right. The only kiss that had ever felt right.

His touch felt familiar. A-million-lifetimes-ago familiar.

They were the perfect kind of wrong.

JERSEY WIGGLED OUT of his arms before he had a chance to catch his breath. She sat on the edge of the bed with her head down.

"You okay?" He rested his head on his propped-up arm. Ian didn't know how to describe sex with Jersey other than a war of sorts, maybe between them, maybe between her mind and her body.

Anger.

Anguish.

Addiction.

They screwed like junkies—powerless to the pull, in denial of the effects, and destined to do it again and again.

She thought he was her truth, but he knew it was a lie.

"Yeah. I'm fine." She straightened her back, inhaled

sharply, and stood, padding to the bathroom without looking back.

The door shut, and Ian slipped on his jeans, fishing his phone out of the pocket. A string of missed messages from Max and Ames cluttered his screen. On a deep sigh, he clicked on them and scrolled through the chaos and panic.

The good news? No one's talking about the lip-sync scandal. The bad news? The world knows a homeless woman is at your hotel. They know she has a record. They know she killed a man. They know she assaulted two of your employees.

This isn't good, Ian.

He tossed his phone aside since the rest of her messages were nothing more than her frustration over him not responding to her or answering her incessant knocking at his door.

The toilet flushed. The faucet ran for a long time. Then Jersey opened the door to the bathroom. Her hair was a little wet in front like she washed her face. A white terry cloth robe covered her body. And a sadness resided in her eyes.

Ian sat on the edge of the bed with his hands folded between his legs. "I don't trust Chris." He held no hesitation or regret in his voice.

Jersey stopped halfway between the bed and the bathroom. "I don't trust anyone."

He tried and failed to hide his slight grimace. What had he done to lose her trust? Or was he a fool for thinking he ever had it at all?

"I think he's telling people about you."

She lifted her eyebrows as a cryptic grin played along her lips. "What's there to tell? And who would he tell? He has nothing more than a first name, a disfigured body, and one friend who happens to be in Switzerland."

"I don't know. It's just a feeling, a vibe I get when I'm around him. But you're my new news story, the next chapter in my saga, and I have no clue how this happened. Do you?"

He studied her—every blink, the focus of her gaze, the curve of her spine, and the tension in her jaw.

"No."

He nodded slowly, lips twisted, eyes unblinking. "Can I trust you?"

"No." Her answer fell from her lips with no emotion but complete resolution.

It knocked the wind out of him for a moment.

Jersey untied the sash to her robe and slipped it off her shoulders, letting it pool at her ankles. As Ian searched for a response, she pulled on her clothes and tied her hair back into a ponytail.

"Why?" he finally asked, feeling the ache of disillusion in his chest.

She stood between his legs and pressed her warm palms against his cheeks for a few seconds before dragging her fingers through his hair. "The first time Mr. Fisher touched me—made me touch him—I cried for hours. G carried me from the basement to her bedroom. I told her how I trusted him because the lady with social services promised it was a good home and I could trust the

Fishers. G told me to trust no one. Not ever. She said trust is what we do when we have no other choice. Death or trust? Go with trust, but you might end up dead anyway."

"G sounds like a cynic."

Jersey squinted.

He twisted his lips. "Someone who has little faith in mankind."

"I suppose it's hard to have faith in mankind when you spend your whole childhood with men who are anything but kind."

Ian rested his forehead against her chest, his hands on the back of her legs, and he closed his eyes. She continued to run her fingers through his hair. Ian loved that so much he tried to keep from moving or speaking. Could a killer's hands bring such pleasure, calm nerves, soothe souls?

Yes.

Her stomach growled. Ian ignored it. It growled again. He looked up, ending the perfect moment. "When did you last eat?"

"Not sure. On the plane. They offered me food all the time. And drinks. Everything was free. But it was weird traveling on a big plane with so many people. Not as much room to myself."

He chuckled. Maybe he wasn't supposed to trust her, but he liked her. He liked her in a way that made him feel more vulnerable than he'd ever felt in his life. Horrible men tried to rob her of her innocence, but they didn't succeed. Jersey had a light, an innocence that no one could take from her.

"You're unknowingly a plane snob."

"A what?"

"Your first plane was a private jet, an experience most people never get. It's the most luxurious way to travel. Really wealthy people, including ego-driven rock stars, travel that way. You flew here first-class commercial. It's how most fairly well-off people travel. You had all the luxuries of a commercial airline. But …"

She kept her eyes slightly squinted—the innocent side of Jersey Six.

"A majority of people travel coach. They get pretzels and pop, maybe one meal on an international flight. The seats are smaller and recline approximately two inches, less legroom, and no warm towels before your meals." He leaned up and kissed her neck. "I've spoiled you."

Jersey blinked several times, jaw slack. "Huh. I had no idea."

"I'll send you home coach, just so you can experience all forms and comfort levels of air travel."

"Mmm…" Jersey nodded several times, concentration etched into her expression. "When I go home …" she whispered as if she didn't say it for his ears.

"But I'm not sending you home—yet." He pulled her closer, forcing her to fall into him, straddling his lap, arms around his neck. "I haven't shown you the world—yet."

She returned a sad smile and a slow blink while letting her gaze fall between them, chin down. "Coop, I'm afraid."

His hand slid around her neck to the back of her head, pulling her closer, so his lips grazed her ear. "So am I," he whispered.

CHAPTER TWENTY-FOUR

Paris, France
Esc-sur-alztte, Luxembourg
Amsterdam, Netherlands
Berlin, Germany
Cologne, Germany
Gothenburg, Sweden
Stolkholm, Sweden

FIVE WEEKS AND eight stops after Jersey arrived in Switzerland, they hit the tour's halfway point in Liverpool, U.K. It didn't matter that Jersey refused to call herself Ian Cooper's girlfriend. The media stamped her with that label and a lot of other labels that were much worse. But … they didn't know her name and that was a silver lining for the Ian Cooper camp.

No name meant no way to dig up more dirt on her than what had already been mysteriously leaked about "the woman in his bed." Jersey gave Chris a little bit of credit for not entirely destroying her in his attempts to bring down the rock star. She liked being a no name to the media.

Ian let Max and his manager know that Jersey wasn't

going anywhere, and they needed to deal with it along with the rest of the world. He kept her close to his side, holding her hand, kissing her at will with no concern for the flashing cameras and gossip frenzy.

Jersey played the part, drawing him into her world, priming him for a confession. She took her clothes off anywhere, and at a moment's notice, whenever Ian felt the need to have her—which was often. It was her favorite part of the plan—and the most dangerous part. Every time she let him inside of her, he took a piece away. As the weeks passed, she felt herself changing, weakening, missing those pieces that held her together and kept her strong. Resolute.

"Ian! Ian! Ian! Ian!" It didn't matter where they were in the world, the chant was always the same.

"They want you," Jersey said, buttoning her jeans as Ian pieced himself back together following their precon-cert ritual which involved something quick and dirty that Max insisted they finish in under fifteen minutes.

Three minutes, forty-two seconds was their record.

"More than you?" he asked with his signature smirk firmly in place. Ian excelled in cocky. Really, he excelled in all things.

"Probably." Jersey shrugged, hiding her grin.

He charged toward her, picking her up while continu-ing his forward movement until her back slammed into the door. His mouth took hers, and she kissed him just as eagerly without having to think.

They were always explosive.

Always ready to attack each other.

Always insatiable.

And always in trouble with Max.

"Tomorrow is the day, right?" he mumbled over her skin as he kissed his way down her neck, his hand sliding up her shirt, yanking the cup of her bra down. "Tomorrow is the day I stop needing you so fucking much. Right?"

"Tomorrow …" Jersey echoed with little conviction as her head fell back against the door.

Bang! Bang! Bang!

"Showtime! Let's go." Max maintained a flawless record of perfectly timed announcements.

Ian let Jersey slide down the door until her feet found the ground. He grinned, fixing her bra as she made a few adjustments to his hair and straightened his shirt.

On a begrudging sigh, he opened the door, taking her hand and following Max toward the stage with Shane bringing up the rear.

Max handed him his in-ear monitor and headed up the stairs to the side of the stage.

"Wish me luck, Jersey," he yelled in her ear over the roar of the crowd exploding as the rest of the band took the stage.

"Luck, Coop." She grinned.

He kept ahold of her hand and made his way up the stairs, stealing one last kiss at the top before grabbing his guitar and strutting into the spotlight.

Jersey watched on with adoration, even if she refused to acknowledge it. Max draped her arms over Jersey's shoulders from behind her. "You've stolen their dreams,

Jersey." She laughed. "Look at them. You've taken their rock star, all of him. And they know it."

"You came to me
Cracked and worn
Strong and fierce

Needing something
With nothing to give"

Ian sang a new song, closing his eyes, gripping the microphone, face wrought with pain.

Jersey glanced around to see if any of the crew looked at her, but they didn't. They watched their guy make love with his voice—his lyrics—to thousands of fans. A single spotlight shone on him, making it feel incredibly intimate as he sang an acoustic song with just the raw notes of Bryson on the piano.

"Are you the beginning
Or are we the end

Who will love the unlovable
Who will make something of nothing
Who will cry for you when you're gone

Let it be me
Let me be the one
The one who cries for you
Let my hand guide you
Let my heart love you

Everyday I'd miss you
Let it be me
Let me be the one"

Jersey sucked in a shaky breath, shoving her hands into her pockets as she blinked back an onslaught of emotions. Anger being the strongest emotion. Why did he sing those words?

"When there's nothing left to say
And surrender finds its way
When trust is all that remains
And you give in to your fear"

Ian turned his head, gripping the mic close to his lips while ensnaring Jersey's gaze. He held it hostage, along with her breath and next heartbeat.

"Let it be me
Let me be the one
The one who cries for you
Let my hand guide you
Let my heart love you
Everyday I'd miss you
Let it be me
Let me be the one"

He repeated the chorus again. The venue fell silent before the last line. Eerily silent. Then he sang the last five words alone, bringing everyone to their feet, hands in the air clapping, screaming, shaking the entire venue.

Ian grinned. "Thank you, Liverpool! I hope you liked my new song, 'Unloved.'"

Just as Jersey swiped at an errant tear, Ian glanced her way again. She hated that he saw it.

Unloved.

"I'm nothing…" she whispered *"…insignificant … forgettable … no one would miss me if I died. No one would look for me if I were lost. No human has ever cried for me."*

"I am unloved."

After his final song, he took the bottled water from Max in one hand and laced the fingers of his other hand with Jersey's, leading her down the stairs to the green room.

"You hungry?" He released her hand and shrugged off his sweaty shirt, slipping on a dry one.

"Coop …" she whispered.

He glanced up, zipping his bag.

"It's me. You wrote that song for me. I am unloved." It hurt to say those words. In front of thousands of people, he exposed every single one of her insecurities. Could she kill her greatest weakness?

He hiked his bag over his shoulder and closed the distance between them with calculated steps. On a long inhale, he bit his lips together and nodded. "Yes. I wrote that song for you." Leaning down, he pushed her hair away from her ear and brushed his lips across it. "But no, you're not unloved."

Jersey's fingers curled into the hair on the back of his head, holding him close so he couldn't see her reaction.

He kissed her neck just below her ear, and she blinked away the rush of vulnerability.

On the way back to the hotel, Jersey gave her attention to the streets of Liverpool. Ian squeezed her hand every few minutes. She remained still, not squeezing back, not looking at him, not uttering a word.

"What's wrong?"

"Nothing," she mumbled without a glance, without a single blink.

The lie hung in the air between them, making it hard to breathe.

"Have you ever done something really horrible?" she murmured.

When he didn't answer, she turned her head, studying his pensive expression through the shadows and flashes of night lights flickering through the windows. His brows pulled inward as he nodded slowly.

She forced a swallow in spite of the desert in her mouth. "How horrible?"

Ian's gaze shifted to the front seat. He never seemed to care about Shane's presence, often talking about anything without concern. He clearly trusted Shane, until that moment.

Jersey didn't push him, fearing he might clam up. She had him where she needed him. He all but said the words "I love you." If he meant it, he would tell her *everything*. She had little knowledge of love, but the part of her that could imagine it believed it was all or nothing.

At the hotel, Ian locked himself in the bathroom, turning on the shower, leaving Jersey and her question without any sort of acknowledgment. After concerts, he rode an adrenaline high, and they barely made it to the room before he was deep inside of her, half naked, and insane with need.

She liked that Ian, riding the high with him, feeling so wanted—so needed. But that Ian was nowhere to be found. Had she already lost him?

Nick arrived with food, much earlier than Jersey was used to seeing him. It's as if he knew Ian wasn't fucking her against every surface of the hotel room.

"You're fast tonight." She fished containers out of the sacks.

"I was told to be quick. He used the term *starving.*" Nick pulled down the bed, setting out his alcohol, wipes, and needles on the nightstand.

"He's in pain?"

"I think he's always in pain." Nick shrugged.

The shower stopped running.

Jersey stared at the closed door. "I need you to leave."

"What?" Nick murmured like he was half listening to her while continuing his routine.

"I need you to leave," she repeated with more of an edge to her voice.

He stopped his busy hands and faced her. "How long do you need?"

"We'll see you tomorrow."

"But he asked me to—"

"Listen, I know you work for him, but if you want all of your body parts to work for you, then I suggest you leave before he comes out of the bathroom." Her mouth thinned into a line. "It's not personal, Nick. Okay?"

Flitting his gaze between the bathroom door and Jersey's ridged body with clenched hands, he nodded once and exited the room.

A few minutes later, Ian emerged from the bathroom, wearing nothing but a pair of black shorts and wet hair. He glanced around the room as Jersey shoveled pasta into her mouth from her seat at the kitchenette table. "Where's Nick?"

"How horrible?" She wiped her mouth with her arm and took a drink of his fancy bottled water.

"*Nick.* Jersey ... where's Nick?"

"I told him we'd see him tomorrow."

"You can't just—"

"How horrible? Just answer the fucking question."

Ian didn't flinch. His expression remained stoic, numb like his emotions. Jersey knew about numb. Numb was how you navigated life after killing someone.

Good.

Bad.

It didn't matter. Taking a life changes a person forever, like brutally taking away someone's virginity. Everything after that is nothing more than a dead string of events, marking time until the next life—a clean slate.

"Do you know what stands between me and you?" he asked, grabbing a gray T-shirt and pulling it over his head.

She narrowed her eyes.

"Your best friend." Ian grabbed a bowl of pasta and peeled off the lid, looking for a fork, a napkin, his water … looking at anything but Jersey.

"No. What stands between us is you not sharing anything about your past. I've told you everything about mine. I told you I killed a man—"

"No." He chuckled, while shaking his head. "Max told me you killed a man. Try again."

"I didn't deny it."

"It's public record, Jersey. There *is* no denying it."

The game. It needed to end.

She didn't have a weapon with her, but she had her fists and a need for revenge that outweighed self-preservation. If she wasn't afraid of the consequences, then why was Ian Cooper still alive? Did he *have* to confess?

Yes.

He did. He had to say it. She needed to know why. And how. How does a monster write a song for a homeless girl? How could he feel deserving of the fame and money?

Air … how could he feel deserving of air, of life?

Jersey pushed her half-eaten bowl of pasta to the middle of the table and affixed her gaze to Ian. "When I was fourteen, they placed me in a home with three other foster kids. I was the oldest. For the first time in my life, I felt like I belonged. I felt loved."

She drew in a shaky breath and let it out slowly. "But more than that, I felt safe. You see, this couple, they weren't the first to say the words *I love you*. They were the first to actually do it—love me like parents should love their child. They gave me a family, a family that didn't have fucked-up secrets. They hugged me, but never inappropriately. They didn't watch me shower or dress. They didn't crawl into my bed at night and tell me how special I was for letting them touch me."

Ian swallowed hard; his face warped with pain.

"I dreamed, Coop. Not just of getting out of a bad situation. Not of anyone dying so I didn't have to be abused. I dreamed real dreams. Dreams of a future. Friends coming over for sleepovers. Shopping for prom dresses. Being adopted and having real parents. Choosing a college. Getting a job. Buying a car …" She grunted a laugh. "A driver's license. I dreamed of having freedom. The fucking American dream."

He opened his mouth to speak, but she wasn't ready for his meaningless "I'm sorrys." She didn't want an apology. Jersey wanted a confession and an explanation. When she watched him take his last breath, she needed to know there was nothing left to say.

"Their names…" she continued before he interrupted "…were Charles and Dena Russell. I should have been Jersey Russell." She shook her head a half dozen times. "No. Not even that. Not Jersey. Nothing to remind me of how worthless I was to my mother.

"I mean … who leaves their baby at a fire station? And then why show up months later, acting like you're ready to be a mom when you're high? Why ruin your child's chance of being adopted into a good family by holding on to some stupid string of hope that you're going to get your shit together?"

"Jersey …" Ian's voice cracked.

"No." Her eyes burned with unshed tears. "You're not allowed to feel sorry for me. I … I was going to have a family. Shortly after they placed me with Dena and Charles, my birth mom died. She OD'd. And since there was no record anywhere of my biological father, the Russells would have been able to adopt me. And…" she blew out a quick breath and lifted her gaze to the ceiling "…I would have been Rachel or Abigail … maybe a Heather. Heather Russell. Something common, simple, normal."

Nothing.

Ian gave her absolutely nothing.

Not a flinch.

Not a blink of recognition.

Not a drop of blood draining from his face at the mention of Charles and Dena.

Was he innocent?

Or ruthless?

"Do you know how they died?" She pinned him with a look, daring him to move. Daring him to lie. Daring him to run one more step from the truth and the consequences.

"I'm having Chris removed from my house."

Her eyebrows lifted up her forehead. "Excuse me?"

Ian gnashed his teeth. "I don't like him texting you, calling you, filling your head with lies."

And just like that, Jersey's world tipped onto its side. Kind Ian vanished, and the monster emerged. She crossed a line, and he wasn't ready to let her see what was on the other side. He wanted to get rid of the gatekeeper.

"How horrible, Ian?" She pushed away from the table and stood, balling her hands.

"Now I'm Ian?"

Her nose burned with emotion, tears like acid, rage like an inferno. Every inch of her body vibrated with anger. "It was an early Friday morning. Charles and Dena took their usual morning walk together. They trusted me to stay at home with the three younger kids. We were usually still asleep by the time they returned.

"Hand in hand. That's how they always walked, like sharing their love with abandoned children only intensified their love for each other. They were never gone more than an hour. I knew … I just knew something wasn't right. It was almost lunchtime when several cars parked out front; two of them were police cars. I don't remember their exact words. I just remember the ones in my head. *You're not getting real parents and a new name. You're not going shopping for a prom dress. You're not going to college. You're once again … unloved.*"

"You're not un—"

"I am!" She pounded her fists on the table, knocking the glass bottle over, sending water running off the edge of it.

The ghost of sympathy on Ian's face hardened into something else, something she couldn't quite identify.

"Lyrics don't mean anything, if you don't give me everything. And even if I want to let myself believe that Chris loves me, I know it's because I'm all he has. Our love isn't real. I'm not a choice for him. I'm just his only option. But some day he will remember everything, and he will find his family. But for now, he is the only truth in my life because, even if it's not much, he's giving me everything he has to give."

She closed her eyes, jaw clenched, and took a slow breath. "Someone ran them over. They killed them. They drove off. They got away with murder. They put three young kids back on the fucking market, probably destined to land in a shitty home. And they evicted me from *my* home, my whole goddamn life!"

After her echo evaporated and a cloud of silence filled the room, Ian stood, meeting her hard gaze. "I'm sorry."

Her nose twitched with anger. "I don't want an apology." Each word teetered on the edge of control, grating past her throat to find her lips.

Ian grabbed the back of his neck and just kept his hand there, soothing some physical pain or holding himself together. She wasn't sure.

"What do you want?" he asked.

"A confession." Her chin tipped up a fraction, eyes narrowed.

"From whom?"

"You."

"What is my confession?"

If she said it, there would be no going back. Her access to Ian Cooper could end in a matter of seconds. And maybe that was okay. The time had come to end it. To end him.

"For the record," Jersey whispered, glancing down at the mess on the table. What was left of her heart crumbled, disintegrating into dust, into nothing. "I think I could have loved you."

Thump! Thump! Thump!

Jersey jumped as they turned toward the door.

Thump! Thump! Thump!

"Ian!"

He brushed past Jersey, opening the door. Max charged inside. "Why haven't you answered your phone?"

Ian nodded toward the bathroom. "I left it on the vanity after my shower. What the hell is going on?"

Max held up her phone and the video playing on the news app. Ian narrowed his eyes at the screen, slowly taking the phone from her hand, lips parted. The volume wasn't turned up enough for Jersey to hear it well.

"I'm sorry," Max whispered.

Jersey remained statuesque in the corner of the room. She confessed to him something that was only meant for him to hear right before he died. But he didn't die.

"Cancel the rest of the tour," he said with no emotion to his voice.

"Ian—"

"Cancel it!" He shoved the phone back into her hand. Eyes pinched shut, jaw muscles flexing.

"Jeanine said the neighbors were out of town. Had he not been there—"

"We're going home. Now."

Max nodded slowly. It was a rare moment when she let her vulnerability surface—at a loss for words, at a loss for control.

"Jersey—" Max took a step toward her.

"I'll tell her." Ian interrupted Max again.

She backed up to the door, giving Jersey a sad smile before leaving them alone.

Whatever he watched on her screen should not have changed the course of their fate, but it did. Ian silenced Max and unarmed Jersey with a look, a tone, a new side she had not seen before. It made her feel like someone pummeling her into the ropes, the way Racer did to her so many years earlier.

After several minutes, Ian turned, meeting Jersey's gaze. "My house is on fire."

Jersey flinched. "Chris …"

"He's fine. Saved my dogs. A real fucking hero on the news right now."

Fire. The man who survived a horrific accident and lost everything but his actual heartbeat had to escape the jaws of twisted fate again.

Jersey despised the contempt on Ian's face. Only a monster would show so much anger toward a hero. Ian's life was spared, but only temporarily. Jersey knew what needed to be done. As soon as they returned to L.A., she planned on digging his grave amongst the rubble of his house.

CHAPTER TWENTY-FIVE

Jersey: *We're on our way home. What happened?*

She shot off a text to Chris on their way to the airport.

Chris: *Gas explosion at the neighbor's house. The wind carried the flames to Ian's house. So tragic.*

Jersey stared at his message, trying to decipher the meaning and the context of his words.

Jersey: *Where are you?*

Chris: *Another neighbor's house. The Blevins. I'm a hero at the moment. On every news channel. Saved the dogs. Called 9-1-1. Warned the other neighbors to evacuate. I've already had people offer to adopt me, feed me, house me. Better late than never, right?"*

Jersey: *He did it.*

She stared at the three pulsing dots on the screen. Did Chris understand what she meant?

Chris: *Not news to me. But I'm glad you've seen*

Jesus.

Jersey: *?*

Chris: *The truth. Why haven't you done your thing?*

Jersey: *Because you had to be a hero.*

Chris: *Sorry. I didn't think you'd grow a pair and do it.*

Jersey: *Fuck you.*

Chris: *Love you too. Have a safe trip.*

Jersey: *Do you?*

Chris: *?*

She stared at the screen, keeping it tipped away from Ian's line of sight. Not that it mattered, he seemed content with ignoring her.

Jersey: *Love me. If you got all of your memory back tomorrow, and you found out you have a life waiting for you, would you love me?*

Chris: *Absolutely. If you asked me to leave my imaginary wife and kids for you, I would do it in a heartbeat.*

Swiping out of the message screen, she tucked the phone into her bag and tipped her head back, closing her eyes.

As soon as they were in the air, the flight attendant closed the curtain, giving Ian and Jersey privacy. Jersey leaned her seat back. Ian watched her from the wide sofa that doubled as a bed, the bed where they usually had sex.

"I'm not taking my clothes off for you." She frowned, holding his unreadable gaze.

He blinked a few times, not looking like a man who cared if Jersey took her clothes off for him. "Finish telling me what you were going to say before Max interrupted us. On the record you said, 'I think I could have loved you.' There was a *but* coming. Finish it."

"Not now," she whispered, exhausted from a long day. Almost twenty hours without sleep.

"It has to be now."

"I'll finish it if you tell me how horrible the thing is you did."

"Horrible enough to leave that life behind." For the first time, she could see lines of regret on his face and hear it in his weak voice.

"Tell me."

He closed his eyes and mumbled, "Not now."

"JESUS ..." MAX frowned as they pulled into the driveway.

Half of Ian's house looked charred. The other half seemed untouched. Chris traipsed through the front yard from the Blevins's house with Ian's dogs. Ian climbed out and greeted Lola and Foxy while Chris opened Jersey's door.

She fell into his arms, her mind riddled with the events and revelations of the previous twenty-four hours.

Ian glanced at her, looking like he could murder someone. Jersey didn't care. His days of killing would soon come to an end, and so would hers.

"I missed you." Chris squeezed her.

"Missed you too. I'm so glad you're okay. You had to be freaking out. I mean …" She looked him over when he released her. "Did it trigger any emotions or memories?"

Chris eyed Ian and shook his head.

"Were you here when it happened?"

"Yeah. I heard the explosion, but I didn't know where it came from. I ran outside, and that's when I saw the neighbor's house. I called 9-1-1 while running toward the fire. I had no idea if anyone was home, but I wanted to make sure they got out. The doors were locked, and before I knew it, the side of Ian's house was in flames." He spoke to Jersey but kept his gaze on Ian, just a few feet away, the whole time. He seemed distracted by Ian.

"So I ran back over here and rescued the dogs. The fire sprinklers turned on right after I got through the front door. It appears most of the damage inside is from water and smoke."

Jersey's gaze followed Ian as he walked around the taped-off perimeter with Shane and Max.

"Hope they know they're not supposed to go inside until the fire chief gives them permission," Chris said.

Jersey didn't respond. Her thoughts felt like sludge.

Tragedy.

Murder.

Shock.

Lies.

Deception.

Love. That was the hardest emotion to handle.

"What's up with the rest of the tour?" Chris folded his arms over his chest and leaned against the vehicle.

She shrugged. "I think it's been canceled. I heard them talking about a major setback on top of the already bad publicity. And supposedly his record label could drop him or sue him."

"Thanks to us."

Jersey inwardly cringed. Why did ruining Ian feel worse than killing him?

"Had we known this would happen, we might not have had to do any more than sit back and watch fate do its thing."

Chris chuckled. "Are you kidding me?"

She shot him a squinted look. "What do you mean?"

"Jesus, Jers ... I thought we were just role playing for shits and giggles and the proximity of the enemy." He nodded toward the house where Ian, Max, and Shane were out of earshot.

"What are you—"

He pivoted, putting everyone else at his back, at least twenty yards away. Looming over Jersey, he waited for her to look up at him. "Listen, my very best friend in the whole wide world, I fear you grossly underestimated the level at which this game of revenge needs to be played. We agreed to destroy him in every way. You have been trying to fuck him to death, while I've been doing real things to make his life miserable."

Jersey's mouth opened, but nothing came out.

"You sliced open a man's torso and watched him bleed out. You don't get to give me the doe-eyed look of shock for starting a little fire."

"A-a little fire?" she stuttered, pointing toward the neighbor's house. "*You* did this? Why did you blow up *their* house?"

Chris twisted his face, pulling his head back in disbelief. "Um … duh, I'm pretty sure setting Ian's house on fire would have drawn negative attention and suspicion toward me. But…" he held up his finger like the best idea in the world just popped into his head "…Ian's house being collateral damage and me saving his precious dogs—even if he's too much of a dick to say thank you— was a brilliant idea. Don't you think?"

"No! You—"

"Fuck. Fuck. Fuck it all anyway! You love him, Jers." He pressed his palms to the side of his head.

Her face wrinkled as she swallowed her anger and his bitter-tasting accusation.

"And you're right, Jers, about what you said awhile back. Giving a life and taking a life for someone are two different things. I don't know if I can go all the way and actually kill him. So this…" he nodded toward the rubble "…is as far as I can go. I double and triple checked that no one was home next door because I wasn't willing to actually let someone die. Deep in my conscience, I carry this awful feeling that whatever happened to me…" he held out his scarred arms "…probably didn't end well for someone else."

Jersey watched as Ian, Shane, and Max crossed the

tape and entered the house.

"Jers, I didn't lose my future when Dena and Charles died. I wasn't still living with them. I can grieve them and feel anger toward the man who killed them, but I lost my future in a fire. My anger is not motivated in the same way yours is. What happened to them is tragic in my mind, but it happened to *them*. And … it happened to you. Demand the truth and decide what you can live with. My part is done. I'm going to sit back and watch him suffer through all of this. How long he suffers and how his suffering ends is up to you."

Jersey rubbed her eyes and ran her fingers through her hair.

"Are you going to tell them they shouldn't be in there?" he asked.

She shook her head.

Chris pushed away from the car and started walking toward the house.

"Where are you going?"

He sighed. "To warn them. I have to. My conscience is full."

A few minutes later, they funneled out from the front door. Jersey shared a nervous smile, like she would have gone in to warn them had Chris not already been headed that way. She reserved her I-don't-give-a-fuck-about-anyone smile for another time. Ian set Foxy and Lola down and pulled his phone out of his pocket, reading something on the screen.

"You can stay with me," Max said.

Ian shook his head. "Paul Blevins said they're on their

way to the airport. He's sorry they missed seeing us and sorry about the fire. They'll be in Italy for three months. He said we're welcome to stay at his house. Apparently, he showed Chris everything about the security system."

Jersey frowned at the way Ian said Chris's name with such disgust. On the upside, his attitude fueled her anger toward him, and that was what she needed to carry out her plans.

Ian slipped his phone back into his pocket and scrubbed his face with his hands.

"Do you want me to take your bags over there?" Shane asked.

Ian nodded, letting his hands drop from his face on a big sigh.

"Want me to take your dogs back to the neighbor's house?" Chris asked.

"I don't want you to touch anything that's mine."

Everyone froze, eyes wide, lips parted. Ian didn't even look at Chris when he said it, as if Chris wasn't worthy of a single glance.

"This isn't his fault." Max broke the awkward silence.

Chris's eyes flitted between Max and Ian. Jersey kept her attention on Ian and his awful side exposed for all to see.

"You're tired, Ian," Max continued. "We all are. I'll send some food over to their house. You should grab a shower and sleep. Then we'll start sorting through this tomorrow."

Ian stared off into the distance, squinting against the setting sun. After a few more awkward seconds, he nodded. Jersey picked up Lola and eyed Chris until he got her silent plea to pick up Foxy. They headed toward the Blevins's while Shane climbed into the SUV to take the bags next door.

CHAPTER TWENTY-SIX

"YOU CAN GO." Ian stared at his house, feeling Max's judgmental gaze on his back.

"It's insured. No one died." She tried to reassure him.

"You can go."

Max waited a few seconds before grabbing Ian's hand and giving it a squeeze.

"Thank you," he whispered.

"For what?"

"For not asking." He glanced at her.

"About what?"

"My past."

"Because it's painful?"

He returned his attention to the house. "Because it's ugly."

As promised, Max made sure food was delivered. Jersey and Chris gave Ian the silent treatment, taking their food upstairs to eat while Ian ate in the kitchen with the dogs.

After he took them outside to do their thing, he locked up and climbed the stairs. At the top, Jersey glanced up, with her bag over her shoulder.

"Shane put my bag in the same bedroom with yours.

But I'm staying with Chris because *I'm* not yours. Not yours to touch, to control, to own."

"I never said you were," he replied in a defeated tone.

"What you said to Chris was about me. Everyone knew you were pissing on me like I'm some possession of yours."

Ian stood still, unblinking, with a blank expression. "What I said to Chris was about *me*." He ambled toward her, shaking his head while squeezing past her in the doorway to the bedroom. "Stay out of it, Jersey. You're in over your head this time."

Within seconds, he stumbled forward, flinching from the sharp pain in his lower back from her foot landing there. He turned toward her, quickly ducking to avoid her fist flying through the air.

"Jersey, what the fuck?" He grabbed her arm.

She used his hold on her to pull him closer, pounding her left fist into his face. Ian took a step back, wiping the blood from the cut along his cheek bone. Jersey held up her fists and gnashed her teeth. "Careful, Coop, I think you're in over your pretty, little head. But when I'm done with you, there won't be anything pretty about your face."

Ian's head jerked back. "What did he say to you?"

She smiled. "Chris? He said he couldn't kill you. His conscience is full. But mine has room. I can kill you for taking something of mine. I can kill you for ruining my life."

"W-what …" Ian shook his head. "What are you talking about?" His heart sank into his stomach, a nauseating pain. "I didn't take anything from you." His voice cracked because … he loved her. "Everything is for you. I want to give you the world, the pieces that were taken from you, the life you never had. Jersey, I want to give you back your dreams."

With blood trailing down his cheek, he shook his head and whispered, "I love you."

Her eyes turned red with tears. "Why? How?"

Ian didn't know which would destroy her first, the anger or the pain. He hated how much she blamed him for something. What? He didn't know. It made no sense to him.

Jersey swallowed hard, refusing to let go of a single tear. "How could you leave them there to die?" She bit her quivering lower lip. "Who … who does that?"

"Leave wh—" Ian's words died, leaving his mouth open, choking on disbelief.

No.

She couldn't think *he* did that.

Ian's gaze shifted over her shoulder to the hallway. Where was Chris? Surely, he heard them.

"Jersey … just stay here." He took a step toward her.

Smack! Thunk!

She pummeled his face and torso. He pushed her away to get a better angle and two extra seconds to hug her to him, trapping her arms. Tipping his chin up to keep her head from thrashing into it, he carried her to the balcony of the master bedroom and shoved her onto the floor of it harder than he wanted. But he needed to buy a few seconds to shut the door and lock it.

"Ian!" She punched and kicked the glass.

He knew it wasn't going to last very long, so he took angry strides to Chris's room and threw open the door, shutting and locking it behind him.

Chris glanced up from his book, reclined on the bed.

Chris … rage burned Ian to his very core. That wasn't even the fucking murderous bastard's real name.

"She's screaming, and you're reading a fucking book. Why is that, *Chris*?" Ian squinted, tipping his head to the side.

Chris shrugged, marking his spot with a bookmark. "She can take care of herself. You'll realize this very soon. If your face is any indicator, you probably already know this."

Ian shook his head, resting his hands on his hips and staring at the ceiling. "How the fuck are you still alive? And why not just turn me in? Why use her? Why tell her this grand lie? So she'd kill me because you're too fucking weak to try to do it yourself? Why the name? She wouldn't have known your real name. But it was a nice touch since you're clearly just trying to fuck with me."

Chris sat up straighter, easing his legs off the side of the bed. "You … know me?"

Ian returned a pointed look, not amused by the game any longer. No longer curious about Chris's intentions. He just wanted answers.

Chris pressed his hands to the side of his head, grimacing like something in his head physically hurt. "When did you recognize me? How? Why didn't you say something? Are you really that fucking heartless? I … I believed you. I believed that it was an accident. But running was wrong. You should have stopped, called for help, but you didn't. I told you to turn yourself in, but you didn't. You shed your past, changed your name, and you got all of your goddamn dreams while other people lost everything because of you."

Ian narrowed his eyes, cocking his head an inch to the side. "Kessler, what are you talk—"

"Kessler!" Chris shot up from the bed, pacing the room. "That's it! I couldn't remember your name. I just knew it wasn't Ian Cooper. Kessler … Kessler?" He snapped his fingers over and over.

"Lockwood," Ian whispered in disbelief. Speechless because the scene playing out before him was insane. Indescribable.

"Lockwood!" Chris stopped on a gasp, releasing it slowly like he could finally breathe. "Kessler Lock-wood …" He closed his eyes. "That's it." Opening them, he nodded. "You changed your name."

Ian cocked his head to the side again, rubbing his forehead while rapidly blinking. For months, he stood guard over his whole fucking life, stood guard over Jersey. For months he wondered if it was real or an act, a cat and mouse game. A bomb with a ticking clock. Was the amnesia real? Ian went to great lengths to hide his past. And for months the man before him wielded the power to expose everything, *if* he remembered.

The big fucking *if.*

That if kept Ian from saying a word to Chris—making the first move. That if kept him from telling

Jersey. That if kept secrets. That if dictated his future.

Ian had his answer, and there was no *if.*

"Why does Jersey think I killed Dena and Charles Russell?" Ian asked, numb because he felt certain he knew the answer.

Chris stopped mumbling to himself and glanced up. "Because I told her. When I saw you at the hotel, I remembered you. We were friends. What happened to you? It wasn't fair of you to ask me to keep that kind of secret. I told you to turn yourself in." His words began to lose control again as his hands fidgeted, legs paced.

Ian took slow steps toward him, cornering the rabid animal. Chris stopped, making eye contact with Ian while puffing out breaths like someone having a panic attack.

"*Your* name is Kessler Lockwood."

Kessler's face stiffened as he tried to shake his head. For months, Ian wondered if it was real or just a game. It *was* a game, just not the one Ian could have ever imagined. But he should have known. There had to be a reason Kessler told everyone his name was Chris.

"N-no. You're Kessler. I'm Chris. A-and I don't remember my last name, but I remember Marley's, and I remember boxing there." He shook his head over and over. "I remember playing basketball with you, and I remember you bought me a really expensive pair of shoes because your family is rich. I had nothing, but you befriended me. You came home from college. You were high. You thought you hit an animal. If you just would have gone to the police, they would have understood. But you didn't … because you were high."

Ian didn't want to believe it was real. Real didn't get him a confession. Real didn't convince Jersey. Real was pretty fucking complicated. But he had no choice. He believed the man before him had a brain injury that scrambled his thoughts, stealing some, replacing others. Ian believed Kessler was mentally messed up past the point of return.

"My name was Chris Faulkner." Ian worked hard to control his level of rage, each word jagged, slow, and deliberate. "I grew up in foster care. My last home was with Charles and Dena Russell. I lived with them for two years. Charles encouraged me to play basketball. That's where I made friends with you, Kessler Lockwood. *You* bought *me* an expensive pair of shoes because *your* family was rich."

Kessler shook his head, pinching his eyes shut. "No. No!"

Ian bit his lips together, narrowing his eyes. "Your memory is pretty good; it's just not of *your* life … it's of my life. Some fucked-up part of your brain has remembered everything I told you about *my* life. You didn't want to walk in my shoes then—hell, you didn't want *me* walking in my own shoes because you were embarrassed of my low social status. *That's* why you bought me shoes. I can't let you walk in them now. You can't have my shoes or my life. And you sure as hell can't have Jersey."

"No. No … no … no!" Kessler pressed his hands harder against his ears. "You're lying to save yourself. She's going to kill you. She won't believe your lies. She loves me! She loves me! She loves—"

Ian slammed him against the wall. "Don't think that I don't know that you're the one who tried to ruin me these past few weeks." Ian punched him once. "The lip-syncing. Leaking everything about Jersey." He punched him again, drawing blood.

Chris didn't try to fight back; he just kept yelling. "No! No! No!"

"The fire … you started the fucking fire. How could you be so stupid?" Another punch. "That's your specialty. But you don't fucking remember, do you?" Ian didn't stop.

Even when Kessler fell to the ground, Ian grabbed his shirt and punched him until he was unconscious, then he kicked him in the ribs.

Ian was a boxer.

Marley took him in, trained him to deal with his anger, and sent him on his way when Ian could no longer hear the demons of his past taunting him.

With burning, bloodied knuckles from beating Kessler's face, Ian wiped his hands on his shirt. "Why didn't you die?" Ian whispered to the lifeless body. He headed back to the other bedroom to unlock the door for Jersey, but she wasn't there.

With the door still locked and the glass intact, it meant she climbed down to the ground or jumped.

CHAPTER TWENTY-SEVEN

J ERSEY HOBBLED THROUGH the wreckage of Ian's house, cringing at the pain in her ankle from the second floor drop off the balcony. She needed her knife. Ian's master bedroom took the brunt of the damage, which was where she left her knives. Tossing aside pieces of wood and drywall from the collapsed ceiling, she trudged her way toward the closet.

Her foot kept landing on uneven surface, causing shooting pain in her ankle as she pitched things left and right, searching for the remains to the drawer that had her knives. So much stuff was new to her. She didn't remember seeing plastic containers before the fire, but they were scattered everywhere as if they came from nowhere.

Jersey glanced up. Teetering between two rafters was another plastic storage container. Ian must have kept stuff in storage above his closet. After relentless searching, she found the drawer and her knives. She wiped her favorite one off with her shirt and slipped it in the back of her pants. Holding the other two knives in her hand, she turned back toward the bedroom door.

It was time to kill the rock star.

After one step, she paused next to a plastic container

with half of its contents spilled onto the rubble.

She squatted next to a stuffed bunny—brown and missing an ear. No longer thinking about revenge, she let the two other knives fall to the ground and picked up the bunny.

"You dropped it."

She jumped, whipping her gaze toward Ian's voice. He stood at what had been the entrance to his bedroom.

Why did he have the bunny? *Her* bunny. What did he do? Jesus … who else did he hurt?

All the fear vanished. She knew it would when the time came—when certainty revealed itself, when all of her reasons for living disappeared.

Her face contorted into its ugliest form as she dropped the bunny, retrieved both knives, and slowly stood. "You killed them."

His face drew into a painful mask of regret as he shook his head.

"Stop denying it!" She threw one of the knives.

His hand flew to his ear, blood rushing down his neck from the missing piece she expertly sliced with the knife.

Ian grimaced, removing his hand from his ear, letting it bleed out. "You dropped it—the bunny."

She didn't give a fuck about the bunny and how he knew she dropped it. Nothing made sense anymore, and she just wanted her senseless life to end … but not before his.

The second knife landed squarely in his thigh.

"Fuck!" He seethed, bending at the waist while stumbling forward a few steps.

Jersey retrieved her last knife from the back of her jeans as tears ran down her face. "The next one is going in your heart," she whispered.

"Bunnies…" he grunted, grabbing his leg just above the knife "…still hop with one ear."

Jersey shook her head, gripping the knife firmly in her hand as his image blurred behind her tears.

CHAPTER TWENTY-EIGHT

Sixteen years earlier ...

"J ERSEY! DON'T MAKE me come get you," Mr. Fisher bellowed from upstairs.

She retreated to the farthest part of the fort maze, hugging her bunny, chewing on one of its ears as nerves gobbled her up inside, making her feel sick to her tummy.

G stared blankly at her from a few feet away, curled into a ball, one eye swollen, her lower lip cut at the corner. Mr. Fisher kept her upstairs longer than usual. Jersey thought it meant she'd be spared that day. G always tried to take the brunt of Mr. Fisher's sick needs in an effort to keep Jersey untouched.

That day, Mr. Fisher spared no one.

"You little bitch, I hate it when you make me come down here for you."

Jersey chewed harder on the bunny's long ear as her body shook and her gaze pleaded with G. But G had no life in her single-eyed gaze. She looked dead, except occasionally her whole body would jerk and she'd groan like something shocked her—pained her.

"Fucking little cunt!" Mr. Fisher ripped off the blankets over the fort and grabbed Jersey's arm, yanking her to her feet.

Smack!

He backhanded her, his tarnished class ring cutting open the skin high on her cheek. Jersey cried, hugging her bunny to her with her free hand.

G made a noise, like an animal caught in a barbed wire fence, as she stumbled to her feet, lunging at Mr. Fisher.

Smack!

He dished out the same punishment to her, sending her abused body back to the ground. That's when Jersey noticed the blood along the backside of G's light gray sweatpants.

Mr. Fisher hurt G … he hurt her badly that day.

"I hate this fucking bunny! Stop chewing on its ear like a goddamn dog!" Fisher jerked on the bunny, but Jersey held it tightly. When he jerked it harder, she was left with nothing but the wet ear. He tossed the bunny's body off to the side and dragged Jersey up the creaky wooden stairs. His breath reeked of booze, and a foul body odor clung to his clothes.

Hazel lucked out that day. Mrs. Fisher took her to the doctor after Mr. Fisher complained about her incessant cough. Jersey envied Hazel's illness. Of course she didn't know what it was, maybe it was something awful that could kill her, but still … she envied Hazel that day.

Mrs. Fisher never abused them, but she never helped them either. She feared her husband as much as everyone else.

After Fisher tied Jersey's hands behind her back, exposed her most private parts, and stroked himself for what felt like an eternity in Hell, he forced himself into her mouth, *stroking her hair*, making her vomit. Then he fisted her hair and smacked her several more times for vomiting on him.

She stumbled down the stairs, blinded by her tears, throat bruised and burning, running straight to her bunny missing its ear, and she wept … not because of the abuse to her. Jersey wept for her bunny.

When her tears stopped, G picked her up, swaying a bit on her unsteady legs, and carried Jersey upstairs to the bedroom. G laid her in the bed and knelt beside it, brushing Jersey's hair from her face, inspecting Mr. Fisher's brutal work.

"M-my bunny …" Jersey hiccupped. "Only h-has one-one e-ear."

G's mouth pulled into something resembling a crooked smile and a grimace, probably because of the cut on her lip. "Bunnies still hop with one ear," she whispered.

It was the most she had ever heard G talk. A whisper. Five words to take away Jersey's pain. Who took away G's pain?

CHAPTER TWENTY-NINE

Present

*B*UNNIES STILL HOP *with one ear.*
  Jersey looked down at the one-eared bunny. Next to it, peeking out of a wet, soiled envelope was a photo. She slowly squatted next to the bunny and retrieved the photo with her left hand while her right hand continued to grip the knife. The photo shook in her grasp—*she* shook.

"G …" Jersey whispered, letting her watery-eyed gaze slide over the school photo of G. Her long, scraggly hair hung in her eyes. Her lanky body dressed in a plain red tee and jeans. No makeup. No smile. You could barely see G's eyes.

Jersey wondered if G hid behind her hair to hide her shame.

"Why do you have this?" The pain carried more weight than her pride, sending more tears down her cheeks when she blinked. "What did you do to her?" She tore her gaze away from the photo, meeting Ian's grimace as he continued to clutch his leg.

As if his pain no longer mattered, he studied her, torturing her with that look—the one that made her feel like his whole world. But she wasn't. She was his punching bag, his toy, his most tortured victim.

Ian coughed, trying to clear his throat. "I cut her hair so the police wouldn't unfairly judge her. I cut her hair so her next foster parents wouldn't belittle her and call her a *girl*. So they wouldn't buy *him* feminine clothes, sodomize *him,* and stick tampons up *his* ass to absorb the blood. I cut *his* hair so *he* could play on the boys' basketball team because *he* wasn't a girl ... G was a boy. His name was Christian Guardian Faulkner."

Ian continued to obliterate Jersey's world. "Mr. Fisher said he wasn't worthy of the biblical name, Christian, or a protective name, Guardian, so he called the boy G. And since the boy had long hair, he treated the boy like a girl. And when the boy tried to correct him, or have an opinion, or say a single word to anyone, Mr. Fisher beat him and raped him."

"N ... no ..." Jersey sobbed, the knife shaking in her hand. G was the first person to really care for Jersey—to *love* her. G kept Jersey alive. G told her to *be brave and run fast.*

G remained in the forefront of Jersey's mind every day. When Jersey fought, she fought for G, imagining every face she punched was Mr. Fisher. Not a single day passed where Jersey didn't think of G, wondered where she was, if she was even still alive. Not a day passed that Jersey didn't silently thank G for saving her.

"I left that life," Ian continued. "After two years with the Russells, playing basketball with my friend Kessler

Lockwood and watching him blow a basketball scholarship because of drugs, I changed my name. I followed my passion. And a few months ago, I found the girl who has haunted my dreams for over sixteen years. I found the girl who mattered more to me than my own life. She did sixteen years ago, and she still does at this very moment."

Ian swallowed hard, sucking in a sharp breath as he put his hand behind him and eased to sitting with a hard *thunk* and another painful "fuck!"

"I …" he seethed, his clenched hand covered in blood, "let that life go because I killed a man to save the girl with the bunny."

"If he killed them, it wasn't intentional. He's not a killer and neither are you. I think you might take a bullet for me, but I don't think you'd actually take a life for me."

"No …" Jersey shook her head over and over, covering her face with her hands, just her tortured eyes peeking at him over her fingertips.

Ian was G.

Guard-ian.

And he took a life for her.

"No … no …" The tears flowed freely, blinding her, drowning her thoughts, blurring reality.

Reality … she had no concept of what was real.

"Jersey!"

Her gaze shot to the door, Chris's voice and pounding footsteps drawing nearer.

"Jersey …" Chris stopped at the doorway, face swollen and bloodied.

Her vision blurred as her ears rang, bringing on a

wave of nausea from her stomach tightening. She blinked several times before her gaze shifted from his face to Ian's bloodied knuckles. Everything stopped. Jersey felt catatonic.

At first, Chris sighed with relief before he homed in on Ian and his bloodied ear and the knife impaled in his leg. "Jersey ..." His wild eyes shifted to her as she slowly grabbed the knife again.

It felt numb in her hands. Everything felt numb. "Your name is not Chris ..." she said in a lifeless voice, wrestling with disbelief and the shocking reality.

"It ... it is." Her friend pressed his palms to the side of his head, vigorously shaking it while stumbling over his words. "He's ... that person is ... he's ... he's a liar. Using ... Jers, he's using me to save himself. You were right. He's known all along. He's playing us. He's playing *you!*"

Her pulse slowed and an ache settled into her throat as she witnessed her friend unravel. She gave him a sympathetic nod.

Ian used both hands to apply pressure to his leg. "Kessler drove a black Charger."

"See!" Her friend pulled his hands away from his head and held them up in revelation. "Kessler ... Kessler drove a black Charger. I told you, Jers ... I told you." He pointed an accusing finger toward Ian. "For the love of god, Jers ... just finish it."

She looked at Ian as he glanced up at her with resignation in his eyes. "He did." He grimaced tightening his hold on his leg. "Kessler drove a black Charger. He was strung out on drugs. He killed Dena and Charles. He didn't stop to see if they were still alive. Then he drove home to his parents' estate, parked his black Charger in one of six garage stalls, and set the house on fire. They were inside, still asleep that morning. They didn't make it out."

"No!" Her friend pulled at his hair, bending at the waist, squatting into a ball. "No! No! No!" He tugged and pulled, pinching his eyes shut.

Jersey watched more blood spread into the faded fabric of Ian's jeans.

"NO!" Her friend shot up, eyes bloodshot with rage, a jagged board grasped in his right hand. "It ends now," he gritted through his clenched teeth, taking a step toward Ian. "I love you, Jers. You are mine. He killed them. He played you. You let him inside of you. But you don't have to be a whore anymore." He took another step toward Ian. "I'll save you. We ..." he wrapped his other hand around the piece of wood, cocking his arms back like a baseball player readying his swing.

She gave Ian one last glance.

"Be brave and run fast," he said as if they were his final words. Even in the face of death, he protected her. He risked everything for her. That's what he did because he was her *Guardian*.

Kessler swung his jagged board, but it fell to the ground less than a foot from Ian's head. *He* fell to the ground with Jersey's favorite knife lodged into his left eye.

She put her friend down like a rabid animal. It didn't feel like revenge; in spite of everything, it didn't feel good or right. He wasn't in his right mind. The demons won.

"Jersey," Ian whispered her name with a weak voice.

She didn't look at him. She *couldn't* look at him. How could she not know? How could she not see it? Digging her phone out of her pocket, she dialed 9-1-1.

"Hi. There's been an accident." Jersey dropped her phone before pressing *End*. She dislodged the knife from Chris's eye.

He jerked, bellowing in agony.

More tears burned her eyes. She thought of all the books he read her, his soothing voice, his comforting touch, but soon they faded, suffocated by the cry of agony. Jersey covered her eyes with her arm, the bloodied knife molded in her hand.

Ian grunted as Kessler covered his bloodied eye and lunged for the knife in Ian's leg. Jersey grabbed Kessler's hair, jerked his head back, and cut his throat from shoulder to shoulder.

"We are terrible people," she whispered, releasing him to the ground, sending him to a different life where he might find a wife and children. A good job. A beautifully boring and completely normal life.

With the bloodied knife, she ripped Kessler's shirt and used part of it to tie a tourniquet around Ian's leg.

"Jersey?" Ian reached for her arm.

She gently pulled away, still unable to look at him.

Too much shame and guilt crushed her conscience. She did this ... all of it. She brought down a rock star.

CHAPTER THIRTY

J ERSEY SAT ON the front steps. The police arrived. The paramedics arrived. Even a fire truck arrived.

They asked her a million questions. She answered none.

They carried Ian out on a stretcher as they put her in the back of a squad car. For a brief second, she made eye contact with the rock star.

He took a life to save hers.

She returned the favor—but not before she broke him.

He knew it was Kessler all along. Why didn't he say something? It didn't make any sense. He knew *her*.

Nothing. Nothing made sense.

The next morning, Max arrived at the jail with an attorney, Isabel Higgins. She asked Isabel to give her and Jersey a few minutes alone.

"You stabbed my guy and removed part of his ear." Max let out a deep sigh. "He said Chris … or I guess Kessler did it, but I'm not stupid."

Jersey stared at the table between them.

"He's having surgery on his ear today."

Jersey continued to stare at the table.

"He said you saved his life."

Still no response.

"But it's a sticky situation since it would appear you first tried to take his life. I know this. The police don't know what to think yet, but I know. Ian's not admitting that, just that you're innocent. And he said you were aiming for Chris, who he now refers to as Kessler, and that's how his ear got cut. He said Kessler's fingerprints should be on the knife that they pulled from his leg. Is that true?"

Jersey slowly glanced up at Max, but she didn't have any words to say—or the right ones. Max returned a disappointed frown. "They haven't charged you with anything … yet. Isabel is here in case they do, but Ian gave them his account. If your account of the events matches his, then they'll let you go. It's that easy."

"I killed Chris …" She closed her eyes and shook her head a few times. "Kessler."

Max nodded. "I know, but who tried to kill Ian?"

"Me," she whispered, feeling that heavy numbness settling over her body again, slowing her thoughts, echoing voices.

Max rested her elbows on the table, dropping her head and threading her fingers through her silky, black hair. "Why is he protecting you?"

"Because he is my guardian," she murmured.

Lifting her head, Max squinted. "What do you mean?"

"My protector. My defender."

"I know what guardian means. I just don't know why

he's willing to lie for you. Why he's willing to risk everything to protect you. He won't tell me. It's this line that no one is allowed to cross … except you. You crossed it. I just want to know what's on the other side of it. I just want to know what I'm not seeing because your past is not filled with fancy birthday parties and trips to the carnival."

Jersey returned a somber expression.

Max studied her for a few minutes before biting her upper lip and nodding in tiny increments. "You're it." She grunted a laugh, averting her eyes to the ceiling for a few seconds. "I told you he just appeared out of nowhere, landing on the world's biggest stage with no past, seemingly no life before stardom. But you're it."

Returning her gaze to Jersey, Max nodded one more time, pressing a hand to her mouth. "You're his past." She swallowed hard, letting her hand slide from her mouth to her neck. "I once asked him if he gave you a kidney because I just couldn't figure it out—the unwavering attachment and fierce instinct to have you by his side no matter what. I think he gave you more than a kidney."

Jersey turned her head, focusing on a dark stain on the shiny floor, maybe spilled coffee.

Max pushed her chair back and stood. "Take the kidney, Jersey."

ISABEL STOOD NEXT to Jersey as she gave her account—Ian's account—of the events. They released her a short while later.

As soon as she exited the jail, Shane took one arm and Max took her other arm, helping her to the SUV as Jersey hobbled on her bad ankle.

"Where are we going?" Jersey asked.

"Well, I can't take you to the hospital. There's a big gathering of cameras and reporters around it. But you need to have that ankle checked out. Then Ian wants me to take you to the Blevins's house until he gets out of the hospital. But I'm willing to make sure you get anywhere you want to go. A hotel. Another city or state. Another country …"

Jersey shifted her focus out the window. "You want me gone."

"No. I want you *well*. If you need help, someone to talk to, I want to get that for you. I don't know what it must feel like to be in your shoes. Do you move on like nothing happened? I honestly don't know."

When Jersey didn't respond, they took her to the doctor. An x-ray revealed a small fracture, so they sent her home in a boot. Home at the moment was the Blevins's house.

Marley's was gone.

Her friend was gone.

She had no sense of belonging. Guilt filled her from top to bottom, overflowing with nowhere to go.

Jersey expected Lola and Foxy to greet her, but the house remained still and silent when she opened the door. Max probably had Bria, the dog sitter, come get them after Jersey tried to kill Ian.

Jesus … she was seconds away from killing him.

Jersey slowly climbed the stairs and pushed open the partially closed door to the room where Chris had slept. Blood stained the carpet, but it wasn't beige like Dena's carpet, it was white. And the blood wasn't from an inexperienced social worker; it was Chris's blood from Ian's fists repeatedly hitting his face.

Why? Why didn't Ian say something before yesterday? He knew it was Kessler. He knew Chris was *his* name. He let Jersey talk about her past and the Russells, but he never said a word.

Why? It made no sense.

She eased onto the bed, thinking of Chris, thinking of Ian … thinking of G. *That* was it. All the looks, the despair in Ian's eyes, the admission that he had something to tell her—it wasn't that he killed the Russells. He was G.

And looking back, the familiarity, the sense that they had an invisible connection that felt bigger than a meet cute at a hot dog stand … it all made sense. Ian had always been her guardian, and on a subconscious level, Jersey knew it.

HOURS LATER, A gentle hand rested on the side of Jersey's head. She blinked open her eyes.

Max sat on the edge of the bed and smiled. "Hungry?"

"No," she whispered. Jersey turning down food was a

first.

"My husband is a sales rep for a software company. He travels a lot. So do I. It's what makes our marriage work. Or probably more accurately ... not work. I took the job for Ames, watching his kids, during a rough time in my life. You see, we had a five-year-old son. His name was Ian." She smiled. "Such a great name. He liked to ride his bike up and down our street. It was his first summer riding it without training wheels. I was inside making dinner while my husband pulled some weeds out front and Ian rode his bike."

She curled her hair behind her ear, looking beyond the bed out the window. "I'll never forget the moment I heard sirens approaching our street. I dropped the potato peeler and casually dried my hands, making my way to the bay window in our living room. And that's when I saw it ... my husband knelt beside Ian, cradling his limp body. He didn't come tell me; he didn't have *anyone* come tell me. Because he knew Ian was dead. He knew it because his skull was cracked open and he wasn't breathing. He just knew ..."

Max ignored the stream of tears racing down her cheeks as she inhaled a shaky breath. "We don't even know what happened. Why he rode into the street. The driver of the car said he just veered off the sidewalk so quickly, there was no time to react. Was something on the sidewalk? A worm? Was he chasing a butterfly? Did he just totally lose his balance? We'll never know."

"I'm sorry," Jersey whispered.

Max nodded. "Me too. I ... I don't *know* a lot. I haven't since that day. All I know for sure is that bad things happen to good people. That's it. Nothing profound. Nothing hopeful or inspiring. All these years later, the first thing I think about when I wake up in the morning is Ian. And my heart still breaks. And I still ask *why* to a god I no longer believe in. I have a husband who I never see. A grave I rarely visit.

"When my life hit rock bottom, I ran away. And sometimes I wonder why my husband doesn't come for me. Does he think I blame him? Does he think I'm broken beyond repair? Is he? I don't know the answers to any of these questions. But I know that Ian Cooper would come for you." She grabbed Jersey's hand. "He'd give you the kidney."

Max laughed on a tiny sob and wiped her eyes. "That's not really my point. My point is … bad things happen to good people. You and Ian … you're good people."

A hint of a smile moved Jersey's mouth as she thought about Ian's words. *We're terrible people …*

Maybe good people could do bad things without being truly terrible.

CHAPTER THIRTY-ONE

"SHANE'S BRINGING IAN home later." Max stayed the night with Jersey, helping her take a shower and making her breakfast the next morning.

Jersey sipped her coffee, her leg propped up on a chair.

"Do you care what happens to Chris's—Kessler's body?"

Jersey coughed. "I stuck a knife into his skull before slitting his throat. I think we've established I don't care what happens to his body."

Max nodded, not showing any emotion in her reaction to Jersey's words.

"He was sick. Mentally not well. That's what Ian said."

With a shrug, Jersey shook her head. "Maybe. I don't know." She wondered if Ian truly believed that. Jersey did. The way he reacted to being called Kessler—being accused of killing the Russells—it wasn't defensive. It was denial. Like the idea of it tore him up inside, the way he'd wake from a nightmare. Ian shook Chris's whole world, scrambling everything where down was up and up was down, and he just … cracked.

Max would never know the truth. She would never know that Ian saved Jersey with a baseball bat. The proverbial kidney. Her rock star was raped and beaten, ridiculed, and treated like a girl—but she would never know. Ian went to great lengths to bury his past. And Jersey tried to unearth it. Wake the dead.

JERSEY'S BREATH HITCHED when she heard the door open. Scooting up a bit on the sofa, she waited for the painful, *shameful* moment. Max asked Ian if he needed anything. Jersey couldn't hear his response. After another minute or so, the front door clicked again, and the voices were gone.

Silence.

"Hey," Ian said from behind her.

She closed her eyes for a brief moment. "Hey." One word squeezed by the lump in her throat. It hurt to hear his voice. It hurt to be in his proximity. Everything just *hurt*.

He limped a little, making his way to the chair perpendicular to the sofa. Right in Jersey's line of vision. Ian eased into it, clearly not able to bend his leg easily. Bruises mottled his face, and gauze covered his left ear.

Jersey's fingers traced her lips as her sluggish gaze inched along Ian's body, assessing the damage—assessing *her* damage.

"I'm sor—"

"Don't." Ian shook off her attempt to apologize.

She swallowed her words, nearly choking on them.

They were big words, filled with so much regret. She needed to let them out. Clearing her throat, she met his eyes. "Why?"

"Because you did what you did when you thought I killed Dena and Charles."

"But maybe that doesn't make it right."

"It has to." He turned, averting his gaze to the television screen even though it wasn't turned on.

"When did you know who he was?"

"When I first saw him." His attention floated around the room, landing on his leg. He brushed his hand over the bandaged area that peeked out just below his shorts.

"Why didn't you say something? Why let this go on? Why not tell me? Why hire him to work for you? It makes no sense."

He rubbed his temples and ran a hand through his hair, cautiously avoiding his ear. Jersey's eyes filled with tears as her gaze snagged on it.

"Jersey …"

She shook her head, swallowing regret and fighting back the flood of emotion. "Your ear …" The words fell from her lips on a painful sigh.

He gave her a tiny smile. "Bunnies still hop with one ear." His words reached into her chest and ripped out her heart.

"G …" She covered her face and cried into her hands.

He lumbered to his feet, scooped her up in his arms, and released a restrained groan as he sat on the sofa with the weight of her body balanced between his arms and his good leg.

She waited for his words.

They never came.

He didn't tell her everything would be okay. G never told her that. G never lied. G offered his arms. His warm body. G threw himself in front of a bus for Jersey and took up arms with a bat, but he *never* promised everything would be okay.

The tears dried up, and she fell asleep in his arms, like she'd done so many times before. When she woke, he was gone. She followed the soft noises to the kitchen, hobbling in her clunky, black boot.

"Sleep well?" Ian set two bottles of water on the table next to boxes of Chinese takeout.

Jersey nodded, limping to the table.

They ate in silence, sharing an occasional sad smile but mostly focusing on their food or the pool out back that was twice the size of Ian's pool, decked out with a slide and diving board. After dinner, they climbed the stairs at a snail's pace. Jersey stopped at the door to the room where Chris had stayed.

She bit her lips together to keep her emotions from running out of control.

"You're allowed to be sad," Ian said, reaching for her hand.

She nodded slowly, using her other hand to blot away a tear before it escaped. They shuffled down the hallway to the other guest bedroom. Jersey brushed her teeth while Ian sponged his body off, avoiding his bandaged areas. She didn't sneak a single peek in his direction. Instead, she spit out her toothpaste and crawled into bed.

As soon as he joined her, shutting off the lights and getting into bed with her, both on their sides facing each other. Jersey lifted her hand, running it through his hair. "We need to talk."

Ian closed his eyes, returning a tiny nod. "We will … later. We need time."

JERSEY GAVE HIM time—weeks.

Weeks of monotony. Weeks of his leg healing. Weeks of his ear healing. The plastic surgeon worked miracles rebuilding his ear. Underneath his shaggy hair, it looked completely normal.

Jersey spent her days with the dogs, watching the re-construction of Ian's house and hitting a bag he set up for her in the Blevins's garage. Occasionally, she sat by the pool and listened to audiobooks on her phone. A truly remarkable invention and the very best gift from Ian.

His record label calmed down, after he had to cancel the last part of his tour, because he promised to get to the studio and start working on a new album.

Sometimes they held hands, sometimes he kissed her on the head while she stood in front of the fridge perusing for a snack, and every night, he spooned her body to his in bed.

No intimacy.

No kissing.

She missed the kissing so much.

His unspoken words grew into this gigantic barred

fence between them. They could see each other and find *some* physical contact, but they just couldn't connect. He stayed in his cell, and she stayed in hers, afraid to push him, afraid of losing him.

Her G.

Her protector.

Her life.

"Ian's different." Jersey and Max took Lola and Foxy for a short walk one evening since Ian worked late and Max used any excuse to not be home with her husband. Jersey still had the boot, but she had to get out and move around for a bit.

"How so?" Max stopped as Lola pissed in a small patch of grass.

"He's distant. I know you don't want to hear the graphic details of our sex life, but the *different* part is that we're not having sex. We're not kissing. We're not doing anything. I don't know why I'm here. He hugs me at night, like a stuffed animal or body pillow. I listen to books during the day, work out, and just exist in his life. But as what?"

"They've been working hard on this new album. He's feeling pressure from the label after canceling the rest of the tour. I can promise you he's not cheating on you."

"Cheating on me? I'm not worried about that. We're not … well, I don't know what we are or are not. Roommates, I guess. I mean, Chris—Kessler—used to sleep next to me and hug me. But we were just friends. If Ian's fucking someone when he's not at home, then I'd say I'm jealous but not mad. I mean … whatever. Sex is just sex.

Maybe that's it. Maybe I'm overanalyzing things. Feeling trapped in the house. I should get some sex if I want it, right?"

Max stopped, gawking at Jersey.

Blink.

Blink.

"He loves you!"

Jersey nodded slowly, eyes squinted. "Maybe. But I'm not talking about love. I'm talking about sex. And I'm talking about *talking*. He won't talk to me. It's like he's avoiding me at all costs. I know you're saying he's busy, but when you guys left without me to finish the tour, he found time to talk to me, even if it was just a few minutes on the phone. He *wanted* to talk to me. He doesn't want to talk now."

Max nodded, moving forward as the dogs pulled on their leashes. "Want me to talk to him?"

"Yes. No …" Jersey sighed. "No. I don't want him to know I said anything to you. He's too protective of his personal life. I don't want him to not trust me."

"I don't think he's sleeping with anyone else. I really don't."

Jersey laughed. "It's not about that. I know that's hard for you to believe, but it's not. If he found someone else to meet his needs in whatever way, I wouldn't blame him. I tried to hurt him. He owes me nothing. But I guess I just want to know. If it's time for me to walk, then I'll walk. I feel like he's holding on to me out of pity. Like he lost a bet and I'm a ratty looking dog who needs to be walked and fed every day."

Max chuckled. "That's not it. I don't know what it is that's eating at him, but I know he loves you. Even if you can't fully wrap your head around what that means. You are the center of Ian Cooper's world. I just think he can't see straight at the moment. But he will."

JERSEY WAITED UP that night for Ian. It was almost 12:30 a.m. when he came in the door.

"Hey." She smiled, pulling her earbuds out and nodding toward the kitchen. "I have food for you. Are you hungry?"

He tossed his keys on the kitchen counter as she turned on the light over the dining room table.

"Pasta. And lots of olives." Jersey smiled.

Ian returned a weak smile. "I just ate."

Jersey deflated, sitting in front of her plate of lukewarm pasta. She jabbed her fork into the spaghetti and twirled it. "Know who taught me to use a knife? Who taught me to hit a target with my eyes closed?"

"Axel Smith. Ex-abused foster kid, ex-Marine turned social worker. He only showed the worst ones. Us, Jersey … we were the worst ones, the ones most badly beaten. He did it not so we'd take a life, so we could save a life."

She lifted her gaze. "H-how do you know that?"

"Because he taught me too."

Her head jerked back.

He looked drained, like he didn't care if she believed

him or not.

"Prove it." She pushed out of her chair and grabbed a kitchen knife, pushing it toward his limp hand.

"I'm tired, Jersey. Not tonight." He turned, ambling toward the stairs.

Jersey threw the knife. It landed on the cherry banister an inch from his hand. Ian grabbed the knife and shot it back at her, landing squarely into the wood floor between her feet, leaving less than an inch from each foot—perfectly centered. Bull's-eye.

"Put the pasta away. I'll eat it for breakfast." He headed up the stairs.

Jersey stared at the knife for several seconds. Then she squatted, removing it from the wood. Easing back onto her butt, she bent her legs and rested her arms on them, dropping her head and closing her eyes.

They shared a roof and a bed, but Ian left her long before that. She didn't know where he went or if he'd ever return.

CHAPTER THIRTY-TWO

"You've NEVER SOUNDED better." Ames grinned at Ian as they finished their third song in two weeks. "This album is dark as fuck, but I think it's going to blow your fans away."

Hector, their producer, nodded. "Yeah. I think we should stab you in the leg and cut off part of your ear more often."

Ian held the headphones up to his ear and listened to the second track while glancing at Alex, Jordan, and Bryson, all tipping back beers, grinning like fools because they knew it was good. Not just good. It was their best work. And thanks to Ian's flood of inspiration, it was effortless. They had twelve more songs to go, and no one showed signs of exhaustion. Except Ian. But he kept that buried, giving them the impression that he was on fire, smoking with the perfect lyrics, instead of burning in his own personal hell.

"Food." Max smiled, pushing through the door of the tiny house that they used as their studio. She set the bags down, and everyone pounced. "A minute?" She nodded toward the other room.

Ian grabbed a sandwich and followed her. "What's

up?" Even with Max, he made it all look good. He thought it would eventually be good if he just kept pushing forward.

"You okay?"

"Yeah." He took a bite of his sandwich. "Why wouldn't I be?"

She bit her lips together, studying him for a few seconds. "Everything okay with Jersey?"

He shrugged. "Sure. You see her as much as I do. You should know."

"Is that a problem?"

"What?" He narrowed his eyes.

"That I see her as much as you do? I mean do you ever wonder if you're letting your time get too out of balance?"

He chuckled. "I'm making an album. I have a deadline. This is nothing new."

"You've never kept a girlfriend through making an album."

"Jersey's different." He took another bite.

"How so?"

"She's not needy."

"Wanting to be with someone doesn't make them needy."

"Is this coming from you or her?" He tossed the rest of his sandwich in the garbage by the sink. The direction of the conversation ruined his appetite.

"Me." Max returned a tight-lipped smile.

He didn't know if she was being honest with him. But Max rarely lied, so he took her at her word.

"You have a husband who you never see. Yet you tell everyone that's what makes your marriage work. I know I'm not the first Ian you think of when you wake every morning and go to bed each night."

Max frowned.

"Everyone has their limits. Their reasons. Things that motivate them. Things that hold them back. I won't question yours if you don't question mine."

Dropping her gaze to her feet, Max nodded.

"WHERE ARE YOU going?" Jersey asked as Ian buttoned his shirt after taking a shower.

It was a late Saturday afternoon. She had seen Ian that week for less than an hour, except at nights when he crawled into bed well after midnight from long days at the recording studio.

"I'm meeting the guys, Ames, and a director for dinner to discuss a music video."

"Lucky them," she mumbled, ghosting her fingers over the arm of the black blazer on the bed.

"What do you mean?" He grabbed the blazer, standing again in front of the full-length mirror to slip it on.

"I mean…" she plopped onto the bed, staring at her stupid boot that she had to wear for two more weeks "…I've been waiting for almost a month to discuss things with you. Maybe I need to contact your assistant and see if she can pencil me in on your busy calendar."

"What do you want to discuss?" He turned toward

her, tugging on the cuffs to his shirt as his gaze swept over her quickly before finding something—anything else to focus on.

This was his new normal. Don't look directly at Jersey for more than two seconds. Don't give her more than two minutes of your time each day. Don't give her the opportunity to ask questions and demand answers.

It wasn't like she would leave. After all, where could she go with no job and no skills?

"I want to talk about Kessler."

"Why? He's dead." Ian walked out of the bedroom.

Jersey's mouth fell agape. That was it? *He's dead?*

"Are you serious, *Christian Guardian*?" She chased after him as fast as her boot would let her go.

He descended the stairs. "My name is not Christian Guardian. Legally, it's no longer that. It's Ian Cooper."

Jersey hopped down the stairs on her good leg, finding it the quickest way to get there. "Oh, that's super awesome for you."

Ian grabbed his keys and wallet from the table just inside of the front door.

She continued, "Shedding your skin like a snake and slithering away. I'm still *legally* Jersey Six. A fucking fantastic name. Jersey Six, whose mother didn't want her. Jersey Six, who sick fucks liked to touch and sometimes rape. Jersey Six, who killed a man ... oh wait ... that's right, Jersey Six has killed *two* men. I'm one up on you, Coop ... G ... *Ian* ... whatever the fuck you want to be called in your rock star life."

His brow wrinkled as he stood by the door, trapped

by her words before he could *slither* out of the house and avoid her yet again. "Do you want a new name?"

"I want you to tell me why you didn't call Kessler out when you first met him at the hotel or during the many weeks that followed … months … it was months!"

"Jersey, there's no point in going back. I don't want to go back. Do you? Do you really want to go back and wake up the dead?"

"I want you to kiss me."

Ian stood idle for a few seconds before his feet ate up the space between them. He bent down and kissed her on the cheek. She grabbed his face and kissed him on the lips. He pulled away, and so much pain marred his face. It cut her deeper than the knife she threw into his leg.

"Take off your clothes," she whispered.

He shook his head. "We're not doing this. That's in the past. I told you I'm not going back. You don't need to watch me take off my clothes. I don't need to watch you take off yours. You're not a victim anymore, and neither am I."

"I just want sex."

"Maybe later. I have to go."

"I'm having sex with *someone* tonight."

Ian stopped, holding open the front door, glancing at her over his shoulder. "You're not that person." He brushed off her comment the way he'd been brushing her off for a month. "You're in a boot. Just order dinner and rest your foot"

"You have no clue who I am."

"Jersey …" He sighed, hanging his head. "I have to

go."

"Then go." She tipped her chin up.

"You're staying here." He eyed her for a few seconds.

Was it a demand or a question?

"Go." She met his gaze with a defiant one of her own, pushing her glasses up her nose.

"Are you going to hold this against me?" He sighed, his shoulders deflating inward.

"This? What is this? This moment? This night? This week? This life? Are you going to brush me off forever and blame me for standing up for myself? I don't even know how I could hold something against you. I'm pretty sure the day I conspired to kill you was the day I lost all rights to be anything but forever grateful that you didn't have me thrown in prison. So here I am … just waiting. Waiting for you to talk to me. Waiting for your dogs to shit. Waiting for the next book in a series on my audio app. Waiting for the next meal, the next burst of energy to go pound the bag. I'm just waiting, Coop. And it sucks. I'm pretty sure I was less lonely when I had nothing and no one."

"Jersey …" Another sigh. "Your timing couldn't be worse. I … I have to go. We'll figure this out later."

"Later …" she whispered.

Gone. Coop was gone. She lost him. They were just … going through the motions. Not even that. They were idle. Breathing such shallow breaths, she could no longer feel their pulse.

"This could drag on. Don't wait up."

Jersey looked up at him. Nodding. "You either."

He stopped again, just before closing the door. Studying her for something. Maybe the truth? If he wanted the truth, all he had to do was *listen*. She spelled it out for him.

He didn't listen. Instead, he shut the door, got in his car, and left.

CHAPTER THIRTY-THREE

J UST BEFORE 2 a.m., Jersey came in the front door and eased it shut behind her, as if to avoid waking Lola and Foxy. When she turned, the lights flipped on and she froze, staring at Ian perched on the bottom of the stairs. He still had on his jeans and button-down shirt, but the top three buttons were undone, and the sleeves were rolled up to his elbows.

After hours of running his hands through his hair and tugging on it out of worry and frustration, he knew why her gaze settled onto his head for several seconds before sliding to his eyes.

"Where the fuck have you been? Why isn't the location turned on, on your phone? And why have you been ignoring my messages and calls?" Those weren't the words he rehearsed in his head. The rehearsed words came from worry and the perceived relief he'd feel when she walked safely through the door.

But his heart only took seconds to feel relief and gratitude before his brain and ego jumped in to grill her.

She stared at him, looking numb from head to toe. The look she used to have in her eyes after Mr. Fisher took her to his room. Only this time, Ian—*G* didn't rush to comfort her.

"It's in the past, *Ian*. I don't want to talk about it."

"If you went and fucked some other guy tonight …"

"What?" Jersey crossed her arms over her chest. She wore a dress. Jersey rarely wore dresses.

He felt certain she only had maybe one or two that Max bought her for a few parties they attended on tour. It ate at him that she looked so fucking beautiful and it wasn't for him that night. Ian hated himself for leaving that night … he should have stayed. His list of "should haves" was long.

"I've used my body for many things. Sometimes it's fun to actually use it for pleasure. And thanks to technology, that pleasure is just a screen swipe away."

"You cheated on me because I wouldn't take my clothes off for you?"

She laughed. "*Cheated* on you? Are you serious? Did we get married when I wasn't looking?"

"You know what I mean!" He stood, balling his hands.

She inched her head side to side. "No, I don't know what you mean. I know that I used to sleep in the same bed as Chris, and he'd hold me at night, but I wasn't his girlfriend or wife. I know we don't go to movies. I know you're not here very much. I know I eat most meals alone. I know I play with Lola and Foxy. So … maybe there's a title for all of that, but it sure as fuck is not a girlfriend."

The ache in his chest multiplied with each word she spoke. It hurt less when she cut his ear and put a knife in his leg.

"Yes or no? Did you fuck someone tonight?" His words came out jagged and harsh. Desperate … so damn desperate.

"Yes."

Ian rested his hands on his hips and dropped his chin. His heart felt out of control, ready to explode into a million pieces as he chased each breath, burning with anger. "Max will arrange for you to go back to Newark tomorrow." He pivoted and headed up the stairs.

A few minutes later, Jersey appeared at the door to the bedroom. He finished tucking her belongings into her bag and shoved it into her chest. The impact made her stumble back a few steps. Without giving her a direct glance, he closed and locked the bedroom door.

EARLY THE NEXT morning, Ian slipped on shorts and a tee to take the dogs for a walk. At the bottom of the stairs, he heard noises in the kitchen. He took slow steps in that direction and peeked around the corner.

Jersey shoved as much food and bottles of Ian's water as she could into her bag. When Lola barked by his ankle, Jersey froze, glancing up at him.

"Max will be here at nine," he said past the ache in his throat.

"No need." She tried to zip her bag, but it was too full.

He never got around to getting her a new bag.

Jersey hooked the strap over her shoulder. "I'm leaving now." She brushed past him and opened the front door.

"Where are you going?" A toxic mix of pain, anger, and concern gripped his words, making them break apart as he said them.

She paused at the door with her back to him, staring out at the driveway. And then as if none of the thoughts in her mind deserved to be heard, she stepped outside and closed the door behind her.

For a solid five seconds, he fought the urge to chase after her. The sixth second … of course *six* … he opened the door just as she reached the end of the drive. "You have nowhere to go. Why are you doing this?"

Jersey kept walking.

He jogged after her, planting himself in front of her to stop her movements. She stared at his chest, jaw set, eyes unblinking.

"I love you, but you fucked another man last night."

"Sounds like a good topic for you to discuss with your shrink." She tried to step around him.

He stopped her again, and she pushed out a sharp exhale.

"I'm sorry I walked out on you last night."

"I'm not sorry I fucked another man." She knew how to cut him without even using a knife. With a little more force, she got around him and kept walking.

"So … you're just going to be homeless on the streets of L.A. now?"

Jersey was a good fighter. The fact that she didn't jump around with her hands up at her face was her biggest strength. Opponents underestimated her, and she leveled them when they least expected it.

Ian could jump around, taunting her all day long, taking a few swings, trying to provoke her, but in the end, she would be the first to land a solid punch, and it would hurt like hell. So if he wanted to compete at her level, he had to stop jumping around. He had one chance to land a hard hit that would knock her down.

Jogging again to catch up to her, he grabbed her from behind with a firm hold, fully prepared for her to wriggle and thrash to get free.

Then his lips brushed her ear, and he punched *hard*. "I set Kessler on fire."

Knockout.

It was as if every muscle in her body stopped working, like his arms were the only thing keeping her upright. Jersey didn't move any part of her body. She didn't breathe.

He should have told her weeks ago. He should have told her the day he saw Kessler at the hotel. He was so afraid of losing her again. But he managed to do it anyway. She slept with another man, and in true Jersey style, she told him exactly what she planned to do, and he was too stupid, scared, and blind to see the truth.

Still, even if it was too late, he had to tell her. At that point, he had nothing more to lose. "I saw him outside of a club in New York City. I hadn't seen him in years. He was high. Still, I told him I was sorry to hear about his parents. You know … their tragic death. He said he was sorry to hear about mine. I thought he meant my real parents, but then he said, 'The sun was at a bad angle. I thought I hit an animal.' He said he was so fucking scared and his car was dented and had their blood on it, so he drove home, parked in his garage, got high, and set the garage on fire to get rid of the evidence. Only … he thought his parents were still out of town. Little did he know—because he was too fucking high all of the time—that they got home late the night before. While I gagged on his meth-induced confession, unable to see straight or even breathe, a car pulled up, he got in, and I lost my chance to even the score.

"He killed the Russells *and* his own parents in one fucking morning. Both deaths were unintentional, but in so many ways … unforgivable. I tried to let it go. I couldn't bring back the dead, and I had no idea where he was at. So I put all of my focus into music. I became a fucking rock star. I had everything … *almost* everything. Except revenge—justice. So I hired a private investigator to find him, and it took *years*. Then one day, they delivered a file with notes, dates, photos, and locations. It was him. I let it leak that I was taking a vacation, staying at an undisclosed location in France, to avert the media. At the last minute, I faked an illness. I told Max to take a vacation, get on the plane, and let the paparazzi think Ian Cooper was in France. I told her I needed to just hole up and get better.

"So Max, the one person who kept constant tabs on me, left for France. Shane took his family to the Grand Canyon since I wasn't leaving my bed, and I drove from L.A. to Newark and found Kessler at his usual spot that the investigator put in his report. Of course, he was selling drugs. Then I followed him to a rundown shed behind an old warehouse. When he snorted his last line and passed out, I emptied a can of lighter fluid on him and lit his pathetic ass on fire.

"When he started to scream and yell, I didn't look back, not once—the way I imagined he didn't look back after killing Charles and Dena. But then ... he called my name. I glanced over my shoulder to the human inferno and gave him the finger."

Ian felt Jersey's heart booming in her chest, her breaths labored just from his words.

He kept his lips next to her ear. "I should have told you, but I didn't know if his amnesia was real. I kept waiting for the other shoe to drop. I thought *he* was the one who was there for revenge, not you. I tried to kill him for the same reason you tried to kill me. We are the same, Jersey. Only, I am capable of loving someone, but I don't think you are." He released her, waiting for her to turn toward him, to say something, but she didn't. So he walked back toward the house ... he set her free.

CHAPTER THIRTY-FOUR

JERSEY SPENT SEVERAL nights in a homeless shelter, digesting Ian's revelation.

He lit Chris on fire.

He didn't know if the amnesia scenario was real.

He was waiting for Chris to make his move.

He had no idea the move was Jersey's, and it involved killing the world's biggest rock star.

Jersey heard that some guy fitting Shane's physical description had been asking around about her. So she made sure she never stayed more than one night in the same place. Ian and Jersey were terrible people. And she was incapable of love. Ian said it. And she had no way to argue with him.

After all … what was love?

"Do you need help finding a job?"

Jersey turned to the woman's voice. The long-haired blonde looked about Jersey's age.

"I'm Natasha, a student. And I'm part of an outreach project to find jobs for people who need them. We offer help with resumes and interview practice, as well as transportation and financial assistance to get you on your feet."

Jersey stood from the homeless shelter cot and pulled her hair back. She wanted to beat a bag, knock fists with Judd, listen to Chris read her a story, watch Ian perform to thousands of fans. But that life was over. On a good day, she got a workout in at a park and avoided any unwanted advances from some questionable people she encountered.

"Yeah." Jersey nodded. "It would be great if you could help me find a job. I … I didn't graduate. And I—"

Natasha waved off Jersey's insecurity. "Don't worry about it. I'll gather all of the information from you, and we'll find something to fit your interests and skill level. Okay?"

"K." Jersey looked at her feet, returning another tiny nod.

As promised, Natasha took Jersey back to a building on campus. She entered Jersey's information into the computer, a little surprised to see that Jersey had a recently issued passport with so many stamps in it already.

"You wouldn't believe me if I told you," Jersey said as a response to Natasha's silent, raised-brow question.

How many people in homeless shelters traveled the world with rock stars? Maybe more than she imagined. After all, she met a woman the night before who used to be married to an NBA player and lost everything, including a roof over her head, in their divorce.

A week later, Jersey had a job waitressing at a diner. Her first official job. During the next few months, Natasha helped Jersey manage her money, open a bank account, and get a cellphone with a prepaid plan. Her world expanded with access to apps. It made navigating public transportation easier, as well as accessing her bank account, contacting her employer, and messaging Natasha.

"I love this song," Natasha said as she ate lunch with Jersey at the diner during her break.

"I hate it." Jersey frowned as the number one song on iTunes, "Unloved," played over the speakers for the millionth time that day.

"How can you hate it?" Natasha's food nearly fell out of her mouth. "I mean … I don't follow music that much, and I have no idea who sings it, so for me to like it, that means it has to be amazing."

"It's Ian Cooper. I used to sell merchandise at his concerts. He's kind of a dick."

Natasha lifted an eyebrow. "You said this was your first job."

"Officially, yes. Ian paid me in cash … and sex." Jersey smirked.

"That's the most unbelievable lie I have ever heard." Natasha rolled her eyes. "But I like where it was going. Please … tell me more."

"Is this a regular check-in with me, or are we friends?" Jersey asked, sipping her coffee.

"Both. I'm here to see if you need anything. But you're usually pretty self-sufficient, so it leaves time for the friend thing. Do you have any friends?"

Jersey shook her head. "I used to have one, but he died."

"Oh, I'm sorry. Was it sudden?"

Jersey shrugged. "It happened quickly, but I saw it coming. He had a lot of issues."

"Was this while you were sleeping with the rock star?" Natasha grinned.

Jersey mirrored her grin, finding Natasha's complete disbelief in Jersey's story quite funny. "As a matter of fact, it was."

"Mmhmm ..." She narrowed her eyes. "Ian Cooper ... I feel like ... was he in the news awhile back? Did his house burn down?"

"Yes, but we weren't in L.A. We were in the U.K. on his world tour."

Natasha flipped her hair over her shoulder and giggled. "Yes, you were with Ian Cooper on a world tour when his house burned down. Keep going ..."

Jersey grinned at Natasha over the steam of her coffee. "How do you think I got all those stamps in my passport?"

Wiping her mouth with a napkin, Natasha eyed Jersey, studying her for a few seconds. "Okay, I'll play. So you traveled with Ian, his house caught fire, and you returned to L.A. Correct?"

Jersey nodded.

"Then what happened? You had a falling out and you ended up in a homeless shelter?"

"Exactly."

"What was the falling out about?"

"Oh, just the usual stuff. He'd been so busy in the studio and meeting with important people about videos and shit like that. I was feeling lonely. So I asked him to stay home one night with me and have sex, but he didn't. I told him I was going to have sex with *someone* that night. He thought I was joking." She shrugged. "I wasn't."

Natasha blinked a few times before laughing. "That's your story? Ian Cooper wouldn't have sex with you, so you found another guy to have sex with? And then what? He got mad because you cheated on him and you broke up? Which…" she held up her hand "…for the record, no woman in her right mind would cheat on a rock star, right? It would be a step down. Unless you slept with another rock star … or an actor. But what are the chances of that? So that part of your story just ruins the rest. It's too unbelievable. You have to keep it a tiny bit believable if you want to keep your audience engaged."

"Well, I didn't cheat on him. We weren't married. And I wasn't his girlfriend."

"Oh …" Natasha sported a sly grin. "Gotcha. That's a relief. Cheating is just awful. Not so much flirting, or even a kiss that could lead to something, as long as someone stops it. But going as far as to have sex is unforgivable."

Jersey set her coffee cup down and traced the rim of it. "Why? It's just sex."

"Sex is intimate, sacred in some ways."

"Sacred?" Jersey's head tipped to the side.

"Yeah, like special. The pinnacle of intimacy."

It wasn't. Not for Jersey. Sex had been used as a weapon, a punishment, a bargaining tool, and a means to barter for goods.

"Someday you should make things right with *Ian.*" She used air quotes with his name. "Bad relationships follow you around. They bleed into all your future relationships. It's uh …" She glanced up at the ceiling, lips twisted. "Bad karma … bad luck. If your head is right, and you feel confident about moving on, you should go make things right with Ian. Find closure and make it peaceful."

Jersey held her fingers up in air quotes. "Why are you doing this every time you say his name?"

Natasha returned the hairy eyeball. "On the off-chance that your Ian is not *the* actual Ian Cooper. Which…" she nodded, squinting her eyes into a weird expression "…I totally believe you. I'm just saying other people might find it a bit unlikely."

Jersey glanced at the clock behind the counter. "Listen. My break is over. But I'm interested in this karma thing. I think I have a lot of bad karma in my life. I'm willing to try to make things right with Ian, but I don't remember where he lives. I'm not great with directions."

"Do you have his address?"

"No. Do you have it?"

Natasha chuckled. "Are we back to talking about the rock star?"

"Yes."

"Sure. I can probably track down an address and get you to his house. Shall I pick you up after work?"

"Yeah, that would be great. Thanks."

Natasha stood, shaking her head while grinning. "Oh girl … you sure are entertaining." She set a twenty-dollar bill on the table. "What time are you off?"

"Seven."

"Then I'll see you at seven."

CHAPTER THIRTY-FIVE

"T HAT'S HIS HOUSE." Natasha pointed past the gate
from the street. "I'm not sure he's living there
since there's still construction going on." She narrowed
her eyes a fraction at Jersey, clearly still not buying the Ian
Cooper story but indulging Jersey just the same.

"He was staying at his neighbor's house." Jersey
pointed across the street. "But it appears like they're home
again from the looks of the kids playing with their toys
out front. Hmm … this is fine." She opened her door.
"I'll get out and see what I can find out. If he's not
around, I'll find my way back or call for a ride."

"You sure? I don't mind staying."

Jersey poked her head back into the car. "Because you
don't believe me?"

Natasha shook her head and laughed. "No judgment
here."

"Go home. I'll send you photos for proof if I find
him."

"Yeah, you do that."

As Natasha drove off, Jersey typed in the code to Ian's
gate, and it opened. She surveyed the perimeter before
ringing the doorbell. No one answered. She tried to open

it. It was locked.

Traipsing across the street, she waved at the neighbor whom she'd never met, but Chris had. "Hi. I'm a friend of Ian's. Jersey. I stayed here with him for a while right after the fire." She gripped the iron bars to their gate. She knew their code too but decided not to freak them out quite yet.

The short-haired brunette nodded, padding toward the gate while messing with her phone. The gate opened. "Hi. I'm Eve Blevins. It's nice to meet you." She held out her hand, and Jersey shook it.

"You too. Say, I'm looking for Ian. He's not still staying with you by any chance, is he?"

"No. He's renting a place now, I believe."

"I see. Do you happen to know where that is?"

"No. Sorry." She gave Jersey a sad smile.

"Do you happen to have his phone number? I had it in my old phone, but I left it behind a couple of months ago, so I don't have his number now."

Eve bit her lower lip and nodded slowly. "Um … don't take this personally, but I'm not really comfortable giving out his personal information."

"Oh. Sure. Yeah, um …" Jersey glanced around, looking for another solution.

"But if you have a new phone now, I'd be willing to send him your number, and he can contact you if he wants to."

"Okay. That works."

Eve brought up another screen on her phone and typed in Jersey's name. "Okay, what is it?"

She gave Eve her number. "Tell him I just want to leave things good between us. Karma or something like that according to my new friend."

New friend.

Jersey inwardly smiled. She had a job, and she wasn't screwing her boss. She had normal hours. Coworkers who weren't jealous of her relationship with their boss. A phone that she bought on her own. And money in the bank to go toward rent at some point. And most nights she found a place to sleep at a shelter. Oh … and she had a friend.

"I'll just tell him you'd like him to call you when he gets a chance."

"Thanks." Jersey smiled.

Eve's thumbs moved across the screen of her phone. Then she held it up for Jersey to see. "There. Message sent."

Nerves teased Jersey's stomach like they did when she arrived in the neighborhood, like they did when she rang his doorbell, like they did when she first met him.

Message sent.

She hoped to get the chance to talk to him again, and suddenly that made her body do really crazy things inside.

JERSEY MEANDERED DOWN the winding road of the valley, finally ordering a ride before the sun set any lower in the sky. It took her back to the diner where she had a locker to keep her things until she found something permanent.

After retrieving her bag, she hopped on the bus to head to the shelter.

Her phone chimed as she stared out the window. She didn't recognize the number which meant it had to be Ian. Her tummy flipped in one direction and then the other direction as her pulse doubled in response.

"Hello?"

Silence.

"Hello?" she repeated.

"Hey."

Nothing could have prepared her for hearing his voice after so long—months that felt like years.

"Hi. Um … I went to your house. I see it's still not fixed."

"Not yet." He sounded tired.

She bit the end of her thumbnail, fighting the nerves. Why so many nerves? It was closure. Making things right. Finding good Karma, whatever that meant. "So I was talking to my friend, Natasha. She goes to college and she helped me get a job, but that's not my point." She closed her eyes and pinched the bridge of her nose. Who was the blubbering girl failing to articulate her reason for contacting him?

"You have a job?" Ian still sounded tired, but his voice held a smidge more life or curiosity.

"Yeah. I'm not selling out stadiums or anything like that. But it's a job. I wait tables at a diner. The tips are good."

The line went dead for a long moment.

Jersey cleared her throat. "So, Natasha thinks it's

good to end relationships with no hard feelings. Like making things right before closing a door. Karma … something or another like that. I'm not really skilled in that area, but she seems pretty smart, so …"

"So …" Ian echoed. Maybe it wasn't exhaustion in his voice. Maybe it was something else. Anger? Sadness?

"I think we left things … not so great. Do you think … I don't know … maybe we should say whatever needs to be said so things are good?" The girl who had zero experience with relationships made a terrible attempt at fixing one. Just to end it properly? She didn't know. It sounded weird when she thought of it like that.

"Where are you?" he asked.

"On a bus."

"Where are you going?"

"Shelter."

More silence.

"Jersey …"

She missed him. And she hadn't even realized just how much until she heard his voice. "Don't feel bad or sorry or whatever. It's fine. It's not a bad place. Better than Marley's, really. I'm actually happier than I've been in a long time. I don't know. Maybe ever. And I'm saving up for a place. Natasha said she could match me up with a roommate."

"I'm happy for you, Jersey."

"Yeah." She pressed her hand to her chest, rubbing the ache as her other hand clutched the phone.

The bus stopped, and Jersey got off.

"Where's the shelter?"

She crossed the street. "Opposite corner of Mission Church."

"Can I pick you up in thirty minutes? Take you for a drive and talk?"

She nodded for several seconds before realizing he couldn't see her. "Yeah … yes. That's good."

"See you soon." He disconnected.

CHAPTER THIRTY-SIX

H E PULLED UP in his blue sports car with the top down. Jersey pressed her hand to her tummy to calm it. Ian made casual sexier than anyone—gray shorts, blue tee, messy hair, and sunglasses. And that lopsided smile.

"Hi." Her voice shook as she opened the door and plopped down into the luxury leather seat.

"Hey." Ian held his smile, but it faded a fraction when he glanced over her shoulder to the group of guys huddled outside of the door to the shelter, smoking their cigarettes. He sped off into traffic as soon as she clicked her seat belt.

She waited for him to say something, but he didn't. The wind made it difficult to have a conversation without yelling, so she leaned her head back and let the breeze play in her hair as he drove them up into the hills. Darkness enveloped them by the time he pulled off the road. As the car crept forward, a spectacular view of lights below them, including the Hollywood sign, came into view.

"Wow …" She broke the silence.

Ian shut off the car and unfastened his seat belt. "Not a bad view. It paints a much more beautiful picture than what's really there." He pressed a button, reclining the back of his seat a few inches.

Jersey released her seat belt and felt the side of her seat, hitting the wrong switch the first time before finding the one to recline her seat.

"So … you told your friend, Natasha, about us?"

She chuckled, staring at the smattering of stars in the sky. "I tried. I'm ninety-nine percent sure she doesn't believe me." After a few minutes, she rolled her head to look at him. "I didn't know what we were. After Kessler died, I didn't know what we were."

Small talk felt wrong, and she wasn't great at it anyway. Jersey held a bunch of emotions in her mind, weighing heavily on her conscience.

Ian rolled his head to meet her gaze.

"I felt kept," she continued. "Like your need to protect me was all that mattered. But I don't need protection. I'm not the little girl you saved from Mr. Fisher. And I didn't feel loved. I didn't even feel wanted. I just felt … kept. Like one of your awards you have in a glass case. I needed the truth. I needed you. But you wouldn't give me either one."

"But I did love you." His eyebrows pulled together.

Jersey's shoulders lifted. "Then it wasn't the love I wanted. I wanted the love you gave me in the dark, in the bathroom, when I told you my deepest secret."

He studied her for a moment. "That you were going to miss me?"

She nodded. "It was when I knew killing you would kill me too. It's when my heart begged me to just walk away."

"But you didn't truly love me back."

"I could love you or kill you, but I couldn't do both."

Ian's lips twisted as he nodded slowly, gaze focused. "You fucked another man, Jersey." Agony … that's what was in his voice. Unshed tears filled his eyes.

"I was waiting for you to love me. I was feeling pretty fucking *unloved*."

In tiny increments, he shook his head a half dozen times, focusing back to the sky. "Yeah, well, welcome to my world."

Jersey climbed out of the car and walked closer to the steep drop-off. A few seconds later, Ian's car door clicked shut, and clumps of dirt and brush crunched beneath his feet as he approached her.

"I don't know much about love." She crossed her arms over her chest, focusing on the sea of lights. "I think Dena and Charles loved me. And I think G loved me. Sometimes, I even think *Chris* loved me.

"I don't really think sex is love. I know people say 'make love,' but I've never felt it. Even with us, I sometimes wondered if that's what we were trying to do, but I couldn't make love to someone who took my life. And that's what I thought … I thought you took my life from me."

"So what is love to you?"

She quickly wiped a stray tear from her cheek and sniffled. "When Dena used to braid my hair and tell me what a strong young woman I was and how I was going to do amazing things in life … change the world. That was love. And when Charles promised he would never do anything to lose my trust, never be anything like the men before him; he made sure my bedroom door had a lock on the inside that no one could open from the outside because he wanted me to feel safe. That was love."

More tears escaped. "And when G carried me upstairs and tended to my wounds ... when she told me one-eared bunnies still hop ..." Jersey's voice cracked. "When she picked up that baseball bat after ... Mr. ... Mr. Fisher crossed the final line, when he took my virginity." A sob escaped, and Jersey covered her mouth to catch it. "That was love."

"Jersey ..."

She held out her hand to keep him from coming closer and shook her head. "You not talking to me was not love. Why did you think it was okay for you to know my secrets but not okay for me to know yours?"

He rubbed the back of his neck. "I was ashamed of what I did to him. It wasn't right. It wasn't going to bring Charles and Dena back."

"Ashamed?" She jerked her head back. "You tried to kill him. I *did* kill him. What does that say about me?"

"You killed him to save my life."

She laughed as pain bubbled to the surface. Making things right for Karma was a lot harder than she expected. "I was so fucking close to killing *you* because I thought you killed Dena and Charles."

"Not the same, Jersey!" Ian ran his fingers through his hair, tugging it a bit. "I stumbled into your life. You didn't hunt me down. And you wanted to kill me for more than just them. You wanted to kill me because you thought I stole your life, your future." Ian laced his fingers behind his head and looked up at the sky. "I had everything. No one stole my future. I hunted a man down and lit him on fire. And unlike you, I didn't have a single emotion that played in my conscience. Not a moment's hesitation. Not one unshed tear."

"I let you into my life—into my bed—just to kill you."

He shrugged. "Kessler was my friend. I knew his parents, and they were kind to me. He was fucked up on drugs. I had the means to get him help, but I didn't. I set. Him. On. Fire." Anguish grew in his eyes. She could see it when the glow of the city lights reflected off his face.

"You should have told me." Jersey shook her head.

Ian gazed out over the city. "It was a lie. Until I told you the truth, it felt like a lie. So I didn't want to tell you—make it real, make it true. I just wanted it to go away. I've spent so much time trying to make my past just … go away. I wanted to be the one thing in your life that wasn't *terrible*. So I kept you. And I waited for …" He shook his head. "I don't even know."

"You waited too long," she whispered.

"I know. I lost you. I lost you to the arms of another man."

"You didn't lose me." Her tone gained momentum as anger nipped at her. "You gave me up. You were going to send me back to Newark. I *told* you what would happen if you left that night. I begged you to stay. I begged you to love me."

"I did love you!" He held his arms out to the side for several seconds before letting them flop to his sides.

"You wouldn't kiss me." She fisted her hands.

"You fucked another man, Jersey."

"You wouldn't kiss me." Her voice remained steady in spite of the pain and anger just beneath the surface, desperate to be heard, to be felt.

"It's not the same," he said slowly through gritted teeth.

"It's more," she whispered as hot tears escaped her burning eyes. "When we kiss … *that's* love. I didn't let that other man kiss me." She shook her head as her lips trembled. "Why … why wouldn't you kiss me? L-love me? Why wouldn't you just love me?" A sob ripped past her throat.

Ian stepped closer, his hand inching toward her face. When his thumb brushed along her tear-stained cheek, she leaned into his touch. He took another step until there were no more steps to take. "I should have told you. I'm sorry."

Her body shook as she tried to swallow back the flood of pain.

"I shouldn't have left that night. I'm sorry."

She forced her gaze up to his, blinking out more tears. His thumb brushed down her cheek and traced her trembling lips.

He blinked, eyes wet with emotion. "I should have kissed you. I'm sorry," he whispered each word as if something in his chest tried to suffocate them.

They were raw, real, and painful to hear.

"I looked for you. Shane looked for you."

She nodded slowly.

"Ian Cooper would come for you … He'd give you the kidney."

"A part of me has been searching for you for sixteen years."

"Coop …" Jersey rested her hand over his hand cupping her face. She guided his fingers over her lips, closing her eyes. Her heart beat so fast; she felt certain it took flight. And that fluttering feeling in her tummy returned, so much stronger than before. Every cell of her body felt alive.

In the next breath, his fingers disappeared, and his mouth took their place. It sent a warm rush of emotion through her body, making right of so many wrongs. For the first time in twenty-four years, Jersey let herself fall— completely fall in love with the first person who ever showed her love. For her, love was no longer an action, an emotion, or a promise. Love was a person.

Ian was love.

He kissed her mouth, her cheeks, her neck. "Feel that, Jersey? Do you feel my love?"

"Yes …" She curled her fingers into his shirt, holding him close.

"Let's go," he whispered over her ear before taking her hand and pulling her toward the car.

He kept ahold of her hand as they backed out onto the main road again. A few miles down the road, Ian turned into a secluded drive nestled into the woods.

"Where are we?"

"My temporary house." He pulled the car into the single garage stall and closed the door behind them. "The realtor is a friend. They're having trouble moving it. The price is too high. So I'm renting it until either it sells or my house is finished. My recording studio is just a mile from here, so the location is good."

Jersey climbed out and the light went out. "What happened?" She shut the door and stood still in the pitch-black, windowless garage.

"Light burned out. It was flickering earlier."

"I'll use my phone—"

Ian startled her, running his fingers down her bare arms, eliciting goose bumps. She couldn't see anything, but she felt everything.

"Missing you has been a most excruciatingly painful full-time job," Ian whispered, dragging his lips along her cheek.

"I missed you too … but don't tell anyone."

His lips turned into a smile against her mouth. "Your secret is safe with me."

"Coop …"

"Yes?" His hands guided her shirt up her torso.

She lifted her arms as he pulled it over her head. Her hands searched for his stubbly face, cupping it as she lifted onto her toes to put her lips a breath away from his. She shivered when his fingertips feathered down her neck to her bare back. "I've spent my whole life waiting to love you."

He paused for a few seconds.

Time stood still.

Darkness became their new light.

He kissed her—he *loved* her. His hands removed her bra. Hers pushed his shirt over his head.

Ian held her to him, his chest warm against her breasts. He kissed down her body, slowly peeling off her shorts and panties, his lips following the path of his hands.

So long ago, he touched every inch of her without ever laying a hand on her. Because Ian was love before Jersey knew what it meant to be loved.

She rested her hands on his shoulders to steady herself in the dark as he took his time exploring the curves of her body. When their mouths fused again, she unfastened his shorts. He slid them over his narrow hips along with his briefs, his lips never leaving hers.

He palmed the back of her thighs and lifted her up.

"Coop ..." she breathed his name against his ear when he pushed into her.

They paused like a statue. Time stood still, like nothing would ever matter as much as that moment.

"Jersey?" Ian rested his forehead against her shoulder, his warm breath brushing along her chest.

"Yes?" Her breaths chased each other as she held tight to the moment, never wanting anything more than to feel so completely filled by him. Ian chased away the bad and filled it with good. He slayed demons, built dreams, and gave kidneys.

He was everything. He had *always* been everything.

"I love you," he whispered. "*All* of you. So every part of you is as sacred to me as your lips. Do you get that?"

She closed her eyes as he brought her a tiny bit closer, filling her a tiny bit more. Then she remembered what Natasha said about sex being sacred. "I … I think so."

"We're going to go inside … so I can kiss *all* of you. Then I need you to promise to never let anyone touch you where my lips have been." He held her to him, toeing off his shoes, taking slow steps toward a door she couldn't see, kicking his feet out of his shorts and briefs.

Dim light brought new life to the moment as he opened the door and carried her through the shadows to the bedroom. He shut the door and pressed her back to it, thrusting into her over and over while their mouths moved together. They went from the door to the dresser, the dresser to the bed, the bed to the shower.

Every time his lips explored a new area of her body, he made her promise. And she did, writhing beneath his touch, drowning in his words—his commitment to give every breath to her—Jersey promised herself, her whole being, to Ian Cooper.

Her Guardian.

CHAPTER THIRTY-SEVEN

"I CALLED YOU for closure." Jersey wrapped a blanket around herself as she approached Ian sitting in a chair on the deck shrouded by trees.

The sun started to peek over the horizon. After waking to an empty space next to her in bed, she needed to make sure they were still *them*.

Wearing jogging pants, a white tee, and sipping a cup of coffee, he glanced over his shoulder and smiled that perfectly lopsided grin. "This *is* closure."

She leaned over his shoulder and snapped a quick selfie with him.

"Ah hem …" He lifted a curious brow at her.

"I have to prove something." She sent the picture to Natasha while sitting in the chair next to him. He smirked, handing her his cup of coffee. Jersey blew at the steam and took a sip. "It is?" She handed the coffee back to him. "Is it closure?"

"Closure is not a good word." His mouth twisted as he watched the birds flutter and jump from one branch to the next. "As much as I've tried to bury my past, lock that door, pretend that it never happened, I can't. You're my past. And for you to be my future, I need to let our lives be whole. Acknowledge the pain, accept what happened, and show gratitude that we are in fact survivors. I don't know ... maybe my story could help people."

"You set a man on fire."

"Okay, maybe not *all* of my story will be helpful." He cringed. "I had issues, even with the Russells. They loved me. They fostered my love for basketball. But Fisher changed me. The day you watched me beat him with a baseball bat, the day you dropped that bunny, the day I told you to be brave and run fast ... it changed me at an elemental level. I struggled with self-identity. Forgiveness. I just wanted to be someone else.

"Music let me be someone else. It's hard to explain, but sometimes a talent can feel like its own person, its own thing or existence. I suppose you could call it an alter ego on the stage, like Ian Cooper was the talented part of Christian Guardian Faulkner. It was fun to let Ian out on the stage, so much fun that I never wanted to go back to being that other guy. So ... I didn't. But I also didn't go back to anything or anyone else. I didn't visit the Russells, or friends, or anything associated with that life. I just didn't think I could hold on to any pieces. And when I heard about their deaths, I regretted it. When I saw you in Newark ... I regretted it. Had I kept in touch with them, I would have found you. And when they died, I would have saved you."

"Saved me?"

"Yes."

"How? Were you going to adopt me?"

He shrugged. "Sure. Why not?"

Jersey laughed. "Daddy Ian. It's a little …"

"Don't." He chuckled. "Now you're making it weird."

"Had they adopted both of us, we would have been siblings."

"Jersey … stop." He shook his head, hiding his grin behind his coffee mug.

She tugged the blanket around her tighter. "Did you know Charles and Dena had a dog named Cooper? He died of cancer. It was years before I was with them, but I saw a picture of him. He was a German Shepard. Did they have him when you were there?"

Ian nodded slowly, keeping his focus on the trees and the birds.

"Oh my god!" Jersey laughed, reaching over to put her hand on his arm. "I get the Ian; it's from Guardian. But Cooper … did you name yourself after a dog?"

Ian rolled his lips together, narrowing his gaze a bit while keeping it focused away from Jersey.

"Coop? Did you name yourself after a dog?"

"*A dog* makes it sound crazy. Cooper was more than just *a dog*."

Jersey giggled, bending at the waist, holding her belly. "That's the best … it really is. God, I love you, Coop." As her laughter settled, she glanced over at him.

He watched her with a bit of amusement and something else, maybe an uneasy disbelief? "Do you?" he asked with a stifled confidence. An Ian she didn't know. Not the Ian who owned sold-out venues of screaming fans.

Her smile deflated a bit, feeling his vulnerability

squeezing her heart. "Yeah, I do. I love you, Coop. I meant what I said … I've spent my whole life waiting to love you."

Ian laced his fingers with hers, giving her hand a firm squeeze. She took his coffee from his other hand and set it on the little table. Then she crawled onto his lap, straddling it. Her favorite place to be.

"I don't want to close the door to our pasts either. If we leave it open, it just shows how strong we are. It means we know we don't have to run anymore *because* we are brave and strong. And sometimes I might want to look back to discover things about you in the now, like you named yourself after a dog." She grinned.

He slid his hands under the blanket, palming her naked ass. "Watch it."

Jersey giggled.

Ian's gaze settled on her face and the scar beneath her eye. He leaned forward and kissed it. "Fisher's ring cut your eye and left a scar. It's how I knew for sure it was you that day at the hot dog stand."

She nodded.

"I'm going to discover why you say you like olives but won't eat them." Ian twisted his mouth.

Jersey glanced over his shoulder, her brow slightly wrinkled. "The wife of the man I killed. Her name was Sharon. She was oblivious and evil in her own way. And a drunk. One day I saw her sitting in the kitchen, drinking something with olives in it. A martini. I'd never had an olive before. I asked her what they were, and she pulled one out and handed it to me. The gin burned my tongue, but I liked the salty olive. I still do, but they just bring back bad memories."

Ian nodded slowly, brow tense. "I'm going to take you to Tuscany. We'll stay at a vineyard … I know a guy." He smirked. "We'll drink wine, eat pasta with our hands, and I'll feed you olives until the only thing you think of when you see one is *me*."

"I'll check my work schedule. Which …" She pulled on his arm and glanced at his watch. "I open this morning. In an hour." Jersey tried to stand.

Ian pulled her back to him. "Play hooky. Let's go back to bed and do what terrible people do."

"No. Sorry, Coop. I have a job. I like it. I want to keep it. So you'll have to be terrible with someone else today." She wriggled out from his hold on her and rewrapped the blanket around her body.

Ian frowned. "I fear we're still not on the same page. I don't want to be terrible with anyone but you. And I don't want you—"

"To let anyone touch me where you've put your mouth?" She glanced at him over her shoulder at the doorway, a flirty grin on her face.

That erased his frown.

"I get it." She rolled her eyes. "I think that leaves maybe my left pinky toe."

"No." Ian shook his head. "I covered that. ALL of that. ALL of you."

"No." She strutted toward the bedroom. "I have a left pinky toe to offer the right guy. So—COOP!"

He scooped her up and threw her onto the bed. She

kicked and giggled as he wrestled with her leg.

"Eww ... don't do that."

He sucked her left pinky toe and bit it for good measure. Then he kissed his way up her naked body, tangled in the blanket.

"Coop ..." She grabbed his hair before his mouth did any more damage to her resolve. "I have to go to work."

His tongue slid up her inner thigh. "What's our record?"

She squirmed, intent on getting to work on time but tempted by his mouth's ascent. "Three minutes, forty-two seconds."

He grinned, a wicked gleam in his eyes. "If I can beat that, will you get to work on time?" He kissed an inch higher.

Jersey tightened her grip on his hair as her pulse began to race. "On your mark ... get set ..."

EPILOGUE

Ten years later

"WHAT'S THE WORD of the day?" Ian knocked on the door to Jersey's office.

She swiveled in her desk chair—her favorite spot in their 4000-square-foot penthouse in Central Park West, New York.

Tucking her bobbed hair behind her ear, she shot him a sexy look over the frames of her glasses. "Recalcitrant."

"Sounds hot." He prowled toward her.

She leaned back, folding her hands on her lap. "It's very sexy. It's an adjective meaning stubborn—defiant of authority. Difficult to control or manage."

"Sounds like my wife." Ian sat on the edge of her desk, pulling her leg up to massage her foot—perfectly manicured with pink polish on her toenails that matched her fingernails.

"Sounds like the author who wrote this manuscript." Jersey nodded toward her computer screen.

"Still working on the same edits?"

"Yep." She sighed. "This girl is brilliant. She's eighteen and writing with the imagination of a soul that's passed through a million lives. She's meticulous with her world building, a literary savant. I have no idea where her mind goes to create this stuff. It's incredible. But she's oblivious, or allergic, or something … to punctuation!"

Ian chuckled.

"I'm serious. She's recalcitrant!"

"I'm sure, babe." He could not have been more proud of the girl with the bunny. She honored her past by chasing her dreams, not letting a single thing that happened to her define her as a person or cripple her ability to achieve anything.

Jersey toured with Ian and a private tutor to get her diploma. Then she attended college, pursuing her dream of "working with words." It took her down many roads which ultimately led to freelancing for several of the Big Six publishing houses. On the side, she followed her other passion—narration. Ian set her up with her own booth in their home to narrate books.

Jersey's dreams of boxing died after a shoulder injury, but she could still kill a fly a hundred yards away with a knife.

"How are you alone? Where are the kids? How many do we have today?"

Ian pursed his lips to the side. "Let me think … seven. Maybe eight. I lose track of the youngest one. What's her name? I can't remember. But it's Friday, so they're in school. Except the youngest one … dammit! What's her name?"

"Abby? Something like that." Jersey tapped her finger on her chin.

"Is that it?" Ian rolled his eyes to the ceiling.

"I think so." Jersey giggled. "We're terrible people. After all these years, we're still terrible people."

They knew her name, Abigail Lola Cooper. Lola after their favorite ratty dog who died. It seemed like the better choice of the two names. Two-year-old Abby had dark hair and dark eyes like her mom and dad. The only biological child they had together. A true "oops" child. The product of insane amounts of sex.

After devoting so much of their time to taking in foster children, they chose not to have any of their own. The world had plenty of children who needed loving homes.

But then … oops happened.

"Max took her to the park."

"Max shouldn't be taking care of anyone but herself." Jersey shot Ian a tiny frown.

Max never divorced her husband. Jersey and Ian wondered if it was the couple's destiny to live in sadness, feeling unworthy of anything more for the rest of their lives.

"Well…" Ian shrugged "…I know she's officially a widow now, but I'm pretty sure she lost him many years ago. That's why she refuses to stop and grieve like everyone keeps telling her to do. I think she did that a long time ago. There's nothing left to grieve."

"Well, Abby loves her. And it gives her something to do since her rock star is too damn lazy to put out a record or sell out huge stadiums."

"I am." He yawned. "I'm getting old. I need daily naps. I'm cold all the time like my blood isn't circulating.

I bruise easily when you beat on me. Thank god tomorrow is my last concert. I might have to take an intermission to deal with my prostate issues."

"I might have to trade you in for a newer model."

He nodded. "I wouldn't blame you." Ian grabbed her other leg and started massaging her other foot.

"Your last concert, Coop. Are you having second thoughts?"

"Nope. Not even a little."

"What are you going to do with all of your spare time?"

"Hmm ... good question. It's not like we have seven, nine ... a hundred kids or anything like that. And my wife hasn't been riding my ass to write a book with her about our life. And the outreach program you started totally runs itself." He rolled his eyes. "So ... I'll probably spend my days shooting hoops, screwing my wife, and watching Netflix."

She eased her foot from his grasp and stood, planting herself between his legs, arms wrapped around his neck. Brushing her lips over his, she grinned. "Solid plan."

THE COOPER CLAN of ten, plus Alex, Jordan, Bryson, their wives and kids, Max, Shane and his wife, along with Ames and a few people from the record label all crowded into the green room before the final, sold-out concert.

Ian tapped his glass bottle with a drumstick while whistling to get everyone's attention.

"Quiet down. Don't make me yell, or I won't have a voice to sing my final songs."

Everyone laughed before the room quieted with the exception of a few young kids making their playful noises. Jersey's eyes burned with emotion as she watched her husband struggle to keep his own emotions in check as he glanced around the room with such gratitude.

"I love—" Ian choked up, blinking back the tears while swallowing hard and pressing his fist to his mouth for a few seconds. The women in the room started sniffling. Even his bandmates weren't immune to the moment as their eyes, too, reddened with emotion.

"I love this dream. The fact that I've had the honor of living it with all of you is just beyond words, or lyrics, or any truly expressible emotion. Every choice we make changes the course of our lives. Don't ever take that for granted. I was in the right bar on the right night." Ian smiled at Ames. "And it changed my life forever. Years later, a young man carrying equipment for me saw my Marley's Gym T-shirt, and because of that moment of my life literally crossing his path, I drove to Newark and found my wife. It's that simple. A different T-shirt would have led to a different outcome. So tonight we sing. And tomorrow we welcome a new path full of possibilities. But we never forget. We never stop looking back to regain perspective, to find gratitude. Thank you."

The room exploded with applause, wiping tears, hugging the family that Ian Cooper created through his nearly twenty years of performing. Minutes later, everyone started filtering out of the room. Where there would be an after-party, the kids went home, and the band headed toward the stage, until it was just Ian and Jersey.

He looked at his watch. "We have no time for our ritual."

She grinned, walking into his embrace. "Because you're too long winded in your old age."

"Probably." He kissed the top of her head. "Walk with me." Ian took her hand, and they walked to the stage through the deafening roar of the crowd shaking the whole venue.

"Ian! Ian! Ian! Ian!"

Jersey wiped her eyes and smiled as they stood at the bottom of the stairs to the stage.

Ian kissed her slowly as if thousands of fans weren't demanding their rock star. He closed his eyes, pressing his forehead against hers for a few seconds as if to pause time. Then his mouth brushed her ear, sending chills along her skin. "Wish me luck, Jersey."

She gripped his shirt, holding him to her for an extra breath, an extended moment. When she pulled away, a smile reached her ears. "Luck, Coop."

The End

Acknowledgments

Thank you to every reader who takes a chance on my stories. You've made my dreams a reality.

To my family, you ground me, inspire me, love me when I'm bitchy and stressed. You give me space when I need it, and hold me together when I'm falling apart. My love for you is infinite.

Thank you to my keeper of all things, including my sanity, Jenn Beach, for your inspiring levels of awesomeness, including a beautiful cover for this book. I honestly would be lost without you.

To my alphas and betas—Leslie, Kambra, Sian, Shauna, Sherri—thank you for sacrificing your reading pleasure to wade through the shit I call my first draft.

Max, thank you for seventeen books! It's a pleasure to work with you and an honor to call you my friend.

Monique, thank you for being my number one bitch and an invaluable member of my editing team! You always go above and beyond.

Amy, Bethany, and Shabby, thank you for loaning me your eyes through the proofreading phase. Your support is appreciated more than you know.

Thank you to the amazing team at Social Butterfly for

getting this book into so many hands. It's a pleasure to work with you.

Paul with BB ebooks, as always, thank you for your formatting services.

To my Jonesies, you are my people and I couldn't adore you more.

Finally, thank you to Cleida for asking for a rock star!

Also by Jewel E. Ann

Jack & Jill Series
End of Day
Middle of Knight
Dawn of Forever

Holding You Series
Holding You
Releasing Me

Transcend Series
Transcend
Epoch

Standalone Novels
Idle Bloom
Only Trick
Undeniably You
One
Scarlet Stone
When Life Happened

Look the Part
A Place Without You
Naked Love

jeweleann.com

Receive a FREE book and stay informed of new releases, sales, and exclusive stories:
Monthly Mailing List
jeweleann.com/free-booksubscribe

About the Author

Jewel is a free-spirited romance junkie with a quirky sense of humor.

With 10 years of flossing lectures under her belt, she took early retirement from her dental hygiene career to stay home with her three awesome boys and manage the family business.

After her best friend of nearly 30 years suggested a few books from the Contemporary Romance genre, Jewel was hooked. Devouring two and three books a week but still craving more, she decided to practice sustainable reading, AKA writing.

When she's not donning her cape and saving the planet one tree at a time, she enjoys yoga with friends, good food with family, rock climbing with her kids, watching How I Met Your Mother reruns, and of course…heart-wrenching, tear-jerking, panty-scorching novels.